The Last Thread

Ray Britain

The Last Thread

Published by Ray Britain www.raybritain.com

ISBN: 978-1-9998122-2-5 (eBook)

ISBN: 978-1-9998122-3-2 (Paperback)

Cover design by Dominic Jones Photography
www.dominicjonesphotography.com/

eBook formatted by www.bluewavepublishing.co.uk/

DEDICATION

For my wife and children, each of whom has made me a better person.

And for the men and women of the police services of the United Kingdom, the finest in the world who, unarmed, and too often unappreciated, routinely and selflessly put their selves in harm's way in the service of their communities.

.

ACKNOWLEDGEMENTS

First and last, I am grateful to my wife and family for their patient support as I wrote this story over two winters and a summer, patiently ignoring my erratic hours when an idea, the story, a sentence, or simply a word drew me back to the keyboard.

My sincere thanks go to Gina, Hilary, Karen and Lisa for their kind advice, support and comments of the draft manuscript. Any remaining typos, errors or grammatical howlers are entirely my responsibility.

I am grateful to Dominic Jones for accepting my commission for the cover image. Understandably, he and his wife were a little cautious about joining me one morning to arrange rope around a tree in publicly accessible woodland. Thankfully, no one came past.

Finally, but by no means least, thank you to Peter at Blue Wave Publishing for his boundless patience and courtesy in answering my many questions as a 'newbie' Indie author.

CONTENTS

Ray Britain

THE LAST THREAD

PROLOGUE

The boy's hand was slipping from his grip.

Reaching out as far as he could, Stirling tried desperately to grasp it tighter but the boy's weight, balanced tenuously on the edge of the bridge, hung out over the space below. The boy's cold fingers clutched desperately at him inside his hand as he hung there, suspended between life and death, his slender body sagging with cold and exhaustion. His dark grey eyes filled with terror.

Stirling was aware of his own ragged breathing as he shouted hoarsely to the boy to hold on, frustrated that no one was helping but they were still too far away.

Looking across the space between them, Stirling saw a calm peace fall across the boy's features and a vague smile form as he looked deep into Stirling's eyes, relaxed his hand and let his fingers slip away.

Horrified, his perceptions intensified by adrenalin, Stirling watched the boy fall slowly away from him, every detail sharp as the boy strained to keep eye contact as he wheeled slowly through the air until the wind and momentum caught him and he fell swiftly to smash onto the cold tarmac below. A low sickening crunch of flesh and bone echoed grotesquely under the concrete span of the bridge.

Transfixed, his hands gripping the cold railing, Stirling watched the boy's body twitch feebly, a leg drag slowly across the ground and then lie still. A dark pool of viscous blood began to form under the cruelly misshapen head as his life wept into the tarmac to mingle with the rain now beating down hard. A failing pulse oozed blood from the boy's ear as his heart fluttered against death.

A woman's scream pierced the mourning wind funnelling below the bridge, followed by urgent shouting. As his mind tried to order events, confused, Stirling looked around for the woman who had screamed.

Seeing no one, he turned back to look below as two officers in yellow jackets emerged from under the bridge and ran to the boy's side. One was female. Was it her who screamed? The man crouched at the boy's side checking for signs of life as she watched, hands at her mouth, sickened by what she had witnessed. The officer looked up to the young woman and spoke sharply. She knelt to help him turn the boy and they began a futile attempt at resuscitation, but Stirling knew it was hopeless. He had met death before.

Squinting his eyes against the rain, the male officer looked up at Stirling, gave a grimace and shook his head.

Stirling stared at the boy's disfigured face staring sightlessly up at him, untroubled by the rain plastering his fair hair across his features, one arm thrown out above the head, the fingers clutching emptily, both legs shattered and splayed absurdly like a thrown doll. The white polo sweater had slipped up to reveal the boy's abdomen, its fair skin smudged with road oil.

Pushing himself off the railing, Stirling turned from the heartbreak below and lifted his face to the cold rain and sucked in air. Through force of habit, he checked his watch.

7.28 am.

 С੪ ୨১

February: Monday - 6.25 a.m.

Annoyed at the interruption he snatched up the phone, 'Stirling!'

'Mr Stirling?' A man's voice, hesitant. Late twenties, early thirties.

'Yes, DCI Stirling.' Glancing at the clock, he wondered who was bothering him. He had come into the office early to avoid interruptions to prepare for a difficult meeting that morning.

There was another pause. 'Inspector James, sir. Duty Inspector in the Force Control Room. Sorry to bother you but we need a negotiator at an incident close to HQ.'

'I'm the duty Senior Investigating Officer this week, not the duty negotiator.' Stirling knew he sounded irritable, but it was not the first time he had been contacted wrongly. He knew the on-call negotiator was Tom Simons, he had checked the rota only the night before.

'I'm aware of that sir, but one of my team saw you on CCTV driving in. The duty negotiator is an hour away and we need someone urgently. There's a young lad, fifteen or so on the outside of the motorway bridge just down the road, by the rugby club. I've had to close the motorway and although my first consideration is to save life, it's causing some serious operational problems. Would you help us sir, please?'

In truth, the decision couldn't be simpler. Someone's life was at risk, so he would turn out immediately. He needed his position covered at the meeting but that wasn't James's problem.

Stirling shifted into quick-time decision making. 'I'll call in on my way there. Have a printout out of the log and whatever Intel' you have of the boy. Name, background checks, the usual. I'll be with you in a few minutes.'

'Thanks sir. I'll get the duty negotiator on his way too, so he can take over from you if it goes on for a while.' James's relief was clear.

'Start planning for a long day, Inspector, in case we can't get him back over the railing quickly. Get another negotiator briefed and ready but keep Simons coming towards me, I may need him. The media will be there soon so think about extended cordons to keep them away, and us safe. And remember to brief the duty Chief Officer. Who is it?'

'Deputy Chief Constable McDonald, sir, I'll call him next.'

Stirling groaned inwardly. McDonald had arrived in the force on promotion a year ago and was disliked. James was newly promoted and needed to establish a reputation for dealing with a crisis calmly and efficiently, a regular occurrence in the control room where reputations were made, or broken, in a short space of time.

'A word to the wise, Inspector. Don't call him straight away or you'll have more questions left unanswered than answered which you'll find to be an uncomfortable experience with McDon ... *Mr* McDonald. Put everything in place and get it moving along before you call him. He'll still think of something that you haven't but thank him for his advice and be sure to smile as you do it!'

There was silence at the other end and Stirling imagined the young Inspector working out if this was helpful advice, or if he was being set up. Deciding it was help, he answered gratefully, 'Thank you, sir. Everything will be ready when you get here.'

The phone went dead in Stirling's hand as James got on with his instructions. Looking up at the wall clock, Stirling noted the time out of professional habit, even though the incident log would show the time he'd been contacted and read through what he would need. The motorway network was already fouling up and with the rush hour imminent, there would be huge pressure on the force to get it running again as quickly as possible with scant public sympathy for the distressed soul standing on the parapet. He had not asked which bridge to go to but assumed that 'down the road' meant Junction Six, next to the rugby stadium where several arterial routes fed in and out of the M5.

Putting his papers into a drawer, Stirling was concerned. Budget cuts meant he was expected to do more, with less people. He needed more investigators and specialists in the Major Crime Unit, but he was competing against some wily colleagues who, like him, had been discreetly lobbying the CID command team and Chief Officers at every opportunity. To miss the meeting would ruin months of preparation.

Grabbing his coat, Stirling glanced out of the window. On the far side of the car park a long row of tall, stark trees filtered the weak morning light of a cold February sky filled with dark clouds, heavy with rain. A gusting south westerly was tossing the tree tops, tugging at the remnants of last year's crows' nests above which the resident colony flapped and dipped. Stirling could hear their raucous cawing even from this distance. The weather looked ominous, but he knew that anything he needed was in the boot of his car in two "go bags." One for his day job of Senior Investigating Officer, SIO, the other for the voluntary role of Negotiator, each containing the basic tools and clothing he could need in the opening hours of a call-out.

It took only a minute to drive to the other side of the HQ estate to the modern glass-fronted building of the Force Control Room. Swiping his "access all areas" ID card, Stirling pulled open the heavy glass door and cast a quick glance across the long room with its many work stations, each staffed around the clock by communications personnel who handled the treadmill of thousands of telephone calls and radio transactions each day. Across the room there was a low hubbub of mingled conversations.

Picking out the person he was looking for, Stirling made his way through the room towards a raised dais at the far wall set below the large digital clock which governed the operational heartbeat of the force. Behind the work station on the raised platform sat Inspector James, the Duty Force Inspector in an open-necked white shirt. Although Stirling had heard of James, he had not met him and thought him young for his rank, late twenties at most.

Hearing the buzz of the security door opening, James looked across the room and watched Stirling making his way towards him, noticing how several of the female operators tracked his progress for longer than necessary, yet never pausing in their message taking and conversation. One, a good-looking woman in her forties with a certain reputation, smiled to her colleague opposite and arched a knowing eyebrow as Stirling passed between them.

James knew something of Stirling's reputation. Silhouetted for a moment by the morning light flooding the entrance lobby behind him, Stirling's physical presence was apparent, even from a distance. A sportsman himself, James recognised a self-assured lightness of movement that spoke of a man who kept himself physically fit. He had heard in the staff crew room of Stirling's reputation for enjoying the company of attractive women. Nothing more disreputable than idle chit-chat that gathered embellishment through retelling. Of more interest to him was that Stirling was generally well liked and respected, professionally.

Drawing closer to him, James thought Stirling to be about thirty-five with watchful, dark brown eyes under strong eyebrows and black wavy hair pushed carelessly past his ears. A well-cut, dark blue suit, white shirt and a red silk tie completed an impression of a man who took care to appear professional without any overt vanity. James thought that when he escaped from the Control Room, he might like to work for DCI Stirling.

Considering James's age, Stirling assumed him to be a rising star in the firmament of the accelerated promotion scheme, his short-cropped hair seeming to accentuate his youth, rather than add any welcome gravitas. Stirling was generally sceptical of the so-called *"fast trackers"* as, too often, they were promoted without sufficient operational experience. However, once he had realised he was not interested in the politics of the chief officer roles, he had become more relaxed about younger officers overtaking him in the promotion boards. Stirling was happiest doing what he had joined up for, to help people and, when the justice system defied its predisposition to leniency, to put criminals in prison.

James held out a sheaf of papers for Stirling. 'Morning, sir. Thanks for coming out so quickly,' said James. 'We've precious little info' at present but the Intel team next door is working on it. I'll get anything else to you as soon as I can.'

James was referring to the twenty-four-seven intelligence cell next to the control room which browsed national systems to provide real-time intelligence to officers deploying to incidents so that they arrived as well briefed as possible. Stirling scanned the incident log quickly, picking out key information to understand what had been done so far. Detailing every action and deployment to that moment, the log's most recent entry was James's call to him. With no name for the person on the bridge, he was unsurprised to see no intelligence was available at this early stage. James described the measures he had taken and that his next job would be to call DCC McDonald. Listening to James, Stirling could hear an underlying tension in the young man's voice who knew his actions could be under scrutiny later.

'What time did this all start?' asked Stirling calmly. His own demeanour would set the tone for those around him.

'First call came in at 6.16am from a lorry driver on the southbound who saw him standing on the bridge, leaning over the carriageway. We've had a lot more calls since. The first patrol car got there within a few minutes, but the lad keeps screaming he'll jump if they come too close, so they're standing off.'

'Have they been able to talk with him?' he asked

'No. He's on the outside of the railing on the north side of the bridge, near to the rugby club. But because he can walk along the edge over the southbound carriageway, I've had to close the motorway in both directions, and all the access roads. You can imagine what that's doing for the road network.'

James pulled a face and gave a hard blow to expel some tension. Stirling knew the pressure James was feeling. It was an exposed role with few Inspectors prepared to do it. As James talked, Stirling scanned a bank of CCTV monitors on the far wall, one for each junction of the motorway. Some showed the motorway empty and further away, long standing queues where the backlog was already building. The camera for the junction he needed was dark with a white static haze travelling across it.

James followed Stirling's gaze, and explained, 'Sods law. That camera was disabled a couple of days ago by someone working in the roadworks. The incident is already clogging up all the main routes around the area and up into West Midlands. Very soon we're going to have a major transport problem throughout the region.'

As the main corridor between the north and south-west, even if resolved reasonably quickly the blockage would cause huge delays. With thousands of disrupted journeys, the force would come under pressure to resolve the problem quickly with scant public concern for the boy on the bridge, and none for the force which would be damned in the media, whatever it did. The Chief Officers would exert their own pressure too as they began fielding calls from politicians and the media.

Smiling at the young man, Stirling said wryly, 'So, no pressure then?'

'No, none at all,' James replied with a lightness he didn't feel, but drawing comfort that they were in it together.

Looking at James over the papers, Stirling assessed his mettle. Perhaps he had what was needed when the soft stuff started hitting the fan. He folded the pages and stuffed them inside his jacket pocket ready to leave.

'Okay, I'm on my way but I need as much info as possible of the lad's background, *anything* might be important. But I don't want any family or friends brought to the scene, that's very important, d'you understand?'

Seeing the puzzled look on James's face he explained. 'We don't know why he's there. Until we do, we avoid introducing anyone who might be the reason for him being there. Got that?' Stirling demanded. He didn't have time to explain the competing psychological and emotional factors involved and needed James to rely on his professional advice.

James showed recognition. 'Good job you said, or it would have seemed a good idea. If we do identify anyone, I'll have them taken somewhere where we can debrief them but keep available to you.'

Stirling nodded, pleased that James grasped things quickly. He turned to go as another thought occurred to him. 'Contact one of our psychologist specialist advisors. The numbers are in the system. Give whoever's available a brief and that I may need them later. I need to get a feel for the situation first, though, to see if this person does want to jump, or if it's attention seeking. I'd usually call them myself, but you can explain why I can't.'

'Okay sir, good luck.'

Stirling turned to go, glancing at the clock to note the time.

6.55 a.m.

He met no other vehicles in the narrow lane leading from HQ to the motorway, but the short journey gave him little time to think. He knew no more than when he was first called so a sophisticated strategy was out of the question. He would have to rely on his training and experience.

Parking amongst a row of police cars, Stirling could see the youngster some fifty yards away. Rummaging in the boot for a digital recorder, he was struck by the silence with only police radios occasionally breaking through the quiet. At this time of the morning there would usually be a constant roar of noise rising from the motorway below and vehicles sling-shotting in and out of the access roads, all now blocked off by marked police cars, their blue strobe lights flashing. Shrugging on a thick rainproof, Stirling looked across to a Sergeant some distance away and beckoned him across. The Sergeant walked over with a studied nonchalance which annoyed Stirling immediately. Overweight, his bright yellow jacket open of necessity either side of a spreading gut, Stirling recognised him as an old-school traffic cop who had spent too many years sitting in patrol cars, nurturing a contempt for senior officers and making sure he got through his shift whilst doing as little work as possible.

'You the scene commander, Sarge?' asked Stirling, still getting his kit together.

With a smug smile, the Sergeant answered, 'I was, but not now you're here.'

'Sorry?'

'Well, you're a DCI, so you're the senior officer on scene.' He spoke with the smug arrogance of many years' service and a smile that said, "Over to you, pal."

Stepping forward, Stirling gave him a hard stare. 'Sarge, you're the Bronze Commander until a more senior uniformed officer takes over from you. As the Negotiator, I'm here as a specialist to support *you*. I can offer you advice, if you need, but *you're* responsible for this scene. You got that?' Stirling demanded.

The Sergeant eyed Stirling truculently as he thought of arguing the point, but many years' experience got the better of his instincts. He answered Stirling's questions with as little civility as could be deemed acceptable about how he had deployed officers around the incident. Two officers in hi-vis jackets were standing about twenty metres from the lad, keeping an eye on him but keeping their distance.

Nodding in their direction the Sergeant said, 'My lads have had to keep away because he kept screaming at them. There's more officers nearby if you need them.'

'Do we know his name yet?'

The Sergeant gave a dismissive shrug, 'Don't think so, nothing's been said over the radio.'

There was a flat disinterest in the man's voice, time served and cynically indifferent to the outcome. Irritated at his attitude but without the time to take him to task, Stirling decided there was no more to be gained and to approach the boy. Some distance away he saw an ambulance parked and hoped they would not need it.

He gave the Sergeant a last instruction. 'Tell your officers I'm going to speak to the lad now, but they're to stay back *unless* I call for their help.'

'Yes, sir.' Stressing the second word, the Sergeant stared at Stirling with years of practiced insolence before sidling away to give instructions over the radio.

Setting off towards the railing, Stirling clipped the microphone to his lapel, gave the recorder a final check and slipped it into his jacket pocket. If the worst happened, at least the Coroner would have more than his best recollection of what was said. Stirling paused to speak briefly with the two officers, their collars turned high against the rain which was now falling heavily, driven into their faces on a cold wind. Keen to help in whatever way they could, Stirling was impressed by the contrast in their energy and professionalism to that of their supervisor.

After waiting to make sure the boy had seen him, he began walking slowly towards him. Looking up at the sky and feeling the rain on the back of his neck starting to trickle uncomfortably under his collar, Stirling thought the foul weather could work in his favour. As he became more cold and uncomfortable, the lad might be encouraged to climb over the railing with a promise of a hot drink and dry clothing. Meanwhile, he began the negotiators mantra: Why here? Why now? Why today? If he found the answers to those questions, he might find a way to get him back to safety.

The boy watched his approach intently, possibly curious as to why someone in ordinary clothes was coming to talk to him, and not one of the policemen. Closer to him, Stirling thought the lad to be about fifteen, but it was hard to be certain with his features obscured by thick, wind drawn blonde hair. Standing with his heels on the outer ledge of the bridge and his hands gripping the railing behind him, he was looking north as if preparing to dive. As Stirling got close, the boy began to stare down to the tarmac twenty feet below. He had only to release his grip slightly, or slip, and he would fall to suffer serious injury, but more likely his death.

The boy turned and shouted something, but his words were snatched away on the wind. Indicating he couldn't hear, Stirling shouted across the space between them.

'I've been asked to come and talk with you. I'm not going to try and grab you. I'd just like to talk with you. Is that okay?' Stirling smiled, trying to reassure him he was not a threat, his calm front concealing an intense focus on everything about the young man; his body language, facial expressions and, if he talked, to hear the underlying emotions.

Stirling took a few more cautious steps forward until he was close enough to speak to him over the wind without frightening him. He was immediately struck by the depth of colour in the boy's eyes, a deep, dark grey colour he had never seen before and wondered if they were contact lenses. The boy was lightly dressed for the weather and time of year in a baggy, red checked shirt over a white roll neck sweater, both hanging loose over jeans. He was shivering severely. Did that mean he hadn't planned to be here, was careless to his needs, or just too poor to possess suitable clothing? Stirling was concerned the boy could lose his grip through numbed fingers. But he had seen people with serious mental illness endure freezing temperatures for hours, seemingly immune to what everyone else around them was suffering.

'Who are you?' shouted the boy harshly, his eyes flitting between Stirling and the road below. A young voice, softer than Stirling had expected, with fear in the grey eyes.

'My name's Stirling, I'd like to talk with you. Can I come closer? So that we don't have to shout?'

Searching Stirling's face for any sign of deception, he appeared to think about it for a moment and looked over to the two officers some distance behind Stirling. He jerked his head in agreement and watched carefully as Stirling slid his hand along the rail until he was only a few feet away. Between them the wind thrummed through the railings and a fluttering noise caught Stirling's ear. Searching for it, he saw a torn polythene bag thrashing amongst some brambles on the embankment.

'Will you tell me your name, please?'

The boy stared at him suspiciously and shook his head dully, a deep sadness now visible through the veil of wind driven hair before he turned to look down at the road again.

Stirling knew he must get the boy's focus off the road below, from imagining how he would harm himself and thinking about something more positive.

Smiling kindly, hoping he had his attention, Stirling asked, 'How long have you been here?'

The boy shrugged his shoulders and looked away, up the empty lanes and across the bare fields. Barely audible, he shrugged as he answered, 'About an hour. No one took any notice.'

'You must be very cold.' He wanted the boy to recognise his discomfort and the risk.

Again, a distracted shrug and a shake of the head.

'What is your name, or what name d'you like to be called by?' Stirling smiled, making sure it showed in his eyes, that he could be trusted. He needed to establish a rapport quickly.

The lad looked at him searchingly as he wrestled with the convention of the invitation. I tell you my name, you tell me yours. Opening his mouth to speak, the boy hesitated and closed it again, shook his head and let it fall forward so that his face was obscured again by the drape of hair.

Stirling urged himself on, keep talking, keep trying to reach him. Speaking as softly and reassuringly as the wind allowed, he said, 'Okay, that's not a problem, but I'm concerned for your safety, hanging out like that? Your arms will get tired and you could slip. Will you turn and face the railings? Please?'

The lad looked at Stirling again as he thought about the request. Moving quicker than Stirling had anticipated so that he thought he was about to fall, the boy swung himself round to face the railing, holding it with both hands. A small win.

Staring at Stirling, the boy shrugged his shoulders indifferently and said in a quiet voice that Stirling barely heard, 'It won't make any difference.'

'Why are you here? What caused this?'

Lifting his head to face him, the boy was crying as he struggled with whatever was going on in his head. 'Because everything in my life is *shit*! People treat me like *shit*! My whole *life* has been *shit*. Everyone *lies* to me.'

The bitter words tumbled out, his face twisted with anguish before dropping his head again to weep quietly. Inside the veil of hair, the boy appeared to be talking to himself, but Stirling could not hear the words. Stirling was framing his next words to find out the underlying problem and about to speak when the boy leaned out backwards, his knuckles white from the tightness of his grip.

Stirling shouted, 'Careful! Lean in or you'll slip!' trying not to sound as alarmed by the suddenness of the movement as he felt. The heightened tension had started a familiar separation in Stirling's brain which he often experienced in dynamic, high risk situations. Fuelled by adrenalin, his awareness was now acute, one side thinking laterally and calmly, noting minute detail as the other "motor" side drove on the functional elements of the task; seeking the boy's cooperation, reduce the risk of him falling, ask him who had lied, whatever words seemed appropriate. Somewhere too, his brain registered cold rain slapping on the back of small hands, slender fingers, no rings, troubled grey eyes peering through strands of fair hair, a slight cleft to the chin, wet clothes sticking to his body.

Stirling considered moving forward to try and grab him but knew it was too dangerous. He might misjudge his grab or miss him altogether and knock him off balance, causing him to fall. From the corner of his eye a flicker of movement amongst some scrub like bushes on the far embankment caught his attention. Certain he had seen something move, he glanced across briefly but could not see anything and assumed it had been another piece of litter swept by on the cold wind which flapped and tugged at the lad's shirt. With so much wind noise he wondered how much of the conversation the microphone would pick up.

'I'd like to help you. How can I do that?' he called over the wind.

The lad turned his grey eyes towards Stirling, gave an apathetic shrug and began to look carefully around him, triggering a memory of something he had learnt during his exchange training with the FBI. Someone settled on ending their life often take a long, last look around at the last image they will see. Alarmed, Stirling realised the boy was scanning. He must act swiftly.

'How will you get back over the railing when you're ready to?' It was an intentionally oblique question, to disrupt his thoughts, to make him think towards the solution and could lead to more conversation.

The lad turned his head slowly to look at Stirling with a new calmness that concerned him. Cautiously, Stirling extended his right hand.

'Lean back in. Please? Just talk with me?'

The lad stared at the outstretched hand for several seconds and then, warily, stared into Stirling's eyes before pulling himself in. Tentatively, he reached out a hand. Was he reaching for help? He'd experienced it before when just a simple touch of human kindness had prevented someone from jumping. Stirling stepped forward and took the boy's hand in his own, keeping hold of the cold railing with his free hand. The boy's hand felt small, soft and cold. Stirling gave him a reassuring squeeze, holding it as tightly as he dared to avoid frightening him. Closer now, he noticed the full mouth and fair skin between the wet hair through which the grey eyes watched him warily. There was a depth to their colour that struck Stirling again.

'Thank you. Will you tell me your name now?' asked Stirling, smiling as he spoke, projecting a calm he did not feel.

The boy said nothing as he looked into Stirling's eyes. Without warning, he let go of the railing and fell back, one foot perched precariously on the parapet, slipping as his weight twisted him away to hang over the void.

The unexpected movement caught Stirling by surprise. Seeping between their fingers, the rain made his hand slippier still as the boy's weight drew him slowly from his grip.

Reaching out as far as he could, Stirling tried desperately to grasp it tighter …

*

7.28 a.m.

Fighting down the nausea rising in his throat, Stirling sucked in the cold air, only vaguely aware of the two uniformed officers now at his side, their voices agitated and too loud with high emotion. Their voices seemed far away. One of them was shouting into his radio, looking towards someone Stirling could not see, waving an arm in the direction of the road below. At the edge of his vision, a paramedic scrambled down the embankment towards the boy.

The face of the younger of the two officers at his side was white with shock, his eyes fixed on the body. Stirling wanted to put a hand out to reassure him but knew he must master his own emotions first. The officer looked at Stirling, bewildered. Incidents like these had a familiar routine and pattern to them; the police turned up, cordoned off the area and played a slow game until everyone packed up peacefully and moved on to the next job. The officers would have seen death often enough but always after the event, usually in the community, and always sanitised within procedures that kept it impersonal, leaving them largely untouched. But to witness violent death was different. Stirling knew it would return to them unbidden, all their lives, triggered by a scent, a stray noise, a song or a random word. Stirling's own back catalogue of such memories was substantial already.

Seeing the Sergeant walking towards him, Stirling pushed himself off the railing. Glancing down again, he saw the paramedic checking the boy for vital life signs. Another paramedic joined the first and after some moments, reached out to stay the efforts of his colleague and gave a shake of his head. Drawing another deep breath, Stirling forced himself to regain his self-control and to function as an SIO.

Looking the Sergeant in the eye, willing him to say something insubordinately unprofessional, Stirling began giving firm orders. 'Sergeant. This is now a crime scene! I need you to contain and preserve it until someone can take over from me as SIO. Understood?'

Aware of the serious turn of events and keen to keep his own involvement as clean as possible, the Sergeant nodded his understanding, yet volunteered nothing. Stirling tasked him with the essential things which needed to be done to protect the scene, his experience overriding the shock. Happy to take instructions rather than to think for himself, the Sergeant relayed Stirling's instructions to the two officers at the railing who were pleased to have something more constructive to do than stare at the shattered body.

Fishing his mobile out of a coat pocket, Stirling pushed the pre-dial button giving him direct access to James's desk, bypassing the switchboard.

'James? Stirling. You're aware of what's happened?'

'Yes, we had an update by radio a moment ago. I understand he jumped … or fell. He's died?'

'That's about the sum of it. It's a teenage lad about fifteen or sixteen, I think. We need to find his family before social media finds them first. I'm in command here for the moment but as I'm involved in it, you'll need to get an SIO down here to take over from me. And get the duty Silver Commander out to take over the operational side of things.

'If you haven't already contacted the HQ media team, you'd better do so quickly. There's going to be a lot of media interest in this. I'm surprised they're not here already. Stuck in the traffic, hopefully.'

James confirmed a couple of points and was about to end the call when something else occurred to Stirling. 'Have you contacted PSD yet?'

Stirling was referring to the Professional Standards Department which investigated complaints against the police, and of misconduct.

'PSD sir?' James didn't understand the relevance.

Stirling held his tongue. It was not James's fault he was inexperienced. 'Anyone who dies within a police-controlled incident is in our constructive care and control, so the Independent Police Complaints Commission, the IPCC must be informed. The Chief will formally refer it to them later, but we usually give them an early alert. The duty officer for PSD will put in a discreet call ahead of the formal referral. It helps them to plan their response.'

Finishing the call and with nothing to do for the moment, Stirling suddenly became aware of how cold he was and began to shiver. Just cold? Or the onset of shock? He knew he must keep himself busy but all he could think of was the way the boy had stared into his eyes. What was he trying to communicate to Stirling, or was he reading too much into the eyes of a troubled mind? He kept re-running the conversation. Conversation? Hardly that, just a few words exchanged which reminded him of the tape recorder. Unclipping the microphone from his lapel, he pulled the recorder out of his pocket. It was still running. He was tempted to play it back but could not risk accidentally erasing it with cold, clumsy fingers. He switched it off.

Everything was there. He would have to live with the consequences.

Someone was shaking his shoulder. 'Doug! Come away. You can't do any more here, let them get on with it,' said a voice at his side.

Turning his head away from the paramedics packing away their equipment below, life all too obviously extinct, Stirling saw a familiar face at his side. He watched the lips moving but his attention was elsewhere, still trying to process the events leading to the boy's fall. He began to look back over the railing when the grip on his arm tightened and pulled him firmly away.

'Doug!' The voice was urgent, trying to penetrate his awareness. 'Come on! I'll take you back to HQ. You need time to yourself before the media circus gets here. It wasn't your fault!'

Looking intently at the face in front of him, Stirling couldn't work out why his friend and colleague of many years, Detective Inspector Bill Edwards, was there.

Shaking his head, he said, 'Bill? I thought I'd got his attention, but he just stepped away from me. He smiled at me.'

Stirling looked into his colleague's face as if the answer could be read there. Finding no explanation, he looked at his right hand, flexing and uncurling his fingers, still able to feel the cold fingers slipping through his own.

'I'm taking you back to HQ.' Edwards insisted. 'The Silver Commander's here, let her get on with the job.'

Looking around them, Stirling asked, 'Who is it?' his professional instincts returning.

'Inspector Murray. She's got bags of experience and will make sure all evidence and witness details are secured for the post-incident review and inquest.'

Taking his arm, Edwards began to steer Stirling towards his car. 'Let's get away from here before some cub reporter tries to splash your face all over the news.'

Stirling protested, pulling his arm from Edwards. 'Okay, but I'm waiting for the SIO to take over from me.'

'That's me! I was turning into HQ when they called me, so I came straight here. I'll speak with Murray and then I'm taking you to HQ. You might be suffering shock'. He could see Stirling was already in a mild shock but knew he would take a lot of persuasion to see a medical professional.

Stirling walked towards his own car, accepting Edwards's offer to drive. Feeling the cold rain driving into his face, Stirling looked up at the dark clouds scudding over them and tried to remember when, exactly, it had started raining. Hunching down into the passenger seat, Stirling pulled his coat around him, aware that he felt very cold. Some distance away, Edwards stood talking with a stocky woman in a yellow coat who kept breaking off to give directions into her radio. Both had their backs to the car, with Edwards looking at him occasionally with concern through the rain smeared windscreen, but Stirling took no interest. He could not stop playing the looped tape inside his head, analysing every sentence he had spoken with the boy, holding them up to scrutiny to identify what he had missed. His many years' experience as a Negotiator told him he had done all that he could in the time available, but he was left feeling that he had missed something.

The driver's door opened and a blast of cold air jolted Stirling from his thoughts. Slamming the door shut, Edwards looked over and studied him critically before telling him what he would want to hear.

'Everything's in hand, scenes of crime are here. She'll have to open the motorway as soon as possible.' He paused, asking cautiously, 'Did you tape it?'

'Of course I did. It's standard procedure,' replied Stirling, too forcefully.

Edwards ignored the over-reaction. 'Good. That should help to clarify things later, hopefully.' Holding his hand out towards him he added, 'I need it Doug, it's evidence.'

Stirling looked at Edwards's outstretched hand, contemplating the request. Reaching into his coat pocket he handed over the slim silver recorder. 'Take good care of that Bill.'

After checking the recorder was switched off, Edwards put it in a jacket pocket. 'I'll book it into evidence as soon as I've finished at the scene.'

Pushing the start button, Edwards selected gear and pulled away from a growing line of emergency vehicles.

*

A small knot of curious motorists and people from nearby business units had gathered to watch at one of the cordon tapes which fluttered and sagged under the wind. It was the only significant noise apart from instructions being shouted between the officers. Unable to see what was happening on the motorway below and chilled by the cold rain, some had already begun to drift away, back to the warmth of their offices and cars.

At the rear of the group, a man wearing a drab green parka coat with the hood drawn over his head, ostensibly against the rain but in truth to conceal his features, pointed a telephoto lens towards the car pulling out of the line of police vehicles. The camera shuttered rapidly as it captured Stirling's departure.

The photographer smiled, pleased with his morning's work. The few police officers at the scene had been too busy to notice him slipping down the embankment and working his way into some bushes from where he had photographed the whole thing, including the boy falling to the ground and now, he had the face of the last person to speak to him. A police negotiator, he assumed, who he had seen hold out his hand to the boy and suddenly move forward.

Knowing the police would take an interest if they suspected he had anything of evidential value, the photographer secreted the camera under his coat and ambled away from the cordon. The yellow jacketed officer nearby was too preoccupied with keeping his back to the rain to notice him go to a battered old car ramped up on a kerb. Fighting down his rising excitement, the photographer began calculating how much money he could make if his pictures were taken up by the nationals. He had a scoop, surely? And then there were the global internet syndicates too. It would make a lucrative change from the mundane community news he covered each day, from which he scratched a meagre living.

Pulling the driver's door shut, its dry hinges creaking with neglect, the photographer reviewed the images he had captured of the boy's death. Used to covering sports events, his camera was already set to a fast shutter speed and he had reacted instinctively when the boy leant out before falling. Scrolling though the review screen, he breathed a sigh of relief at the fifty or more images tracking the boy's fall. Even though he was concealed in bushes, he had kept the subject in frame with only slight blurring at the margins which he would crop out.

Shocked, uncertain of what he had witnessed for a moment, he had lowered the camera to stare at the body. Hearing a scream, he had photographed the two officers running out from under the bridge where they had been out of sight. Lifting the camera again, he had photographed the negotiator's face.

Enlarging the face until it filled the screen, a storyline formed in his avaricious mind: "Bridge Death! Pushed by Police?"

Taking a quick, furtive glance around outside, the photographer chuckled to himself mirthlessly, and said aloud, 'I'm about to make you famous, pal.'

Putting the key into the ignition he turned it, more in hope than expectation. The engine coughed into life at the third attempt but instead of cursing it as he usually would, he smiled in anticipation of scrapping the old nail and accelerated away.

*

The drive to Headquarters only took a few minutes. Staring through the side window, Stirling saw little of the sodden fields sliding behind gaunt hedgerows as they swept up the narrow lane, wipers rhythmically beating aside the rain. His mind had already turned to the post-incident enquiry when others, free of the demands of swift decision making and blessed with acres of time, and that most critical commodity of 20-20 hindsight, would unpick his every decision and action.

Edwards tried reassuring him that he had done the best he could, that it was impossible to save each one. Stirling knew he was right, but it didn't make him feel any better. As well as both being SIOs, their "day job", both were experienced Hostage and Crisis Intervention Negotiators, a voluntary role in which they were often exposed to danger during the miserable hours of the night when more risk averse colleagues stayed safe in their beds. Misunderstood by most cops, and despised by some, negotiators were often thought of as a tedious impediment to getting on with the sexy stuff of breaking down doors. Stirling had lost count of the times he and Edwards had worked together as negotiators, working for the safe release of hostages held at knife or gunpoint, occasionally by the "mad and bad." More often, though, it was about talking to sad, vulnerable people, trying to bring them back to safety from high buildings or any number of dangerous situations that people intent on self-harm got themselves into.

They both had their fair share of war stories, of working in dangerous locations, in miserable conditions. But when, like today, their efforts were unsuccessful, every action would be critically examined, each sentence parsed and analysed before a Coroner's inquest. All for which, it being a voluntary role, police negotiators were rewarded with the handsome fee of nothing at all.

Most of the people they met were simply seeking attention or making a cry for help, and responded well to a friendly face and voice, to someone prepared to listen. Very few were absolutely determined to die and could often be identified within a few seconds of talking to them. He had not experienced the usual sense of foreboding and no matter how many times he re-ran it, he could think of nothing more he would have said or done differently. There was simply no time to establish a rapport.

Edwards broke into his thoughts. 'What did you have planned for the day? You need to reschedule things, for a few hours at least.'

They had grown up in the Service and their career paths had occasionally brought them together. They worked hard, and as younger men had played harder still, been drunk together a few times and got into scrapes, but without any career damaging repercussions. When investigations and Edwards's family commitments permitted, Saturday afternoons might find them together enjoying a shared passion for rugby, loyally supporting the local premiership club in and out of the relegation zone. A year ago, they had both applied for promotion to the DCI post in the MCU, but it was Stirling who had been successful, leaving him awkward at beating a friend to the job. Both had been equally qualified for the role but, in typical fashion, Edwards had made sure he was the first to congratulate him, to shake his hand and pledge support.

Stirling dragged his thoughts back to the question. What had he planned for the day? All he could think of was the boy's eyes that had seemed to hold him, searching for something, now constantly falling away from him in slow motion.

'I had an office day lined up. The annual budget blood bath is this morning and there's the trial coming up. The QC's asked for some late enquiries to be done before the trial.'

'Which one, the girl who went under the train?' asked Edwards.

'That's what the accused wanted everyone to believe, except she was dead long before the train mangled her,' he answered dispassionately, as he remembered the young woman's terrible end.

Edwards brought the car to a halt. 'Okay, I suggest you get yourself a hot brew and I'll get back down there before anyone screws up the scene.'

Stirling looked up, surprised to see the familiar light stone facade of force HQ in front of him, now washed to a darker colour by the dull morning light and rain.

Edwards passed over the car keys. 'I'll get a lift back down there.'

'Thanks Bill,' said Stirling, looking up at the building and wondering if he could get to his office without meeting anyone.

8.24 a.m.

As Edwards set off towards the control centre, Stirling walked quickly towards the Ionic columns standing guard beside the wide oak doors of the main entrance. Pushing the heavy door open, he stepped into the high-ceilinged reception hall and strode past the reception desk. Intent on reaching his office quickly, he ignored a cheery "Morning, sir" called to him by the receptionist. She would think him rude, but he was in no mood for small talk and would explain another time.

Running up the wide staircase, taking the shallow treads two at a time, Stirling knew how quickly operational chit-chat circulated and wanted to avoid talking about what had happened, for now at least. Reaching the top of the stairs, he was turning towards his office when the door leading from the Chief Officers Command Suite swung open and a familiar figure walked through, clearly looking for a conversation. Stirling gave an inward groan as Deputy Chief Constable Ian McDonald stepped towards him.

McDonald had a higher opinion of himself than anyone else had and took an unfortunate pride in his reputation as a disciplinarian. As the Deputy, McDonald's portfolio included the Professional Standards Department, so anything which engaged the IPCC fell to him. Since arriving from a large metropolitan force the previous year, McDonald had already damaged several officers' careers, and trashed the career prospects of a highly respected senior detective. McDonald was distrusted by everyone that Stirling respected, which was good enough reason for him to be cautious. Controlling his reactions, Stirling offered a brief greeting that he hoped would imply he was busy and could move on, but the Deputy wanted to talk.

A short man in his late forties, McDonald had probably once been athletic but was now thin and unhealthy looking, with a greyish pallor caused by more than simply working indoors for too long. McDonald was a heavy smoker, unusual amongst police officers these days, and the rasp in his voice only served to accentuate his habitual brusqueness. A hawkish nose underlined by a precisely trimmed moustache made Stirling wonder if McDonald had ever served in the military.

'Morning DCI Stirling. A problem down at the motorway, I hear?' McDonald's clipped tone wasn't enquiring so much as making a statement.

'Yes, sir,' replied Stirling. 'I'm afraid we were unsuccessful in saving a boy's life.'

'We? I believe you were on your own?' McDonald replied with an implicit challenge. 'The Duty Inspector's given me a *full* briefing.' There was an edge to McDonald's voice, his jaw set, head tilted back to look up to Stirling who stood several inches taller than him.

Feeling his hackles rising, Stirling answered with a harder edge than he intended. 'Sorry, sir. I thought *we* always made a collective effort and I doubt he could have given you a *full* briefing. I've only just left the scene. Inspector James only has verbal information on which to advise you.'

As he spoke, Stirling felt his anger rising. An inner voice urged caution, but he expected better from a Chief Officer. McDonald had heard the anger too.

'I see, Detective Chief Inspector,' McDonald replied tightly. 'Then I look forward to reading more about it as soon as possible. By end of the morning, latest. There'll be a referral to the IPCC this morning.'

Having just tried and failed to save someone's life, and sensing no concern for his welfare, Stirling dismissed any further concern for McDonald's sensibilities. 'I've arranged an informal referral already through the duty PSD officer. I imagine you'll hear more at your morning briefing, sir,' Stirling said, bluntly.

'Ah, yes, of course. That would be the correct thing to have happened.' McDonald had stiffened, irritated at being corrected and remembering to rebuke whoever in the PSD had not already briefed him.

Stirling could see that he had caught McDonald off guard, making him more dangerous. McDonald stood looking up at him, expecting more information which Stirling was not going to provide until he'd had time to collect his thoughts.

'I must make up my notes sir, so please excuse me.' Without waiting for a response, Stirling turned and walked off towards his office.

*

McDonald watched Stirling's back departing down the corridor, angry that he had been dismissed from Stirling's company, rather than the other way around. Deciding he would take a close interest in the case, he turned back towards his office and thought about who he could appoint to lead the force's input to the IPCC's investigation. Someone ambitious, suitably qualified, but who he could manage. A name came to mind, together with something he had overheard recently.

In the Chief Officer's Secretariat, a dark-haired woman in her early thirties had just arrived for work and was putting away her coat and bags in a cupboard. Seeing the Deputy at the door she greeted him brightly.

Ignoring the greeting, McDonald ordered brusquely, 'See if Superintendent Shaw is in yet and put her through to me when you get her.'

Without waiting for a reply, McDonald walked on into his office and closed the door, leaving the woman still holding her coat above the coat hook, stunned at his rudeness.

The Deputy's office was a large room at the corner of the first floor of the original mansion house building. McDonald stared out through the tall sash window across the countryside as he thought through the imminent IPCC investigation, asking himself if it was an opportunity, or a threat to his career. Looking through the rain smeared glass to the motorway two miles away, he saw it was still empty. Normally, it would be a constant stream of vehicles, night and day. He was tempted to send a message to whoever was in charge down there to get it opened damned quick, but decided not to. Instead, he might use it to obliquely undermine a colleague at the Chief Officer's meeting that morning. The recently appointed ACC needed to be kept in her place.

Half an hour later, McDonald was still fuming at his dismissal by Stirling, when his thoughts were interrupted by the telephone ringing on his desk.

'Superintendent Shaw at Kidderminster for you, sir.' McDonald didn't encourage the modern trend of addressing senior officers by first names, not even by his PA.

'Put her through!'

*

Although Stirling's own office was fifteen miles away, where the MCU's teams of investigators, specialists and the HOLMES system were based, whilst finalising the trial papers he was using an office in a red brick wing of the main building. Designed with an eye to function, rather than form, the wing sat back from the main building like an ugly relative standing hesitantly in the shadow of its elegant sister, aware of its own offence. The offices still had the original windows fitted which bore testament to the craftsmanship of the day, but meant the rooms were frequently cold in winter. Under each window, heavy radiators warmed the draughts.

The wing had served many purposes over the decades and for a long time had been the living quarters for women officers attending training. Few men had succeeded in outwitting the stalwart women sergeants who had patrolled the morals of their young charges, even if some were not especially worried about their virtue being protected.

Shutting the door, Stirling slumped heavily into the large swivel chair behind the desk and pushed himself around to stare out of the window, hands thrust deep into his raincoat pockets. The window rattled noisily in its frame and rain disfigured the landscape. Low leaden clouds reaching to the horizon reflected his mood perfectly.

It was not the first time he had "lost" someone in a negotiation, but this one was scratching at his soul. Was it because it was a young lad, or something else? What had he missed? After many minutes' reflection, Stirling swung his chair around and pulled a bound notebook towards him. He might make better sense of it as he wrote up his notes which he would have to submit that day. A formal statement would have to wait until he had recovered himself and was sure he had everything in the correct order of events. The Coroner's inquest and the boy's family would be better served with an accurate account and no vital omissions. Thinking of the boy's family, he wondered if they knew yet.

Absorbed in writing up his notes, Stirling only heard the slow tread of footsteps approaching his office when they were just a few feet away. Stopping to listen, pen poised over the page, he knew only one person with that distinctive tread and waited for the door to open. Instead, there was a knock and silence.

'Come in,' he called, thinking he was mistaken.

The door opened slowly to frame a familiar and welcome figure. Detective Superintendent Dave Pearson paused to study him before stepping into the room, closing the door behind him. Taking one of the two seats opposite Stirling's desk, Pearson crossed one leg over the other and sat with his hands folded in his lap, all the while watching Stirling keenly.

'Morning, Doug. I heard a few minutes ago. Thought I'd come and see how you are?' A pause, 'No fun losing someone like that.'

Pearson's concern was sincere and in marked contrast to the Deputy's manner earlier. Stirling was pleased to have someone he could talk with as an equal and who had been through similar experiences himself. Pearson understood both the personal cost, and the professional risk.

Dave Pearson had been his boss for several years and they trusted each other completely. Stirling smiled privately as he noticed a familiar, slightly shabby tie tied in a small knot, one of only half a dozen worn by Pearson together with four suits which gave him options in blue, black, grey and a dark green affair that he seemed particularly proud of. A renowned workaholic, Pearson would never waste time on something as frivolous as shopping, so his wardrobe reflected Mrs Pearson's interpretation of Service attire. Today, suitably, he was in black, giving him a funereal look which accentuated a thin, slightly stooped frame caused through too many hours bent over case papers, reports and a computer keyboard.

Stirling had met Mrs Pearson a few times over the years, but only very briefly. He remembered a pleasant woman but so unremarkable in features that if required to, he would struggle to describe her. More usually, he had spoken to her on the telephone when calling Pearson outside office hours to discuss something urgent, but the phone was always swiftly handed off to Pearson, preventing polite small talk. The Pearsons did not socialise together in police circles and some of the office wags mischievously questioned if she existed at all, playing a running game of fantastically speculative tales of Pearson's supposed double life of champagne, fast cars and even faster mistresses, all completely at odds with his quiet, slightly dour nature. But always in good humour. Everyone had great respect and affection for *"the old man."*

'How are you feeling?' Pearson asked.

No questions about what had happened at the bridge, or a hundred other operationally related questions he could legitimately have started with, just a concern for his welfare. Stirling smiled thinly as Pearson hunched down in the chair, watching him with the half-hooded eyes which intimidated many.

'I've had better starts to the day, Dave.'

'Want to talk about it?'

'Yes, and no. I'm happy to talk about what I did. I'm sure I did things correctly, but I'm still confused ...' Stirling shook his head slightly, '... disturbed really. I was struggling to hold onto his hand anyway, it was wet and slipping away. But, I felt him let go of me, quite clearly. And as he let go, he smiled at me. Faintly, but very definitely. There was something in his eyes too, I'm not mistaken about it. It was as though he was ... I don't know, leaving something with me ... a message.'

Stirling noticed Pearson watching his hands. Looking down, he was surprised to see that, unconsciously, he had been re-enacting the boy's hand slipping through his own. He looked back to Pearson and raised his hands in a gesture of frustration. 'I know that sounds daft, but that's the impression he left me with. I can't explain it any better than that.'

Pearson said nothing as Stirling leant back in the chair and put his hands into his pockets out of sight. Pearson sat quietly waiting for him to speak again, the silence hanging between them. Stirling understood what Pearson was doing and surrendered to the opportunity to talk.

'He was just so very young Dave.' He shook his head, 'Perhaps that's why I feel like this? We don't get many situations like that, with youngsters, thankfully. But what a waste! What the *hell* was going on in his life, or not going on for that matter to make him give up like that? I'm angry with myself that I couldn't stop him, but I barely got chance to speak with him ... I feel as though I've failed!'

Stirling could hear the anger and emotion in his voice. Breathing out loudly to release the tension, he looked across at Pearson, seeking a response, some recognition. 'You've been there Dave. You know how it feels.'

Years before becoming a Negotiator himself, and before he got to know Pearson well, Stirling had been told of an incident in which Pearson was the negotiator. The police had arrived at a remote farm with the farmer sat in the middle of a field cradling a shotgun, intent on killing himself. Heavily in debt, he was about to lose his home, his livelihood and his family through divorce.

The armed response vehicles were committed elsewhere so at great personal risk, Pearson had walked out to the centre of the field where the man was sat, holding the shotgun under his chin. With no body protection, Pearson spent two hours trying to persuade him to put down the gun and not give up on life. Despite apparently gaining a good rapport with the man - they had even shared some humorous anecdotes together - the man thanked Pearson for trying to help but couldn't see any way out of his problems and blew his brains out, spraying Pearson in blood and gore.

Stirling had only ever heard the story from others and had never raised it with Pearson. Those who knew Pearson well told Stirling it had affected him deeply and he was never quite the same afterwards, his previous easy humour and sparkle diminished. Noticing Pearson's gaze drift somewhere behind his left shoulder, Stirling was beginning to understand how that could be. Pearson knew what Stirling was referring to but showed no emotion. Instead, a mask fell over his face and when he spoke, his voice was soft and controlled.

'We do the best we can Doug. We follow our training and procedure as far as circumstances allow us to and apply our experience. Usually, it works out well, but you know as well as I do that some people can't be helped. It doesn't stop us trying and when it works, we feel good. Today's the other side of that coin.'

Stirling nodded silently, acutely aware of his own despondency.

Aware he might be exposing his own wounds, Pearson coughed and stirred himself in the chair. 'Besides, we know nothing about him yet, do we? Why was he there? Drugs? Mental health or family issues? Let's find out more about him first before you beat yourself up too much.'

It was sound advice. 'You're right, I know, but it's impossible not to be affected.'

'Bill Edwards has gripped the scene and will manage it until he can hand over to the IPCC. They'll either take full control with one of their own SIO's or supervise someone appointed from the force. Right now, I want you to finish writing up those notes and then take the day off, a few days if you need it.' Pearson looked at him, raising his eyebrows in enquiry.

Stirling pointed to his notes. 'I've almost finished. Thanks for the offer Dave, but I need to keep busy.'

Pearson gave him a long, shrewd look. 'Okay, you're clearly not falling apart so it's your call, but you'll have to accept a mandatory referral to Occupational Health for a psychological assessment.'

Stirling smiled, ruefully. 'Since it was me who worked so hard to get it in place for the negotiator team, I can hardly avoid it for myself, can I?'

'No. Hand your notes into the investigation as soon as you can, and I'll keep the dogs off your back. McDonald will be all over this like a rash and only too happy to add more scalps to his lance if he scents blood.'

Pearson levered himself out of the chair and took another long appraising look down at Stirling. 'If you need to talk, off the record, let me know. I've been there. It's lonely, personally and professionally. Particularly with others picking over your actions with the science of applied hindsight.'

Standing up, Stirling reached across to shake hands, holding his hand firmly to emphasise his appreciation. 'Thanks Dave.'

With no more needing to be said, Pearson left, closing the door quietly behind him. Stirling turned to watch grey columns of rain dragging over the fields beyond the estate as he listened to Pearson's steady footsteps along the corridor, and halt. A low conversation ensued with someone in an office and the footsteps continued again, until lost to earshot. Stirling knew he could depend on Pearson's counsel if needed. Although something of a legend in the force, Pearson rarely spoke of his experiences, letting others do the storytelling.

Stirling read through his notes again to be sure he had included everything, and that the sequence was as accurate as he could recall it. Deciding he could add nothing more, he signed each page and put them inside an envelope. Stuffing his mobile into a pocket and pulling on his coat, he strode along the corridor towards the secretary's office. Turning the corner brought him to Pearson's door, open as usual. Looking up from a spreadsheet, Pearson raised his eyebrows in a silent question.

Holding up the envelope Stirling said, 'I'll make sure they're handed to Bill Edwards personally. I'd like to get out of the way to the MCU, if that's okay with you?'

'Who's covering for you at the meeting with ACC Crime?' Pearson tapped a thin finger on the spreadsheets. 'It'll be tough enough getting this budget through with all the cut backs. If you're not there it might go against you. Against us.'

'I was in early this morning preparing but after what's happened … can you cover for me? Extenuating circumstances?'

Pearson thought it over for a moment. 'You're asking for a lot of money here. Don't expect to get everything you've asked for.'

'It's a strong business case with demand projections for the next three years. If the force doesn't invest in investigating major crime, and its reputation, I can only do so much. I gave ACC Tanner a peek at the business case last week when I was briefing her about a trial we've got coming up, so the ground's prepared and she's a strong supporter of the MCU.'

'Okay, but Steph Tanner has to be seen to be fair.'

'Thanks. I owe you.'

'I'll add it to the list!' Pearson grumbled, already re-immersing himself in the papers.

Stirling continued down the corridor and turned into the CID Secretariat where a woman was sat at a large desk which dominated the room and from which she could screen the entrance to the Detective Chief Superintendent's office. It was a brave man or woman who tried to speak with the DCS without first checking in with Beryl Loveridge, his formidable secretary who had served the force loyally since leaving secretarial college at the tender age of seventeen. Now forty-three, Beryl Loveridge was in awe of nobody, not even the Chief Constable of the day - she'd seen enough of them process through the force - and gave short shrift to anyone she thought to be a threat to the reputation of "her" CID Command Team. Hard working and highly competent, she ruled her roost with a shrewd eye and did not suffer fools gladly. However, beneath the façade, she had a compassionate nature.

Hearing footsteps enter the room, Beryl looked up with a prepared frown, ready to deter any frivolous enquiry. On seeing

Stirling, her face softened immediately, and she gave him a warm smile, until she remembered what Pearson had told her.

'Dougie, I'm so sorry to hear about what happened. Such an awful thing to have seen, and so young. His poor family too. How are *you*?' Beryl's questions were sincere, moving easily from a genuine concern for the dead boy's family to his own welfare.

'I'm okay thank you Beryl, but I can't talk about it,' he replied, shrugging his shoulders.

Lowering her voice, she said, 'Stirling, I know you would have done all that was possible. As tragic as it is, he took himself there in the first place. You tried. Not many would put their selves in your place.'

As much as he enjoyed Beryl's company he wanted to get away quickly. Holding out the buff envelope he asked her to copy the notes, email a copy to him and hand the original to Bill Edwards personally.

Taking the envelope from him, she placed it on her desk and patted it protectively. 'I'll hand it to him myself.'

Stirling stood undecided for a moment looking at the envelope on the desk, concerned about it reaching Edwards safely. But Beryl's efficiency was legendary, so he thanked her and left.

*

Watching Superintendent Shaw nodding frequently, her jaw setting ever more firmly between agreeing in the appropriate places to the voice at the other end of the line, from the other side of the desk the other voice sounded terse, to say the least. Shaw was trying to wind up the call.

'No problem sir, leave it with me. As it happens, he's here with me now. We were just about to chat through some divisional issues and ...' The voice interrupted brusquely, giving instructions before Shaw resumed, 'Yes sir, I'll get his work handed over for a couple of weeks ... longer? That's going to leave me thin on the ground ...'

There was another terse interruption before she could speak again, trying to maintain an even tone. 'I'll get him to you this afternoon ... this morning? Yes, sir.'

The conversation appeared to have ended abruptly as Shaw held the phone away to study it for moment before slamming it into the cradle.

'Ignorant bastard!' she muttered under her breath and looked at the heavy-set man in uniform who had been sat in front of her desk throughout the conversation. Superintendent Jenny Shaw would have preferred that Chief Inspector John Ballard was not present during the call as she could have been more forceful with the Deputy, but the presence of a more junior officer had prevented that. Shaw had enough service to know how to politely tell a Chief Officer to put his suggestions where the sun didn't shine, if the occasion called for it.

'Problem, Ma'am?' Ballard asked, eyebrows raised and curious to know what he had been selected for.

Leaning back in her black leather chair, Shaw drummed the fingers of both hands on the desk edge as she studied Ballard. 'That, if you hadn't already worked it out for yourself, was the Deputy, as bloody rude as ever. What we did to deserve him, I'll never know!'

Unwilling to be drawn into criticism of a Chief Officer, Ballard asked, 'It sounded as if I must go to HQ, to meet with him?'

'He wants you for a post-incident review of something that happened this morning. He's asked for you explicitly, but I'm not sure why. There are other people in more suitable roles who could do it instead of taking someone from my divisional command team which I can ill afford. Any idea why?' Shaw fixed Ballard with sharp blue eyes that held his unwaveringly.

Ballard affected a blank look as he looked at her. Superintendent Jenny Shaw was a short, stout woman in her early fifties who wore her salt and pepper coloured hair cut short in a practical style that tended to accentuate her strong build and suited her temperament and reputation for getting things done. Shaw had grown up in the force since joining as a cadet at seventeen, and proudly claimed that like a stick of fairground rock, if you cut her in half you would read the name of the force running through her. As tough as tin tacks and possessed of formidable energy, Shaw set and expected high standards of everyone under her command, and woe betide whoever fell short. Most people in the division liked her and respected her and the few who did not were the few loafers and coasters every workplace suffers. With such long service, she was extremely well networked throughout the force too.

Ballard shifted uncomfortably under Shaw's inspection, as if she was reading his soul. Believing his talents had not been valued in his previous force, Ballard had transferred into the force on promotion to Chief Inspector five years ago, hoping to improve his fortunes. Since arriving, he had worked hard and volunteered for anything that might raise his profile, but his efforts to gain promotion to Superintendent had come to nothing. The first time, he consoled himself that the Chief Officers simply needed to see more of his capabilities and he would soon be on his way to taking his seat amongst them, where he fully deserved to be. But as each year went by without promotion he had become increasingly bitter, seeing shadows in the dark and perceiving an old pals network conspiring to hold him back. That others considered him to be incompetent and vainglorious would never occur to him. And the peer review of the investigation he was leading last year had not helped his cause. Until then he had only known of DCI Stirling by reputation, but Stirling's peer review had identified policy decision errors and missed opportunities that, Stirling had claimed, would have expedited the investigation and saved time and money. Ballard was still aggrieved that his explanations had not been heard.

Clearing his throat, Ballard asked, 'Did he say what the post-incident review is about Ma'am?'

'Not much. The IPCC is being called in after a death in our constructive custody this morning. A suicide intervention on a bridge over the motorway close to HQ. A negotiator was there but the chap jumped. Or fell. McDonald expects the IPCC to provide oversight to an internally appointed SIO.' Shaw paused to watch Ballard's reaction. 'He wants you to be the SIO. You've done the course, so you're qualified, but you don't have much experience in the role ...' Shaw saw Ballard bridle at her words, '... so you'll be working under their supervision, but reporting to the Deputy. He'll be keeping a close eye on it anyway because PSD's in his portfolio.'

Ballard was delighted but didn't want Shaw to see. He frowned with concern. 'I see. It sounds very interesting. And challenging too, of course. It's always difficult enquiring into the work of a colleague but, of course, I will show complete impartiality.'

Shaw's eyes gave nothing away as she listened to the pompous reply. She knew Ballard was delighted to be selected and wondered how he would react to the next piece of information.

'The focus of the enquiry will be on the police response and the negotiation strategy. Particularly, the negotiator who was speaking to the person who died.' She paused, 'DCI Stirling.'

Ballard's eyes flared so slightly that someone else might have missed it, but not Shaw's astute gaze.

'Oh?' replied Ballard, keeping his voice level and his faux concern in place. 'That must have been very difficult for him, at a personal level. I don't fully understand the work of our negotiators, but this will give me a chance to learn more about the role.'

Seeing no reply from Shaw was forthcoming, he decided to manage himself out of the room as quickly as possible. 'So, I'm required at HQ this morning, Ma'am?'

'Yes. Delegate as much as you can to your Inspectors and I'll arrange for your divisional call-out to be shared out amongst the command team. Any questions?'

'No Ma'am, thank you.' Ballard rose from his seat and walked to the door before turning to look back at Shaw. 'I'm sorry, Ma'am. Do you still want to discuss what we were meeting for this morning?'

Shaw glanced down at the papers under her hand. She had intended to haul Ballard over the coals regarding the poor performance of his teams, which meant his poor performance, but it would have to wait. Shaking her head, she replied, 'If it's still important when you get back, we'll pick up then.'

'Thank you, Ma'am.'

*

After the door had closed, Shaw sat thinking for some minutes as she tried to work out why McDonald would have asked for Ballard, who had little investigative experience. Even allowing for his naked ambition, which everyone was painfully aware of, it didn't explain why he had been requested.

Usually, if the force's reputation was at risk, it would use its best people to limit the chance of any further cock ups. Putting someone like Ballard to lead the investigation was risky, even with oversight from McDonald and the IPCC. Like all chief officers, McDonald had a heavy daily schedule and would be unavailable to give moment to moment direction and advice, and some of the IPCC's investigators had proved to be of variable quality. Shaw picked her mobile up from the desk and scrolled through her contacts until she found Pearson's number.

'Dave, it's Jenny.'

'Morning Jenny, good to hear from you. How can I help?'

'You need to know about a call I've had this morning.'

*

Pulling the door shut, Ballard looked up and down the corridor passing Shaw's office. Seeing no one, he allowed himself a broad smile and started towards his own office with a lighter step than when he had arrived. Delighted at the opportunity to raise his profile with no less than the Deputy Chief Constable, he was already planning how to clear his desk and delegate the worst aspects of his work to his Inspectors. The sooner he could get himself off to HQ, the better.

He was pleased to escape from the beady eye of Jenny Shaw who took far too much interest in his business for his liking and had been critical of his performance recently. He had been expecting a roasting this morning and although it might still be waiting for him when he got back, he would make sure it was delayed for as long as possible.

Ballard felt McDonald might be a kindred spirit. Neither of them was originally from the force and were unshackled by professional relationships developed over many years. In Ballard's view, such relationships only got in the way of change and modernisation which he always embraced enthusiastically. Particularly if his career could profit by it. Any concern Ballard might once have felt for colleagues he had put aside as unhelpful to his career, believing a dispassionate attitude to be the only way in which a senior officer could operate in modernising public services. Somewhere along the way Ballard had also ditched any concern for the public part of public service, considering it to be a varied and unpredictable commodity which he knew he must engage with on occasions, but to be avoided as far as possible. Particularly the tedium of public meetings with their inherent risk of having to meet with angry members of the public and community groups, delegating as much as he could get away with to his Inspectors and Sergeants.

Arriving in his office, Ballard began calling each of his Inspectors, passing over projects he had volunteered for, but had become bogged down in and would now prefer to be free of. Giving instructions on what he could be contacted for in the event of a decision being required of him, he made it clear they should sort things out themselves. Thereby, absolving himself of responsibility if the wheel came off. A telephone call to the Deputy's personal assistant identified the first available diary slot would be late morning, so he busied himself in making telephone calls to find out what had happened earlier.

Several calls later, Ballard was feeling increasingly optimistic.

*

After dropping Stirling off, Edwards had returned to the scene to check on progress, making sure every aspect of the evidential process was being completed thoroughly, despite pressure to reopen the motorway. The body was still screened over and an undertaker's black van stood nearby.

He needed a decision as to how far he should take the enquiry before handing over to the IPCC. Like any other public body, Edwards knew they were strapped for people with a heavy caseload. Meanwhile, he had a body but no identity and the calls he had taken from the force's media relations team were becoming more urgent as the media machine demanded to be fed. Edwards had agreed an initial holding statement with a promise of more to come as soon as possible, but it would only buy a little time. The boy's age was attracting interest. At the cordon, he could see a small group of journos gathered together, swapping information. Of greater concern was the dynamic of social media which would swiftly overtake them all, if had not already. He would be lucky to identify the boy's family before they found out by other means.

A swift but thorough search of the scene and its surrounds by Task Force officers for any physical evidence had recovered nothing. Edwards pressed the TF team leader, a grizzled Sergeant with close shaven grey hair, if he was certain there was no mobile phone. The Sergeant looked at Edwards as if his parentage was in question before assuring him they had searched where a phone might reasonably be expected to have landed, if thrown from the parapet. No phone or phone parts were found. A quick check of the boy's pockets revealed a handkerchief and a housekey only which had been bagged by the SOCO team. Edwards was surprised at the absence of a mobile phone.

The Coroner had given permission via the Coroner's Officer to remove the body to Worcester Hospital two miles away. The undertaker's van pulled forward and two men efficiently lifted the broken body into a black plastic body bag. Zipping it closed, they lifted their anonymous cargo into the van's interior and stood talking quietly with one of the officers for a few minutes, looking at the bridge above and then to the roadway at their feet without a trace of emotion.

Once the van had sped away, a fire unit hosed away the coagulated blood whilst Edwards agreed the scene hand over to the Silver Commander, and the job of reopening of the motorway. At every approach road, long queues of cars were waiting for life to resume.

Very soon, thousands of people would travel over the spot, oblivious to, and uncaring of an anonymous boy's death.

*

Swinging into the parking bay, Stirling braked to a hard stop beneath the three-storey building, of which the Major Crime Unit occupied two entire floors. Switching off the engine, his mind consumed by the events of the morning, Stirling could remember nothing of the twenty-minute drive. Peering up at the windows of the MCU above him, Stirling saw a face disappear from a window and the vertical blinds swing slightly. His arrival had been announced.

Stirling took his time climbing the stairs, his footsteps echoing off the tiled steps and bouncing down the open stairwell. Normally, he took them two at a time to reach the top slightly breathless, a small way of monitoring his fitness, but this morning he would give people time to escape rather than feel awkward in his company, unsure what to say for the best.

Reaching the top of the stairs he pushed through the outer swing door into another short corridor where his small office lay to the right. Dropping his briefcase on to the desk and pulling off his overcoat, Stirling looked through the window blinds down into the car park he had just left to see three detectives emerge from another door and walk to their cars. Perhaps they had been leaving anyway.

Deciding he should get on with it, Stirling made his way down the short corridor to the main office and pushed open the door. He was surprised to see some of his team waiting for him and, at their centre, Detective Sergeant Jon "Geordie" Heal with a mug of tea in his hand, wearing a cautious smile.

Holding the mug out to Stirling, Heal welcomed him in his distinctive singsong Geordie accent. 'Morning boss, we thought you might need this. It's been a difficult start to the day.'

Stirling took the mug reactively and looked about the room. Ten or so men and women of his team had waited for him to arrive to show their support. They were a mixture of investigators, HOLMES specialists, analysts and other staff, most of whom had worked in the MCU for some years. Stirling wasn't sure what to say, but before he could reply, Heal gestured around at the team who were waiting for Stirling's reaction.

'We know you can't talk about it boss, what with the IPCC and all that, but we want you to know we're behind you and not have to tip-toe round you, pretending nothing's happened. It'll be weeks before the investigation reports its findings, and then there'll be the inquest. We thought you'd prefer things to be as normal as possible. So, we thought a hot brew and get on with the morning briefing as soon as possible would be best? It's Monday morning, after all!' Heal gave a tight, forced smile, trying to keep the atmosphere light.

Stirling cleared his throat to speak. 'Thanks Geordie, everyone,' he answered, 'That's very much appreciated and you're right, business as usual. But let's not forget a young lad died this morning. There's a family grieving for a lost child. So, not too strong a show of support outside the building, please. It might be misread. Okay?'

There was a murmur of agreement as Heal looked around at his colleagues before turning back to Stirling. 'We understand that boss. We can't help them from here, but we can support you.'

Not trusting himself to speak, Stirling took a swig of the tea to mask his discomfort. It was a welcome response, but he wasn't surprised. Most of them, particularly the experienced detectives, had witnessed some gruesome tragedy or other and had their own memories boxed away. Speaking briskly Stirling began to get the ball rolling.

'Okay, briefing in five minutes. Geordie, keep it tight, headline stuff only and restricted to supervisors unless you think it's important for someone to be there. In my office.'

Looking around at the faces he lifted the mug in salute to them and added, 'Thanks.'

Back in his office, Stirling switched on his computer and searched for the incident log for that morning, muttering his annoyance when he found he could not access it in the usual way. Bill Edwards and James had secured it, as they should.

The investigation had started.

*

11.37 a.m.

Formally named the Chief Officers Command Suite but more commonly known as "the landing," Ballard had only visited it once before, and that was when he had been carpeted after Stirling's review. Originally, the wide landing area had served the large, principle bedrooms of the old manor house. From the landing, painted out in pale regency green with a high, white ceiling above, six oak doors led to spacious offices for each of the Chief Officers, the largest of them all, the Chief Constable's. On the walls hung ancient oil paintings of the building's former aristocratic owners.

Arriving early for his meeting, Ballard sat in one of several brown leather chairs clustered around the hushed landing wishing he was part of the steady procession of senior officers and staff entering and leaving the offices, standing to confer quietly about meeting decisions or share a relaxed joke before drifting back to their offices elsewhere on the HQ estate.

Occasionally, a chief officer in shirtsleeves crossed from one office to another or into the PA's office, nodding briefly to Ballard as they gathered up their next meeting group. Ballard enjoyed the acknowledgement, assuming they knew who he was and the importance of his appointment as SIO. He intended to become a familiar figure on the landing in the weeks ahead as he met regularly with the Deputy to report on the investigation. Ballard hoped he might even see the Chief Constable himself, but as he considered the possibility and being asked a question he could not answer, he began to worry if he really wanted to. He did not want to appear uninformed of whatever topical issue the Chief might have on his mind and anxiously tried to recall what the headline news items were that morning.

With a nervous twist in his gut, Ballard hoped the Deputy would see him soon and looked towards his office, willing the door to open. He had been kept waiting for over half an hour. Just then, the PA called across to him pleasantly to say the Deputy was free and he could go in. Ignoring her smile, Ballard gave a curt nod, walked to the office door and knocked, waiting to be called in. A barked command impatiently called "Enter" and he stepped into the room with a tentative smile, unsure of what to expect.

McDonald sat behind a large antique desk with papers piled at each corner and more stacked on the floor at the side. Absorbed in reading a report and without lifting his eyes, McDonald pointed to a chair in front of his desk and continued reading. Ballard settled himself into the chair and as he waited for the Deputy to speak, sat looking around the room imagining his own occupancy of it in the future. Five long minutes later, McDonald put down the paper and looked across at Ballard, studying him for a moment before speaking.

'Thank you for coming Chief Inspector.'

Ballard smiled. 'I'm pleased to help, sir.' There could be no doubt of his sincerity.

McDonald studied Ballard appraisingly. 'Yes, well, I have a challenging job for you, but you wouldn't be here if I thought you were not up to it. Have you been briefed?'

'Not entirely, sir. I understand it's to do with the death at the motorway this morning whilst we had constructive control over the subject?'

'Yes, broadly. Consequently, there has been a formal referral to the IPCC who agree my proposal that the investigation is conducted by us, but under their supervision. D'you know what that entails?'

'I think so, sir. We appoint an SIO from the force and they provide day to day oversight by their own SIO. The IPCC signs off on all key investigative policy decisions.'

'Yes, that's about it. However, I will be taking a *very* close interest in this Chief Inspector. I want to be sure the correct procedures and tactics were followed. If there's to be any criticism of our response I want to know as *soon* as possible. So that we can improve our response in the future, of course.' The last sentence was added a little too quickly, thought Ballard, but gave no indication he had noticed.

'I understand, sir.'

McDonald said he had given instructions for a small team of people to be provided by divisions - Ballard knew that would make him unpopular with Divisional commanders - and for some office space to be allocated within the PSD at HQ. Ballard would report directly to him each day, or any time he thought the Deputy should be aware of any significant developments. McDonald agreed Ballard's proposal that the investigation would not be put on the HOLMES crime investigation data base as it would be relatively small scale. With several other major investigations already running, the specialist staff needed to resource HOLMES would be difficult to get hold of.

As they neared the end of the conversation, the Deputy fixed Ballard with a beady eye and asked, 'You know DCI Stirling, I think?

Ballard considered the question. McDonald would know about Stirling's review of his investigation the previous year, and of the criticism in the report. 'Yes, sir. DCI Stirling carried out the SIO peer review of an investigation I led last year.'

Never taking his eyes from Ballard, the Deputy asked, 'You felt aggrieved?'

Ballard thought quickly. If the Deputy doubted his suitability he would not have spent so much time briefing him, only to send him home now. 'I *was* disappointed with his observations. I felt he'd misunderstood aspects of my decision making and the challenging circumstances I was working in. But, I can assure you it will have no effect on my enquiry, which I shall approach with an open mind.'

McDonald stared at Ballard, searching for something. 'Hmm, yes, well, that's what I wanted to hear, of course. So, is there anything else you need? No?' Reaching across the desk, McDonald handed Ballard a piece of paper on which he could see a name and telephone number scrawled. 'Your contact at the IPCC. Get hold of them straight away and call me later.'

McDonald picked up the report he had been reading earlier, leaving Ballard to understand the meeting had ended. Thanking the top of McDonald's head and gaining only a grunted reply, he left the room.

*

As the door shut, McDonald put down the report and reflected on the meeting, concerned if Ballard had the skills to do the job thoroughly. He was keen enough, that was clear, and McDonald knew exactly what was motivating the ambitious officer. But did he have the ability? To be sure there was no risk to his own career if things went pear-shaped, he decided to keep himself closely involved. Picking up the phone, he pressed the internal communication button to the PA and asked for Pearson to be contacted. A few minutes later, the PA called to say Detective Superintendent Pearson was in a meeting with ACC Tanner and would not be available for some time. McDonald snapped impatiently that he did not care who Pearson was in a meeting with, or where, but that she should get him on the phone immediately.

Ten minutes later the phone rang again, and the PA connected McDonald. There was a momentary silence as each waited for the other to speak.

'Pearson?'

'Sir.' After being dragged out of a critical meeting, it was as courteous as Pearson could muster.

'I've appointed Chief Inspector John Ballard as our SIO to work with the IPCC. Arrange a smooth handover from your people to him, will you? As quickly as possible.'

There was a long silence. McDonald could hear the man's breathing and grew impatient for a reply.

In a slow, measured tone, Pearson answered, 'Chief Inspector Ballard, sir? An … *interesting* choice. He doesn't have much SIO experience. Are you sure he's the best person?' Realising McDonald would think he was doubting his judgement, which he was, Pearson added, 'For the force, I mean? The investigation is likely to be quite high profile.'

'Yes, I'm aware of that thank you, Superintendent. Ballard will be working out of PSD and I'll keep an eye on things from here. I want a formal handover as soon as possible.'

Pearson considered arguing more but knew it would be pointless. McDonald had made up his mind and would not want to lose face by changing his decision.

'Very good sir, I'll see to it. But, as things progress, if you have any concerns I'll be happy to help in any way I can. Discreetly, of course.' It was an olive branch. Pearson's first concern was that the investigation was carried out efficiently. Untangling poorly executed investigations was always problematic.

'I doubt that will be necessary, thank you.'

McDonald ended the call, thinking it unlikely he would be seeking advice from Pearson, who he considered to be well past his shelf life. Another of the force's "characters" he would like to move on towards their pensions.

*

Pocketing his mobile, Pearson stood outside the CID conference room and thought through the conversation. He disliked McDonald, and not just because of his gratuitous rudeness. He didn't trust him and together with the information received from Jenny Shaw, scented an intention to work against the interests of one of his best SIO's. Stepping back into the meeting, Pearson worked his way around the long oval table at which sat each of the CID's Detective Superintendents and Detective Chief Inspectors, with one notable exception, Stirling. At the head of the table sat

Assistant Chief Constable (Crime & Operations) Stephanie Tanner in white shirt sleeves, the silver rank insignia prominent on her shoulder epaulettes, still shiny and not yet dulled through long wear.

Tanner was respected by everyone under her command for her professional competence. Recently turned forty and considered an attractive woman by most men who met her, she had established a strong reputation as a fair minded, no-nonsense leader who did not trade on her gender or looks. With blonde hair cut short in a stylish, business-like bob and a fringe above dark brown eyes, Tanner had an ability to look well-groomed in any circumstances, whatever the hour of day, and however long the day had been. Having worked through the night alongside Tanner on several operations, dealing with difficult "life at risk" operations, Pearson had come to admire her stamina and coolness under fire. She had earned the loyalty of her teams by trusting them to get on with their jobs, confident in their skills and experience but always accepting the buck stopped with her.

Arriving on promotion from a large metropolitan force about a year before, soon after McDonald's arrival, it had since become quietly understood that neither of them liked the other. Although careful to conceal it from general view, rumours of their differences in Chief Officers' meetings had inevitably leaked to senior officers and percolated on down to the CID team in general. For their part, the HQ CID team liked Tanner enormously. She had earned her spurs the hard way through leading high-profile murder investigations that had attracted extensive national media coverage. Consequently, her face was well known before she had set foot through the door. Their only concern now was how long they could keep her before her abilities led inevitably to promotion in another force.

Edging his way around the meeting room and tuning his ear to the heated debate around the table, Pearson returned to his seat next to Tanner. Aware of who had demanded him to be called out of the meeting, she looked at him with a concerned frown. As the discussion continued without interruption, Pearson leant in slightly to whisper they should speak after the meeting.

*

They had retreated to Pearson's office where they could talk without interruption. Waiting for coffee to arrive, they discussed the disputes and agreements from the budget meeting. Tanner had supported Stirling's bid for most, but not all the additional posts for the MCU. Her view was pragmatic; faced with difficult choices, she believed the public had a reasonable expectation that the force could investigate murder and organised crime efficiently.

Turning to his conversation with McDonald, Pearson described the actions taken to hand over to the IPCC. Tanner listened carefully, occasionally asking a question for clarification or checking some detail whilst making notes in the black day book resting on her lap, the usual accessory of good investigators. When he had finished, Tanner sat deep in thought, repeatedly circling a name in her notes.

'Has Ballard enough experience for something like this, Dave? It seems straightforward enough, but these things can unravel unexpectedly, and from unexpected quarters. He wouldn't be my first choice, in fact, he'd be a long way down the list.'

'I agree,' answered Pearson. 'With some close supervision, he'll do an okay job, but he's very ambitious. My concern is he'll use the investigation to harm Stirling's reputation, because of last year.'

Seeing Tanner's puzzled expression, Pearson explained. 'As a newly qualified SIO, Ballard led an investigation last year into a suspicious death. It was before you arrived in force, so you wouldn't have been aware of it. It was a straightforward investigation intended to let him get his feet wet, but it dragged on. There was a strong feeling that Ballard was milking it to polish his reputation rather than dealing with it efficiently, so we sent Stirling over to do the usual twenty-eight-day, peer to peer SIO review. Stirling's report identified several ways in which the investigation could have been completed far sooner. Even allowing for Ballard's inexperience, it was obvious he was making a meal of it and using it to raise his profile. He was *very* unhappy with Stirling's report and challenged it. His challenge was not upheld, and he received *words of advice.'*

'A bollocking in other words then. And you think Ballard might try to settle a score?'

'Highly possible. Probable even, if the opportunity presents itself.'

Cautiously, Tanner asked, 'And the Deputy's role in this, Dave?'

'Hard to tell. McDonald's a strange fish and doesn't seem to like anyone who's been here for most of their service. Rather than seeing the strengths of long standing professional relationships in cooperating with each other to get things done, McDonald thinks it's all a bit incestuous. Stirling is one of the best SIOs we have but he doesn't suffer fools gladly, whatever their rank. I don't think the Deputy has Stirling at the top of his Christmas card list. I don't expect you to comment on that Steph, but you need to be aware.'

'Okay. Make sure Stirling has all the support he needs. The boy's death will affect him more than he might yet understand, as we know from experience. I'll keep a weather eye on things at my end, but we should keep in touch.'

Pearson nodded his agreement.

'I heard this morning that Stuart will be off for some time, so I'd like you to continue to cover his desk, please. The Chief has agreed my request to promote you to Temporary Detective Chief Superintendent. If you're doing the work, and taking the flack, you deserve the appropriate recognition.'

Pearson had been informally covering Stuart Mann's desk for some weeks now, following the diagnosis of a serious illness.

'Let's hope he makes a good recovery,' replied Pearson, sincerely. He had no desire to benefit from a colleague's ill health.

Pearson walked with Tanner to the exit where they shook hands, her grip as firm as always. Back in his office, he thought through events for a few minutes. Fishing his mobile out of his pocket, he called Bill Edwards.

*

11.56 a.m.

Standing at the bedroom door, hand resting tentatively on the door handle, she listened for any sound inside. Hesitantly, she knocked and called out her daughter's name before opening the door and entering the bedroom. Across the darkened room she saw the bed was empty, the quilt thrown aside and lying half on the floor. She could not tell if the bed had been slept in or not.

Walking to the window she pulled open the curtains and turned to look around the room, looking for any sign of it having been occupied overnight. There were none of the usual glasses or dirty plates on the side table, no phone or laptop chargers carelessly trailing across the floor at the bedside, the usual hallmarks of occupation. On the dressing table, tubes of makeup, scents and the trappings of a teenager lay scattered across the surface in the same careless disorder she had last noticed. Some family snapshots usually stuck into the edge of the mirror frame had been taken out, but that could have been done days ago. She wasn't sure.

Katrina Martin had got up early as usual and pottered about downstairs, assuming Cassandra was sleeping in, again. But it was almost midday and she ought to be up. And shouldn't she be at college? She had probably stayed at a friend's home, but Cassandra usually sent a cryptic text at the very least, no kisses or smileys to soften concern, just bare detail which rarely invited a reply. Trying to think the best of her daughter, she decided she must have forgotten, or had left it too late to text, knowing she would have been asleep. More likely, a conscious indifference to her Mother's concerns, yet another small but painful cut.

Cassandra's nature had changed since she had started at college the year before. Katrina Martin believed it was due to the new friends she had made, and not the sort of people she thought Cassandra should be mixing with.

With a sigh of impatience, she left the room and walked back down the wide staircase, pausing at the window of the half-landing to peer over the landscaped trees at the end of the driveway, hoping to see Cassandra walking towards the house. Continuing down, she crossed the entrance hall into a spacious, modern kitchen and switched on the kettle. Turning to rest against the counter, arms folded with one hand plucking at her lower lip, she pondered her options, paying no heed to the local radio station burbling away in the background. More problems on the roads. A crunch of footsteps on the gravel drive caused her to lift her head and listen, hoping to hear Cassandra's footsteps in the hallway but heard only the clatter of the letter box, followed by a slew of letters falling across the tiled floor. Walking back to the hallway, she collected the letters and shuffled through them. All business correspondence and none for Cassandra.

Standing in the centre of the wide hallway, she looked up to the open landing above her hoping, irrationally, that Cassandra might emerge from one of the spare bedrooms. It was two days now since she had gone to meet her friends. Reassuring herself she would be home after college, Martin returned to the kitchen, made coffee and went to stand at the bank of sliding doors. Looking out over the terrace to the countryside beyond, she could see little more than half a mile as a succession of heavy rain showers drew drab veils over the landscape. She worried about Cassandra again. She would not have a coat with her, as usual. The weather depressed her further and she wished again she could just leave.

The house was too big for just the two of them, but all their memories were here. The last in a small community of executive homes, each sitting remotely in large gardens and remoter still from each other's lives, they were far enough outside Worcester to justify a claim to county living, yet close enough to access its independent schools, its heritage and excellent shops. After buying the plot, almost twenty years ago, they had had the house designed to their own specification and she had always taken pride in pointing out its bespoke design features, in the days when they used to host visitors. How the staircase rose from the wide black and white tiled reception hall, turning onto the mezzanine landing above which gave a view back down into the hall. The open plan kitchen dining room fitted with the most expensive kitchen then available, replaced twice since and now in the current vogue of creams and black marble work tops, all sitting on black porcelain tiles. And the wonderful view from the terrace over the long garden providing a manicured foreground to open countryside and the distant, flat-topped bulk of Bredon Hill.

But now, the house was sterile. Happiness had leached out of it in recent years. When had she and Cassandra last been relaxed in each other's company, talking as they once had about anything and everything? She had always looked forward to Cassandra's teenage years, determined to be a friend and able to discuss anything. Unlike the stifling atmosphere of her own teenage years when any discussion of boys, sex, contraception, or anything remotely challenging was brushed aside by her own mother. Something had changed as Cassandra entered her teenage years and they had become strangers, simply occupying the same living space. The carefree, articulate girl, pre-disposed to laughter from an early age had become increasingly serious and self-absorbed, spending more and more time in her bedroom or in the company of friends rather than be at home. She was trying to pinpoint when her behaviour had changed when the house telephone rang loudly.

'Hello?'

'Hello, Mrs. Martin? … It's Alice. Can I speak with Cassie please? She's not answering her mobile.' There was a soft laugh at the other end.

'Alice?' she asked, vaguely remembering a girl with long, untidy hair and torn jeans. The accent had a hard edge. Embarrassed by their wealth, Cassandra did not bring friends home very often,

'No, I'm sorry Alice. She's not here. I thought she might have stayed with you, or another friend, perhaps?' Her words trailed off, hoping for more information. Hearing only silence, she offered more. 'Her bed hasn't been slept in.'

Hearing only breathing as the other girl worked out what to say, she tried again. 'Alice, are you still there?' She heard her voice rising, concern mixed with irritation. Cassandra should not put her through this stress.

'Um, sorry, no, Cassie's not with me. She's not come into college today so we was wondering if she was sick, or summat.'

Martin forced aside her irritation at the girl's poor language, 'When did you last see her? Please tell me, I'm concerned.'

There was a long pause at the other end that suggested the girl was thinking what to say. 'We haven't seen her since Sat'day, in town. We was in town shopping like, but split up. I was like meetin' my boyfriend and she like, said she was gonna see a friend but, like, wouldn't say who.'

'What time was that?' asked Martin, wondering how many more "likes" the girl could squeeze into a sentence.

'Dunno, 'bout three.'

'Can you call around your friends and find out where she is please, Alice?'

There was hesitation the other end before the girl answered, 'Okay. But she's like, been a bit moody lately.'

'And you'll call me back Alice? I need to know she's okay.'

The girl gave a vague undertaking to ask Cassie to call her and was gone. She wanted to ask more questions, but the girl did not want to talk any longer.

Replacing the phone, Katrina Martin wondered if Alice was hiding something. She had met her a couple of times when dropping Cassandra off, or collecting her from a small semi-detached house in a nearby village. She realised suddenly that she did not know any of Cassandra's friends, and those she had met, she thought unsuitable for her daughter.

*

1.37 p.m.

Edwards had been waiting in the small parking yard at the rear of the mortuary for some time when Ballard arrived and parked nearby. Ballard got out and looked around, unsure of where to go until he saw the flash of headlights from Edwards's car and began to walk across. He had seen Ballard before in force SIO meetings but didn't know him well. He had, though, seen and heard enough of the man's posturing in those meetings, and through the accounts of others, to have formed a low opinion. That, together with Pearson's words of caution earlier.

Watching the heavy-set man walking towards him, he thought Ballard was carrying more weight than was good for him and the large, florid face suggested high blood pressure. Edwards leaned over and opened the door to let Ballard in out of the rain which was still falling intermittently. Dropping heavily into the seat and pulling the door shut, Ballard looked ill at ease. Taking Edwards's outstretched hand, he shook it unenthusiastically.

Edwards introduced himself, 'I don't think we've met properly before, Bill Edwards.' Feeling the limp, clammy hand, Edwards completed his estimation of Ballard's worth.

'Chief Inspector John Ballard,' the younger man replied with unnecessary formality, looking at him with defiant eyes that faltered as they met Edwards's steady gaze.

'As you know, I've been appointed as SIO to this investigation and I require from you all information you have, as soon as possible, together with a verbal briefing. I may require you to meet with me again to clarify any matters, or any inconsistencies.'

Edwards bridled at Ballard's pompous manner and the unnecessary use of rank. Senior detectives didn't worry much about rank and titles, understanding that respect was earned, not put on with a uniform, or badges. Usually, between fellow CID officers, if introductions required the mention of rank it was usually as a reference to roles and responsibilities rather than any reliance on its own importance, with suspicion attaching to those who made too much of it.

Looking stonily at Ballard, he saw a man in his early thirties with a complexion which had reddened further since getting in the car. Uncomfortable, thought Edwards, noticing Ballard's green eyes flitting about, unable to hold his gaze. Edwards's many years' experience in dealing with people at all levels of society drew him to the swift conclusion that Ballard was ill at ease with himself and lacked confidence, hiding behind rank and relying on bluster to get him through when necessary.

In the uncomfortable silence, Ballard continued, 'You should also know that I'm reporting directly to the Deputy Chief Constable, Mr McDonald, in this investigation,' ending his introduction.

Edwards continued to look at him coolly. Was this a threat, or did Ballard need to draw on an authority he did not possess himself? Masking his contempt, Edwards answered dryly, 'Really? I thought the IPCC was supervising it. Supervising you, that is.'

Ballard was taken aback by the quiet insult. 'Well, yes, they are,' he blustered, 'but as the professional lead for PSD, the

Deputy has a keen interest in all matters which could adversely affect the force's reputation.'

'And not his own reputation, of course,' replied Edwards cynically.

Ballard's eyes narrowed. 'I'm not sure if I have your full cooperation, DI Edwards. How soon can I have your report?'

Edwards stared hard at Ballard, struggling to conceal his contempt. 'It's under your fat arse, Chief, Inspector, John Ballard,' drawing out the words slowly and deliberately.

Ballard stared blankly at Edwards for several seconds as he absorbed both the insult and the information. Leaning sideways to reach under himself, Ballard pulled out a buff envelope and held it in front of him, turning the envelope in his hand suspiciously before looking back to Edwards who smiled coldly.

'You got in very quickly.'

From the look in Ballard's eyes, he realised that if they were not enemies before, they were now. He began to regret winding him up in case it made things worse for Stirling. Ballard returned his attention to the envelope and pulled out the contents as Edwards described the contents and the duplicated schedule of contents stapled to the front.

'I'll be grateful if you'll sign a copy of the schedule to confirm what you've received please, Chief Inspector.' Edwards held out a pen.

After checking through the papers, Ballard signed the schedule and handed it back to Edwards, who folded it and tucked it inside a jacket pocket. 'I've included a list of witnesses which I suggest you should see as soon as possible, with an order of priority. The highest priority is to identify the lad and contact his next of kin. Nothing's come in through the media coverage yet.'

'Thank you, Inspector, but *I'll* determine the order of priority, *when* I've had an opportunity to read through the papers.' Ballard spoke tetchily, feeling his seniority was not being respected.

"Of course you will, you prick," thought Edwards as a car driven by a man he recognised parked at the far side of the yard.

'Well, Chief Inspector, John Ballard,' Edwards could not resist rubbing a little more salt into Ballard's discomfort, 'You'd better be quick because that's the Pathologist and he doesn't hang about.'

Without waiting for a reply, Edwards got out and walked over to the metallic black Audi sports car bearing recently issued registration plates and stood waiting as the driver finished a phone call. When he got out, he greeted Edwards with a warm smile. 'Hello Bill, we haven't seen each other for a little while. How are you?'

Edwards liked Doctor Khan, who he had met at many post mortems in recent years. Edwards thought Khan to be in his mid-forties, but looked younger. Not particularly tall, he had a naturally lean physique, due to a busy schedule driving around the region as one of the small team of Home Office appointed forensic pathologists, and long, anti-social hours. Khan was dressed immaculately in a dark blue suit, looking as though he had just left a boardroom, rather than another post mortem. Above all else, Edwards liked Khan because he was efficient. He turned up at short notice whenever and wherever he was needed, in the middle of the night if necessary and gave clear, unequivocal evidence. He was an excellent witness at trial and had established a good reputation throughout the region.

'I'm fine thanks Dr Khan,' Pointing at the new car Edwards added, 'Times are hard, I see.'

Khan laughed. 'It belongs to the bank, they just let me drive it,' he said with a wink. 'I'll get my stuff out of the car and we can get inside, out of this rain. I'd have been here earlier, but got stuck in Crown Court. Most unusual, of course,' he added humorously.

'Delays, in court? Surely not?' replied Edwards with mock amazement, both of them frequent victims of glacial court proceedings.

Khan lifted a bulky leather briefcase out of the car and they began walking towards the mortuary building chatting together comfortably. Edwards noticed Ballard hesitating a little distance away, unsure of which way to go. Extending his arm towards his own car, Edwards locked it remotely to shut off any possible retreat, obliging Ballard to either stand in the rain or follow them inside. Without waiting to see which option he chose, Edwards went inside with Khan.

Clutching the envelope of papers, Ballard hurried after the two men. Angry that he had not been formally introduced at the first opportunity, he mentally scoped Edwards into his investigation, alongside Stirling. After wandering around unfamiliar corridors, Ballard found Edwards and the Pathologist in a small office fitted out simply and functionally with two chairs and a small desk. Khan and Edwards were already seated and talking together, obliging him to stand awkwardly near the door, waiting for conversation to turn to him.

Looking up at Ballard, Edwards made the necessary introductions, explaining that his own role was to ensure continuity in handing over the investigation. Khan smiled professionally up at the Chief Inspector. Ballard opened his mouth to speak but Khan had already turned back to speak to Edwards.

'Have you a résumé of the circumstances at the scene please Bill, any photographs, and what you hope to achieve with this examination?'

Reaching inside his coat, Edwards pulled out an envelope and handed it to Khan. 'It describes the circumstances in which the boy died this morning, our efforts at the scene to save his life and his transfer here.' Khan leafed through the album of proof photographs dispassionately, making notes as Edwards spoke.

'Although obvious, we must determine a cause of death, evidence of any substance or alcohol abuse, anything he consumed which might have impaired his ability to function, and whatever else you consider relevant as we get into it.'

Turning to Ballard, Khan asked, 'Anything you wish to add, Chief Inspector?' and smiled pleasantly. Ballard was unsure if the pathologist was enjoying a private joke with Edwards or whether he was simply being professionally polite.

'No thank you, Doctor. DI Edwards has covered the key points,' Ballard answered, trying to assert his authority.

Khan turned from Ballard to Edwards who returned his gaze, betraying nothing. But Khan was no fool and had sensed the tension between the two officers. 'Okay, well, we'd better get on with it then. Is the body ready?'

Edwards was rising to go and find the mortuary technician when a stooped, pallid looking man arrived at the door wearing surgical greens over white wellington boots which trailed damp footprints across the polished flooring. The technician confirmed the body was ready to be examined and left.

'Are you coming into the examination room Bill, or going into the gallery?'

Khan was referring to the glazed viewing gallery along the length of the examination room which gave an elevated view down onto the examination tables. The gallery reduced the risk of any cross-contamination of the body and allowed those not directly required in the post mortem to watch proceedings. Directly beneath the windows were more steel tables on which organs were weighed and dissected for internal inspection, particularly useful for medical students. An audio link allowed the gallery to listen to the examination whilst separating them from the worst of the cloaking, throat lining odours of death and decaying bodies. In Edwards's opinion, bodies which had been in water were amongst the worst for smell. Eels got into every orifice and the stench could overwhelm even the hardiest professionals. Worse still, were his memories of babies and children.

'I'll come in with you, it'll be easier to talk.' Edwards turned to Ballard, raising an eyebrow in enquiry.

Ballard stood stock still, unwilling to be in the examination room but aware it was a subtle test of his character. 'I will too, thank you,' he decided.

Edwards and Ballard got themselves gowned up in protective clothing and fluid proof gowns kept for visitors, and then each selected a pair of white wellington boots. Neither spoke a word to the other. With only their eyes visible above paper masks, Edwards led the way into the long, white tiled room.

Edwards breathed in the familiar sour, odour of death in the cooled room, underscored with industrial strength disinfectants. He had been to more post mortem examinations than he cared to remember, but never enjoyed them. Once started, he knew the needs of the investigation and professional interest would quickly take his mind off the worst aspects of the process. The lab technician stood quietly checking over the tools of his trade laid out on a steel trolley, next to an examination table furthest from them, on which the boy's body lay.

As essential as the role was, Edwards was always intrigued as to how someone got interested in working with the dead each day and what they talked about at night: "How was your day, dear?" "Oh, the usual, only three today," as they tucked into steak and kidney pie.

Waiting patiently at the far end of the room, a female SOCO stood with a camera to record injuries and whatever else the pathologist considered of interest, to receive the boy's clothing and record and seize forensic samples taken from the body. To her side was a table on which lay tamper proof evidence bags and clear plastic phials into which swabs, and other physical samples would be placed as the examination progressed. Moving to her side, Edwards cast an experienced eye over the SOCO's preparations and silently nodded his approval. He recognised her as one of the local divisional team but did not know her name, the shapeless crime scene suit and mask making her even more anonymous.

Khan entered the room and breezed down to the examination table chatting cheerfully to the technician who returned simple, direct answers to his questions. Moving to stand at the table, Khan and the two officers stood looking down at the body, still fully dressed as Edwards had instructed. He wanted the pathologist to see the boy exactly as he was. The weather conditions might prove relevant. The boy's hair, still damp from the rain and stained with dried blood had fallen back from his face. Even allowing for the terrible damage to the side of the face and skull, he looked younger now than Edwards had previously thought.

Without taking his eyes from the body, Edwards spoke across the table to Khan. 'We have no identification for him yet. Fifteen or so we thought, but difficult to tell. He's very fresh faced. That's all he was wearing, and it was very cold so, very little protection from the elements. Hypothermia may have played a role, perhaps? He'd been there for a good while before we were contacted, so we assume he'd walked there from somewhere. There are no dwellings near the location, so he would have been cold already if he walked any distance to get there.'

Khan was walking around the slab, looking at the boy's body. The legs had been straightened but one foot lay at an impossible angle to the lower leg, the joints smashed. Blood from the ears had dried in dirty, crusting trails across the cheeks and neck, smudged where he had been handled. From an ear, brain matter had been extruded by the force of impact. Edwards was thankful the boy could not have suffered, or for no more than a few seconds.

Standing on the other side of the table, Khan said aloud, but to no one in particular, 'Hmm, this might be interesting.'

Reaching up to the microphone suspended above the table, Khan looked around to be sure everyone knew they were now being recorded. Looking at Ballard to check he understood, Edwards saw he was staring at the body, his usually florid face now very pale. Noticing Edwards studying him, he looked away from the body.

'You okay?' asked Edwards.

'Yes,' replied Ballard. His voice had lost its bluster.

'Been to one of these before, Chief Inspector?' asked Edwards. He guessed Ballard had about ten years' service. Unlike when Edwards had joined, and officers routinely attended a post mortem as part of their probationary training, in these more caring times it was optional. Looking at him now, Edwards reckoned Ballard had opted out.

'Um, no, but I'll be fine,' he replied.

Edwards pulled out a packet of strong mints and offered him one. 'You might want a couple of these. They'll help to mask the smell.'

Ballard looked down at the packet suspiciously and shook his head. 'I'm fine. The smell is not that bad, really.'

Edwards glanced at Khan who was doing a poor job of hiding his amusement. Turning back to Ballard, he said, 'I don't mean *now*, we haven't started yet! It's going to get a lot worse.' Edwards gestured towards the long window, 'It's okay to watch from the gallery.'

Seeing Ballard's reluctance to accept anything from him he shrugged his shoulders, fed himself a mint under his mask and offered them towards the SOCO who shook her head. Khan pressed the record button and began his examination, speaking loudly so that the microphone would capture everything for later transcription. Walking around the body he methodically recorded his observations of the external appearance of the boy, visible injuries and apparent skeletal damage, calling the SOCO photographer in and out of the examination, as required. Once completed, he turned to the technician and nodded, signalling the removal of clothing.

 Everyone stepped out of the way to allow the technician to move around the body freely. No one spoke, each alone with their thoughts of the tragedy lying mute and shattered in front of them. Edwards thought of the boy's parents and his own kids. Almost grown up now, but there had been times when the challenges of raising teenagers had deteriorated into blazing rows, doors being slammed and the occasional tearful flouncing out of the front door. His daughter, usually, who would return hours later, truculent and resentful. It hadn't been easy, made worse by the long hours spent working on murder investigations all over the force area for weeks at a time. But there had never been any likelihood of something like this happening.

As the technician removed each item of clothing, starting with footwear and socks, he handed them to the SOCO who placed each item into separate evidence bags, noting down its description, sealing the bag and signing it to start the trail of evidential continuity until the end of whatever judicial process concluded the boy's existence.

Cutting up the side of the red checked shirt, with Khan helping to roll the body each way, the technician pulled it out from under the body, handed it to the SOCO and turned back to cut away the white polo shirt, now dirty with dried blood and road grime. Working with quiet method, he cut up the side of the shirt to the neck, preserving the garment as far as possible. Seeing him struggling to cut through the seam of the roll neck collar, Khan stepped forward to help, obscuring Edwards's view. Edwards saw both men stop working and look at each other.

Khan spoke quietly. 'Bill?' he called, stepping aside and beckoning Edwards and Ballard forward.

Standing alongside Khan, Edwards looked down at the boy lying on his back, the white shirt cut open and pulled aside.

Edwards was shocked to see small, but undeniably female, breasts.

Edwards was confused. How could everyone have failed to notice it was a girl, and not a boy? And if not straight away, surely it should have been noticed when she was being worked on by the paramedics, or at any point until she arrived here? Khan called the SOCO forward.

Khan turned to the SOCO. 'Photograph this please, to show the sequence in which gender has been revealed?' The SOCO stepped forward and as the flashlight bounced brightly around the tiled room, Khan broke into their thoughts.

'I did wonder actually, Bill, when we came in. Soft feminine features, but I wanted to see what the examination would reveal. It may yet prove to be a male if he, she, had begun a programme of gender re-assignment with hormone treatment for breast augmentation. But they'd have been very young to start something so life changing. Personally, I suspect not.' Looking to the technician he instructed, 'Remove the remainder of the clothing please and we'll see, shall we?'

The tight jeans were cut away to reveal a pair of red, women's panties. Following their removal, there could be no further doubt. A female in her mid to late teens.

'That's what I enjoy about this job, every day is interesting!' said Khan cheerfully, looking across at the officers.

Ballard asked how the girl's gender could have been missed. Studying the corpse with professional interest, Khan replied, 'Well, she's slender with *very* small breasts and not wearing a bra. Either she didn't bother, or didn't need to. Her family might explain that.'

Still confused, Edwards asked, 'But what about when they were treating her at the scene? Surely they'd have noticed during CPR?'

Studying the body, Khan suggested, 'Well, usually, yes. But after hitting tarmac from that height, she died mercifully quickly. Look at her injuries. I doubt if the paramedics spent much time working on her, if at all. They're very highly trained with considerable experience. They know what can or can't be done. Some are trained to pronounce life extinct too, nowadays. Saves calling out scarce doctors to declare the all too obvious.' Khan pointed to the white sweater. 'With that roll neck collar, even the most observant person is unlikely to have noticed the absence of an Adams apple. In the tension and stresses of the incident, all quite forgivable, I would suggest?'

Standing either side of the frail, naked body as the photographs were taken, Khan was about to resume the examination when Edwards, who had already recalibrated the needs of the examination, spoke.

'This changes the complexion of the investigation. Why she was there? We need to establish if she was sexually active or if there are any signs of sexual trauma.'

Khan looked at Ballard, his eyebrows raised in silent question. Ballard nodded his agreement. Painfully aware that Edwards was far ahead of him in his thinking, he knew he should be taking a more decisive lead, but was unsure what to say.

The examination continued quietly and efficiently with everyone absorbed in its detail, quietly discussing issues as they arose with Ballard remaining largely silent in the background. Khan described for the audio recording the nature of the many fractured bones and injuries as photos were taken with a small ruler held alongside to provide scale. Head hair was cut and plucked and placed into evidence phials, as was plucked, cut and combed samples of pubic hair.

Khan remarked, 'There's no obviously different coloured hair amongst her pubes, but forensic examination will determine that more conclusively.'

Scrapings from beneath every fingernail were taken with a wooden scrape; swabs from inside and around the mouth for DNA profiling, and for the presence of other fluids, semen a possibility. The girl's legs were parted and to allow swabs to be taken from the vagina, anus and inside the uterus for the identification of semen, if present. Reaching across to the metal trolley, Khan scanned the instruments before picking up a clear plastic speculum, explaining the internal examination to establish if the girl had been sexually active. As the girl's legs were pulled open and the tube inserted,

Edwards felt for the poor girl's indignity, even in death. He was conscious of the SOCO standing nearby, but whatever she felt was hidden behind her mask and her eyes betrayed nothing.

Straightening up, Khan stepped back and looked at Edwards and Ballard. 'The hymen is ruptured and fully healed so, sexually active for some time, I'd say. We'll examine the internal sexual organs in a little while. That's the external examination complete so if anyone's squeamish, now's the time to make a tactical withdrawal.'

Edwards shook his head. Ballard stared at them uncertainly before he too shook his head. The SOCO officer had no choice, she had to remain.

The next few minutes passed quickly as Khan cut a deep Y shaped incision at the neck and drew the scalpel quickly downwards, efficiently cutting a deep wound over the sternum, through the soft abdomen and lower belly to a few inches above the mound of blonde pubic hair. Khan opened the wound and pulled back the thin flesh and subcutaneous fat. With a deft adjustment of the scalpel, he began to trim flesh and muscle from the ribcage to reveal dark haemorrhages where bleeding caused by the impact had clotted amongst muscle tissue. Edwards thought of his local butcher.

As the abdomen opened, a thick cloaking odour slid over the room, striking the back of Edwards's nose and throat as it crawled into his lungs. He slipped another mint into his mouth and crunched on it to fill his nostrils with the cool menthol flavour. It masked the odour, to a point, but not entirely. It didn't matter how many of these you went to, he thought, you never got used to it. A young body, still quite fresh, meant the smell was not as unpleasant as many he had attended.

Dropping the scalpel into a tray with a loud clatter, Khan took from the technician a set of stainless steel croppers and began to remove the sternum by cutting through the cartilage and bone either side to separate it from the ribs and create a cavity large enough to work inside. Khan stood considering the open chest cavity as he held out the ragged-edged bone for the technician to take from him, who casually dropped it on the table between the girl's feet.

Absorbed in the process, Edwards's barely registered the soft groan behind him and turned only at the sound of Ballard's body striking the ground to see him lying prostrate on his back, his face a pale, sickly grey colour. For a moment, everyone stood looking down at the prone body, wondering if he would get up.

'Haven't had that happen for a while,' said Khan cheerily. 'You'd better check if he's hurt himself. I thought I heard him bump his head?'

Edwards looked down at Ballard, unhappy at the prospect of having to give mouth to mouth resuscitation. Muttering an obscenity under his breath, he knelt beside Ballard's inert body and put his hand to the back of his head. There was no obvious damage. As he studied Ballard's face intently, irritated at the inconvenience he was causing, the man beneath him stirred.

With a low groan, Ballard opened his eyes and blinked against the glare of the white lights above him. Regaining his focus, a bewildered look crossed Ballard's face as he struggled to understand why Edwards was looking down at him. As the awful realisation struck him, he gave a loud groan, not of pain but at the shame of his situation and struggled up into a sitting position, shrugging off Edwards's attempt to help him.

'I'm alright!' he snapped, ungraciously. Passing a clammy hand over his face, he cautiously probed the back of his head as he saw Khan and the technician studying him impassively above their face masks. Edwards noticed the SOCO officer had turned away and was fiddling with her camera, embarrassed probably. Shifting his eyes back to the opened body, Ballard felt a fresh wave of the nausea he had been trying to control for several minutes before fainting. Swallowing hard against a strong desire to vomit, Ballard got uncertainly to his feet and stood there, swaying slightly, one hand clamped over his mouth. Concerned he might fall again, Edwards reached out a hand which Ballard slapped away and stepped back, glaring at him.

Turning to Khan, he said, 'I'm sorry for any inconvenience Doctor, but I think I'll get a drink of water. I'll watch the rest of the examination from up there.' He gestured to the gallery and turned towards the door.

'That's fine, Chief Inspector,' said Khan heartily to Ballard's retreating back, and returned to his work.

As they heard the door close, Khan and Edwards exchanged a look, each aware the microphone was recording. Khan's eyes twinkled as he gave a low chuckle. Edwards rolled his eyes and shook his head in reply and returned to watching as the pathologist delved with both hands inside the open body.

The examination continued routinely with the heart, liver, lungs and other organs all removed, weighed and dissected to see if any disease was present. There was none, but all were badly damaged from the impact. The liver had burst. Edwards knew that even without the extensive brain injury, yet to be revealed, without swift surgical intervention the injury to the liver alone would probably have proved fatal. Khan moved to the lower abdomen. Reaching inside, he began to detach the womb and uterus and lifted them out, laying out the bloodied tissues and membranes next to the body. Edwards was moving around to see more clearly when Khan paused to lean on the edge of the table with both hands and studied the organ below him. Lifting the scalpel again, he deftly cut open the womb and a soft spurt of fluid flowed across the cold steel table.

Inside the membrane sac lay a tiny foetus.

The room was silent. Distantly, Edwards could hear a radio playing, probably in the technician's office. He had not noticed it before, but it now seemed all too loud, the jangling pop music discordant and intrusive to the growing tragedy. He could hear his own breathing sucking at the thin paper mask as a deep sadness swept through him. Looking up at the face of the girl, he wondered if she had known and if she had, how desperate were her circumstances to kill not just herself, but her baby too? The foetus' translucent skin still had an embryonic appearance, the head disproportionately large to its one-inch body, the arms and legs still forming. The eye, a dark spot that would never see the world it was destined for.

Khan was the first to speak, quietly, 'Between nine and ten weeks, approximately, the point at which the embryo becomes a foetus. Your investigations with her family might narrow down when conception occurred.'

Nodding silently, Edwards began to recalculate new lines of enquiry; health centres, family planning clinics, and then remembered it was now Ballard's problem. He could not help speculating how many lives would be affected by the girl's death, and that of the baby. Had the child been known about, and had its announcement been well received? Considering her age and actions, he thought it unlikely.

Khan looked at Edwards questioningly, who murmured they should continue.

Making a clean cut around the rear of the head inside the hairline, the pathologist peeled the scalp from the skull and pulled it forward until it lay in an inverted mask over the girl's face. The technician moved forward with the small circular saw and began cutting around the exposed skull, creating a circular lid. As the room began to fill with the smell of burnt bone, Edwards remembered Ballard and looked up into the gallery where he stood, shoulders hunched, sipping at a plastic beaker of water and the mask now hanging loose under his fleshy chin. He still looked pale and when he noticed Edwards watching him, glared back.

Replacing the saw on the side trolley, the technician picked up another tool and prised open the cap to expose the damaged brain.

Stepping to the head of the table, Khan studied it briefly before carefully cutting it free and carried it to an examination table below Ballard. There, he weighed it before slicing it through several times, laying each slice open in flat cross sections. Edwards considered the thoughts, the memories, emotions and experiences that had inhabited the grey matter until that morning.

Khan summarised his conclusions clinically. 'No apparent disease of the brain, such as tumours. I can't comment on any psychological issues, obviously, but there's considerable physical trauma consistent with her striking the ground on her left side which, again, is consistent with the severe damage to the head and body. Death was caused by severe trauma to the brain and to internal organs. She was probably alive for a *very* short time after impact but, thankfully, would have been unconscious. I doubt she experienced any further pain.'

Suddenly recalling something from his SIO training, and anxious to contribute, Ballard pressed the intercom button and directed a question down to Khan. 'We should consider toxicology Doctor, in case she was under the influence of drink or drugs?'

Khan exchanged a look with Edwards before looking up to Ballard and answered smoothly, 'I'm *so* sorry, Chief Inspector. I should have mentioned it before. I took blood samples and stomach content samples earlier whilst you were … ah … indisposed. Judging by the state of digestion, her last meal was consumed many hours before she died and included chips and a curry. Hair follicles taken from the head will tell us if she has used substances in recent weeks, for how long and what they were.'

Suspecting he was being patronised, Ballard nodded his understanding.

'We'll tidy away here Chief Inspector and catch up with you in the office, if that's alright with you?' Khan said to Ballard, pointing in the direction of the exit doors. Without waiting for a reply, he walked over to speak with the SOCO where Edwards was already checking through the samples, making sure everything was documented accurately.

Ballard watched as the technician began gathering together the internal organs and other human detritus, putting it all inside a large clear plastic bag which he stuffed inside the abdomen. Fitting the bone cap back in place on the open skull, he pulled the scalp back into position and began to sew it back into place. Unless a next of kin looked very closely, with her hair washed out they were unlikely to notice, unlike the crude stitching which would close the body before she was returned to the mortuary fridge to lie with strangers.

As they walked towards the exit, Edwards took a long last look at the girl's ruined body, wondering what life may have held in store for her.

After stripping off their protective clothing, the three men crowded into the small office again to discuss reporting lines and procedural points. Ballard revealed his inexperience again by asking Khan to supply him with the results of toxicology by the end of the week. Dealing him a patient smile as if responding to a dull-witted child, Khan explained that with the pressure on forensic laboratories, toxicology usually took some weeks to be completed and, in any case, it was not his responsibility. Acutely aware he was out of his depth, Ballard bristled and after some blustering comments made his excuses and left without the customary handshakes.

Khan waited for Ballard's footsteps to disappear through the outer door before turning to Edwards. 'He's not one of yours, surely? He's not out of the usual CID mould.'

Edwards shook his head, embarrassed by Ballard's performance in front of another professional. 'Between you and me, he's a bloody idiot. Just my opinion, though. I don't know him well but the Deputy's put him in charge so he's not my problem. I just hope he manages the girl's family kindly, when we find out who she is.'

Khan said nothing. He knew many of the SIOs in the region and was always impressed by their relaxed, good humoured company, underlined always by a calm professionalism. It wasn't his place to comment on a member of another agency, but he was deeply unimpressed with Ballard.

*

Stirling put his mobile back on the desk and stared vacantly at the paperwork he had been working on when Edwards called. Closing his eyes to think clearly, he saw again the grey eyes, the haunting smile and felt the hand slipping through his fingers. A young woman, and pregnant. He had failed to save two lives.

How could he have not realised it was a girl? Thinking back, Stirling realised bitterly that he had allowed himself to succumb to mindset, or groupthink. From the outset, someone had thought the girl to be a boy. From then on, with no information to the contrary, every communication had reinforced the first assumption. When he reached the boy, the girl, there was no time to reappraise the information yet, with hindsight, he had registered something about her complexion. But had he realised, would he have used different words, or acted differently? Stirling did not think so.

The laughter of two detectives passing his door interrupted his thinking and he knew he should leave the office. Standing at the door to the incident room, Stirling waited until he caught Heal's eye and beckoned him to his office, gave him the results of the post mortem and told him he was leaving for the rest of the day. Assuring Stirling he would keep everything ticking over, Heal disappeared back to the main office.

Grabbing his coat, Stirling headed for the stairs, imagining how the information was unfolding amongst the team. Pulling out of the car park and into the traffic flow, he suddenly wondered where exactly he was going. After a moment's thought, Stirling set course for the one place where he was certain of being alone.

Home, where there was rarely anyone to speak to.

*

Driving from the mortuary to HQ, Ballard seethed with rage, mixed with anxiety, that he had harmed his reputation by fainting in front of Edwards, a friend of Stirling. Edwards had made him look a fool in front of the pathologist and the SOCO. He wondered who she was and decided to find out.

At the PSD office, Ballard began organising the small team of people that had begun to filter in from divisions. Mindful of insulating himself from any future criticism, Ballard settled on his usual strategy of setting the overall direction of the investigation, delegating as much accountability and decision making as he could to more junior staff, allowing him to trade on their skills and experience whilst presenting a facade of decisive leadership. He knew that, ultimately, he was accountable for everything, but he could deftly mitigate any serious difficulties by pointing to the failures of others. Recognising the need for some top cover, he would make sure McDonald signed off key policy decisions before they were implemented and would do the same with the IPCC lead.

Watching the last member of his team arrive, Ballard allowed himself a smile of satisfaction. This enquiry was just what he needed to gain the promotion he was long overdue and if he could damage some of the opposition along the way, all the better.

*

Stirling had considered taking a long walk in the lanes near his home but with neither the will nor the weather for it, had stayed in and brooded gloomily.

He was tempted to open the malt whisky he kept for an occasional tot and got as far as unscrewing the cap when he remembered his Father's words, that no solutions are ever found in the bottom of a glass.

Bill Edwards called twice. Stirling ignored the first call but answered the second a few minutes later. He knew Edwards was checking to see he was alright under a pretext of keeping him briefed. Declining the offer to come over and keep him company for a while, they agreed to speak the following day.

Throwing the phone aside, Stirling sat in the darkening room trying to close out the endless loop of images playing in his head.

6.47 p.m.

Preparing a supper for which he had no appetite, Stirling ignored his mobile ringing in the lounge until it rang for the third time. Someone was persistent in wanting to speak to him. Swearing loudly, Stirling walked through to the lounge. Picking it up, he saw it was Edwards.

'Are you at home?' Edwards sounded concerned.

Irritated at being bothered again he answered tautly, 'Yes!'

'Have you got the TV on?'

'No. Why?

There was a momentary silence. 'Doug, a media shit storm's blown up. There was a photographer hiding nearby this morning. He's got the whole thing, the girl falling from the bridge right through to the impact and then the officers with her body.'

Stirling could hear the anger in Edwards's voice as he described the pictures, thinking through the new development.

'You still there?' asked Edwards.

'Yes, I'm thinking. That's disgraceful, and tough for the family too, but it shows what happened and that we tried to help.' He knew the family would be a long way behind the media's interests.

'They don't give a toss about the family but that's not the problem.'

'Well, what is then?' asked Stirling, imagining the photographs.

'Switch your TV on and watch the rolling news channel. It's being repeated every few minutes until something else knocks it down the agenda. Doug, they've got your face all over it and you're not going to be happy with the headline. Call me if you want to talk. I'm at home.'

Stirling rarely watched TV, so it took a few moments to find the remote control. Standing in front of the small screen in a corner of the room, he searched for the twenty-four-seven news channels. He didn't have to wait long until the bridge appeared behind the presenter's shoulder. The presenter's mouth moved with the story, but he barely heard what was being said as he studied the images. Taken from below and upwards to where he had been standing, he could see himself leaning forward, his hand inches from the girl as she slipped from him, daylight visible between their fingers.

The headline crawling from right to left along the bottom of the screen told him all he needed to know of the media's angle:

"Girl pushed to death by police? Investigation launched."

Watching the story as it developed currency, Stirling's emotions ranged from shock, to nausea and, finally, to an impotent rage. As time went on he realised he needed to analyse the pictures and media coverage and pressed the record button.

With bitter cynicism he watched an interview with McDonald, standing alongside a dour faced individual from the IPCC who blinked uncertainly into the glare of the media lighting. In the background, shifting sideways to keep himself in the camera shot stood Ballard, nodding sagely in agreement with his master's voice as McDonald extended sympathies to the family, promising a "full and thorough investigation" under the IPCC's supervision.

No details of the deceased were being given out until all next of kin had been identified and spoken with. When pressed by someone behind the camera whether the girl was pushed,

McDonald had become increasingly terse in his responses. Stirling did not believe it was out of any loyalty towards him, more that McDonald would like to have thrown them all out of the building.

Stirling sent Edwards and Pearson a text to say he would call them in the morning. Even though he thought it unlikely the media could get his mobile number, he was taking no chances and switched it off. It was the first time he had removed himself from contact for more than ten years.

Working into the small hours of the morning, Stirling played back the images repeatedly, making sure he had missed nothing. Even allowing for the photos being a succession of freeze frames, they were consistent with his memory of events; from his arrival close to the girl, moving closer to her and then the damning pictures of his desperate lunge to save her which were open to misinterpretation. Or misrepresentation.

Stirling studied his own face, saw the desperation he had felt, his mouth open as he called out to her, and detesting the public exposure which he had sought to avoid for so many years. The photographer had got lucky. Stirling could even grudgingly admire his coolness in keeping the lens steady. Remembering the glimpsed movement amongst the bushes and angle of view, he had quickly worked out where the pictures were taken from. But how could they suggest he had pushed her? He was there to save a life, not to let it go.

Stirling had never felt so alone.

Waking with a start, Stirling's head hurt immediately. The stiffness in his back reminded him that he had fallen asleep on the sofa. Shivering despite being fully clothed, he pulled the blanket back over him and worked his tongue which felt too big for his mouth, trying to create some saliva.

Squinting through his hangover, Stirling looked at the half empty bottle of malt whisky on the table next to the sofa, trying to recall when exactly he had opened the bottle. His resolve to have just the one glass had led to several large ones and the dull ache behind his eyes grew in intensity as he came fully awake. He had seen every hour until four that morning until the alcohol had overtaken his insomnia. It was now almost nine.

Pulling the blanket tighter around him, Stirling tried to collect his thoughts. He would like to have someone to talk with, and to hold, but who that could be, he had no idea. It had been a while since there had been anyone in his life. Looking around at the simple arrangement of his possessions he tried to remember how long it had been since a woman's hand had touched his home, or him. He preferred it that way and while he missed the physical comforts, he did not miss the emotional entanglements.

A weak sun was slowly brightening the room and as the shadows dissolved, he closed his eyes against the throbbing pain in his head and dozed off again to wake an hour later. Switching the television on, he lay there flicking through the channels, drawing some small comfort that the story was already being bumped down the schedule. The girl had still not been named, which surprised him. After an hour of watching the same endlessly re-cycled information, Stirling switched the TV off, resolving never to watch or read anything more of the subtly negative, inferential language being used by some of the on-scene reporters.

What was done, was done. The images in his head would remain vivid and troubling enough.

CŁ ŁO

March

Standing in a cool breeze outside Worcester Crown Court was a welcome change for Stirling after several weeks of being stuck at home on so called, "gardening leave."

The media attention had swiftly resulted in him being put on restricted duties, removing him from involvement in anything directly or indirectly operational. Consequently, he'd had limited involvement at the end of the phone answering questions of a technical nature about the prosecution case for the trial in which he was a witness.

Stirling had railed futilely against the decision but with McDonald holding the levers, there was little Tanner or Pearson could do to help. Ballard's investigation was moving at glacial speed and the few leaks there had been from the investigation had not filled Stirling with hope. Even though the media's attention had swiftly lost interest, the images haunted Stirling night and day, so he had made sure to avoid any discussion or enquiries about the girl's death, preferring to deal with it whenever Ballard got around to interviewing him. Ballard had postponed two appointments, claiming further enquiries were necessary. Stirling had privately discussed making a complaint of abuse of process and was now biding his time.

Standing outside the Shirehall, Stirling was enjoying discussing the evidential twists and turns of the trial with the Queens Council who was prosecuting the murder trial for him. After five days of listening to the evidence, the jury was out and they expected a verdict soon.

The QC had needed a cigarette break, so they were standing in the car park under the statue of Queen Victoria who frowned stonily across Foregate Street. Drawing heavily on his cigarette, the QC stood with a wig the colour of old ivory tucked under his arm as the wind drew his black gown around him. They discussed what had gone well, and where the defence had scored against them. There was no doubt the man was guilty, and there was enough evidence to convict him, but they had been in the game long enough to know how fickle juries could be, bogging themselves down sometimes in irrelevant detail and losing sight of key evidence.

Stirling and the QC had known each other for years through various trials and chatted together companiably, their conversation ranging from technical points of law to a shared interest in the varying fortunes of the local premiership rugby club. Both had played as younger men and that experience had cemented their professional relationship. Playing rugby from a young age on muddy, half frozen pitches in the teeth of British winters had a way of forging character and temperament. But as the knocks and bruises of Saturday afternoons took longer to heal, and the imperative of being able to work on Monday morning grew more insistent, both had surrendered to the inevitable and were now content to watch others do combat.

As they talked, the QC's attention drifted to somewhere over Stirling's shoulder. With a murmured apology and smiling broadly, he stepped away from Stirling who turned to follow the QC's gaze.

Walking purposefully towards them, a woman was shifting the weight of a hefty bundle of papers from one arm to another as she passed under Victoria's scowl. Stirling immediately recognised the lawyer's dress code but, unlike some female lawyers he had met, there was nothing dowdy about this young woman. Dressed in understated elegance in a tailored black jacket and skirt over a crisp, white collared shirt, she exuded purpose and self-confidence. Black hosiery led the eye to stylishly sensible black shoes suitable for spending long hours standing in a courtroom. As she shook hands with the QC, apparently oblivious of Stirling, he discreetly admired her figure and strong, raven black hair which she had gathered back with a crimson red velvet tie, her only concession to colour, and all the more striking as it mingled with the wave of her hair which hung below her collar.

Remembering he was there, the QC introduced him. 'Ms Patel, this is DCI Stirling. We're in a murder trial together waiting for the jury to make up its mind.' Turning to Stirling, he explained, 'Ms Patel has brought me instructions for my next case starting here tomorrow, if our jury ever reaches a decision.'

With professional politeness, Ms Patel flashed the briefest of smiles at Stirling but barely glanced at him as she and the QC stepped away until they were out of earshot. With nothing better to do, Stirling watched the woman as she talked with the QC. He guessed her to be about twenty-six, fairly tall at five feet ten in her shoes with a nicely proportioned figure. There was a confidence about her in the way she stood facing the QC, which was attractive too; feet apart, speaking calmly and articulately to the older man without any unnecessary deference as she shook her head and appeared to correct him on some point of detail. The QC listened, nodding thoughtfully until after several minutes he took the bundle from her. With a glance at Stirling, the QC drifted slowly back towards him, drawing the young lawyer along who continued talking earnestly, gesturing with her hands as she emphasised a point until they were stood by him again. As the QC outlined his intentions in the case, Ms Patel stood with her arms folded, following his words closely.

Closer to him, Stirling could study her face in profile. A perfectly straight nose above a full, sensuous mouth which set firm as she listened one moment, now puckering slightly as she frowned in concentration and chewed slightly at her bottom lip. Very little make up, and with no need.

The conversation came to a natural conclusion. Looking between her and Stirling, the QC asked, 'D'you two know each other?'

Shaking her head, she turned and offered her hand. Stirling felt slender fingers, cool skin and was pleasantly surprised by the firmness of her grip.

'Stirling. I'm based at HQ.'

She had recognised him immediately from the news coverage but said nothing. Raising an eyebrow, she waited for more information.

'I lead the Major Crimes Unit, the MCU. You might have heard of it perhaps, Ms Patel?'

Now that she was facing him and watching him candidly, Stirling felt a pleasant flip in his gut as he saw her eyes properly for the first time, a startling dark green with honey gold flecks around her pupils. Seeing his reaction, Stirling saw the merest hint of a smile in her eyes and felt he was under a shrewd scrutiny as she studied his features in return.

'Ayesha, please. Ms Patel sounds so stuffy, unless we find ourselves against each other in court.'

The warmth of her smile encouraged Stirling to ask which solicitors practice she worked with and about the range of work she did. As they chatted, the QC tactfully moved away to study the bundle of papers, watching from the corner of his eye with amusement. Keen to keep Ayesha talking, Stirling was about to ask another question when a court usher appeared at the top of the steps leading to the court entrance. Standing between the tall Doric columns flanking the main entrance, he called out his and the QC's names as he searched for them and announced the jury's return.

'It's been a pleasure to meet you, Ayesha. I'd really like to talk with you some more, but I have to go back in there,' he pointed after the QC who was already hurrying up the steps. He gave a regretful shrug of his shoulders but kept eye contact with her.

Firmly shaking his hand again, she held onto it a little longer than necessary. 'Yes, and it's a pleasure to meet you, too.'

The sentence had lingered. Was there an expectancy in her voice as she looked up at him? A smile played at the corners of her mouth and there was amusement in her eyes. Stirling wasn't sure if she was making fun of him or waiting for an invitation. She was quite a bit younger than him. Was she enjoying waiting for him to make a fool of himself?

'Ayesha, I must go but can I buy you coffee sometime, soon? You're very busy I ...'

'I'd like that very much, thank you,' she interrupted. 'You know where I work, give me a call!'

Without waiting for a reply, Ayesha smiled and walked away without a backward glance. Watching her weave between the parked cars, Stirling thought there was a deliberateness in the sway of her hips, but his thoughts were interrupted by the usher calling him querulously from the top of the steps.

'DCI Stirling. You're needed, sir. Now!'

The twelve men and women of jury was filing into the courtroom when Stirling entered. At the noise of his clattering arrival on the bench behind him, the QC turned and gave Stirling a conspiratorial wink. Stirling was unsure if it was in expectation of the right verdict, or the encounter in the car park. Suspecting it to be the latter, Stirling smiled.

Feeling a quickening in his chest which had nothing to do with the trial, Stirling focused his attention on the jury.

A bewigged Clerk to the Court with a splendid beard and steel-rimmed glasses rose to address the foreman of the jury, his voice booming louder than necessary in the hushed courtroom. 'Ladies and gentlemen of the jury. On the indictment of murder, have you reached a verdict on which you all agree?'

A timid looking man rose at the corner of the jury box and with a nervous glance towards the dock, answered that they had.

'On the indictment of murder, how do you find the defendant? Guilty, or not guilty?' the Clerk demanded.

'Guilty.'

*

They had agreed to meet in a popular, art themed café close to the cathedral, with walls covered in an eclectic range of arty photos, each with a small biography of its creator and a smaller label advising the curious of their considered value. The café was busy with tourists, shoppers, and friends catching up.

Sitting alone at the rear where he could see the door and the room, Stirling was the only man there. Ayesha was ten minutes late. Second thoughts? Around him sat young mums, talking and texting with toddlers in pushchairs at their side. Mothers with daughters, taking respite from their shopping, and each other. Mothers with others, quieter, looking about them with slight nods and gestures of disapproval or irritation, exchanging a roll of the eyes and muttered critiques. A smaller number of women wearing the confidence of understated wealth looked bored as they cast cool appraising glances about the room. On the far side of the room, one had stared at him candidly over the shoulder of her companion, smiling faintly when she caught his eye and lifted her left hand to make an unnecessary adjustment to her hair, ensuring he saw there was no wedding ring. It was a speculative smile, expected to be returned, but Stirling turned to look elsewhere. From the corner of his eye he saw her stiffen at the snub and return her attention to the other woman who had not stopped talking, murmuring agreement whilst darting sharp, glances over the other woman's shoulder.

A jangle of the old-fashioned bell above the door turned curious heads and Ayesha was there, looking around the room, frowning when she could not see him. Spotting him stood at the rear of the room, she gave him a broad smile and worked her way around the crowded tables to reach him. The belted, fawn coloured raincoat she was wearing was covered in a film of moisture from the fine drizzle that had been falling most of the morning. Ayesha slipped off her coat and threw it carelessly across the empty chair on the other side of the table before sitting beside him in a breath of greeting, apology and a light, spiced perfume. Registering the scent, the energy and freshness about her as she explained the delay - a difficult client - Stirling was pleased she had taken the seat next to him, and not across the table as she might have done. On the other side of the room, Stirling caught sight of the smart woman watching them, calculating the relationship.

The café had been Ayesha's suggestion. Close enough to her office to slip out between appointments but not so close that any of her colleagues were likely to see them together. She had explained that she tried to keep her work and private life separate. Stirling was pleased they shared the same view, explaining to her that the police service was disgracefully gossipy and sometimes too interested in colleagues' lives.

'It's not so difficult to understand,' he explained. 'Our stock in trade is people and their lives, so it's inevitable that some of my colleagues spend too much time gossiping about other people's affairs.' He shrugged his shoulders in apology, but she laughed it away.

Resting a hand on his arm, suggesting a tactile nature, she answered, 'It's not so different amongst my profession and as a young woman in a largely male practice, some of our senior partners show a little *too* much interest in my personal life.'

Enjoying the touch of her hand on his arm, Stirling asked with concern, 'No more than paternal concern and interest, I hope?'

'Not entirely. One of them is un-reconstructed 1980's, a little too touchy-feely when we're near to each other.'

Stirling made a comment about sexual harassment in the workplace before reminding himself that he barely knew her, and Ayesha could almost certainly stand her ground.

Ayesha smiled, 'Don't worry. I made it *very* clear he should keep his hands to himself and he keeps his distance now. As for the others, they're just old school, very paternalistic and protective but charming with it. Anyway, the work is intense and the hours long, so I don't have time for a private life.'

Their conversation flowed easily until long after their coffee cups were empty and keen to keep her company, Stirling ordered more from the passing waitress. Waiting for the cups to be exchanged their conversation paused momentarily and Stirling briefly scanned the room through force of habit. Most of the tables had exchanged their customers for new, but the two women opposite still sat talking, heads leaning forward across the table in an intense conversation. The woman with her back to him was hunched forward, resting her head in one hand and reaching across the table with her other hand to hold the hand of her elegant companion. The woman with her back to him seemed to be crying, her shoulders shaking slightly as the elegant woman leaned forward, talking quietly to her, irritation creasing her brow as she tilted her head to look up into the other woman's face. Noticing Stirling watching them, she glared at him. He looked away, returning his attention to Ayesha.

An hour after she had joined him, Ayesha looked at her watch, her eyes opening wide with surprise. 'My God, is that the time? I must go! Sorry, but I've an important client due soon and I can't be late.'

Stirling picked her coat up from the seat and led the way to the door where he turned and held the coat open for her to put on. Ayesha looked at the coat with a flash of irritation. Seeing his reaction, she immediately regretted her annoyance.

'I'm sorry, I don't think anyone's ever offered to help me on with my coat. Not since I was a child, anyway.'

'Ah, sorry, I forgot that such courtesies aren't always welcome.' Smiling apologetically, Stirling held the coat out to her.

Taking it from him she considered it for a moment and handed it back. 'It's a very nice gesture, thank you. I'm just not used to it, but I could get used to it, perhaps.' She laughed lightly.

Stirling held the coat open again as Ayesha slipped it on and turned to face him. Reaching forward, Stirling lifted the lapels lightly until the coat sat evenly over her shoulders, as she looked up at him.

'Thank you, kind sir,' she said, mocking him good humouredly.

Ayesha stood facing Stirling, smiling as she studied his features, heedless of people squeezing past them as the café began to fill with lunchtime diners. Stirling saw something thoughtful going on in her mind. He wasn't sure what it meant but he understood the warmth of his own feelings towards her. Over the last hour he had seen that behind the cool, professional front Ayesha presented to the world, there was a warm, caring personality. Strong willed, certainly, and proudly independent without a doubt, but that was part of her attraction.

Hearing her gentle mockery, he said ruefully, 'You have an ability to make me feel slightly clumsy.'

She laughed, answering perkily, 'Good! I don't want you taking me for granted now, do I?'

Watching her buttoning up the coat, Stirling was pleased to hear an implicit invitation to meet again. Pulling the belt tight, Ayesha moved to leave the café. Stirling opened the door and held it open for her to pass in front of him. She looked at the open door for a moment before stepping past, restraining a grin and making him feel awkward again.

The rain had stopped but a cool breeze whipped around them as they turned in the direction of her office. Walking as closely to Ayesha as he could whilst stepping around the puddles filling the worn flagstones of the side street, he knew he had only a few more steps when they must part company.

'So, would you like to go out to dinner one evening, soon?' he asked.

Over their heads, the cathedral bell began to toll midday across the city. Ayesha continued walking without answering. He knew she had heard him. As the silence lengthened, Stirling began to feel uncomfortable and cursed himself for thinking this beautiful, intelligent young woman would want to spend a full evening out with a man some years older than herself.

'Sorry Ayesha, I thought we were getting on well. If you don't want to, I understand,' he added, apologetically.

Ayesha stopped suddenly and turned to look up at him with a puzzled expression, the wind dragging her hair across her face. Lifting a hand to pull it from her eyes, a strand caught in the corner of her mouth. Stirling wanted to reach forward and brush it back but kept his hands in his pockets in case he committed another faux-pas. Believing it to be the last time they would speak, he prepared to put a brave face on it. They would shake hands, say something pleasant about how nice it had been to meet each other and then part company, each walking away as quickly as dignity would allow.

Frowning, her green eyes darker in the overcast light, she asked, 'I've asked around discreetly and no one knows what your first name is. Everyone refers to you as Stirling. Your family name is Stirling, DCI Stirling. But that's not your first name, is it?'

The question took Stirling by surprise. It wasn't the first time he'd been asked but it was out of step with an invitation to dinner. Perhaps she wasn't sure about him?

He shrugged. 'It's not a common surname. I've some Scottish heritage on my father's side. Most people call me Stirling as a familiar term, a nickname if you like. A bit like the racing driver, Stirling Moss?'

Ayesha gave him an amused, quizzical look that said, "I haven't a clue what you're on about."

Stirling laughed, 'Yeah, before my time, too. Good friends call me Douglas, or Doug, a family first name. I never use my real birth name.'

Ayesha nodded as she looked from him along the street and glanced down at her watch. She went to speak and hesitated. Thinking he should allow her to say "no" gracefully, Stirling continued.

'Ayesha, I'm sorry. I misread the signals. If you don't want to go out to dinner then perhaps another coffee sometime, when you're not so busy?'

He knew it would not happen but wanted to spare her the embarrassment of saying no. He might just as well have said, "Let's do lunch sometime."

As Stirling went to speak again she looked up at him, recognition dawning and put a restraining hand on his forearm. 'And what should *I* call you? Stirling? Douglas or Doug?' Ayesha was looking at him with amusement, searching for something.

Stirling wasn't sure if this suggested another meeting or if it was simply a curious, professional question. 'I don't mind, whichever you prefer,' he smiled, trying to project a nonchalance he didn't feel as he waited for her decision.

Ayesha tilted her head and puckered her mouth as she looked at him, holding his gaze firmly. As the bell reached the end of its peal, the wind fluked along the narrow street and tugged at her hair again. Somewhere, a mother was scolding a child, but it seemed far away as he watched her mouth soften, teeth part and smile broadly.

'I would *love* to go to dinner with you. I was just trying to figure out when. I can't make it this week and I'm committed for the weekend. How about next week? It's your invitation, but could it be anywhere but Worcester please, for privacy?' Holding her hair back from her face against the wind, she asked, 'Sorry, is that rude?'

'No, that sounds perfect. I can't guarantee we'll remain unseen, but I'll consider it a mission!'

Grinning with delight, Stirling reached out to shake her hand. Ayesha looked at it for a moment and gave a slight shake of her head. Stepping in closely, she reached up and kissed him lightly on the cheek.

'You are a bit old fashioned ... Douglas.' Ayesha's eyes were twinkling. 'Or shall I call you Dougie?' Speaking slowly, exaggerating each syllable for effect, she continued, 'Doug-las. Dou-gie. I'm not sure which I prefer?' raising an eyebrow.

Smiling good naturedly, he answered, 'You'd better get going or that demanding client will play hell. I'll call you.'

Ayesha smiled, held his gaze for a moment and walked off briskly down the street. Watching her go, Stirling hoped she would turn to look back at him, but she turned a corner and was gone. Putting a hand to his cheek, he remembered the soft touch of her lips which had caught him by surprise.

Stirling cast a swift look about the street to see if anyone had been watching the exchange. Seeing no one, he walked in the opposite direction, hands thrust deep into his coat pockets as he passed in front of the café.

Checking over his shoulder before crossing the road, Stirling failed to see two women emerge from the café and stand in its entrance to shelter from the wind. As the younger woman fiddled with the zip of her thin coat, her companion watched Stirling reach the other pavement in a light run. Calmly buttoning her coat, she stared after him, willing him to turn round so that she could see his face again.

Responding irritably to a tug at her arm, the two women walked away, their arms linked and heads bent into the breeze.

*

Dinner was a success. After picking Ayesha up from outside her apartment in a new riverside development close to the Diglis Basin within earshot of the cathedral, he had driven them to a village lying astride the old Roman Saltway, close to the Warwickshire border. Far enough from Worcester to meet Ayesha's concerns, and a menu expensive enough that he was unlikely to meet another copper mid-week. The pub had been transformed from a spit and sawdust watering hole for locals into a gastro pub, with decor stylish enough to offend heritage purists.

Chatting together at the bar as they waited for their table, Stirling tried not to let his pleasure seem too obvious. But it was impossible not to admire the fall of Ayesha's thick, black hair, its natural wave catching the light as she turned her head. Dressed simply in jeans and a white cotton shirt that gave effect to her figure, Stirling had noticed the envious, sidelong glances of other men in the bar, and some women too. He had noticed too the estimating looks of the women as they studied the attractive young woman with a man some years older.

Sat at a table in a corner from where he could see the room, Ayesha had been relaxed as they chatted about her work, her ambition to become a partner when the time was right, how hard she would have to work to achieve it and a little about her family. Her parents had migrated to the UK with the expulsion of Asians from Uganda by the tyrant dictator Amin, who, for good measure, had confiscated their families' assets too. Her parents had arrived as youngsters with their respective families with nothing to call their own, but a determination to succeed in the country which had given them a home. Their families had worked hard and an arranged marriage had followed. Although a successful marriage, Ayesha wasn't certain there had ever been any romantic love involved.

The fourth of five children, Ayesha had wanted to study law from a young age. Her parents had worked hard to give their children the best education they could afford. As her father's business in the textile trade grew, they had put their children through private schooling, encouraging them towards the professions. Her eldest brother was a successful surgeon in London and her younger sister was just coming to the end of medical school with aspirations of specialising in an obscure branch of medicine she didn't understand. The other two brothers had gone into the family business bringing a renewed energy that was helping to expand the business.

'So, do you lead a double life between your professional life here and when you're at home?' he asked. Seeing her quizzical response, he explained, 'I mean, you dress to please yourself, you live independently, very different to your parent's generation I imagine?'

Ayesha looked at him thoughtfully. Seeing Stirling's interest was genuine, she answered, 'My parents went through a lot of trauma as kids and had to work so hard to succeed here. Unlike some families who turned inwards to their own community for the old, familiar certainties, my parents chose to embrace the freedoms the UK offered. Sure, if there's a family wedding or celebration, I'll be there in traditional clothing, and I absolutely love all that stuff. But, it doesn't define me. My parents were determined we should live our lives as we wish to. Luckily for me, they've never employed the double standards that some young Asian women suffer. I've been treated exactly the same as my brothers and I'm grateful to them for that. They have only one expectation of me, that I work hard and I'm successful in my career. My private life is my own, but out of respect to them I'm discreet in my relationships because more conservative family members would try to embarrass them. My parents are liberal minded, but others are not.'

As she had explained all this to him, speaking thoughtfully, pausing occasionally to select her words, Stirling had watched Ayesha's face soften when she spoke of her parents, and heard the pride in her voice as she described the achievements of her siblings.

Ayesha looked across at Stirling, watching for his reaction. 'Well, does that help you to understand me better?'

'Yes. It helps me to understand what drives you, and I admire your determination. You're highly intelligent, which I find as attractive as ...' he hesitated, wondering if he was about to step into another minefield, 'well ... your attractiveness. If I'm allowed to say that to a modern, professional woman?' Stirling smiled, teasing her.

Ayesha smiled, accepting the compliment without any faux modesty. 'So, Douglas … hmm, I'm still not sure about that,' she said, continuing with a dry irony, 'Does that burnish your liberal credentials? To know you're dating a girl from a respectable, middle class Asian family?'

Ayesha waited for his answer, smiling faintly, but there had been an edge to her voice. Stirling had caught a whiff of social politics behind the question and grinned back at her.

'Ayesha, I'm delighted to know we're dating and I shall see you again. Soon, I hope.'

Ayesha's eyes narrowed with wry amusement as she realised he had turned her words against her and laughed.

'Your eyes fascinate me,' said Stirling spontaneously, against the flow of the conversation. 'They're the most wonderful dark green and those tawny flecks, they seem to change colour with the light. They're unusual for your heritage, aren't they?'

'You're not the first to ask. My family tell me there was an aunt on my Mother's side with the same eyes. If you know anything of the history of India, you'll know it's been invaded many times throughout history, including your own East India Company! And trade too, of course, so for thousands of years there've been many contributions to our gene pool.'

Stirling reached forward and took her hand in his. Returning the pressure, Ayesha enjoyed the warmth of his hand enfolding hers and wondered what the possibilities might be with this strong minded, but guarded man.

As they chatted, she tried to understand what it was about him that intrigued her. In his mid-thirties, she guessed, Stirling was a few years older than the men she usually dated. Although relaxed and attentive, she felt there was a reserve about him too, something always held back. Whilst Stirling showed a lot of interest in her and asked many questions, he skilfully deflected many of her questions about his past. He had made it clear he wasn't married, her first concern. But there remained a vague air of mystery which, whilst intriguing, left her wondering if she should be concerned that he avoided talking about himself, unlike many men she had known. Yet, when he became enthused about something, or a subject, he talked quickly and articulately, his eyes sparkling with good humour and with a force and strength that suggested dependability and reliability.

As Stirling leaned forward to listen to her, resting his chin in the cup of a hand, Ayesha saw warmth in his dark brown eyes, but a sadness too. She knew about the girl's death at the bridge but as he had not mentioned it, she felt she couldn't.

Dropping Ayesha off outside her apartment, she had not invited him in. Preferring to get to know her better first, Stirling was pleased not to have to say no.

April: Good Friday - 7.56 a.m.

She was late. Would she come?

Looking at his wristwatch he saw it was almost eight and went over the conversation again, puzzled why she had wanted to meet so early. Looking around the open expanse of ground and the surrounding fields he wondered again, and why here? He fidgeted nervously, tapping his forefinger on the steering wheel. Did she suspect something? The money had all gone, if it was to do with that.

Drifting back to another time, he looked around at the fields bathed in the clean edged morning sunlight. At the edges of the pastures, a soft wind ruffled the hedgerows, fast greening over after a long, wet winter. Cloud shadows chased up the incline towards the copse, remnants of the spring shower that was drifting through as he drove down. Dotted about the wide, stoned hardstanding lay muddy puddles. He had parked at the far side of the clearing to be able to watch cars travelling down the narrow, rutted track leading from the main road a mile away.

For a hundred metres in each direction the land had been scraped into levels in readiness for building. Beyond the cleared ground white surveyor's post levels marched away, half covered in grass, but still describing the intended scale of the development. Scraped clean of vegetation, the rich dark soil which had supported generations of farmers now lay dormant, overgrown with wild grass and weeds. Dotted about were remnants of former crops that had seeded down, stirred into life by the recent warm weather. Thinking about the lost money made him grip the wheel tighter.

The telephone call had been brief. He had reluctantly agreed to meet and was regretting it now as he checked his watch again, thinking he should leave. The sun was warming the car's interior, making it stuffy, so he tilted the quarter light open to let in some fresh air. Running his fingers over the burred walnut fascia, he enjoyed the smooth feel of it under his fingers. As the cooler air stirred the interior and lifted the scent of the old leather seats, evoking many memories, he thought again about her call. She had been amongst the best of them, sexually feral, beautiful, but life moves on.

A sudden concern came to mind. Turning the ignition key, he checked the fuel gauge. Very low, but enough to get home.

Narrowing his eyes against the glare of the sun on the bonnet, he looked up the track to see a car travelling down slowly, dropping in and out of the ruts and splashing water over the verges. He followed its progress until it stopped at the other side of the cleared ground where she sat looking across the space between them. Who should go to meet the other? He would let her come to him.

Looking in the rear-view mirror, he ran his fingers through his still thick, wavy hair, studying the silver streaks and persuading himself again that they added something. Unsure yet of what she knew, he wanted her to think him attractive still. He felt his arousal stirring as his mind roamed the possibilities.

Staring across to the highly-polished saloon, the sun shimmering on its windscreen hurt her eyes and made it difficult to see if there was anyone inside. A cloud shadow passing across the ground dimmed the glare for a few seconds to reveal his outline behind the wheel. Seeing him again made her nervous and suddenly sick with fear. She was alone, and it was so isolated down here.

Wiping damp palms down her trouser legs, she reminded herself why she had come and felt her hatred gnawing at the pit of her stomach. It had seemed so clear in her mind before, but why had she insisted on meeting him here, of all places? Looking around, she remembered it as it had once been, beautiful, but scarred now and ugly. But isn't that how life treats beauty, she thought, bitterly. Held up for transient admiration before crushing it into the dust, swiftly discarded in favour of the next attraction. That had always been his style.

She wondered again how anyone could have loved this vain, emotionally shallow man. He had been an attentive lover, handsome to the point of beauty with his unruly blonde hair and eyes that held a woman captive, seemingly able to read her soul, which she had been tempted to give him freely. The implacable anger returned at the thought of how he treated the people who loved him, interested when he must satisfy his needs, toying with their emotions, arrogantly confident of his charm but detached, cruel.

Opening the small clasp handbag on the passenger seat, she checked for her mobile phone. Rummaging inside and realising it was not there, she felt a rising panic as she searched under the seats in case it had fallen there, then remembered she had left it at home on charge. Looking across at the car she again thought of leaving but after another look inside her bag, decided to stay.

Opening the door, she stepped out and stood, resting her hand on top of the door and looked across the open space, uncertain. Looking around, a new sadness struck her as she saw that all trace of its former use had been erased, scratched from the soil that had once given it purpose. And then she felt a cold satisfaction that everything had been so completely obliterated and consigned to the past.

Taking a deep breath, she pushed the door shut and walked slowly towards the other car, able now to see his outline at the wheel. Lifting her eyes above the car briefly, she followed the slope of the field upwards to the stone wall enclosing the wooded copse which stretched along the length of the crest, stitching the hillside to the blue sky. Shivering at a memory, a new fear gripped her as her doubts resurfaced.

Reminding herself of what had brought her here, an icy determination stilled her stomach and she felt the anxiety slough away, cold hatred returning as she thought of the pain and the humiliation.

She needed to look him in the eye. To know, for certain.

With a practised eye, he studied the movement of her hips in the tight, faded jeans as she approached, head bent forward slightly so that her hair partially obscured her face. He wondered if he would still find her attractive. A clutch handbag in the crook of her arm drew his eye to her breasts which swayed with her step under a thin wool sweater which were fuller than he expected, but put it down to her being older. He had not seen her for some years, but she was as slender as he remembered.

Feeling a tingle of excitement, he reached down to adjust himself as his body stirred at a memory and in expectation. Checking the rear-view mirror, he ran his fingers through his hair again, his heartbeat lifting as he wondered if he might yet feel her skin under his hand again. But, how much did she know?

Seeing him lean over to open the passenger door for her, she hesitated and examined the rear of the car. It was empty, the brown leather seat reminding her of other times. And of other women. Slipping agilely into the passenger seat, she pulled the door shut and turned to look at him. Meeting his eyes, she looked for something there, contrition perhaps, but saw only the familiar, charming smile falter as he registered his surprise, a puzzled look in the usually calm, seducing eyes. He leant back as he studied her face.

'I was ...' his voice trailed away.

Ignoring him, she said nothing and turned away to stare out of the windscreen. Looking at the ruined landscape, she exhaled a long sigh and said sadly, 'It used to be so beautiful here.'

'Yes, it was. But things never remain the same, do they?' he replied, still recovering from his surprise. Studying her profile, he tried to gauge her mood.

'No. But anything beautiful you touch always turns to ugliness,' she answered coldly.

He said nothing, still cautious. Waiting for her to speak, he watched her breasts rising and falling slowly and her nipples, brushed by the cool air outside, pressing through the soft wool. He wanted to reach across and touch her.

Breathing in the familiar scent of the leather seats she noticed his after shave, the one he had always worn. With a slight shock, she wondered how she could have missed that trace scent and felt the hatred bubbling up again. Turning to face him, she looked into the familiar eyes and realised she was no longer afraid of him. Half turned towards her, his arm hooked over the back of his seat, she sensed his uncertainty, whether to say something or to let her take the lead. She watched him draw his eyes from her breasts and compose his features into sincere, melting his eyes in the way he always could when it suited his purpose. In her lap, she gripped the clutch bag, opening and closing the clasp fastening.

She asked, 'Why did you agree to meet?'

'Well, I thought ...' He stalled, unsure now what the meeting was about and cautious. Play it open, he thought, keep it friendly. 'No matter, we've been friends for a long time, so why not?'

'Friends?' She laughed contemptuously. 'And we know how you treat *friends*. Even those who loved you,' she said, scornfully.

Surprised at her own calmness, she searched his face for a sign of regret or contrition but saw only his confident arrogance returning. She could read too, the calculation as his eyes travelled over her body, smiling at her with open interest. Surely not? After all the harm he had caused, could he really be considering *that*? Or was he mocking her? She had never been able to completely forget him.

'You arrogant bastard. How could you even consider it? You think I don't know, but I do. I know everything, and I hate you!'

Explaining what she knew, about the depth of his treachery, she saw his self-assurance melting away until he sat shaken, unnerved by the intensity of her vitriol.

He began to give wheedling, self-justifying excuses but in the face of her stony features, he fell quiet. Then, with a smile of growing satisfaction at the pain it would cause, he told her everything: how long it had gone on for and the intimate details she would not want to hear; how well it had compared, and all with the added spice of knowing how much it would hurt her when discovered. Finally, the pleasures he had enjoyed.

'So, there you have it, darling. That's what happened,' adding maliciously, 'and there's absolutely nothing that you can do about it.'

Sickened by the details and the degradation, and shocked at his arrogance in absolving himself of blame, she sat stunned and still.

Feeling he had regained the upper hand and recovered his dominance, he waited for her to respond. His eyes fell again to her breasts and he casually edged his hand along the back of her seat.

The sudden movement and scream of animal rage came without warning. Unable to free his arm, he barely saw the sunlight flash on the blade as it arced upwards into his face to plunge deep into his left eye, destroying the optic nerve as the point exploded inside his brain in a kaleidoscope of blinding, splintering light and unspeakable pain.

Roaring in agony and blinded by the blood and fluid flowing through the fingers of his free hand, he could not avoid the blade as it flashed again. Cartilage crunched as the blade sliced through the bridge of his nose to destroy his right eye, spattering another spray of blood and fluid across the windscreen.

Clutching at his face with both hands and screaming in terror, he could hear the woman screaming incomprehensible obscenities as she lunged and stabbed, striking wherever he was exposed and defenceless. Unable to protect himself in the confined space and trapped in his seat, he felt blows to his head, his neck, his body, vaguely aware too of blows aimed at his crotch. As he reacted increasingly slowly to one blow, another struck him somewhere else until he could respond no longer. A primitive instinct made him curl and turn away from the attack which only served to offer his back. With his senses diminishing through shock and the damage to his brain, he was only vaguely aware of hysterical screaming coming from above him as fresh blows rained on his head and neck.

Gasping for air bubbling through a punctured lung, he no longer felt the blade piercing his body as the blows became ever more remote.

Kneeling in the passenger seat, she realised he was no longer moving and lowered the knife, massaging her wrist which throbbed from repeatedly striking bone. Panting deeply through exertion and rage, her breath sawing in her throat, she stared at the knife uncomprehendingly and back at him, unable to remember how it had started.

Gulping for air, she felt her senses alert and incredibly alive as she looked with a detached fascination at her bloodied hand holding the smeared knife, gazing at the blood sprays around the car interior and across her clothes. Running her tongue across her lips, she could taste his blood and was surprised she felt no revulsion, only curiosity. Hesitantly, she leaned over to listen to his breathing as it grew weaker, fluid rasping noisily in his throat and jumped back, startled, as he gave a final convulsion, stopped breathing, and died.

In the heavy silence, she realised how warm it was as strong sunshine warmed the car. She sniffed the air, smelling her own sweat and the cloying, sickly-sweet smell of blood. Another odour supplanted the others as his muscles relaxed and the stench of faecal matter rose into her nostrils.

Horrified, she scrabbled at the door and stumbled out, falling to the ground where she knelt on all fours, retching bile. Drawing the back of her hand across her mouth, she felt his blood smearing her mouth and retched again. Turning to sit on the ground, she stared at his body across the seats, half expecting him to stir, trying to grasp what she had done, looking dazedly from the knife, to the body, and back to the knife.

Shocked at her loss of control, she had never experienced anything so primitive and visceral. A tremor shook her body as she remembered the pleasure of plunging the knife into him, again, and again, and again.

Feeling the blood becoming sticky between her fingers, she looked around for something to clean herself with. Noticing the pools of water in the rutted surface she crawled to the nearest of them and knelt to wash her hands. As the adrenalin ebbed, the blood and fluids staining her clothes began to sicken her and she fought down another urge to vomit. Sitting back on her heels, she felt cold and began to shake, tired suddenly.

Obeying an instinct to flee, she took some stumbling steps towards her car before stopping to look back. Why run, only to be discovered later?

Noticing blood still on her hands, she returned to crouch again at the water. Putting the knife down, she slipped her fingers through each other slowly until the blood was lost in the darkening pool, enjoying the cold water on her skin. Cupping water in both hands, she splashed it onto her face and turned her head up to the sky to breathe deeply, feeling the cold water trickle between her breasts and over her belly, her flesh alive and tingling. She laughed, nervously, shaking her head in amazement that she could have done this.

Astonished by her own detachment, she lifted the knife and played the blade in the sunlight as she contemplated what to do, giving an abstract smile as the songbirds sang, unconcerned by murder. The woman took a long, careful look around her and up the long track. No one would come down here for days, perhaps weeks. The entrance was almost a mile away with signs declaring it as private land. Not even lovers came down here, and there were no footpaths across the land.

She decided on what to do.

 C8 80

Easter Sunday

With Ballard's investigation plodding on interminably and scant information being shared with him, things with Ayesha had moved quicker than Stirling had expected.

More evenings out had led to them agreeing to spend time together over the Easter weekend. Later than usual this year with a promising weather forecast, Stirling had invited her to spend the Saturday evening with him when he would cook dinner.

Ayesha could not have known it was the first time a woman had been invited to the cottage for over a year.

Early morning sunlight slanting through the curtains suffused the room in an indistinct, hazy glow. On the far wall of the bedroom, daylight shimmered and danced through the branches and leaves of the tree outside, fretting under a light wind soughing in the roof eaves above them. For the first time in weeks, Stirling had slept without waking.

Without lifting his head from the pillow, Stirling gazed at Ayesha's raven black hair falling across the pillow. He particularly enjoyed the fine tendrils that escaped from her hairline, however thoroughly she tied her hair back for work. Lifting the sheet gently, he followed the contours of her body from the fine hair at the nape of her neck, down her spine to the soft indentations at her lower back to disappear into the cleft of her cheeks. He resisted a temptation to reach out and stroke her.

Lowering the sheet again, Stirling rolled onto his back slowly to avoid waking her. Listening to Ayesha's soft, regular breathing, his mind roamed through the previous evening. It was the first time she had visited his home. As he cooked, they had amused each other with anecdotes but, apart from telling her some funny stories, he had avoided talking of his work.

After a few glasses of wine, Ayesha had pressed him to reveal his true first name. Reluctantly, with threats of punishment if she repeated it, he had told her. He closed his eyes with a cringe as he recalled her stop-eyed astonishment, asking him to repeat it. Rolling about with laughter, Ayesha had apologised and wiped away her tears, struggling to contain her amusement. He had laughed too at his Father's wistful romanticism.

Sitting together in the lounge enjoying the warmth of the fire and its light dancing across the room, the mellow, modern jazz he enjoyed had backtracked their conversation late into the evening. Too much white wine had made driving impossible. Close together on the sofa, in a natural break in conversation, Ayesha had pulled him closer to her and kissed him slowly, her tongue playing lightly in his mouth and then gently bit his lower lip so that he was quickly aroused.

The sex had been urgent, lustful, each thrusting hard at the other as they surrendered to the passion they had restrained until then, gripping at each other's hips and hair. Stirling remembered the sharp, stimulating pleasure of Ayesha's nails urging him into her until they climaxed loudly and close together. Him, arched back with pained pleasure as Ayesha's legs wrapped tightly about him, her fingers tangled in his hair. Her, absorbing the physical tremors coursing through her body, surprised by a deep emotion, her nerves tingling as she buried her head into his shoulder, enjoying the hard thump of his heart against her chest. Both, panting for air and sweat sheening their bodies in the low light of the log embers.

For a long time, they had lain naked on the old sofa wrapped in each other's arms with Ayesha's head resting on his chest. Stirling had enjoyed caressing her skin and playing her hair through his fingers, filtering the light from the fire to watch the hues change subtly. When she had shivered, he had drawn over them the old cashmere blanket he kept for winter evenings. Comfortable and warm again, Ayesha had drifted into a light sleep as Stirling breathed in the scent of her hair, the musky scent of her body mingling with the smell of their sex, smiling as her muscles relaxed and she twitched against him.

They had dozed together for an hour until he could no longer resist the need to flex his arm, deadened by Ayesha's weight lying on it. Lifting her head from his chest, Ayesha propped herself up to look down at him, uncertain of what she would see. Seeing him smile, Ayesha had kissed him and stood up, holding out a hand to him. With their bodies pressed to each other they had embraced and kissed deeply.

Feeling him stirring against her, Ayesha had rubbed her hips encouragingly and without taking her eyes from his, watching for his reaction, had enclosed him in her hand, massaging him until he was fully erect. When Stirling had begun to manoeuvre her back to the sofa, she had led the way upstairs, flirting her hips at him as she went ahead of him. At the top of the stairs Ayesha had stopped to watch him, her eyes sparkling with mischief as she followed the sway of his erection.

'So, you think you're up to it again, do you?' she challenged.

Ayesha had stepped lightly away from his grasp and with a low laugh, had smuggled herself under the quilt to watch his approach. As he approached the bed she had drawn back the cover to let his eyes linger over her as she rested her weight on an elbow, one leg drawn forward to cover herself, but not completely.

Stirling had drawn his eyes slowly down the length of Ayesha's body, printing the moment onto his memory. Sitting on the edge of the bed, he had drawn his fingertips lightly down her spine causing the fine hair of her forearms to stand under his touch, spreading his fingers over the cleft of her buttocks before reaching down to caress the soft skin of her inner thigh, gently probing and massaging until Ayesha had arched in pleasure and drawn him to her.

Their lovemaking was slow, mutual, watching for each other's reactions to a touch, to a caress, each seeking to give pleasure until they had fallen asleep, physically and emotionally sated.

Stirling felt Ayesha stir beside him and watched as she pulled the cover over her shoulder against the cool morning air and settled back into sleep. In a short space of time she had found a way into his heart as no woman had for a long time, deftly sidestepping the defences he habitually ranged around himself. There was a subtle insightfulness and patience, too. He knew Ayesha could see him moving behind the barricades and yet, did not pry.

There was a special quality about her which he was drawn to. Sharp witted, funny, intelligent, and beautiful too. But it was the warmth of Ayesha's personality and emotional honesty that gave her depth, leading him to think a man could make a home in her heart where she would hold it, safe.

Recalling their lovemaking had aroused him again. Rolling onto his side, Stirling moved closer until he was pressed along the length of Ayesha's back, seeking the warmth of her body against him. With her buttocks in his lap, he slid an arm around her waist to cup her breast in his hand and felt the nipple harden in his palm.

Sleepily, she murmured, 'Something's letting me know you're awake,' and pushed her hips back against him.

Kissing her shoulder, he answered, 'Good morning, Ayesha. The sun's up,'

'Really? I've not heard it called that before,' she answered sleepily. Turning slightly, she lifted her leg over his and reached for him.

As Stirling slipped into a doze, feeling the heat of his body pressed against her back, Ayesha smiled at the sensation of him retreating from her.

Enjoying Stirling's warm breath on her neck and his heartbeat slowing to a steady rhythm, Ayesha contemplated why she found him so interesting, intriguing even. She felt a calm reassurance in Stirling's company, unlike any other man she had known. It was not just the sex, as good as that had proved to be. Her family was unlikely to approve of him. The rebellious part of her nature enjoyed the prospect of that meeting. But there were depths to his personality that she suspected would take a long time to reach, or to understand. Was that the attraction?

When he had asked to meet, she had been curious. She was not short of attention from attractive men, wealthy ones too if that had been important to her, which it was not. Taking care not to wake him, Ayesha rolled over to study his face. Relaxed in sleep, he looked younger. Physically strong and good looking, she studied the dark wavy hair that she liked to run her fingers through. The attentive, watchful eyes which seemed able to penetrate her thoughts and interpret her moods so accurately. But it was also something to do with his quiet confidence and mental toughness, together with an intuitive compassion she didn't often notice in men. And there was the dry, sideways looking wit that made her laugh so easily.

Letting her eyes travel over his body, the sheet still drawn aside, she saw again the small, healed scar high on the left side of his chest. Ayesha was tempted to run her finger over it again as she had last night. When she had asked how it was caused, Stirling had glanced down as if he had forgotten it was there before replying obliquely, "Catching a stray bullet isn't always a metaphor" and had changed the conversation.

He was wary of putting his trust in others. Was that life experience through work, a woman, or something deeper? She could only guess at the violence he must have seen and dealt with. That would harden a soul, surely? Ayesha had noticed how, sometimes, a shadow fell over his face as a memory flickered and he might look away, distracted, his brow furrowing before pushing away whatever had intruded and returned his attention to her. The girl's death was troubling him deeply but when she had tried to steer into the subject one evening, Stirling had manoeuvred away from the subject, but with sufficient inference to let her know he felt poorly treated. The subject was clearly not open to discussion.

Watching him sleep, Ayesha felt a fresh tenderness for him and leaned over to kiss him on the lips. Without opening his eyes, Stirling smiled at her touch.

'Morning again,' she said, when he opened his eyes. 'Three times on the first night. Not bad for an old man, but you'll have to do better next time if you want me to visit more often.'

Pulling Ayesha to him, Stirling smacked her bottom lightly and kissed her.

Anticipating what the kiss would lead to, she lifted herself onto an elbow and looked down at him. 'So, does a girl get breakfast here, or must she go home to eat?'

Ayesha came downstairs to find Stirling preparing breakfast. Leaning against the pillar of the lounge archway into the kitchen, she watched as Stirling moved barefoot on the stone flagged floor in quiet concentration. Dressed in a white T shirt hanging loose over faded jeans, the pocket edges and legs frayed through long wear, he paused to reduce the volume of a radio from which a current affairs programme chattered quietly.

On the far side of the modern kitchen-diner he said he had built himself, glazed doors led onto a half-formed terrace. Bright sunshine poured through the doors to lie aslant the room, warming the stone floor. The air was tinged with a pleasing mix of the cottage's timber framework, wood ash from the evening's fire and now, the smell of cooking teasing her hunger.

Noticing her, Stirling stopped and smiled, spatula in hand. 'Find everything you need?'

'Yes, perfect. A great shower, thank you.'

With a grin, Stirling pointed to the oak table for her to sit as he returned to preparing breakfast. Now clothed and without the shared intimacy of their nakedness, Ayesha suddenly felt awkward with the usual anxieties of the morning after. She had felt apprehensive as she came downstairs, uncertain how the mood between them might be, once the night's passion was spent.

She remembered other mornings; an awkward dance of manners with dissatisfaction shambling left-footedly around unspoken embarrassment, laced with misunderstood apologies. The cold light of morning had a way of casting a sharp objectivity on alcohol and lust-fuelled indiscretions. As a younger woman she had had her own share of hasty departures, hurriedly gathering clothes up in an unfamiliar room, offering mumbled excuses about a busy day ahead. But here, she was happy and comfortable in his company. Lost in thought, Ayesha realised Stirling had asked her something.

Shaking her head in apology, she replied, 'Sorry, still half asleep.'

'Is scrambled eggs, smoked salmon and toast okay? Or there's fruit and yoghurt, if you prefer?'

'Yes please, all of it. I'm famished ... can't think why?' she answered, raising an eyebrow.

Stirling smiled. 'It suits you,' he said, pointing with the spatula to the over-sized man's cotton shirt she was wearing. Stirling had not worn it since he had been a young Constable on patrol, many years ago, but kept a couple clean and ironed for female visitors who made an unplanned stay. They had not been used for a long time.

Pulling out the sides of the oversized shirt to form bat wings, she asked, 'Is this an old police shirt Douglas? It's huge!' Turning slowly to demonstrate her meaning, the long shirt tail lifted to give him a tantalising glimpse of her bottom. Crossing the room quickly, Stirling smacked Ayesha's bottom lightly with the spatula and made her jump.

'Ow!' She exclaimed, rubbing her bottom with one hand and stepped forward to hit him playfully on the chest. 'That, DCI Stirling, is police brutality!' She reached up to kiss him, pressing herself against him.

Stirling laughed and pulled her close for an embrace. Reaching down, he lifted the shirt tail and stroked her cheek, before allowing his hand to roam.

Ayesha pushed him away. 'Stop! You've had quite enough already, and I'm famished.'

'So am I,' he replied with a gleam in his eye. 'And you look very appetising in that shirt.'

'Hmm, I don't think you've been fed for a long time!' she replied and crossed the room to look out of the glass doors to the garden. Standing with her leg crooked, combing her damp hair through her fingers, she was unaware of the sun silhouetting her figure through the shirt. With a long, admiring look, Stirling sighed and returned to preparing breakfast.

Raising her voice above the noise of cooking and the radio, Ayesha called across, 'It's going to be a nice day.'

Stirling nodded and continued cooking. Looking across the half-built terrace, past an upturned wheel barrow and a stack of stone slabs, Ayesha's eye followed the line of the garden to an untidy hedgerow beyond which lay fields. In the distance, the Malvern Hills humped and dipped southwards, their green flanks marked with dark swatches of last year's bracken. The garden disappeared around the side of the house to where she thought the front driveway must be. It was almost dark when she arrived and had only a few moments to take in the old, oak framed cottage with red brickwork set back from the road when Stirling had opened the door to invite her inside.

Sat together at a corner of the dining table, they ate in companiable silence enjoying the food and settling their hunger. When they were finished, Ayesha reached across and took Stirling's hand.

'Thank you, for last night. The dinner was lovely and … well, everything else too.'

Meeting her eyes and understanding Ayesha was trying to convey something heartfelt to him, he replied, 'It was wonderful. And this too, you here with me.'

He meant it. It had been too long since he had enjoyed a woman's company without second guessing a commitment he was unwilling to give.

Recognising his sincerity, Ayesha smiled, more for herself than for him. 'Me too. It can be a bit awkward, can't it? You know, the morning after?'

'It can be, sometimes,' and gave her a tender smile. 'But not today.'

Glancing outside Stirling said, 'It's a fine day and I promised you a long walk.'

After reaching the top of Worcester Beacon from North Hill, Stirling led them south along the foot worn, undulating spine of the hills, stopping now and then to point out features of the landscape. To the east, Worcestershire, stretching away across the flat plain of the Severn valley to where the Cotswolds formed a hazy horizon, thirty miles away. To the west, Herefordshire and, to his mind, the more attractive of the two counties with its chequer board of fields, woodlands and hills rippling away to the Black Mountains of the Welsh border. Stirling pointed down to Eastnor Castle, sheltering in its wooded valley to the south west.

Stirling put a steadying hand on Ayesha's arm and stood to listen to the trill of a lark, high above them. He was struggling to pick it out against the glare of the sun when Ayesha pointed to a dark speck, hovering high above them, and laughed delightedly at the bird's joy. Turning to him, she looped her arm through his, reached up to kiss him and prodded him in the chest with a finger.

'You know, Douglas? Beneath that tough hide of yours, there's a nice bloke trying to break out.' She was making fun of him gently, but there was a seriousness to her voice.

'Hmm, you clearly don't know me well enough yet,' he replied, shrugging away the compliment with a self-deprecating smile.

Ayesha gave an exaggerated roll of her eyes. 'You don't like compliments either!'

Laughing, Stirling tugged her hand. 'Come on, or we'll never get a table.'

An hour later they were stamping mud from their boots at the entrance to a hotel near to British Camp. As Ayesha headed straight for the open fire to warm herself, Stirling ordered drinks and food at the bar. Taking a table close to the window where they could watch people coming and going, they chatted amiably about the morning, leaning close to each other to be heard over the hubbub of other diners. Around them sat a mixed collection of walkers with muddy dogs, families enjoying the remains of the Easter holiday and couples of varying ages.

In reply to his surprise when she ordered a traditional ale, Ayesha explained with a shrug, 'Sorry, student habits.' Eyes bright above the rim of her glass, she sipped at the beer and commented on how good it was, amusing Stirling that her many qualities included being a good judge of ales. Impatient of vanity, Stirling also liked the way she simply combed her wind tangled hair out with her fingers and let fall, curling over her shoulders in a semblance of order.

Asked how he knew the hills so well, Stirling explained that, as a boy, it had been an easy destination for a rare family day out in summer. It didn't cost anything more than the petrol to get there and an ice cream for him and his brother at the end of a walk. Since moving back from London a few years before, he walked them a couple of times a year. Ayesha's own cityscape upbringing, with both parents working hard, had left little time to develop an interest in the outdoors and she had made only a few friends since moving into the area. Career minded, her long hours prevented socialising a great deal, so she tended to keep in touch with university friends as much as possible but, already, that network was loosening as her friends married and developed their careers. Ayesha asked about his family, but with his parents having died some years ago, and an older brother who lived abroad whom he rarely saw, there was little to tell. They fell to talking about his role and the work of the MCU.

With genuine interest, Ayesha asked, 'So, how *do* you go about investigating a murder, just follow your instinct?'

'That alone would get you into trouble. Instinct is the accumulation of experience mixed with astuteness, and only ever applied with a healthy measure of common sense. We're obliged to follow national good practice doctrines contained in something affectionately referred to as the "murder manual."'

'Wow! A manual on how to commit murder?' she said, jokily.

He smiled, 'No, how to detect them! Rather than every police force applying its own methods, as would happen decades ago, there's now just one national standard which all SIOs, who are nationally accredited, must follow. The manual's revised constantly to keep abreast of developments, particularly things like DNA and changes to the law. Sometimes, that's around the "dark arts."'

'Dark arts?' she asked in amusement. 'Sounds a bit medieval.'

'Surveillance, informants, the sneaky, sexy stuff that's portrayed fast and loose on TV, but is tightly regulated and people lose their jobs over if they get it badly wrong.'

As Stirling talked, in more detail than he had previously about his work, Ayesha noticed the enthusiasm and pride in his voice as he talked of his team, enjoying the funny anecdotes about some of the "characters" and hoped to meet some of them soon.

Returning to the cottage late in the afternoon, they slouched together in the sofa enjoying the warmth of the fire, talking together and listening to music. With his arm around her, Ayesha shaped herself into Stirling's body, shifted about until she was comfortable and quickly fell asleep. To his silent amusement, she began to snore softly. An hour later Ayesha woke with a start.

Sitting up, she rubbed her eyes awake. 'Sorry, I fell asleep.'

'No problem. You were snoring,' he teased, and laughed at her immediate embarrassment.

'I was not!' she retorted. Looking at him questioningly, she asked, 'I wasn't, was I?'

After teasing her a little more, Stirling asked, 'It's early evening. Do you need to go home, or would you like to stay over?' He hoped for the latter.

Stretching her legs and wincing at the stiffness in her legs, she answered, 'I really should do more exercise.'

'I agree, but what about this evening, do you want to stay?'

Serious now, she asked, 'Would you like me to?'

'Yes, even if you snore! I've a new toothbrush you can have.'

'In that case, how could a girl refuse,' she said, resting her head back on his chest.

⊄ ⊅

Easter Monday: 3.37 a.m.

Steering with one hand, the poacher guided the battered old Land Rover over the rough ground. With his free hand, he reached up and swivelled the headlight mounted on the cab roof and turned it slowly, seeking out his prey.

Having played across them since he was a kid, he knew these fields like the back of his hand. It was different then, when it was a working farm and he'd known the farmer's kids. They went to school together and each year he would help with the harvests for pocket money, working late into warm summer evenings, through the night too if there was a good moon and rain forecast. He had grumbled together with all the other locals when the farm was broken up and sold off, the buildings slowly falling into disrepair and the ground rented out.

The cab was filled with the scent of still warm rabbit fur rising from the footwell where he had dumped his kill, together with smoke from the cigarette habitually stuck to his bottom lip. Across the passenger seat lay his shotgun, broken open with a cartridge in each barrel ready for use. The poacher decided to work his way over to the copse where he could count on getting a few more before they scurried back to the cover of the brambles.

Spread out in the moonlight below him was the abandoned building site with its excavated terraces at either side. Sunday's warm sunshine had lifted the moisture from the ground and now, cool night air had flowed down the slopes around the clearing to create a deep blanket of mist which lay silvery white across the hollow, reflecting the pale moonlight so that it resembled a small lake.

Slipping down into the mist, the bonnet pushed and lifted it like a bow wave, sliding under the windows like a spectral sea. Stone crunched under the tyres of the Land Rover as it bounced in and out of invisible ruts. He was aiming for the track he knew rose at the far side of the clearing to take him uphill to a black line of trees silhouetted against the skyline.

Half way across the clearing, the poacher caught sight of something lying on the surface of the mist. Braking to a halt, he watched it submerge from view and re-emerge as a breeze rippled over the surface, tugging aside the opaque blanket.

Reaching up, the poacher rotated the roof mounted lamp until it shone on the object, unable to understand what he was looking at. Watching it slip in and out of view, he realised it was a car roof sloping down at the rear to disappear deeper into the mist. He waited, expecting someone to get out, or for a courting couple to hurriedly drive away after being woken by the lamp and the clatter of the diesel engine reverberating through the still air. Drawing hard on his cigarette, he thought back. It had not been there two nights ago, and it was unusual to see a car down here.

Turning towards the shrouded vehicle, he drove closer until his headlights and the cab lamp shone fully onto the side of the car. He recognised the distinctive outline of a Jaguar saloon burnt out along much of its length. The rear wheel rims sat on the ground explained the ungainly slant of the car.

Assuming it had been nicked and torched, and no longer expecting anyone to be with the car, the poacher picked up his shotgun through habit and stepped out, leaving the lights on to illuminate the Jaguar. With the shotgun broken over the crook of his arm, he began to casually circuit the vehicle, speculating if there was anything worth swiping from it. He was known as a man who could get hold of things at a sensible price, if no awkward questions were asked.

Estimating the value of the front wheels, the poacher paused to listen to a vixen scream, turning his head to the noise. Half a mile away, he reckoned. Closer to the car, the damp air was laden with the smell of burnt rubber and charred materials. He could see the fire had been concentrated at the rear and travelled forwards, consuming the paintwork across the roof and the main body of the saloon, blackening the windows as it went. It had burnt itself out before reaching the bonnet and front wings which remained largely undamaged. The poacher was surprised it had not burnt out completely, supposing there had only been a small amount of fuel in the tank to feed the fire.

Moving round to the driver's door, he bent to peer through the smoke darkened window. From the far side, the Land Rover's lights illuminated the interior dully, outlining something lying below the driver's door window. Intuitively uneasy, the poacher cast a suspicious look around, over the soft bed of mist undulating about him. Reflexively, he sniffed the air but could only smell the burnt car.

Stepping back, he closed the shotgun barrel with a soft click and slid the safety catch off. Shifting the weapon to his right hand, he reached forward and took hold of the door handle. Yanking it open, he uttered a loud oath and sprang back in alarm as a body slumped towards him.

Somewhere, close by, he heard the screams of an animal being torn to death.

CB ∞

Day 1: Easter Monday - 8.44 a.m.

The sound of his mobile vibrating on the bedside table woke Stirling from a deep sleep. Ayesha was moulded into his body, making it difficult for him to reach it. Peering at the screen he saw it was Pearson calling.

Drowsy and confused why Pearson was calling him, Stirling answered quietly, 'Dave?'

There was a pause at the other end before Pearson spoke, his voice unusually cheery. 'Morning Doug. Able to speak freely?'

Looking down at Ayesha, he saw she was still asleep. 'Hold on.'

Stirling slid out of bed and walked naked to the bathroom, closing the door quietly behind him. Sitting on the edge of the bath he spoke again, 'Okay.'

'Anyone I know Doug?' Pearson asked with a soft chuckle. Gaining no answer, he continued. 'I need you to come in. We've got a suspicious death but it's almost certainly a murder. We haven't had the scene long, so things are still imprecise. An anonymous caller during the early hours claimed he'd found a body in a burnt-out car but was vague about the location and hung up. The call recording has been seized. The location he gave isn't in our mapping software. A patrol had a look around the area where the call was made from, a public telephone box, toured the lanes but found nothing so it was written off as a hoax. When the local beat officer came on duty this morning and read the overnight log, he recognised the place name. He wasn't certain of its location but called it in. The control room put the helicopter up to do a search and they found it fairly quickly.'

Stirling had listened carefully, noting the detail until Pearson stopped speaking.

'Sounds interesting Dave, but I'm suspended from operational duties. If the media hears I'm involved in anything, they'll be all over it. And I can't see McDonald agreeing to it, can you?'

Stirling felt resentment at being prevented from doing what he loved most because of Ballard's showboating incompetence.

'I know, but we're struggling to find an experienced SIO who isn't already bogged down in investigations. I've spoken with Steph Tanner and she's signed off on it.'

Stirling thought for a moment, listening to Pearson breathing at the other end of the line. 'And McDonald? He's determined to bust me if he can. Has he agreed?'

'McDonald's on leave for a week. Tanner and I have worked through what we know about the death so far, which isn't much, and we see no reason why you can't lead this. We've no other SIOs free and you're available. It's her policy decision so if there's any problems later, the monkey's on her back.'

Still cautious, and anticipating problems later he asked, 'And the policy decision to appoint me is recorded, is it?'

'Doug, trust me!' Pearson was becoming irritated. 'Now, unless you're seriously ill or that woman has nailed the doors shut, get your arse to the scene as quickly as you can and grip it. I want a situation report from you as soon as possible, and by no later than eleven. We need to keep Steph Tanner briefed.'

There was a long silence before Pearson spoke again. 'Doug, Tanner's gone out on a limb for you on this one, so don't screw up. Let's look after her?'

'Yes, of course.' Stirling respected Tanner's experience and appreciated her support, but he knew it was conditional on him doing a good job.

As they talked, Stirling went downstairs to find his notebook to write down the limited information Pearson could give him of the scene. Ending the call, Stirling stood deep in thought with his arms folded around the book. He was pleased to be called out to lead a murder investigation, if that's what it proved to be, but he would have to watch his back and keep out of the way of the media, which would be difficult if public appeals for information became necessary. They almost always were. Pearson had agreed for Bill Edwards to be his Deputy SIO which would make life a lot easier.

'So, is this how the nation's finest detectives consider their strategies?'

Stirling turned in surprise to see Ayesha standing at the foot of the stairs, leaning on the oak newel post with a towel wrapped around her and arms folded as she looked across the room at him. Deep in thought, he had not heard her come downstairs and looked at her, bemused for a moment. Following her gaze, he remembered he was naked and smiled.

'Ah! Well, yes, I do my best thinking without my clothes on. Doesn't everyone?'

Looking at the phone in his hand, she asked, 'Work?'

'Yes. Sorry Ayesha, I've been called in. I can't spend the day with you as I wanted.'

'Oh,' she said, disappointed, and walked over to perch on the arm of the sofa. 'But I thought you couldn't be involved in anything?'

'There's a suspicious death and we've run out of available SIOs, so I'm needed. To be honest, I'm glad to get back to work,' and explained where he was going.

Seeing her disappointment, he added, 'It might all be done in a day, or it could be weeks and months. It's impossible to say, but I'll have a better idea later today.'

'It's okay, I do understand. It's just that … I was really looking forward to another day together.' She smiled through her disappointment.

Stirling walked over and took her hand. 'I'm sorry. But you don't have to leave. Your car's here so stay for as long as you like. Just pull the door behind you when you're ready to leave. I don't know when I'll be back as I don't know what we've got yet.'

Stirling leaned forward and kissed her swiftly. 'I need to shower and shave.'

Sitting on the loo seat watching Stirling shower, Ayesha felt a sense of foreboding as he washed her from his skin. As he stood naked at the sink to shave, chatting over the noise of splashing water, Ayesha enjoyed the simple domesticity of the scene. Watching the movement of his muscles in his back and arms, she detected a firmness and decisiveness in Stirling's voice she had not noticed before, transformed from relaxed, funny lover to serious minded professional. And something else, the excitement of returning to what he did best.

Stirling walked to the bedroom and selected a suit and shirt from the wardrobe. Ayesha trailed behind and sat on the bed, propping herself up on a pillow against the brass bedhead to watch him dress. Determined to keep the mood light, she crossed the room to where Stirling stood knotting his tie in front of an oval, free standing mirror. Putting her arms around him Ayesha smiled to him in the mirror, but his face was distracted as he itemised the tasks ahead. He's already left me, she thought disconsolately, feeling the last two days slipping ever further away.

Talking to his reflection, she said, 'I've really enjoyed this weekend. Being together.'

She didn't want to sound clingy, worse still grateful, but did want him to understand her feelings. Stirling smiled at her in the mirror. With a final tug on the tie knot, he slid it into place and turned to hold her around her waist.

'I'm sorry to rush off like this. I've really enjoyed spending time together, and I want to do it again. Soon.'

Although she felt reassured, Ayesha pulled a vague expression and shrugged her shoulders as she reached up to adjust the knot of his tie. 'I'll *try* to fit you in somewhere, but you know how busy we lawyers are.' The smile in her eyes gave her away.

He chuckled, 'Good to hear, but I don't know when it will be. The next few days will be very long and very busy, but I'll call you?'

Ayesha stepped away from him. 'Yes, of course. But, just a reminder of what you're missing, Douglas.'

Unfastening the towel slowly, she held it open and asked, 'And you really must go, right this minute?'

Amused at her provocativeness, Stirling's eyes roamed across Ayesha's body, lingering over her firm breasts and dark nipples, the soft curve of her belly and down to the soft, jet-black hair. Feeling his body responding, Stirling was tempted to caress her. With a regretful shake of his head, he pulled the towel closed and kissed her.

'Miss Patel, you're a shameless siren. I'm truly tempted but, duty calls. Go back to bed and then help yourself to food. Stay all day if you wish to and I'll call you later.'

*

Standing at the bedroom window, Ayesha watched Stirling pull out of the driveway and with a spurt of stones from the rear wheels he was gone, quickly obscured by the curve of the lane leading to the main road a mile away. She turned away and returned to bed, lying on his pillow so that she could smell him and reflected on the weekend.

Waking two hours later, Ayesha was surprised she had slept so long and lay still, hoping to hear him moving about downstairs. But all she could hear was silence, interrupted by an occasional creaking as the house stretched off its old bones under a warming sun. Looking around the bedroom, without him there, she felt a stranger again.

After showering and dressing she went to the kitchen and looked through the fridge and cupboards, surprised to find them all well stocked. Was he always so well organised, or had he stocked up in readiness for her visit? He couldn't have known she would stay for the weekend, could he?

Sitting at the oak table eating yoghurt and toast, looking at the sunshine outside, Ayesha regretted they had not been able to use the day as planned and wondered what to do. Having told her friends she would be with family, and her family she was with friends, she wasn't expected anywhere. If it was not a murder he might come back, but knew it was unlikely. After tidying away and free to examine it more closely, she drifted around the house.

Stirling had told her the cottage was a hovel when he bought it and he'd done much of the restoration work himself, over several years. Many of the original beams had been revealed to keep the character of the original building before adding the kitchen-diner. His furnishings were simple with nothing adorning the walls. Ayesha thought about buying him a picture. Something from the café, perhaps, and tried to remember if he had ever expressed a liking for any of the pieces. Returning upstairs, Ayesha looked into the bedroom next to his. Smaller, and with an unfinished look, it had a double bed made up ready to sleep in, a wall cupboard and a chest of drawers. Looking down the landing corridor she saw a door at the end which she had not previously noticed, set back where the corridor was stepped. Turning the handle and expecting the door to open, she bumped her nose on it as it stayed resolutely shut. She was surprised to see the door had a keyhole.

Ayesha stared at the door and wondered what could lie behind it to justify a key. Why lock a bedroom? Was it a study? But during the weekend she had seen him checking emails at a small desk tucked under the stairs in a corner of the lounge. Even though alone in the house, Ayesha looked guiltily back down the corridor before squatting to look through the key hole. The room was dark. Reaching up, and conscious she was prying, she felt around the frame for a key but found nothing.

Perturbed, Ayesha returned to the main bedroom to sit on the bed and reappraised his room. Occupied with their lovemaking, she had not really studied the room and, for the first time, realised there was nothing personal. No photographs. She considered looking through the cupboards and drawers, but it would be a betrayal of Stirling's trust in leaving her alone. Going downstairs, Ayesha wandered through each room with a fresh eye and saw nothing to suggest that Stirling had anyone else in his life, nor that there ever had been. Not one photograph, anywhere.

Making herself coffee, Ayesha took it through to the lounge and settled into the comfortable old sofa, sipping thoughtfully as she reviewed the last few days and weeks. Listening again to the rheumatic timbers stretching off, she wondered what had brought Stirling back from London and to here, to this remote cottage, unsure if he had told her. She knew she had asked.

Detecting the faint scent of his aftershave when she moved amongst the cushions, Ayesha imagined herself herc in the evenings with him. She liked its remoteness and knew she was already very fond of him, but knowing nothing of his past troubled her.

*

0946 a.m.
Using back roads and lanes, it took Stirling about twenty minutes to reach the scene. A police car ramped up on the grass verge of the busy Worcester to Evesham road indicated the entrance to the scene. Other plain vehicles parked nearby suggested he was amongst the last to arrive. Parking where he could, Stirling got out and was almost mown down by a passing truck, its driver indifferent to the line of vehicles. Feeling the draught sucking at his clothes, he moved sharply to the boot and took out what he would need.

Pulling on a coat, Stirling walked over to a uniformed officer standing at a tape cordon stretching across the gateway to a field. Drawing closer, he could see a track leading away behind the hedgerow which screened it from the road. The officer watched his approach and raised her clipboard ready to take his details or, unsure who he was, to challenge him. Stirling pulled out a black leather warrant card holder and showed it to her.

'DCI Stirling. You were told I was on the way?'

Writing down his name and time of arrival, she shook her head. 'No, sir. I've just been told to record everyone arriving and leaving in the scene log.' Pointing down the track she said, 'It's down there.'

Looking along the track, Stirling saw it ran parallel to the hedgerow for a hundred yards before veering left downhill and out of sight towards a wooded area.

'How far?'

'Best part of a mile, sir.' Looking down at his business shoes dubiously, she added, 'It's quite muddy in places.'

He called Edwards who was already at the scene. After a brief conversation, Stirling waited for the patrol car that Edwards was sending up the track to collect him. It would reduce the number of tyre marks to be eliminated from any they might find as the scene examination extended away from the body. Watching the patrol car bouncing slowly in and out of the ruts towards him, Stirling looked around to get a sense of the scene. Inside the gateway an old wooden advertising sign had been put, or thrown, face down behind the hedge where vegetation and brambles had engulfed it. Above it, two wooden posts stuck out of the hedgerow where they had once carried the sign's message to passing travellers. He considered pulling the board out to see what was printed on the other side. Unwilling to ruin a good suit on the brambles, he decided to leave it until he felt it was relevant. Shouting to lift his voice over the noise of the traffic, Stirling called across to the young officer.

'What is this place?' he asked, gesturing down the track.

She shrugged apologetically. 'Sorry sir, I don't know. Someone mentioned a building site?'

Another truck thundered past the entrance. Remembering his own close brush, Stirling called over again. 'Get some signs out to slow that traffic down or there's going to be another death!'

The officer nodded and began speaking into her radio. Hearing the patrol car behind him, Stirling turned to see Bill Edwards grinning at him through the windscreen. Stirling waited for him to turn it round and got in.

Shaking hands, Edwards said, 'I decided to get you myself, so we can talk. It's quite a long way down the track.' Edwards patted the wheel and grinned, 'It's been a while since I've driven one of these!' He spoke again, more seriously. 'It's good to have you back, Doug. They've kept you out of it for too long.'

Stirling looked across at his colleague, grateful for a few kind words after the weeks of isolation, pleased to have someone he could trust alongside him. Tapping the dashboard, Stirling replied, 'Well, let's make sure we don't foul up or we might find ourselves driving one of these again!'

Chuckling, Edwards put the careworn vehicle into gear with a grating noise and set off down the track, easing the car in and out of the deepest ruts as Stirling gave him a summary of Pearson's call.

'What more have we got, Bill?

'The location's known locally as "The Wern" but you won't find it on any maps. It's a local name handed down through the generations and has lost its original reference. The local bobby could only say roughly where it was. Once the helicopter had given a precise fix from the road, a patrol was sent down and they confirmed the call was bona fide. They're still here.' Edwards tapped the steering wheel, 'Which is how I got this little beauty. One careful owner, neglected by hundreds!'

Looking around the car's battered interior. Used twenty-four-seven, Stirling thought it was anything but a beauty. 'The call was anonymous, wasn't it?'

'Yes. It's a long way from the main road for a courting couple to come down to and if they had, I doubt they'd have known the local name for it. I'm guessing it was a local out lamping for rabbits who found it and didn't want to be answering awkward questions about trespassing. The night shift wrote it off as a prank call.'

'But it does mean the caller was local. Why d'you think they were lamping?'

'The beat officer's heard some gossip about a vehicle crossing the land at night with headlights on and of hearing a shotgun. There are no dwellings for at least a mile in any direction for it to have been legitimate, so I've asked him to make enquiries to ID all the local poachers.'

Stirling looked around the open fields either side of the track as Edwards continued. 'When the patrol got here they found an old Jag partially burnt out, with a bloke's body in the driver's seat. He's been warmed up a bit by the fire but not as bad as some we've seen. There are multiple wounds to the body.'

Seeing Stirling's questioning look Edwards explained, 'Knife wounds, to the head and upper body so far as we can see, without moving him. I'd say he's been there for a couple of days. It was a warm weekend so between the heat and the smoke, and the flies have got to him too, he's not going to win any beauty contests. Until we move him it's a suspicious death, but I'd put a safe fiver on it being a murder investigation before the morning's out.'

The car jolted heavily into and out of a rut. Edwards apologised, 'Sorry. I wasn't paying attention.'

'That's alright Bill, I like my breakfast in my lap whenever possible,' replied Stirling drily, reminding him he had skipped it anyway. 'Have we identified the car or the occupant yet?'

Edwards chuckled. 'I've missed your sarcasm. No, the plates have been removed and unless there are some identifying documents in the car, then we'll have to find the chassis number. It's in good condition, or it was. I don't think there'll be many in the area, unless it's travelled in from some distance away. We might need to contact classic car owner clubs later.'

The interior of the car darkened for a few seconds as the car passed through a small wooded area, emerging into sunlight again on a level section of track which began to curve left, down a steady incline. Stirling was looking across a wide, natural depression in the landscape where, judging by the extensive groundworks a few hundred yards wide, lay the opening ground works of a building site.

Rising from the far side of the hollow, a sloping field rose to a dry-stone wall behind which lay a dense, wooded copse, the wall extending away from view over the hillside. Looking at the dead grasses and vegetation growing across the broken ground, Stirling estimated the site had been abandoned for at least two years, probably longer.

'What is this place?' he asked.

'We think it was intended to be some sort of up market residential development.'

Stirling thought of the sign near the entrance and made a mental note for it to be examined. Stretching away from a central, levelled area and barely visible amongst grass and weeds, white surveyor's stakes indicated the intended scale and levels of the development. He wondered how anyone could possibly have got planning permission for such an extensive development on a greenfield site. A change of noise under the tyres brought his eyes back to the scene in front of him as Edwards stopped at the edge of a wide parking area covered in grey compacted stone. At its edges, the earth had been churned into harsh ridges and channels under the tracks of heavy machinery.

At the far side of the parking area facing towards them sat the Jaguar saloon, its former elegance disfigured by fire and smoke. From a distance, Stirling thought it to be an early 1960s model, possibly older. A white SOCO forensic examiners' transit van was parked nearby, a fluttering tape leading from it to the Jaguar defined the approach path at the end of which stood two SOCOs. Dressed in white disposable examination suits with hoods and masks, from this distance it was near impossible for Stirling to determine their sex as one crouched to take photographs and the other pointed instructions. Below the line of the tape, aluminium stepping plates provided an elevated walkway to prevent evidence being trampled into the ground.

Stirling nodded as he checked off the scene. 'Anything else, Bill?

'Nope. We've got a car and a body, with no identification for either at present. We might get his ID when we move the body and can have a look round inside. Wallet, that sort of thing and once we can examine the car, we should be able to get its chassis number. It pre-dates VIN numbers. An initial search of mispers reveals no one fitting the description of the car, or him.'

Seeing Stirling's enquiring look, Edwards added, 'No missing persons reports for a white middle-aged male. In my view but see what you think when you get over there.'

Waiting at the rear of the forensics van for the SOCOs to join them, Stirling asked, 'Has the Coroner been informed? And who's the on-call pathologist?'

'The Coroner's Officer will let me know when the Coroner's been informed. I expect he'll leave it to us to decide when to move the body rather than come out here on a fine, sunny Bank Holiday morning.' They exchanged a look of understanding. 'When the pathologist calls back I'll put him on to you, but I expect he'll be happy to work off the scene photos.'

Stirling nodded agreement as he looked around to understand the scene. Edwards's experience was invaluable, anticipating whatever Stirling needed to hear. One of the SOCO officers had crossed the plates to meet them and after introductions, began to brief them on what they had discovered so far. With his mask pulled down, Stirling recognised him as a senior team leader from the north of the county.

'We've filmed the scene as it was discovered, and the helicopter observer took some aerial shots of the scene and its location relevant to the main road. I'll chase those up later. We've taken general photos, external and internal without disturbing the body.' The driver's door was pushed shut but not fully fastened. The fire appears to have been set at the rear, in the fuel tank, and burnt itself out fortunately. The interior didn't catch fire properly. Consequently, the body's suffered some heat damage but nothing too severe. But, there's a lot of smoke contamination inside which will limit what we can recover, forensically.'

Edwards interrupted. 'The first officer on scene says he didn't touch the door as it was plain the occupant was dead.' Lowering his voice, he added, 'And probably didn't want to, either.'

The SOCO continued, 'I suspect there was only a small amount of fuel which burnt off quickly before it could heat the car sufficiently to burn out completely. Apart from a small quarter light open slightly on the driver's door, the windows are all shut so there was limited oxygen. But the driver certainly didn't die of smoke inhalation!'

The SOCO smiled with satisfaction at his own joke. Stirling didn't mind the gallows humour. It was a necessary part of the job, of compartmentalising the terrible scenes they witnessed, sometimes daily. Especially the SOCOs who attended murders, road deaths, accidental deaths and the many creative forms of suicide people contrived to remove themselves from life.

Stirling smiled thinly, waiting for more information. The SOCO moved to stand alongside him and scrolled through the images on the review screen of his camera until he found the sequence showing the body.

'There are multiple puncture wounds to the head and body, all consistent with knife wounds.'

'Is the knife inside?'

'Not that we can see, but we haven't moved the body yet, so it might be.'

Looking across at the car, Stirling said he wanted to take a closer look. After pulling new coveralls out of the van for them to put on, the SOCO returned to join his colleague. As they struggled into the shapeless white suits, Edwards's phone rang.

Resuming combat with the coverall, Edwards confirmed it had been the Coroner's Officer. 'The Coroner's been informed, and he doesn't need to visit the scene. He's given permission for the body to be removed when you're satisfied we've finished here.'

Perched on the van door ledge, Stirling nodded as he pulled on plastic over-shoes and vinyl gloves. Standing up, he pulled up the tissue mask and tugged the hood forward over his head until only his eyes were visible, waiting for Edwards to finish.

Standing up, Edwards said from behind his mask, 'I find you strangely attractive in these suits, Doug.'

Telling him bluntly what he could do with his suit, Stirling set off over the plates towards the wrecked car, pausing occasionally to study the heavily compacted stone beneath. He knew there was little chance of recovering anything of forensic value, other than dropped or discarded items which a finger-tip search should find later. Turning his attention to the old saloon he estimated it to be an early "S Type". Stirling had a passing appreciation for classic cars, for their elegance and their history, but he wasn't an anorak about them. His own project was under covers in his garage.

Walking around the car, Stirling confirmed for himself how the fire had been set at the rear. The fuel cap was still open from where the fire had travelled forward to peter out near the front doors, leaving the front wings and bonnet discoloured but intact. Sitting on its rear wheel rims, the car's roofline sloped down at a rakish angle the designers had never intended. Standing at the front of the car, Stirling studied the chrome work of the radiator grill and headlights, all in good condition. Mounted on the bonnet, the iconic Jaguar mascot was frozen mid-leap, snarling as it fled the flames behind it. Where the paintwork was undamaged it was a deep, polished red.

Looking across the bonnet through the smoke darkened windscreen, Stirling could see little of the inside other than the vague outline of a figure slumped low behind the steering wheel. Catching an unpleasant odour on the breeze, he wondered how grim the body would be, prompting memories of some he had seen; carbonised into macabre, tortured postures of their last agony. Edwards was crouched at the driver's door studying the body and the interior. Walking down the nearside to the rear, Stirling put the back of his hand on the wheel rim and the tyre's charred remains, expecting to find some residual warmth if it had burnt out recently. They were cold. Taking another long look around the scene and up the access track, he was struck by its remoteness.

Seeing Stirling's sweep of the scene, Edwards said, 'It could have burnt for a long time down here without attracting anyone's attention.'

Stirling moved round to join him, and Edwards stepped back to let him look inside, murmuring, 'Not as bad as some we've seen.'

Edwards pointed at the smoke darkened glass. 'The quarter light's open which is how the flies found him once the fire extinguished itself.'

The SOCO spoke, 'We'll take specimens of the eggs and larva, maggots to you and me, for entomological analysis, sir. Judging by the development of some of the maggots, I think he's been here for a couple of days, at least.' He spoke matter of factly, devoid of emotion, this body just another interesting specimen on his schedule.

From behind the mask of the other SOCO, Stirling heard a younger voice ask, 'It's about twenty-four hours from the egg being laid to the maggots hatching, isn't it?'

Aware of the process themselves, but allowing him to tutor his young colleague, Edwards and Stirling continued to study the interior of the car and its foul-smelling occupant, giving half an ear to the SOCO supervisor as he provided his colleague with a comprehensive explanation.

'Yes, about twenty-four hours, depending on atmospheric conditions. The weekend's sunshine has kept him nice and cosy so it's a perfect breeding ground. When the maggots themselves mass, they generate their own heat so it's a self-perpetuating cycle as the body breaks down. Blow flies, the ones with that shiny, metallic look to them? They'll find a corpse within minutes of death and oviposit, lay eggs, in clusters of hundreds around any available orifices, nostrils, ears, mouth and open wounds, and we've plenty of wounds here. Other fly species follow on and do the same but have differing stages of development, all of which are scientifically documented so we'll analyse what's eating him, sorry, no pun intended, what's recovered from the body, freeze them and compare their relative growth rates to give us a reasonably precise timeline of death and decay.'

Stirling added, more to himself than to anyone, 'The body has begun to bloat which we could expect after a couple of days as it decomposes, and gases build inside. The warm interior has accelerated that, somewhat. It's going to be very unpleasant when we move him.'

'It smells bad enough in there already,' said Edwards. 'Hope everyone had their breakfast a while ago!'

Stirling stood back to take in small detail to understand what had happened, and how. Photographs were important, but they could never convey the stink of death. The body was bent forward and down to the right of the steering wheel, tight up against where the door had been shut, his left arm still raised to shield his head. Stirling could see several knife wounds to the head with dirty blood crusted around them. Some were open slashes where the blade had glanced across the skull, slicing open the thin scalp. Others were puncture wounds that might have penetrated the skull.

Edwards broke into his thoughts. 'Looks as though he was struck from different angles.'

Leaning in to study the wounds, Stirling caught a full dose of the stench rising from the fluids leaching from the body, faeces strong amongst it. Flies rose from the wounds and buzzed around Stirling's head, some quick and busy, landing momentarily before rising to fuss about another site and deposit another consignment of eggs. Others, fat and slow, blundered around the interior, bumping off the windows. In and around many of the wounds sat clusters of white, lice like eggs and feeding maggots.

Stepping back to draw in some fresh air, Stirling turned to Edwards. 'Seems like a frenzied attack. I can count a dozen or more injuries, and that's before we move him.'

'I'm not sure if the attacker was in the front or if they struck from the rear?' said Edwards, peering behind the body to see if there was anything there to justify his speculation.

'Let's have a look at him from the other side.'

The SOCO led the way to the passenger door and with a gloved hand pulled it open. 'We've taken photos from this side sir, and videoed it.'

Crouching down, they both studied the body from the new angle. Thinking aloud, Stirling said, 'He's hunched over to escape his attacker, to protect himself from the knife.'

Edwards grunted agreement at his side. 'The seat belt stopped him escaping. They weren't fitted when these were being made, though, were they?'

'No,' replied Stirling. 'Retro fitted for safety, probably. There are more wounds to his left arm ... to his thigh ...' he paused to look more carefully, '... looks like there might be wounds to the face too.'

Stirling settled on his haunches, elbows resting on his knees as he looked around the interior. The glove box was open. Any papers which might have given information of ownership had gone.

Looking up to the windscreen he saw the round road tax disk holder was empty and pointed it out to Edwards.

'No tax disc and no papers in the glove box. Someone was determined to delay his identification.'

From the far side, speaking across the body, the younger SOCO interrupted Stirling. 'Tax discs aren't displayed any longer, sir. It's all done online now.' He was trying to be helpful.

'Yes,' answered Stirling patiently, and pointed to the bottom corner of the windscreen. 'But owners of cars like this enjoy all the memorabilia that goes with them. The disc holder is empty now, but I bet the last disc issued to the car was in there, with the registration number printed on it.'

The young SOCO's eyes shifted awkwardly under the stare of his colleague behind Stirling's shoulder and moved off to do something.

'So, what d'you think?' asked Edwards.

'First impressions? I'd say the attacker was here ...' he pointed at the passenger seat, '... and attacked him across the central space. It's a bit tight but there's enough space if you were determined. Perhaps the first blow, or blows, disabled him and he couldn't protect himself from what followed. I've counted at least twenty wounds. There are cuts to the back of the seat too, they missed him a couple of times. They were certainly determined.'

'Or frightened, perhaps?' suggested Edwards, thoughtfully. 'It's a long way from anywhere down here. Perhaps the attacker didn't like what our chap here had in mind.'

'Yes, or frightened enough,' agreed Stirling.

From behind Stirling, the SOCO supervisor spoke. 'The interior's badly contaminated with smoke so the chance of getting the attacker's DNA is remote, sir. We might be able to determine blood spray from the wounds, across the headlining and dashboard as the knife swept back between each strike. If so, it'll help to understand how the weapon was used. We'll recover the car to the examination bay at HQ forensic services, but it'll need a full trailer lift and sheeting over for transfer.'

Looking up to the blackened headlining and the other smoke and dust encrusted surfaces, Stirling was doubtful. 'Authorised. As soon as you get him out, check his pockets for personal effects. Mobile, wallet, the usual. I need an ID quickly.' Crouching down again, he added, 'The keys are missing from the ignition. Look for them when you search the car.'

The SOCO went to join his young colleague on the far side of the car. Stirling spoke over the roof to them, 'Are you able to pull him back so I can see his face?'

With difficulty, the two SOCOs pulled the body back to a sitting position, its head lolling forward and sideways, exposing the face.

'Jesus!' exclaimed Edwards over Stirling's shoulder.

Unable to see what had caused Edwards's outburst, the young SOCO moved to get a better view. Confronted with the ruined face, he turned away and stooped to retch as his older colleague studied the face with a detached, professional interest.

From the ravaged eyes and other wounds, a putrid fluid trickled down the bloated, blood encrusted face. Stirling studied the concentration of cuts and puncture wounds, some of which had clearly penetrated both eyes. What the knife had not destroyed, the maggots were rapidly completing.

Both eye sockets were a seething mass of movement.

Stirling, Edwards and the senior SOCO stepped a few feet away to agree actions as the young man stood slightly to one side, looking queasy. Leaving them to their work, Stirling and Edwards walked back to the van where they removed their masks and hoods. Turning to face the wind, Stirling pulled in deep breaths of fresh air, but the smell of putrefying flesh lingered, woven in with the acrid smell of charred materials drifting on the breeze. What a way to die, he thought. Unable to protect yourself as the knife rained down until, hopefully, unconsciousness had overtaken him. But what had he done to suffer such a violent death? Or was he just unlucky in his choice of date?

'It'll be interesting to find out if he was alive when the fire took hold, or if he was already dead,' Stirling mused aloud. The post mortem would reveal whether there was smoke deep in the lungs or not.

Edwards gave no reply as they watched the SOCOs lifting the body out onto a plastic sheet to complete photography and to search his pockets, finding nothing more than some loose change. There were no personal items inside the car. Stirling agreed for the body to be removed and a radio call brought the undertaker's van down the track.

'Strange he had nothing in his pockets,' said Stirling, as he watched the black van bump its way down the track towards them.

'He's only wearing a sweater, so there were only his trouser pockets to carry anything in.' Edwards replied.

'But how many men go out without their wallet?' replied Stirling.

'I've met quite a few of them at the bar!' Edwards answered drily, 'But it's a fair point. The way he's parked, he would have seen anyone approaching.'

'Was his attacker already here, waiting for him, or did he bring him here? Or her. We need to know a lot more about him and about this place too. Is it a lover's spot, perhaps?'

'Or doggers, sir?' said a young man's voice behind them.

The voice caused both men to look round sharply to see the younger SOCO had returned to the van without being heard. With his mask down Stirling could see a fresh faced young man with ginger hair, freckled cheeks and a wispy goatee beard, a failed attempt at gravitas.

Surprised by the interruption, Stirling asked reflexively, 'Pardon?'

'Dogging, sir. You know, people who like having sex while others watch them. Or like to watch other people having …'

Cutting across him impatiently, he demanded, 'I know what dogging is!' What's your point?'

'Sorry.' The SOCO looked uneasy, wondering for the second time if he should have kept his opinions to himself. 'I've heard some patrol officers talk about it being a problem. They get sent to dogging spots if someone's complained?'

Recognising he was trying to be helpful, Stirling appeared to consider the information. 'Okay, thanks. I'll scope it into our investigation.' Looking across to the car he added, 'Are you all done over there?'

'Nearly. Once the body's gone we'll prepare the vehicle for transfer to HQ.'

After the young man had left them, Edwards smiled. 'Eager young man.' Pointing around the open space, he continued, 'You'd have to be a bloody determined voyeur to come all the way down here to do a spot of dogging, or to find it even! As remote as it is, I think it would be in our systems if there was a problem here with cars coming and going regularly.'

Stirling shook his head in shared amusement. As the undertakers lifted the black plastic body bag into the van, Edwards called to a uniform officer stood by the patrol car who had been watching everything from a safe distance.

'Ever done a body transfer for evidential continuity?'

The officer shook his head. 'No sir.' With only three years' service the only bodies he had seen were sudden deaths in the community. Nothing as interesting as this.

Edwards explained, 'That body is a crime scene. An exhibit, if you like. We want you to follow the undertakers to Worcester mortuary where you will *personally* oversee its transfer to the staff there. It's to remain in the body bag, untouched, except for being correctly labelled by the mortuary staff. Only when it's been secured in a fridge are you released, when you'll provide our investigation with a witness statement detailing that process, is that clear?'

Pleased to be involved in the evidence, the officer replied firmly, 'It'll be done exactly as you say, sir.' He left to speak with the undertakers.

'Not his fault, if he's not done it before, I suppose,' said Edwards.

'No. But we could do with a patrol Sergeant down here.'

'Fat chance! Skeleton shifts on bank holidays, they can't afford the double time,' murmured Edwards as he pulled out his phone. 'Speaking of which, how d'you want to gear up for this? I think we can safely say it's a murder? If not, it's the most determined suicide I've ever seen! The MCU budget is smashed after the last few months.'

The MCU had taken a hammering with several murders and unexplained death investigations. Mindful that Tanner would check everything, Stirling thought about his options. It was a murder, without doubt, and the first few days would be critical in securing evidence.

Ignoring the irreverent humour, Stirling replied. 'It's a murder. Open a new HOLMES account Bill and call in enough of the team to get the incident room up and running and to establish a couple of outside enquiry teams for today. We'll scale up once we know what we've got after the post mortem and, hopefully, an identification. Once we identify our victim, a suspect might be all too obvious and it'll be detected quickly.'

Watching the van depart with the patrol car trailing behind, Stirling listened as Edwards began making his calls. He was a fixer and would get most of what was needed. The rest he would have to fight for himself. Stirling called Pearson, briefed him and got his agreement to an opening budget. Little would get going without budget approval, the bane of an SIO's life.

When Edwards had finished, Stirling pointed around them. 'This is a strange place to meet someone, Bill, even if they travelled together. You'd need to know it was here. It's completely hidden from the main road.'

'It might have been a courting couple. If it was, it didn't turn out very romantically,' adding coldly, 'That was one hell of a lovers' tiff! There are plenty of lanes and lay-bys around here anyway without risking the axles of an old crate like that.' Edwards turned away to take a call.

And why bring a knife to a date, Stirling thought to himself. Unless you're on the game and need to protect yourself?

Holding the mobile to his chest, Edwards pointed up the track. 'The dog team and Task Force search team are ready. Okay to call them down?'

Stirling nodded his agreement and turned to the SOCO supervisor who was walking across to them, his hood pulled back to reveal thinning sandy hair which the wind was blowing about. Behind him, the young SOCO was loading their equipment into the van.

With a backwards jerk of his thumb and a smile, he began with an apology. 'Don't mind him boss, he's new. Incredibly keen but still learning. We're pretty much done over there. No personal items found so far, but I'll confirm it later once we've gone through it at HQ. Everything that might assist his identification has been taken. Not usually the actions of an unpremeditated attack.'

He looked at Stirling for agreement who was staring at the car, deep in thought. The SOCO had something on his mind and persisted, describing to Stirling reports of a drug gang from Birmingham muscling in on local dealers with heavy beatings carried out to establish credibility. Knives had been used causing serious wounds but, as usual, no complaints had been made to the police. Stirling assured him all angles would be considered and thanked him for the thoroughness of his examination.

Watching him walk away to re-join his young colleague, Edwards who had overheard the conversation pursed his lips. 'The attack looks frenzied, but the clearing up after seems calmly done.

As remote as it is, they couldn't rely on not being seen. It's wide open down here. As for a drugs turf war, I don't buy it. A middle aged white bloke poncing round in a car like that dealing drugs would stick out like a sore thumb in our intelligence.'

Unless he was well up the feeding chain and got caught out, reflected Stirling. 'Night or day, I wonder, Bill?' he asked aloud. 'We must find our anonymous caller.'

Grabbing a lift with the SOCO crew up to the main road, Stirling left Edwards to agree search objectives with the Task Force who would carry out the finger-tip search of the scene and the track. After that, they would sector the area and slowly walk the ground for several hundred yards in all directions.

Stirling looked at his watch. The day was slipping by quickly.

12.35 p.m.

After many greetings of "Welcome back boss" and some handshakes, Stirling was not surprised with the speed at which his team had turned out on a bank holiday to get the incident room established and ready to go. Already, they were processing the incident log, extracting key information and identifying lines of enquiry for inputting into the national HOLMES database. Maps of the scene and aerial shots from the helicopter were being put up on the briefing boards as Stirling walked in. Watching what was going on, he saw again the benefit of selecting good people with many years' collective experience, everyone confident to get on with their part of the process, knowing they were trusted to do it well.

Listening with half an ear to the buzz and banter around him, Stirling was starting to enjoy himself as the team agreed how they would share the various roles of "Receiver", "Statement Reader", "Action Allocator", "Indexer" and other roles needed to feed the voracious appetite of the beast named HOLMES, happily "double hatting" roles until a fuller team could be assembled the following day. Keeping the outside enquiry teams busy depended on the incident room converting information and evidence into the next iteration of enquiries and actions, and not getting bogged down in process. It was a delicate balance and always hard work.

Stirling sat in a corner catching up with the incident log to be sure he was up to speed with all information gathered so far whilst discreetly monitoring the room. A bank holiday could mean a slow news day, nationally, so the national media might take an interest in an unusual murder. The regional media certainly would, and that assumed the victim did not have a high public profile.

Stirling became aware of someone standing near to him. Looking up he saw Geordie Heal waiting for him to finish reading. Heal was clearly enjoying the buzz of a new investigation getting underway. Stirling hoped the prospect of double time had appeased the formidable Mrs Heal, Geordie's long-suffering wife, at the loss of yet another family day. Stirling had once seen Mrs Heal lose her temper at a team "do" leaving him glad it was Geordie married to her, and not himself.

'Nearly ready for a briefing, boss. I've told everyone to be ready for one o' clock.'

'Thanks Geordie. See if Bill's on his way. If not, we'll start without him.' He returned to the screen, making notes in his day book as he picked out useful information.

1.00 p.m.

Sat at desks or perched on furniture around the room, every member of the team listened closely, making notes as Stirling summarised the circumstances of the body's discovery and what had been done so far.

'For the moment, our priority is to identify the victim. Where he lived, his lifestyle, friends and associates and recent movements. We need to know more about the scene, too. It's very remote, so why was he there?'

Stirling rattled out instructions for strategy documents for each of the initial key lines of enquiry he had identified to Heal on his return. 'Geordie, I'll want to review the draft strategies ASAP.'

Heal was writing furiously to keep up with Stirling's instructions. Stirling would be surprised if the draft strategies were not already half complete, drawn from a bank of templates on the force system. Seeing Edwards slip discreetly into the back of the room, Stirling gave him the nod to update on the scene. Edwards explained the search objectives and parameters but that they should not expect anything for some time because of the amount of ground to be covered. Setting a time for an end of day debrief, Stirling dismissed everyone to their work and waited for Edwards to join him where he was perched on the edge of a desk, checking through the sheaf of draft strategy documents Heal had handed to him. Heal always delivered.

'Fancy a brew?' Edwards suggested.

Holding up the papers, Stirling was about to decline when his stomach reminded him he had not eaten or drunk anything. Skimming through the drafts, he followed Edwards along the corridor towards the staff kitchen at the other end of the building, passing offices separated from the corridor by glass windows where investigators and specialists would usually be working on investigations, empty now because of the public holiday. Edwards set about making the coffee as Stirling went to sit at a table to continue reading until a mug brimming with scalding coffee was set beside him.

'The post mortem's fixed for this afternoon. It'll be Khan, once he's finished a job in the West Mids. D'you want me to cover it? You've enough to do here.'

Stirling would usually go to the post mortem to be sure he understood the detail, but he could rely on Edwards. 'I'll get there as soon as I can but if I'm held up, you know what we need.'

'The scene search will go into tomorrow, probably. They've sectored the area, working away from the car, but hadn't found anything when I left.' Edwards paused, to let Stirling make a note. He knew Stirling must brief elsewhere later and would be working late into the night writing up the SIO's policy book which described every important decision he had taken, and his rationale for those decisions. SIOs stood or fell by the quality and completeness of their policy book. Stirling looked up and nodded for him to continue.

'Geordie will lead the MCU team as Office Manager, as usual. I've got DS Bob Vale from Redditch division on his way here to lead the outside teams. He did a good job for us last year in that contaminated food extortion job, but it still leaves us a bit skinny on people though.'

Stirling remembered a large ruddy faced man who had been completely unflappable, whatever the pressure, and there had been plenty in that case. 'We'll scale up the outside teams once we know what needs to be done Bill. There's no house-to-house enquiries until we identify the victim and his home address. Any progress on the caller yet?'

'The local officer has an idea who it is, so we might get that soon. The media strategy is down to you and the force media team, I guess?

Stirling agreed and asked, 'Any more info on the building work at the scene?'

'Only what we know so far. It was to be an exclusive residential development a few years back but ran into money problems and the company went tits up. The local officer's no idea who was behind it or who owns the land, but we'll find that out soon enough.'

Edwards confirmed the sign near the track entrance would be examined by the search team. Finishing their coffee, Edwards returned to the MCU and Stirling went to his office. Standing at his desk for a moment, he remembered the last time he was there and pushed the memory aside. Picking up the phone, he called Angie Baines, Deputy Director of the force media team. They had worked together often, and he respected her judgement, and her irreverent, acidic humour. Baines had been a journalist herself for many years before "crossing to the dark side," as she liked to describe her career move.

'Ah, I heard you were back in town, tall, handsome stranger,' was her opening gambit. 'You just couldn't keep away from me could you darling, tell the truth.'

Baines chuckled wheezily at the other end, betraying her twenty a day habit, at the last count. Baines was a formidable drinker too, as Stirling could testify to. He would never forget the hangover he suffered after going round for round with her at a conference two years ago, but the experience had cemented a strong professional relationship.

Stirling joined in with her flirting, 'Angie, you alone carry my heart in your hands.'

Baines gave an exaggerated, whimpering sigh, 'Oh! To be desired! It's what a passionate woman needs to hear.' Shifting seamlessly to her usual brisk manner, she asked, 'Come on then, if you're calling me on a bank holiday, the shit's flying! What d'you want?'

Five minutes later, they had agreed a holding statement giving outline information of the scene without any detail of injuries, appeals for information about the car and of the scene and for the anonymous caller to make contact.

'Oh, and Angie. Keep my name out of it, can you? I need the investigation to function without a side bar of speculation about me.'

Stirling listened to Baines' chesty breathing as she considered the angles. 'I'll do my best, but if they pick up on it, I'll have to respond.'

Putting the phone down Stirling sat back and felt the resentment of recent weeks surfacing. With the media in play, the fun would start and wondered how long it would be before someone made the link between him and the bridge. There had been no significant interest from the media, so far, possibly because of the remoteness of the location. If they got a sniff of the terrible injuries, things would alter. The anonymous caller was unlikely to draw attention to himself by blabbing about his discovery.

Stirling spent the rest of the afternoon working his way through the SIO's policy book whilst he had the time. Once the investigation gathered pace, time lost now could never be recovered. He called Pearson again. Tanner would want reassurance everything was going smoothly. Early in his career Stirling had learnt the value of helping his seniors to manage their boundaries, usually someone further up the food chain.

From time to time, Heal knocked on the door to supply him with coffee, update him on some detail or to seek a decision. Heal's robust good humour was a blessing to any enquiry, keeping team spirit high when the endless, long days became a hard slog and success seemed elusive. Heal would push the team on through the fatigue of the days ahead. Edwards called to tell him the post mortem would start at 5.30 p.m.

After the call ended, Stirling sat thinking through what they knew of the victim. Nothing. The car was important as there would not be many in the area. Stirling went to stand at the incident room door where Heal spotted him immediately and looked over enquiringly.

Impatiently, Stirling demanded, 'Get on to SOCO Geordie. We need the chassis number of that car. It should have been here by now!' He knew his impatient brusqueness was unnecessary, but it wouldn't hurt for Heal and the team to feel some heat. 'Have we started contacting the classic car clubs in the region, especially for Jags? I want to be certain what model the car is so that we can release a specimen image to the media for the early evening news.'

'I'll get straight onto SOCO, boss. We're researching the car clubs but no luck so far. The clubs are run by enthusiasts with their home numbers on the websites. It's bank holiday so I guess most of them are out displaying their cars at events today.'

Heal's response was direct, unfazed by a bit of bad temper. Seeing there were no more instructions about to be barked at him,

Heal went to the nearest desk. Picking up the telephone, he began to punch in an internal number. Stirling cast an experienced eye across the room and seeing everyone was engaged in their task, turned to leave. As the door closed behind him Stirling smiled as he heard Heal speaking forthrightly to someone at HQ. Stirling had heard Heal chasing people for results before, and it wasn't always pleasant. The next time Stirling spoke with Heal was as he strode through the incident room on his way to the post mortem. Seeing him enter the room Heal held his hands open and shook his head in frustration.

'Okay, just keep at it Geordie and contact me as soon as you get anything. I'm off to the PM.'

Without waiting for a reply, he passed out through the far door and ran down the long flight of steps to the car park.

Navigating his way through heavy, homebound traffic, he remembered he had still not contacted Ayesha. He would call her later.

9.32 p.m.

Putting her pen down onto the notebook lying across her lap, Tanner exclaimed, 'Forty-seven?'

'Forty-seven,' Stirling repeated, solemnly. 'Probably more.'

'Good God!'

Tanner leant back in her seat, ran her fingers through her blonde hair and held them interlaced behind her head as she regarded Stirling steadily. It was a posture he had seen her do many times when met with some surprising detail and wanted to think about it. Tanner had travelled in from home for the late evening meeting and was dressed casually in dark jeans and a light sweater.

He and Pearson were in Tanner's spacious office, sitting in comfortable brown leather chairs around a low coffee table, next to a tall sash window that rattled occasionally in its frame. A mile away, the dark countryside was bisected by ribbons of red and white lights as the motorway carried holiday makers and day trippers home through the interminable roadworks. The only concession to functional utility in the plush office were three vending machine coffee cups sat on the table's polished surface. Against the main wall was an antique, glass-fronted book case, its shelves laden with ancient law manuals which inferred a dusty authority on the steady succession of office holders sat below. Along its lowest shelf, national reports and policing publications slewed sideways where they had been put for want of anywhere better to store them, or to be read.

In front of the bookcase sat a faux Georgian mahogany desk, its inlaid green leather top laden with papers and reports awaiting Tanner's attention the next morning. Its burnished side panel glowed warmly in the light thrown from a tall corner lamp which cast a pool of light over the three figures sat around the table. Dragging his chair through the carpet pile to sit down, Stirling had thought about the ageing, damaged furniture his teams had to make do with.

He was briefing Tanner and Pearson on the post mortem results, the images of the body still fresh in his mind. They would always be there, making space for themselves among the other brutal deaths and broken bodies he had boxed up and stowed away in the dark recesses of his memory. Khan had been his usual brisk, efficient self. Many of the wounds and cuts were superficial or not life threatening, having either struck bone or were poorly aimed. Defence wounds to the hands and arms showed the victim had tried to shield himself from the attack, with one finger almost severed. Similarly, his penis. Death had resulted from a combination of severe trauma from a wound to the brain through the left eye socket and a puncture wound to the heart, resulting in a fatal loss of blood. Khan believed the victim would have been unconscious for a while until his heart had given out. There was no smoke inhalation, so he was dead when the fire was ignited. Small mercy, thought Stirling.

The body had not been badly damaged by the fire, with some scorching limited to the back of the shoulders and the rear of the head. Once the body had been washed down they could see that, wounds aside, it was in reasonably good condition. Measuring the external dimensions of the puncture wounds and the depth of penetration, Khan believed the murder weapon to be a narrow, single edged blade of about five inches in length.

The heat from the fire and its effect on body temperature, together with having been shut inside a warm car made it difficult to be certain when death had occurred. Probably two to three days before discovery. Entomological analysis of the fly eggs and maggots would provide a corroborative assessment in due course.

Tanner sat looking at Stirling, waiting for him to continue.

'Forty-seven is what we can count. His eyes were badly damaged in the knife attack and whatever was left of them has been consumed by maggots. We can't know for certain at what point his heart was struck, so he might have suffered a great deal before passing out.'

Each sat quietly as they imagined the scene inside the car and how it might have unfolded for the victim. Tanner sat with her head turned towards the window. Glancing across the table, Stirling saw Pearson's face, impassive, expressionless, his eyes on Tanner. Pearson had seen too much to be moved by such information and could be thinking anything whilst betraying nothing. Stirling wondered if he would end up looking like Pearson if he spent another fifteen years peering into other people's lives. And their dead eyes.

Stirling cleared his throat, prompting Tanner to look back to him. 'Something that strikes me is the concentration of wounds around the victim's eyes which would have destroyed them, even without the maggots. There's a ferocity about it that's worth some further analysis. I'd like to get a psychological profile to inform our thinking of the possible motivation behind the murder. And when we get our offender, it could inform our interview strategy.'

'Agreed.' Tanner didn't use more words than were needed. 'What do we know about the victim?' she asked, leaning sideways on the arm of her chair, pen ready again to make notes. He knew she must brief the Chief in the morning, and McDonald would be back from leave in a few days.

'White male, fifties, possibly older and in reasonably good shape, for his age. The car's not been identified yet, but when we do it should lead to an initial ID. We're trying to contact car owner clubs, but the bank holiday is slowing us down. The media appeal will reveal something, hopefully.'

Tanner nodded, scribbling notes as he continued. 'No one's reported a man of that description missing, yet, so perhaps he lived alone. We think we've identified the anonymous caller and I've got two officers with him now, so we might get more info there.'

Turning to Pearson, Tanner began asking questions about budgeting and resourcing for the investigation and media communications. As they talked, Stirling's gaze drifted out through the tall window which mirrored their meeting against the darkness outside. Beyond the darkened fields, the lights on the motorway drew his mind back into the endless loop of a cold, February morning and a girl's soft hand slipping though his.

'Stirling!'

Tanner's voice sounded urgent, but he wasn't sure why. Turning his head back to her, Stirling saw them both staring at him and realised she must have spoken to him before, without him hearing. Tanner frowned with concern, her head tilted to one side as she looked at him and at his hand. Without needing to look, Stirling knew he had been grasping emptily at the girl's hand again. He had caught himself doing it many times. Pearson looked irritated, his eyes urging Stirling to give his attention to Tanner. Cursing inwardly for letting his attention drift, Stirling realised he had been asked a question but had no idea what it was.

'Sorry, Ma'am, my mind was elsewhere for a moment.' He could hear a low defiance in his voice and cursed himself for that too.

'We were asking if you have sufficient people for the investigation?' said Pearson, drawing Stirling back into the conversation.

Seizing the lifeline, he replied, 'Yes, we're fine for the moment but much depends on tomorrow as we learn more about the victim and whether that will reveal a suspect, or not. I suggest we put divisions on notice of a possible need to supply. It's easier to stand the request down, rather than to start several days into the investigation.'

He had recovered quickly but could still feel Tanner's scrutiny. A heavy silence followed which Stirling wasn't going to break, looking at each of them steadily, aware he must keep Tanner's confidence in him. She was the first to speak.

'I agree, leave that with me. If that's everything, I suggest you and I speak again in the morning Dave, after I've briefed the Chief. If anything changes, let me know.'

Tanner rose in her chair, signalling the meeting was over. As the two men reached the door Tanner called Pearson back. 'Dave, can you spare me a minute please?'

Waiting outside, Stirling knew what was bothering Tanner. She had taken a gamble in appointing him SIO and he had drifted off in his first meeting with her. McDonald, her line manager, would be back in a few days calling her judgement into question which would be career damaging. And there was the small matter of advising the Chief in the morning that her decision was sound, that Stirling was fit for duty.

Pearson emerged from the office a few minutes later and with a silent tug of his head, motioned Stirling to follow him. Once in Pearson's office, he motioned for Stirling to close the door. Both men stood looking at each other. Wondering if he was still leading the investigation, Stirling waited for the old man to speak, determined not to show weakness. It was Pearson who broke the stalemate.

'You okay?'

'Yes. Why?' as if he didn't know.

'You went missing in action back there. Tanner's exposed with McDonald and needs to be confident you're fit for duty. She's concerned. Should I be too?'

There was a stony edge to Pearson's normally softly spoken style. However much he would want to support him, Stirling knew Pearson would side-line him if necessary to be sure the investigation could succeed.

'So, what did you tell her?' Stirling demanded with barely concealed anger. The memory of the girl's face had resurfaced his frustration at Ballard's hapless investigation.

Pearson paused before replying, studying Stirling carefully as he considered the simmering anger. When he spoke, there was a sharpness Stirling had not heard in a while.

'I'm on your side and so is Steph Tanner! But we must know we can rely on you to deliver this. You're the best SIO I've got and I trust you completely. *That's* what I told her! We know how punishing the last few weeks have been but are you sure you're up to this? There's no disgrace in stepping aside Doug, but it has to be *now*, before we get further into the investigation.'

Stirling knew he must calm down. 'I'm sorry Dave. I'm grateful to you both and I won't let you down. You have my word.'

Pearson studied him intently for long seconds. Stirling understood the calculations going through the old man's mind: should he keep faith with him or ask him to step aside; who was available to replace him? Edwards was an obvious and sensible option. After what seemed an age, Pearson walked round his desk and sat down. Picking up the papers he had been reading earlier he looked up and gave Stirling a curt nod. 'Okay. Get on with it then!'

Leaving the building through the night door and breathing easier, Stirling suddenly remembered Ayesha. He should have called earlier but had been too busy and now, was too preoccupied with Tanner and Pearson's concerns to have an intimate conversation.

Driving out through the darkened HQ estate, Stirling glanced at the dashboard clock. Past eleven, too late to call. He hoped she would understand.

CB BO

Day 2: Tuesday - 8.30 a.m.

Most of the faces seated or standing around the briefing room were familiar to Stirling but some of the detectives sent by divisions were unknown to him. He could guess at the irritation their absence would be causing to hard pressed command teams around the force that morning.

Stirling nodded to a couple of people he had known for years, pleased to see them on his team. A low murmur of chatter rose and fell around the room as people caught up with colleagues they had not seen for some time, or years, most of them pleased for a break from the daily routine of territorial policing. There was also the prospect of some overtime too, which would motivate some. A loud burst of laughter identified the location of one of the MCU jokers in a far corner of the room. The usual suspects, thought Stirling, but did not mind. Morale and good humour were vital, in his view.

Heal signalled everyone was in and the chatter fell away as Stirling moved to stand at the status board which covered most of the end wall. On it were displayed scene photographs of the fire damaged car, a single image of the body inside, aerial photographs and a map of the area.

After introducing himself and Edwards for the benefit of the divisional investigators, Stirling started the briefing.

'Good morning. Bill will brief you on what we know so far but, first, I want to set the tone of this investigation. I probably don't need to, but you need to be clear of what I expect. As many of you know, I've been the focus of some media attention recently and there's an IPCC investigation still going on.'

At the rear corner of the room someone muttered in a stage whisper something which included "... that twat Ballard ..." to a low ripple of sniggers from his neighbours.

Ignoring it, Stirling continued. 'With the agreement of the Chief Constable, I've been appointed SIO by ACC Tanner. I'm determined to deliver a thorough investigation to find out why this man died and bring his killer, or killers, to justice. It'll be a team effort. The hours will be long, as always, but no one will be working harder than me or Bill. Remember to get the basics right. ABC: Assume nothing! Believe no one! Check everything! Any questions?'

Looking around the room, Stirling met the eye of each person in turn to be sure they knew his mind. At the back of the room the joker opened his mouth to make some wisecrack but seeing Stirling's steely gaze, thought better of it.

Turning to Edwards, he nodded curtly. Taking his cue, Edwards took his place at the board with a page of handwritten notes in one hand. Stirling moved to sit at the side of the room where he could follow the briefing but was free to think and listen to the contributions of the team. It wasn't how he would normally start a briefing, and it was unusual for him to reference chief officers, but he wasn't in normal territory. He needed to stamp his authority on the investigation from the start and for everyone to be on their mettle.

Glancing occasionally at his notes, Edwards summarised the scene using the maps and photographs on the board, how the body had been discovered, first attendance by officers, SOCO examination, his and Stirling's attendance, scene search, post mortem and the established cause of death. Following Stirling's policy decision, only a general description of the injuries was given to reduce the risk of leaks when speaking with victims, and onwards to the media. The photograph on the board only showed the victim slumped in the car seat. Stirling had to anticipate a suspect interview and hold back information which only the culprit could know.

Edwards explained that nothing of value had been discovered at the scene, so far, and although the search continued there was reducing expectation of finding anything more. The anonymous caller, a poacher, had been identified and interviewed. Edwards nodded to two investigators at the back of the room to summarise the interview.

DC Jaz Cooke stepped forward slightly to make himself seen. The poacher was a local man, Jim Osmand, known in the area as a rogue and something of a hard man but Cooke and his partner, Banner, felt murder was out of his league. Osmand admitted making the call, had given a credible account of his movements in the days leading up to and after the victim's death, they would corroborate the account as far as possible but Osmand was a loner, there might be gaps in his alibi.

Using a green lane across the fields known only to locals, Osmand had driven into the scene from the opposite side of the main track into the site. He was hunting rabbits which he sold for a bit of spare cash. And for the pleasure of killing them, thought Cooke. A few locals still put rabbit on the table. Osmand knew the area like the back of his hand, he'd grown up thereabouts and confirmed a dozen or so "mansions" were to be built there but the firm went bankrupt some years ago and the land had become overgrown.

There used to be an old, run down farm which was sold off years ago, with the land broken up into parcels and either sold off, or rented to local farmers. They had some names. Osmand didn't know anything about the development company. He'd discovered the car somewhere between three and four in the morning of Bank Holiday Monday.

'He drives an old Land Rover. Says he'd gone through there three nights before, Thursday night, Friday morning, when there was a full moon. He's adamant the Jag wasn't there then, and we tend to believe him.'

Cooke looked to his partner for confirmation. The bulky figure of DC Banner, chewing bovinely on a piece of gum at his side, nodded phlegmatically without changing his expression.

Cooke continued, 'Osmand says there was a low-lying mist and had to shine his headlights onto the Jag to see it properly. Thinking there might be something worth pinching from it he got out to have a look round. When he opened the door and saw the body inside, he nearly crapped himself.'

There was a wave of low laughter around the briefing room. An extrovert character who liked nothing better than being at the centre of attention, Cooke was enjoying telling the story, looking around at his audience with a grin and starting to gesticulate with his hands for emphasis.

'Anyway, he shoved the door shut and scarpered but after he'd had a think about it, he made the anonymous 999 call from a village telephone kiosk about twenty minutes later. In his haste, though, he gave the local's name for the place, "The Wern" which is not on our systems, which I've checked again.'

Cooke pointed across the room to the scene photograph on the board. 'Osmand's description of the body matches exactly how it was found by the first patrol on the scene so, we've no reason to believe anything was moved. Or removed. Not by him, anyway. We took a statement from him which is in the system. We've warned him off about talking to the press, but now that it's out, I think he'll brag about it in the local pubs. Especially if he sniffs some cash from the media.'

Edwards picked up the briefing again. Regional television and radio stations were covering the story and a picture of a similar model Jaguar of the same colour had resulted in several phone calls to the incident room hotline.

'So, who's our victim?' Edwards asked, pausing for dramatic tension. 'We've no idea!' Ignoring the rumble of sarcastic groans around the room and smiling good naturedly he continued, 'However, about an hour ago, an anonymous female called the hotline and gave the name of Michael Pemberton, an architect from Worcester, but no address.'

Edwards nodded to a man standing at the rear of the room. 'Sandy?'

A slim, fair-haired man in his thirties stepped forward with several sheets of paper in his hand and introduced himself to the room. 'Sandy Sanderson, Intel cell. There *is* an architect by that name in local directories and online searches. There's no crim' intel on him and everything online is historic from many years ago, local newspaper items and the like but all of the images are poor quality, many in black and white.' Turning back to Edwards, he concluded, 'We're still digging boss.'

'Thanks Sandy.' Looking around the room, Edwards continued, 'So, we apply the detective's maxim: find out how the victim lived, and we'll find out why he died. Today's priority is background and lifestyle. Once we have his address there'll be a search to carry out and house to house enquiries, so we should know more by end of day.'

Catching Edwards's eye, Stirling stood to speak. 'Once we have a firm ID the Economic Crime Unit, ECU, will unpack his finances. Geordie is chasing Land Registry for information about who owns the land. If he *was* an architect, perhaps he had an interest in it? Telephony, who did he speak with in the days before he died? Did he speak with his killer who met him there, or did they travel there together? And what other phones were there at the same time?'

Stirling looked around the room, pleased to see the attention in everyone's faces. 'Any questions? No? Let's get to it then!'

With everyone wandering back to their computer screens or assembling in small groups to be tasked by the team leaders, Stirling retreated to his office, closely followed by Edwards.

'Your opener was a bit heavy. Not your usual style.'

'I can't afford any foul ups on this Bill, so they might as well understand that from the start. We all set for the day?'

Edwards knew Stirling well enough to understand there was to be no further discussion of the subject. Stirling told him of the meeting with Pearson and Tanner the previous evening, omitting his own embarrassment, and asked him to arrange for a psychological profiler to be contacted via the National Crime Agency. Standing to leave, Edwards looked down at Stirling who was already pulling reports and the policy book towards him. He hesitated, wondering if he should say something. Yesterday, Stirling was relaxed, buoyant even, glad to be back to work and doing what he loved most of all. But now, he could see the anger had returned. Stirling looked up at him, questioningly. Instead of saying what he wanted to, Edwards decided to raise something he had been wrestling with overnight.

'There wasn't a lot of room inside that car for someone to swing a knife that many times and get a clean strike.'

'Yes, I was thinking about that too,' replied Stirling, happy to discuss something practical. 'Khan said the knife was single edged. The cuts to the eyes, the ones that we could see, had the cutting edge away from the passenger seat. I think the attacker swung their arm backwards from the passenger seat.' Picking up a pen from the desk, Stirling made a backward swinging movement.

'But the seat would have restricted the swing of the arm, wouldn't it? And if it was someone well built like you, for example, there wouldn't have been much room.'

Stirling thought about it. 'They were heavy blows which might suggest a male attacker.'

Edwards's gaze drifted out of the window as he visualised the scene inside the car before answering. 'A smaller person might do it more easily but there's the matter of physical strength. Could a woman have kept up an attack that long, unless they got lucky with the first strike and incapacitated him?'

Stirling studied the pen, rotating it in his hand as if as if it were something more lethal. He thought back to the post mortem and Khan's description of the wounds to the victim's upper back and the rear of his head, where the knife appeared to have been used in a downwards style.

'Possibly, Bill. The victim was hunched over towards the door. If he turned away from the attack, a natural reaction I'd have thought, the attacker could have shifted around in the passenger seat to carry on stabbing at will.'

Edwards turned back from the window where he had watched the first enquiry teams driving out of the yard. 'Poor bastard. If the first blow was the one through his eye into the brain he wouldn't have had much chance. And he'd have felt most of the attack before passing out.'

'We've seen multiple stabbings before, Bill. They happen incredibly fast if the attacker has lost self-control. Remember the case last year where it was caught on CCTV? We counted over twenty strikes in almost as many seconds!'

Edwards gave an involuntary grimace as he replayed the images in his mind. 'Yes, it was bloody awful to watch. I'll see you later.'

Ten minutes later and struggling to concentrate, Stirling threw his pen down in frustration. With Ayesha's scent on the pillow and the day's events buzzing around his brain, he had drifted in and out of a restless sleep. But, predominant amongst his thoughts was the embarrassment of drifting off in the meeting with Tanner. He was wide awake when the dawn chorus began at four but, too early to get up, had stayed in bed and fallen into a deep sleep until jolted awake by the alarm.

His brain was fogged. He needed fresh air.

10.45 a.m.

As a legitimate means of escaping the office Stirling decided he wanted to look at the scene again with a fresh eye, telling Heal he was going to check on the progress of the scene search.

Bumping down the track, Stirling opened the window and drew in deep breaths of clean spring air to clear his brain, savouring the pungent scent of hawthorn blossom. The good weather was holding and the sun was climbing into a clear blue sky. Stirling felt his mood lightening and thought of Ayesha.

Late the previous evening, in a foul mood and tired, he had sent a brief text of apology. He wondered why he was hesitating to make contact. The familiar inner voice was cautioning against involvement, again.

Ayesha deserved better than a text, but she would be working now so a call was out of the question. He knew it might be days until he saw her again. The opening days of a murder investigation consumed an SIO's life leaving barely enough time for sleep, less still a relationship. He decided to send another message.

Pulling over, Stirling tapped out a brief text and read it through before sending it. It was inadequate, but thought she would understand. Noticing the Task Force team leader standing at the centre of the clearing looking up the track towards him, impatient with the distraction to his work, Stirling pressed send.

*

10.55 a.m.

After walking her client back to the reception desk, Ayesha shook hands and flashed her professional smile before returning along the carpeted hall to her office. Her mobile had vibrated on the desk during the meeting, but she was obliged to ignore it. Leaning her back against the door, she stood for a moment looking at her phone on the desk. Taking a deep breath to control her irritation and hoping to be pleasantly surprised, Ayesha walked over and picked up her mobile. Standing with one hand on her hip, she opened the message.

With a sharp snort, Ayesha exclaimed to the empty room, 'For fuck sake Douglas! Is that the best you can do?'

Tossing the phone carelessly back onto the desk, Ayesha walked to the window. As a junior member of the firm, her office was at the back of the building with a view into a narrow alleyway used only by locals who knew of it, and usually smelt of piss on Monday mornings. Staring down onto the tops of people's heads with her arms folded tightly, she considered this second, impersonal and functional message.

Ayesha had stayed at Stirling's until late afternoon, resting, reading and generally enjoying the quiet atmosphere of his home. Deciding he was unlikely to return until late evening, and with her own work to prepare for the following morning, she had left a note on the kitchen table to say how much she had enjoyed the weekend and to call her as soon as he could. She had driven home happy and relaxed, a light tingle of excitement in her chest at the prospect of seeing Douglas again soon, and at the positive change in her life. Parking in the underground car park, she had taken the lift to her apartment on the fourth floor and set to work, confident he would call her before the evening was out.

Later, as she had watched the sun setting crimson through the willows lining the far river bank, weeping into the water below, Ayesha had wanted Stirling there to share the moment. She loved the view as it changed with the seasons, the river's colours and moods subtly different each day.

She had returned to work, checking her mobile frequently to be sure she had not missed a call or text, becoming increasingly annoyed with herself for allowing a man to distract her so much. Ayesha had considered the possibility that he wouldn't call but after such an intimate weekend, thought that unlikely. She had considered calling him but thought it inappropriate if he was busy.

And she didn't want to appear too keen, either. Stirling had said he would call her, and she had her pride.

Watching the regional news later, Ayesha had reassured herself he was simply too busy to call and felt a vicarious pride that "her man" was leading the investigation. But the late-night text was perfunctory, to say the least, leaving her feeling flat and disregarded. Crossing back to her desk Ayesha picked the phone up and re-read the message, hoping she had missed some nuanced warmth or a cleverly phrased word.

Finding nothing more than the first reading, Ayesha put it down. Disappointed, and too angry to reply, she was mindful enough not to send a hot tempered, emotional response which she would probably regret. She had been treated poorly once before, allowing it to go on for too long until ending it, determined never again to put up with inconsiderate, presumptuous behaviours. And that determination had only hardened over the years as she listened to the stories of frightened and embittered women whilst preparing divorce papers, restraining orders and court injunctions.

The phone on her desk buzzed and a button flashed. Pressing it down, a woman's cool, detached voice announced the arrival of her next client. Pushing aside her mobile Ayesha decided Douglas would have to wait.

Silence had greater volume than a few angry words. And was more deniable too.

*

12.01 p.m.

As he drove back to the MCU, Edwards had called to say there were some developments in identifying the victim. There was nothing to report from the scene and Stirling knew he could have made better use of his time, but felt better for getting out.

It was a tight squeeze for four people in Stirling's office. Edwards stood with his arm and a mug of coffee propped on top of a filing cabinet by the window and Banner and Cooke sat in the two chairs opposite Stirling. Known affectionately to colleagues as "Little and Large," both had worked on many complex investigations and their judgement was trusted, which was why they had been sent to speak with Osmand.

Mick Banner, now in his mid-forties had once been a good sportsman, but a fondness for beer coupled with a poor diet had thickened him out in recent years and he was carrying far too much weight. But Banner's stoic, unemotional style belied a shrewd thinker who could be relied on for a thoughtful assessment of a suspect, or witness. Jaz Cooke, by contrast, was slim and dapper, his hair neatly cut and brushed back from an alert, intelligent face. Younger than Banner by at least fifteen years and proud of his ethnic heritage, Cooke was a quick-witted joker with a surfeit of energy. Invariably dressed in smart suits, he contrasted sharply with Banner who habitually wore a black leather jacket that had seen better days ten years ago, which he usually paired with a loosely knotted rugby club tie on a tight-fitting shirt, the collar button permanently undone. Satisfied that Banner was an asset to the team, Stirling had given up dropping hints and his indifference to sartorial elegance meant Banner could blend into the background of places where Cooke could not.

Stirling opened the conversation. 'Okay, what have we got then?'

Banner kicked off, glancing down occasionally at the notebook in his heavy mitts resting on broad thighs. Cooke jumped in with some sharpening detail where needed which Banner was happy for him to do, each having grown accustomed to the other's style. Stirling listened intently, interrupting them as little as possible whilst jotting down a few notes for his briefing to Pearson later.

The dead man was almost certainly Michael Pemberton, an architect who lived in a large house divided into apartments in St Martin's Square, Barbourne, about half a mile west of Worcester city centre. Stirling knew the square, a mix of late regency and early Victorian period buildings set around a wide communal green. Banner and Cooke had been to the address but got no answer. Enquiries with neighbours indicated Pemberton had lived alone, which the electoral roll confirmed, and junk mail building up in the apartment's mail box in the lobby bore the same name. A uniform officer was guarding the apartment door until a SOCO team could get there and Stirling had authorised entry and search.

Neighbours confirmed Pemberton owned an old red Jaguar using it in the spring and summer only. No one knew where it was kept during the winter. The car had reappeared in the street a week or so ago. After speaking to some surveyors in an office across the square, Cooke said they'd got the impression Pemberton had once been a flashy, charismatic character amongst the local professional community but in recent years had led a quiet life, a bit of a loner even. There were some veiled comments of financial difficulties but a reluctance to say more. Banner agreed they'd been evasive but felt that would change once people were certain Pemberton was the victim. They had not found anyone who was close to him, or who could tell them anything more about Pemberton's lifestyle. Pemberton was a successful architect in his day but in recent years, so far as anyone knew, he had only done small-scale, private commissions. Some thought he was involved with a big company in London some years ago, but nothing more.

Banner and Cooke confirmed they had other lines to follow up and with Stirling's urging to get back to him as soon as they could, they left. Edwards moved across to sit in one of the empty seats.

'Are we ready to do the search and forensics at Pemberton's place Bill?'

Edwards nodded. 'Everything's ready to go. The car ignition key was found in the boot this morning and there are some house keys with it, a bit damaged but they should work. If not, we'll force the door.'

Feeling the familiar excitement of the chase returning, Stirling stood up with a smile, snatched his coat from the top of the cabinet and led the way.

'Come on Bill, let's go and find out who our victim is.'

Following behind, Edwards scrolled through his contacts to alert the officers at the scene.

1.32 p.m.

The keys recovered from the Jaguar had opened the external door to the porch and to the apartment on the first floor. Two Task Force officers were now inside doing a security search to be sure nothing untoward was waiting for them.

Suited again in forensic coveralls and mask, waiting to enter, Stirling looked up at the red brick building. In its Victorian heyday, the house would have housed a wealthy merchant or professional. Standing in a neatly maintained garden a few doors from the church which had given its name to the square, the three floors of the house had been divided into an apartment on each level. Looking back along the square Stirling thought it more a long, rounded off oblong, its wide central green enclosed by an access road serving similar, three storey buildings arranged around it like faithful parishioners under the watchful eye of the church which dominated the square.

Built in Victorian red brick with bands of white stone for simple adornment, the church sat astride the head of the square, its large round clock between twin spires measuring out life's pace for its congregation. For the moment, that congregation included a SOCO van, several police vehicles and a gathering crowd at the taped cordons thirty yards away. On the other side of the cordons, Stirling could see a couple of faces he recognised from the local media. Behind them, a large satellite van was negotiating the entrance to the square.

Nudging Edwards, he commented dryly, 'Smile, you're going to be on TV.'

As they watched, a mast began to extend from the roof and two men set about their equipment. 'Didn't take them long. Someone's called the local radio station I expect, and they've sent it up the line.'

'At least we'll be anonymous in these suits,' replied Stirling. 'Until we try and leave.'

Impatient to begin the search, Stirling returned his attention to the building. On the ground floor, two bay windows identified the original reception rooms. Above them, each floor had two tall, paned sash windows looking across the square. An ugly, functional porch structure had been added to the left side, its utilitarian purpose jarring with the grace of the house.

One of the TF officers emerged from the porch and gave Stirling a thumbs-up. Passing though the entrance porch, Stirling noted three post boxes fixed to the wall before stepping into the reception hall. Clean and carpeted, a broad staircase covered in the same carpet rose at one side of the hall, its shallow treads enclosed by an elaborate wrought iron work balustrade which carried a dark wood handrail, polished smooth through long use. A uniformed officer at the foot of the stairs logged their arrival.

The TF Sergeant described the lay out succinctly. 'Three apartments, one on each floor. The deceased's is on the first floor.'

Stirling cast a look around to confirm his advice and turned to Edwards. 'Who lives in the other two Bill?'

'Banner and Cooke say there's a woman in the ground floor apartment who's away travelling. The top floor is empty, waiting to be let. We've got the agent's details.'

Following the athletically built Sergeant upstairs, Stirling saw the other TF officer outside the open door to the apartment, the keys still in the lock with an exhibit label tied to them. As two SOCO officers shuffled past them to begin filming, laying footplates as they went, the Sergeant described the interior.

'The keys fitted perfectly and there's no sign of a disturbance. No bodies inside. Letters and other papers inside are addressed to a

Mr Michael Pemberton. There's a meal partially eaten on the kitchen table, looks like breakfast. No lights were on when we entered, and all the windows are shut. One bedroom only, the bed's been slept in, but it's not made up. The bedroom curtains are open. There's only men's stuff in the bathroom and wardrobes. Looks like he lived alone.'

'Thanks, Sarge. Organise a search of the grounds of the house please. I'm not sure what we're likely to find, if anything, but it needs to be done.'

'Leave it with me boss,' he replied briskly. With a nod to his colleague to follow him, the two men went downstairs, leaving Stirling and Edwards alone on the landing.

'House to house, Bill?'

'Geordie's pulling a team together from the enquiry teams, but we're light on numbers so the TF will help out, unless they're called away.'

The Task Force was a multi-skilled team. Highly skilled firearms officers with a surveillance capability, they were also trained in aspects of major crime investigation such as house to house enquiries with its complex cross-referencing of occupants' details to be sure no one slipped through the net. With a positive identification now likely, things would move quickly with many enquiries to be made. The next few days would be tough for everyone, but Stirling would drive the teams hard to maintain the initiative whilst things were fresh in people's recollection, uncontaminated by media reporting and gossip.

Waiting impatiently at the entrance to the apartment, Stirling looked down the hallway into the apartment and watched a SOCO stepping along the footplates laid out in irregular trails through the apartment, filming as he went, recording it as found. Ten minutes later, Stirling and Edwards pulled up their masks and entered the apartment.

He wasn't sure why, but Stirling had expected more. Perhaps because of the man's profession, the address in a sought-after area of the old city and a car which would have been expensive to maintain. But, standing inside a large, square lounge with a high ceiling, Stirling was looking at dated furnishings twenty years past their magazine debut and saw a shabby, neglected home.

Either side of the tall window hung once expensive curtains, their hems dragging unevenly across the floor, each held back by frayed cord ties. Stirling thought they had not been closed for a long time. The room had an unkempt appearance and there was a familiar odour, the one that all coppers and public servants become used to within a few months' service of going into dirty homes. The regular course of footsteps could be tracked through the carpet around a large, three-seater chesterfield settee in dark red leather and matching chair, both creased and sagging through long use.

Edwards came to stand next to Stirling and took in the room with a practised eye, commenting ironically, 'Looks like the cleaner's gone AWOL. The bedroom's a mess too, dirty bed linen and clothes on the floor. I haven't looked in the kitchen or bathroom yet.'

Stepping on the plates, they went next door into a room about the same size as the lounge with a similar window overlooking the green. Unlike the lounge, the curtains were drawn open unevenly. Against the main wall sat an Edwardian styled bed with ornate metalwork at each end. A quilt lay where it had been thrown aside from the double mattress. The bottom sheet looked as though it had been slept on for several weeks. At its centre were stain marks.

Stirling crossed the room to a double doored mahogany wardrobe, its antique, bow fronted design suggesting it might have stood there since the house was first occupied. Lifting the drop handles with gloved hands, he pulled open the doors and stepped back to study the neatly arranged clothing inside. To the left, a dozen suits hung alongside casual jackets, trousers and chinos. To the right, a dozen double-cuffed business shirts hung next to casual shirts and polo shirts, all tidily arranged on hangers. On the inside of the left door, a tie rail carried a selection of silk ties, many in striking colours but all expensive looking. Neatly paired and arranged across the floor of the wardrobe sat business and casual shoes, all good quality. Squatting down, Stirling lifted one up and turned it over, noting the stitching and leather soles. Handmade. Putting it back as he had found it, Stirling considered the shelves that formed the centre of the wardrobe, where cashmere sweaters and other expensive woollens were neatly folded. Without touching the central drawer, he knew it would contain silk handkerchiefs, cufflinks and the trimmings of a man who took pride in his appearance and had the money to buy good clothes, or had once been able to. The neatness of the clothes was in stark contrast to the state of the apartment.

Standing astride two footplates, Edwards spoke to Stirling from the other side of the bedroom, 'No photographs or anything personal that I can see, not without opening drawers, anyway.'

Without turning, Stirling pointed at the clothing. 'What impressions do you get from these Bill?' He heard Edwards stepping across the plates and then his breathing sucking at the paper mask.

'All good quality stuff. Those shoes would have cost a few quid.'

'I agree, but you're missing something.' Seeing the incomprehension in Edwards's eyes, Stirling pointed to the rails. 'There's nothing in there that's been bought in the last five or ten years, minimum. Good suits don't date quickly, but casual stuff does.'

Edwards stood looking at the clothing before shrugging his shoulders. 'I'll take your word for it. No one could ever accuse me of being a fashion victim. My wife buys my clothes whenever she and the kids think I need freshening up!'

Stirling saw the humour in his friend's eyes. Edwards was certainly mainstream when it came to his dress code with a selection of "safe" business suits bought from a famous high street store.

'I'm not sure what you're getting at though?' asked Edwards.

'We're told our man was a bit of a character, someone said flamboyant. He's not spent anything on himself for a long time, which would be unusual for a peacock who took pride in his appearance.'

'And still did, judging by the neatness of those clothes. Habits like that rarely die away. It might reflect his financial difficulties, though.' replied Edwards.

Stirling nodded in agreement and scanned the room. 'But domestically, it's all a bit shabby. And not very clean, either.' He pulled down the mask for a moment to sniff the air, making his point.

Looking about the room Edwards offered, 'There's no woman's touch around here, none that's obvious. Might be useful to see what's in those drawers,' and began moving towards a bedside table nearest to them.

Stirling put a restraining hand on his arm. 'Let the SOCOs do their stuff first, Bill. We still need to connect him to this address, forensically. We'll come back later for the evidential search, after SOCO have cleared.'

'Okay.' Edwards looked around the room. 'An architect needs to make drawings and plans. There doesn't seem to be anything for that purpose in here and there's been no mention of a business address. There must be another room here.'

The two men returned to the corridor and followed it to the rear of the building where they found a room first intended as a second bedroom. Below a window overlooking the rear garden and to houses beyond was an L shaped desk which returned along the adjacent wall below a compartmentalised shelving system that covered most of the available wall space above it. The shelves were bowed under the weight of folders, reference books and trade magazines accumulated over many years.

Moving closer, Stirling stood looking at the desk and shelves, trying to understand Pemberton's life. On the desk was a dormant computer screen and keyboard, a cordless mouse crouched at its side. Close by, a desk telephone, greasy with regular use and a mug half full of something coated in a film of scum, edged with spots of furred grey-green mould. Vertical louvre blinds directed natural light across the desk from the south facing window.

Around the desk lay the tools of Pemberton's profession; scale rulers beside a digital distance meter, fine tipped pens and sharpened pencils. Stirling thought the desk drawers would reveal more of the same but resisted a temptation to open them. Looking along the shelves, he saw nothing that seemed out of place in an office like this, but was struck by the absence of anything personal. Just a few photographs of houses and buildings fixed to the spare wall, the styles suggesting past projects and commissions. Looking at the professional publications, Stirling could not see anything issued in the last couple of years.

'There are no plan drawings on the desk,' Edwards commented.

'Everything will be inside the server,' replied Stirling, pointing to the black tower under the desk. 'It looks like a powerful one. Almost everything's done with software programmes and printed off for the client, or for submissions to planning offices. Which gives us another line of enquiry. I want every planning office in the county contacted for information of whatever he's worked on over the last couple of years. Planning officers know all the local architects and they'll know about any professional gossip in the sector too, which might lead us to his client list, if he's had one in recent years. And while we're at it, identify which planning authority covers the crime scene? I'm struggling to believe anyone could have got permission for a development like that on agricultural land. Not without bribing a bucketful of public officials, so there may have been corruption. If any permissions existed!'

Moving back to the lounge, Stirling watched the SOCOs examining surfaces for latent fingerprints to compare against the fingerprints taken at the mortuary, and so link the dead man to the apartment. From the bathroom, his toothbrush should yield DNA. Stirling reminded the SOCOs to keep a look out for anything relating to Pemberton's mobile phone provider and, if they found a mobile, to get it collected for analysis immediately. Stirling urgently needed to find out who Pemberton had spoken with in recent days.

Looking for the bathroom, Stirling wandered back down the corridor. He was not surprised to find it generally grubby with black mould staining around the bath and sink. Above a grimy sink, a white cabinet with mirrored sliding doors revealed the usual items he would associate with a man living alone; disposable razors, shaving foam, squeezed out toothpastes with an overused toothbrush and a near empty bottle of an expensive after shave. Bending down, he opened the door to the cabinet below the sink to see a collection of dusty, under-unemployed cleaning products.

About to shut the door, his eye noticed a small blue packet tucked away at the rear, almost hidden from sight. Pulling aside one of the plastic bottles to see the box more clearly, Stirling recognised a branded pack of tampons. Intrigued, he lifted the box out by its edge and turned it over to see it was half full and within date. So, Pemberton had had female company in the last year, and frequent enough that she had left sanitary products in the bathroom. If it had been a female.

Replacing the box as he had found it, Stirling closed the door and went to the kitchen next door where he found Edwards opening cupboard doors and closing them again. Pulling open the fridge he turned to Stirling. 'Doesn't look as if he was expecting anyone for a candlelit supper. The fridge and cupboards are pretty much empty.'

Stirling told Edwards about the tampons. 'Pemberton was in his late fifties, possibly older. There's no other sign of female occupancy. I'm puzzled why he'd have those in his bathroom.' Thinking aloud, he added, 'It doesn't exclude their use by a man, I suppose, depending on his tastes.'

Behind his mask, Edwards pulled a grimace of distaste. 'I'd rather not think about the detail too much. Lifestyle profiling should reveal if he was gay or bi in due course.'

Leaving the SOCOs to get on with their work, Stirling and Edwards returned to the front door where Edwards began stripping off his coveralls and over-shoes, putting them in the plastic bag put in the porch for their safe destruction. Before removing his own, Stirling peered cautiously down the square to inspect the crowd at the blue and white taped cordons.

A journalist was stood recording her piece to camera with the church behind her to give a backdrop to her report. Stirling scanned the faces of the photographers looking for one face. Unable to see him, he looked around the square studying the gardens. Seeing no one, but unable to rule out the possibility, Stirling quickly stripped off his coveralls. Tapping Edwards on the arm, they walked briskly to their car.

Driving the wrong way around the service road to avoid the media, Edwards nosed his way into sluggish afternoon traffic filing along the Barbourne, turned right and headed for the Ombersley Road and out of town.

On their way to the MCU, Angie Baines called to complain she was being pressed for more information about the house in St Martin's Square. The media had the victim's name and were using it openly. Could she formally confirm it? Without a positive identification, Stirling didn't have that luxury but agreed some caveated lines, "… enquiries continue to confirm identity ... tracing family members …" promising she would be the first person he would call when he had an ID.

'As soon as possible Doug, please?' she implored.

'What's the matter Angie, feeling the heat? What's it like being on the other end of the crap, poacher turned gamekeeper?' He was winding her up, but was sympathetic to her problem.

With good natured rudeness, Baines replied, 'Fuck off and get that ID to me as soon as you can!' She hung up.

Edwards looked across at Stirling who was smiling as he put his mobile away. 'Problem?'

'No, only Angie getting a taste of her own medicine.'

'Ah, that's always good to hear!'

Turning into the MCU yard twenty minutes later, Stirling could remember little of the journey. Looking at the dashboard clock he saw it was almost four.

Fingerprints from the apartment confirmed the body in the mortuary was indeed Pemberton. DNA and dental records would take longer. A formal visual identification of the body was necessary, if achievable, but there were problems in identifying living relatives and Stirling was dubious about presenting that ravaged face to a grieving relative.

Following media appeals for information, calls to the incident room hotline were steady, but no significant information had been given. Some past social acquaintances and business associates had made contact, but none suitable for a formal identification. The descriptions they gave of the man they knew as Michael Pemberton were consistent and there could be little doubt it was him. Stirling approved a media bulletin confirming a cautious identification.

There was no fresh information about the murder scene. Was it a random location, or did it have a direct bearing on the murder? Instinct told him it was the latter. Reports from the SOCOs at the apartment indicated no signs of a disturbance or of spilt blood. They had seized the bedding as he had instructed in case it became relevant to the motivation for Pemberton's murder. Impatient to move the investigation on at greater speed, Stirling got up and went to find Heal. He found him in the main office sat at a screen, reviewing a document.

Heal saw him approaching and recognised the look on Stirling's face. 'boss?' said Heal, with a cautious smile.

'What have we got on Pemberton's phone records?' Stirling demanded, curtly.

Stirling felt the tension in the room rise as keyboards slowed and conversation tailed off. Heal's eyes flitted about the room behind Stirling.

'We're onto it boss, as soon as I get it, you'll get it.' His response was firm, but not a challenge. Confident in his own ability and prepared to stand up for his team, Heal wanted to reassure Stirling that everything was being done as quickly as time and a limited headcount allowed.

Heal continued. 'The Economic Crime Unit need information from the apartment to start their enquiries. As soon as we can get in there for the evidence search, they'll send someone down. I spoke to SOCO an hour ago, they expect to be clear in about an hour. I've got an evidential search team standing by, ready to go in.'

Stirling knew he should not have had the conversation in the middle of the office and relaxed a little. 'Okay. What about Land Registry?'

Seeing Stirling relax slightly, the cadence and rhythm of Heal's north-east accent returned, infusing his next words with good humour. 'Ah, well there might be a problem there now, boss. It's the Easter holiday week for a lot of people, except for us poor suffering fools. You know how slow Government departments are at the best of times? Well, take away some of their staff and it only gets worse.'

Around the room there was some low laughter. 'But, never fear boss, someone I spoke to this morning was foolish enough to give me his name and I'm on his case, believe me!'

Laughing lightly, Stirling replied, 'Geordie, I feel sorry for them already.'

7.17 p.m.

The detective pointed and said, 'Seems our man liked to dominate his women.'

'Or his men,' countered Edwards.

Once the SOCOs had completed their examination, Edwards and Stirling had returned to the apartment with six detectives to carry out the evidence search. A detective was acting as Exhibits Officer, receiving and recording any seizures with a SOCO ready to photo evidence in-situ before its removal. A call from one of the detectives systematically working his way around Pemberton's study had brought Stirling and Edwards to his side.

Pointing to a grey four drawer cabinet in a corner, the detective explained, 'I found this tucked away behind that filing cabinet, boss.'

Lying open on the study floor was a small, brown leather suitcase with a stitched leather handle. Stencilled on one side in faded ink were the letters M.P. Two chrome catches, mottled with age, lay open. The case reminded Stirling of pictures of war time child evacuees and of private school boys in caps and striped blazers. Inside, lay several thin hemp cords, two pairs of metal hand cuffs, leather wrist restraints and black bands of cloth which had to be blindfolds. A brown leather riding crop was visible beneath them.

'How come SOCO didn't consider this?' asked Stirling, turning to the detective next to him.

'The case was locked so they left it for us. I've unlocked it for you,' he replied, with a satisfied look on his face.

Looking down at the broken locks, Stirling answered, 'Yes, so I see. Has anything in there been touched?' He watched the detective's eyes to gauge his response.

'No, boss. Once I saw the contents I realised there might be some DNA on the restraints and called you.'

Nodding his approval, Stirling squatted down, elbows resting on his knees to study the contents. 'It could have been there for years, but we'll need it itemised. Get SOCO to photograph it as it was found, document and photograph the contents individually and then bag it complete. We'll only do DNA sampling if it becomes relevant and there's a witness to compare against.'

'Or victim,' muttered Edwards at Stirling's side.

Edwards organised the SOCO and the detective continued his search as Stirling scanned the cluttered shelves of the study, looking for anything remarkable or out of place to the room's purpose. Seeing nothing of note, he went to the bedroom. Mindful of the discovery of the case, Stirling moved around the room, trying to imprint it on his memory. Something on a corner post of the bed frame caught his attention. Moving closer, he bent to look more closely at the many light scratches on the metal work. Similar marks were visible on each corner post.

Edwards walked in to find Stirling at the foot of the bed, arms folded and deep in thought. 'Anything of interest in here?'

Stirling pointed out the marks on the frame. 'As the suitcase suggested, our man was into bondage and restraint. Whether he was the dominant or submissive, we don't know, but if he was the dom' I wouldn't mind betting he photographed or videoed whatever happened in here.'

Straightening up from a corner post, Edwards looked around the room. 'There's an old wet film Nikon on a shelf in the study but I've not seen anything more modern. There's also a tripod in the study but he could have used that for his work.'

'Or both. We'll be seizing the computer in the study anyway. If there's anything on it, the High-Tech Crime Unit will find it for us.'

Edwards gave him a doubtful look. 'With all the national paedophile investigations, HTCU's got a backlog of several month's work. It'll take a while to get that examined.'

Impatiently, Stirling snapped, 'We're trying to identify someone with a motive for murder, Bill. Even if everything that happened in here was consensual, they're witnesses to be traced and eliminated from the investigation. Beg favours, pay overtime, but just get it done!'

Stirling stalked out of the room to the lounge, irritated by Edwards's occasional pessimism but, in truth, more annoyed at his own bad temper. It was unlike him, and especially with Bill who had been a friend and colleague for many years.

In the bedroom, Edwards bit down his own anger. Stirling was under strain, fair enough, but they had known each other too long for him to be spoken to like that.

Looking around the lounge Stirling saw nothing any more interesting than earlier. A collection of paintings and drawings covered much of one wall and there were no personal photographs on display in any of the rooms. None had been found in drawers or cupboards, so far, which he thought strange. Perhaps he kept family pictures on his computer screen saver.

Working his way around the apartment, Stirling checked on the progress of the team, making sure everything was being done thoroughly and blocking off the rat runs a sly defence lawyer might bolt down if anything was mishandled or done incompletely. Edwards gave him as wide a berth as the confines of the apartment allowed. A Financial Investigator from the ECU had arrived and was working her way through bank statements and other documents discovered in the study, spreading them across the desk in a semblance of order. The service provider details for a mobile phone account had been photographed and messaged to Heal to initiate research.

9.21 p.m.

With each man reluctant to break the mood, an uneasy tension filled the car on the drive back to the MCU, long silences broken only by stilted discussions about forensics and tasks for the next day. On arrival, Edwards went to see Heal to prepare for the morning briefing.

In his office, Stirling stared blankly at the computer screen, chiding himself for his poor temper. It was unusual for him to be so tetchy. Stirling knew he was respected for his direct but good-humoured leadership style. The professional savaging of recent weeks had gnawed away at his temperament more than he had realised. With little sleep and a difficult investigation to lead, he was allowing the tension to show. He needed to get a grip before word travelled upstream to Pearson and Tanner.

If Ballard drew his investigation to a sensible close soon, it would help, but Stirling knew he was stringing it out. Heal had heard that Ballard had given his team leave for the whole of the Easter week, effectively shutting down the enquiry which would only delay progress. Baines was keeping Stirling's name out of the media releases, but it could only be a matter of time before some hack tripped over his involvement and made the link to Ballard's investigation. Stirling could imagine the contrived headlines questioning his suitability to lead the investigation. If that happened, Tanner's position would be undermined, and her support would melt away as she would have to bow to the inevitable pressure. The morale of his team would be damaged too. Stirling knew he needed some early wins.

After calling Pearson to bring him up to date, Stirling continued to catch up on the reports and completed action sheets Heal had put on his desk and updating his policy book. A knock on the door made him look up to see Edwards in the doorway. They agreed a start time for the morning.

'Bill, I was a bit waspy earlier on. I'm sorry.' He meant it.

Edwards looked at him, saying nothing for a moment. 'Okay, but get some sleep, you look like you need it.' Edwards was about to say more but added only, 'See you in the morning then,' and left.

Not forgiven entirely then, he thought. Stirling knew he needed forgiveness elsewhere too. He had handled things poorly with Ayesha over the last couple of days. Picking up his mobile he scanned the messages. Still nothing, and who could blame her? It wasn't as if she had known him for months and understood his hours, or his temperament very well either. She had good reason to be annoyed with him. Stirling considered driving over and turning up at her home unannounced but realised it might not be a good idea. She might have company. He couldn't be certain he was the only man in her life. Imagining the possibility, Stirling felt a sharp pang of jealousy and was surprised at the strength of the emotion. What did that mean?

Walking over to close the door, he scrolled through his contacts to find Ayesha's number. Half past ten, he wondered if it was too late to call.

There was only silence when she answered.

'Ayesha? I'm sorry.' Silence. He could hear her breathing. 'Ayesha?'

'For?'

'For not calling before.'

Another long silence. 'I see.'

She wasn't going to make it easy. 'How would you feel about me coming over to explain? It's late though and if you don't want me to, I'll understand.'

'What, to explain why I've been ignored for two days and treated like some cheap pick up? And if it's just to give me the brush off, forget it. You can tell me now and piss off.'

Stirling listened to the anger in her voice as it rose in volume, venting suppressed emotion. He could hear the hurt too and felt even more guilty.

'Ayesha. I should have called, I know, but it's been … it would be easier to explain face to face.'

He listened to another long silence as Ayesha wrestled with conflicting emotions and anger. He thought of saying more but decided he should let her decide.

'Alright. But I'm upset with you Douglas. I mean *really* angry with you, especially after we had such a lovely weekend together. But if you think you can come here to give me some crappy excuses and then get your leg over, forget it!'

Imagining her eyes bright with anger as she flung the last remark down the phone at him, Stirling smothered a low laugh at the sharp rebuke and said what time he would be with her.

It was the early hours of the morning when Stirling left Ayesha's home. He could have stayed but had chosen not to.

The conversation was difficult, with both stepping gingerly around each other's pride. A frank apology had drawn the sting from Ayesha's anger. Stirling had explained how the opening days and weeks of a murder investigation unfolded and how the mass of concurrent issues to be dealt with left little time for private life. If he drove his people hard, he had to work harder still. It was the same for every SIO in the land if an investigation was to be conducted professionally.

What Ayesha could not understand was why he had failed to call, if only briefly and out of courtesy. She was right, of course. Stirling knew he was out of practice but could not be bound by any set expectations. Ayesha had listened, sceptically at first, but as she began to understand the professional demands on him, the frost had melted slowly until they could talk together calmly.

Facing each other from either end of a settee covered in black fabric, sipping at the white wine she had poured, Stirling answered Ayesha's questions, leaving out only the details he could not share with her. Dressed in loose jogging bottoms, her hair falling loosely over a T shirt with a rock band logo splashed savagely across the front, she sat with her legs tucked under her. Ayesha's questions were thoughtful and insightful, and she soon became absorbed in speculating on possible motives for the murder. After an hour, there was a natural pause in the conversation and Stirling knew he should leave soon.

Running a forefinger contemplatively round the top of her wine glass, Ayesha looked at him, speculating if this was the right moment to raise the issue. Although still bruised, they had relaxed into each other's company.

Cautiously, she asked, 'Douglas, the last few days. You and me. It's not just the investigation, though, is it?'

Watching him stiffen and his eyes narrow, Ayesha saw she had caught him off guard and hesitated, but she could not ignore the problem any longer.

'I don't understand?' He knew exactly what she wanted to talk about. And he didn't.

'It's none of my business, and you can tell me so, but … the girl who died at the bridge. I …'

Ayesha faltered, unsure whether to continue as he leant forward to put his glass on the table. She thought he was about to leave but Stirling sat waiting for her to speak again, looking at her warily. Seeing the stony, guarded look on his face, Ayesha was surprised at how quickly his mood could change. Putting her glass down, Ayesha leant forward so that she could look directly into Stirling's face.

'If you can't talk about it because the investigation's still going on, I'll understand. But it's the elephant in the room and I can't keep tip-toeing around it any longer. I think you're …' she halted, fumbling for the most appropriate word without offending his pride, '... wounded.' She needed him to understand she was concerned and not trying to pry.

Stirling said nothing. After a few moments thought, she watched him stand up and look down at her, his jaw set firmly. With the light behind him Ayesha couldn't see what his reaction was and felt a momentary unease. He really is leaving, she thought, and regretted raising the subject. Instead, Stirling walked over to the glass wall overlooking the street below and to the river beyond, staring silently into the darkness.

Ayesha went over to stand next to him, looking out towards the river together as she waited for him to speak. In the street below a drunken couple argued their unsteady way home, stopping every few yards to hurl obscenities at each other and to point accusingly, the woman wobbling unsteadily on a broken heel. Stirling watched until they were out of sight, alert in case of any violence.

Without looking at her he said, 'I don't know if I can talk about it Ayesha. Not because of the investigation but, because ...'

Stirling's words trailed away as emotion thickened his voice. Ayesha moved closer to rest her body against him. When he spoke, his voice was steadier but heavy with sadness.

'Every time I close my eyes, I see her. A thousand times, more, I've seen her falling away but looking up at me, her eyes fixed on mine, trying to tell me something. It's driven me crazy all these weeks ... not being able to understand. Which is why this investigation is such a godsend. It gives me something else to think about and consumes my time.'

Stirling shook his head ruefully, 'Which is where we started the evening! And all the while, that bloody fool Ballard bumbles along polishing his career. He's probably not looking after the girl's family, either. I offered to meet them, if they'd wanted to meet me, to explain what happened. To help them understand.'

Watching his reflection in the glass, Ayesha saw Stirling's jaw muscles working and heard the anger in his voice. Putting her arm through his, she rested her head on his shoulder.

'I'm sorry for raising it, but I don't know where you and the problem begin and end? I can feel the tension in you, all the time. And a loneliness too, I think.' Stirling didn't answer. 'I want it out in the open and if you can't talk about it, that's fine, but I won't pretend it's not there!'

Ayesha's voice was firm. Stirling looked down to see her watching his face, waiting for his reaction. Touched by her kindness, he put an arm around her shoulders and pulled her more tightly to him.

'Sorry, I didn't know how to talk about it with you. If I'm honest, I don't trust myself to talk about it either.'

'How could anyone talk about something like that easily? You'd have to be made of stone. But I'm not going to be treated as if I couldn't possibly understand. Either we're honest with each other or … well, there's no point, is there?'

'Cops do a good impression of stone, I'm afraid,' he answered, ironically. 'I can't talk about the details for the moment, but you're right. It needs to be out in the open, between us. You're the first person I've talked to about it since it happened. The most disturbing thing is that sometimes, when I think about her, I still feel her hand slipping through my fingers. It's so real I find myself grasping at it unconsciously. I wake up trying to grab her.'

Ayesha frowned with concern. 'Don't you have professional counselling for things like that, post traumatic something or other?'

Stirling turned his head away, looking awkward.

'You haven't been, have you!'

'I went to the first session but then I got busy preparing for the trial, which is how I met you. So, it's not all bad, is it?' Stirling grinned at her sheepishly.

With an exasperated comment on the stupidity of men, Ayesha led Stirling back to the settee. Sitting closer together now, they sipped at the wine as she asked him about his negotiator role. Stirling had passed swiftly over it in previous conversations because it would have inevitably led to talking about the girl's death. Ayesha was curious to know how it worked, in practice. Stirling explained the training he had gone through, the toughest of his career, that it was a voluntary role and described some of the situations he had negotiated over the years. The most frequent deployments were to talk to people threatening to harm themselves and although many were cries for help or attention seeking, some call-outs were dangerous. He had faced men armed with knives and had found himself looking down the wrong end of firearms too.

Ayesha thought of the scar on his chest but left it for another time. 'And who *was* the girl on the bridge?'

Stirling shook his head. 'I don't know. Because of the tone of the news coverage I cut myself off from it before she was identified. Since then, I've been isolated from it by Ballard's investigation and I purposely kept myself busy at home, and in preparing for the trial.'

Ayesha pointed at her laptop on a table nearby. 'I can find out for you if you'd like me too?'

Stirling shook his head firmly. 'No. I don't want to know. Not now. As difficult as it is, I'd prefer she stay's anonymous to me, until the inquest anyway. If I know more about her and her family, it'll only make things worse if I begin imagining her life as it might have been.'

They talked until Stirling noticed it was after one in the morning and said he should leave.

'So, d'you think you could stand being in a relationship with a cop whose hours are long, unpredictable and unsociable? Who will let you down occasionally and is likely to be grumpy, distracted and frequently tired?'

'You're not really selling this to me Douglas!' Something he had said triggered a thought. 'So, we're in a relationship, are we?'

Stirling smiled, 'We might be, if I don't upset you *too* often.'

Ayesha moved closer to him, 'It had better not be *too* often.' Putting a hand on his thigh and kissing him lightly she asked, 'You can stay, if you'd like to?'

Stirling knew the question was not about her own desire so much as a wish to comfort him. 'I seem to remember being told *very* firmly not to come here expecting to get my leg over!'

For answer, she moved her hand up his thigh until she covered him. 'I'm a woman. I'm allowed to change my mind.'

Taking her hand, Stirling moved it away and leant across to kiss her. 'I'm tempted, but I must get some sleep. If I stay, there'll be no chance of that.'

Ayesha held her hands up in mock innocence, 'I promise I won't touch you.'

'The problem is that you're far too desirable for me, not to want to touch you! I'm already reacting at the thought.'

Stirling immediately regretted what he had said as Ayesha glanced down instinctively and smiled. Massaging him and watching the interest light in his eyes, she drew herself closer to him.

Nuzzling the lobe of his ear gently with her lips, she murmured, 'I can't let you go out into the night with that now, can I? It's a matter of public safety, you might lose your concentration driving.'

Although it was said with humour, Stirling saw a sincere warmth in Ayesha's eyes and felt his tiredness fall away.

CB BO

Day 3: Wednesday - 8.30 a.m.

Looking around the incident room and the now familiar faces of the teams, Stirling could feel the investigation settling into its own rhythm. The officers attached from divisions were more at ease with the environment of the MCU and personalities were beginning to emerge as they asserted their humour and ability. Stirling sat to one side as Edwards briefed everyone on the previous day's results and of the priorities for the days ahead that he and Stirling had agreed earlier.

By the time he got home it had meant a short night, but Stirling felt energised, and more relaxed. Smiling at the memory, Stirling was scanning the faces around the room when he noticed a good looking, dark haired woman in her early thirties watching him with amusement from the other side of the room, her eyebrow arched in enquiry as she watched his reaction. Stirling was taken aback by her presence. He had not seen her enter the room and no one had forewarned him. Stirling returned a brief, automatic smile of acknowledgement and moved on to the remaining team members.

Edwards was winding up the briefing and looked at Stirling in case he had anything he wanted to add. Standing up, Stirling moved to the front of the room.

'We know more about Pemberton than we did this time yesterday but little of his lifestyle, who his friends were and, importantly, if he had any enemies. That's our focus so push hard, please. De-brief will be at six this evening. If you're still out on enquiries, call Geordie with the results of your day. Thanks.'

A scrape and clatter of chairs filled the room as the conversation swelled. In a corner, four detectives bantered with each other over football results as they stuffed action sheets and notes into briefcases. Stirling was encouraged by the air of purpose and good humour, proud to be leading self-motivated professionals with, collectively, a few hundred years of investigative experience.

Standing at the door, Stirling waited to catch Edwards's attention as he discussed something with the woman who had caught his eye in the briefing. As Edwards bent to write something on a document for her she looked over his shoulder to Stirling, a smile on her lips, willing him to respond. Once he had finished, Edwards joined him and they walked to the kitchen where Stirling made coffee for them both. More relaxed with each other than the previous evening, they discussed the briefing.

Reaching the end of their conversation, Stirling asked, 'I see Helen started with us this morning. How come she wasn't here yesterday?'

'She was in court. Sorry, I forgot to mention it. Problem?' Edwards knew the backstory.

'I hope not, but keep an eye on her will you, Bill? Keep her busy and as far from me as possible. She's a first-class detective but she's never forgiven me.'

'You're not the only bloke Helen's never forgiven, Doug. She's not the forgiving type. "Hell hath no fury such as a woman scorned", whoever said that.'

'Who scorned who is a moot point, but it doesn't change anything. The investigation's too important to be cluttered with any personal crap.'

Working his way through a file of witness statements half an hour later, Stirling became aware of someone standing at his open door. Detective Constable Helen Williams was smiling at him as she leant on the door frame, arms folded. The smile didn't reach her eyes.

'Hello Doug. It's been a while. You look fit and well,' she said, her soft Welsh accent laden with insinuation.

In a friendly tone, Stirling replied, 'Helen. How is life treating you in Shrewsbury division?'

'Fine, thanks. A bit quiet after the MCU, but the hours are kinder. I haven't seen you in our end of the force for a long while?'

'No' he replied lightly, 'There's been plenty happening this end of the force over the last two years.'

As a young woman, Helen had been a beauty and was still strikingly attractive, though some might now describe her as having a handsome beauty. With two broken marriages of her own behind her, and a couple of other men's too, she had a reputation for getting her man, whoever he belonged to. In a glance, Stirling took in the tailored, white blouse with a deep neckline intended to draw a man's eye to her cleavage, and black trousers that showed her hips and long legs to best effect. Helen always dressed to compliment her figure and readily caught a man's eye. Stirling thought her dark hair was shorter than before, brushed back over her ears and now cut just above the collar. But the intensity of Helen's dark brown eyes remained the same, projecting warmth or shrewd calculation, as required.

Keeping his tone neutral and without taking his hand from the open file, indicating the conversation must be brief, Stirling continued, 'I'm pleased you're with us Helen, we can put your experience to good use.'

'Are you, Doug? Pleased to see me?' she asked sardonically. 'I was looking forward to seeing *you*, when I heard I was to work here. You didn't look so pleased to see *me* back in there.' She inclined her head towards the main room.

'Caught me by surprise, that's all.' Stirling smiled and tapped the file with an apologetic shrug, 'Sorry Helen, but I must get on with this.'

Confident in herself and in no hurry to leave, Helen studied Stirling's face, searching for a hint of encouragement or warmth. Finding none, she straightened up from the door frame, her brown eyes hardening. 'Well, I'll see you later then.'

Listening to her heels clacking on the tiles of the corridor, Stirling waited for the door to close before leaning back in his chair and expelling a long breath. Things might get tricky, he thought, as he recognised the perfume now permeating his office.

Knowing how Helen's mind worked, it would have been no accident that she had chosen to wear it today.

12.03 p.m.

Geordie Heal knocked on the door clutching a note book and a sheaf of papers, waiting to be called in when Stirling had finished his phone call. Waving him forward and pointing to the empty chair opposite, Stirling held up one finger, mouthing "One minute".

'Perfect. A briefing document and photos will be emailed to you before end of day. Thank you, Professor.' Putting the phone down he looked across to Heal.

'We've got some good stuff coming in now, boss. Telephone records from Pemberton's place show he only had one account. We've secured the account data with the service provider, with the necessary legal authorities, of course. They're sending data for the last six months and we'll go back further if we think we need to. How d'you want to prioritise the data?'

'Prioritise all calls to and from his number for the last week as a first tranche, let's see who he was talking to in recent days. Then go back three months, see if the analyst can identify any patterns or spikes. As we identify his contacts and their relationship to him, we can eliminate them from the enquiry as we go.'

Heal scribbled quickly as Stirling spoke.

'What about cell site analysis of his phone's movements Geordie? Let's assume for the moment it was with him when he died.'

'It's being worked on as we speak. I'm expecting something soon.'

'Okay. What else have you got?'

'Nothing more from forensic, for the moment. They're still working on the car in that special bay they've got at HQ but it's a slow process with all the smoke and crap inside. They confirmed his phone and personal effects are not in it, nor the number plates. House to house in the square is still going on, we're trying to catch up with people who were out last night but there's nothing significant, yet. A few people knew him, vaguely, but say he kept himself to himself. Neighbours confirm he owned an old style red Jaguar which he stored somewhere and used taxis through the winter. The Jag reappeared outside the house a couple of weeks ago, when the weather improved. Some of the business people nearby know a bit more about him. The early information is that he hadn't been working in recent years. Statements have been taken.'

Seeing Stirling about to speak he jumped in, 'I know, we need to know where he kept it over the winter. We're onto the taxi companies. Hopefully, he used just one or two companies who can give us an idea of his habits.'

Stirling smiled. Geordie Heal was in the MCU for his experience and anticipation, not just a sharp wit.

Heal continued, 'Little and Large are down at the square, they'll report in if they get anything useful.'

'Finances?'

'DI Croft, ECU is on his way over to see you. They've done some preliminary work on the papers we got from his study and they've got their own avenues too. Says he has some interesting information.' Heal shrugged his shoulders, pulling a face that said he knew no more.

'Proof photos?'

Heal reached under the notebook on his lap and handed across three volumes of photos, each secured inside a blue cover bearing the photographer's details, time and date taken and evidential reference numbers.

'Three albums. One each for the scene, the PM and his apartment.'

As Heal continued to rattle out updates, Stirling began flicking through the photos, pausing to study the injuries to Pemberton's

196

face. The cold objectivity of the still images managed to make them seem worse than they had in the flesh, apart from the awful smell which he could recall as he turned the pages. Aware that Heal had stopped speaking, Stirling looked up to see him staring at the photograph of Pemberton's ruined face.

'You seen these?' asked Stirling.

'Yes, but I haven't seen anything like that before, have you? Back home, it gets vicious between the gangs, especially if some of the migrant criminals start muscling in on the action. Turf wars and human trafficking. Coming from war torn countries they add another level of violence, but nothing like that. And why the concentration around his eyes d'you think?' Heal craned his neck to see the picture better.

'It might be an isolated case of extreme psychopathic violence Geordie, or something more banal. But that's what the profiler will help us with, I hope. That was him on the phone. I've prepared a briefing paper and will need some of these photo copied, I'll let you know which ones. I can't trust this stuff to email so can you get me a motor cyclist sorted out from Force Operations please?'

'No problem boss. Here in an hour, okay?' Heal rose, preparing to leave.

Stirling nodded. 'Land registry?'

Heal sat again, looking crestfallen. 'I'm struggling at the moment, but we're pressing them.'

'If we haven't got anything by this time tomorrow let me know and I'll send it upstairs for a Chief Officer's intervention. But we should try and sort it out ourselves first, if possible.'

A polite call from an Assistant Chief Constable to a senior civil servant in London would grease the wheels of Whitehall machinery but he shouldn't play the card too soon. With nothing more to update him of, Heal left Stirling studying the photographs. He wondered again about the location, so far from anywhere.

His phone buzzed with the arrival of a text. Turning away from the dreadful images, he picked up his mobile to read the message from Ayesha. He laughed quietly and sent a short reply.

1.36 p.m.

Bill Edwards knocked the door and walked in as DI Jon Croft of the ECU was gathering up the papers spread over Stirling's desk. In his dark grey suit, rimless spectacles and neatly cut hair parted to one side, Edwards thought he looked more like an accountant than a police officer. In many respects, though, Croft's work was that of a forensic accountant. Moving closer, he looked down at the papers Croft and Stirling had been looking at, recognising them as copies of bank statements and other documents seized from Pemberton's apartment, the originals safe in their evidence bags.

Croft left and Edwards settled into a chair opposite Stirling. 'Useful?' he asked, jerking his head in the direction of Croft's departure.

'Yes, but there's a lot more we still need to know. Croft's established that Pemberton had several bank accounts. One registered to his business, Pemberton Architectural Services Ltd., with only a small amount of money to keep the account open. No annual accounts have been filed at Companies House for over two years, so the business is effectively dormant. He needs to go further back to see what sort of money was flowing through it in years past. I suspect it was a lot healthier then. There's a current account with a few hundred quid in it, but nothing obviously irregular about the transactions. One of his team is working through it to profile routine spends and anything else that will help us understand his lifestyle.'

Edwards sat back listening closely, hands folded in his lap, nodding occasionally.

'But what is interesting are share certificates, or bonds for a property development company called Fairway, seemingly based in Kuwait, but with possible ties out of the back door to businesses registered offshore in the Virgin and Cayman Islands. Croft's developing the information with the banks and with his office's contacts in the Caribbean.'

Edwards raised his nose and sniffed the air theatrically before asking, cynically, 'Is that aviation fuel I can smell? If it is, it won't be your arse or mine on the plane to the tropics, either.'

Edwards was referring to the enviable reputation the ECU had for foreign travel. Economic crime investigation was a mainstay of modern investigations and vital to tracing career criminals' financial assets, increasingly overseas. Consequently, their enquiries took them to wherever the evidence lay, often in the offshore tax havens of the Caribbean where slippery regulatory controls applied and every day, billions of dollars of dirty money from all over the world was rinsed in its clear blue waters.

Every one of the ECU's financial investigators was a highly skilled and nationally accredited professional, their skills highly sought after in the private sector. But they suffered endless piss-taking from colleagues who, whilst envying the travel and glamourous destinations, would struggle with the painstaking work of analysing complex financial instruments to build a case against organised crime groups, which used the best lawyers that fraud could buy.

'We follow the evidence Bill,' replied Stirling. He knew Edwards supported the necessity but would be thinking of his team who must carry on with the under-appreciated heavy lifting of day to day enquiries.

'Well, I hope you've got the budget from old man Pearson then.'

Edwards was not going to be moved in his cynicism, but he had a point. Stirling filed it away for his briefing to Pearson later.

'Let's see what's needed first, Bill. There's no mortgage on the apartment and we think he'd lived there for many years, since the property was divided up.'

Edwards said he had called in a favour from a colleague with oversight of the Hi-Tech Crime Unit to get Pemberton's computer examined quickly. The HTCU had copied the hard drive to secure its content, which should include any deleted files and Pemberton's browsing history and had started working through it.

As Edwards was about to leave, Stirling said, 'Fancy a beer later over the road, or closer to home if you prefer?'

Edwards recognised it as an olive branch for the previous day's bad temper. He had promised the long suffering but ever loyal Mrs E. to be home earlier that evening but had been Stirling's friend for too long to snub the offer.

'Just a quick one then, over the road. I promised Ellen I'd be home earlier this evening.'

Pointing at an in-tray full of statements and files piled at the side of the desk, Stirling replied, 'Whatever time suits you, I'm not going anywhere soon.'

6.35 p.m.

The rear snug of the Crow's Nest, a careworn pub near to the MCU and known affectionately as the "Shit and Twigs" was used for socials and celebrations, or simply respite after a tough day. It had the benefit of a discreet landlord who had barred the local idiots who would take pleasure in needling any cops that drank there, but had enough regulars to make his business viable. He kept his beer well and sold simple pub-grub at a sensible price. The MCU preferred the back room where they could talk freely without the locals eavesdropping their conversations.

Over their beers, Stirling apologised. Edwards dismissed it lightly in the way that experienced friends do, knowing the next time it could be the other way around. Neither was immune to the stresses of a murder investigation.

Edwards's biggest concern was that the incident room was becoming swamped as the enquiry teams submitted increasing numbers of statements and information reports, all of which had to be read, systematically registered onto HOLMES, inputted, cross-referenced and then reviewed before generating another round of enquiries. And so, the cycle continued, constantly generating work until HOLMES became an insatiable beast, consuming data and man hours but slowly becoming unable to keep pace with the outside world. The SIOs greatest anxiety was always that a key piece of information, or a connection that could solve the case lay hiding, overlooked or misunderstood amongst a morass of data. No wonder that, nationally, there was a shortage of experienced investigators willing to take on the responsibilities of the SIO role. There were easier routes to the senior ranks with less career risk and a far better social life.

Standing outside the pub, Stirling and Edwards shook hands amiably. A cool, freshening wind which heralding rain ruffled Edwards's thinning, sandy hair.

'Give my regards to Ellen please Bill. All's well with her and the kids?'

'They're all fine, thanks and yes, I will. She wants you to join us for supper soon. You know she's got a soft spot for you Doug. Well, I hope that's all it is!' Edwards grinned.

'Once we've got this job out of the way, I'd like that very much Bill. See you in the morning.'

They parted company and Stirling strode off, back to the MCU.

9.56 p.m.

The desk lamp threw a short pool of light over the desk as Stirling wrote up the policy book, leaving much of the office in a half gloom. Light from the corridor slanted across the floor to fall against the end of his desk. Apart from some distant, occasional conversation in the incident room next door, the building was quiet. Stretching his fingers to release a growing cramp, Stirling looked up to the clock above the door. Almost ten, he would call Ayesha before it got too late.

'Hi, how's your day gone?' she asked, her voice warm but with an undercurrent of concern. As they chatted, Stirling imagined her curled up on the black settee until a loud clatter of something metallic followed by swearing and an apology, revealed Ayesha was in the kitchen. As he waited for her to clear up whatever was now on the floor, Stirling considered driving over to see her, but the pile of reports insisted he stay. After some banter about her language, their conversation fell into a comfortable stride. Stirling sat back and put his feet on the desk, his back half turned from the doorway.

They had been talking for some time when a movement caught Stirling's eye. Turning his head, he saw the corridor light casting a still, partial shadow across the floor of his office. He hadn't heard the outer door open. Lowering his voice, he waited for the shadow to step forward, thinking it must be one of the team still working next door.

'Hold on, I think someone's waiting to talk to me,' said Stirling, turning the phone to his shoulder to prevent Ayesha hearing anything work related.

The shadow moved and Helen Williams stepped into the doorway, looking from him to the phone in his hand with a thin smile. 'Sorry, am I interrupting? Don't let me get in the way of your private life, Dougie,' she taunted.

Ending the call with a promise to speak the next day, Stirling quickly retraced their conversation as to what Helen may have overheard.

'Helen. Working late?' he said, warily, not bothering to hide his irritation at the intrusion on a private conversation. He should have shut the door.

'Oh, you know me, Dougie. I can always be relied on to get the job done. It's what you used to say of me, remember? But I'm sure you've said it to many others.'

Helen entered the room without invitation and took the seat opposite him. Putting her briefcase down at the side of the chair, she sat back and crossed her legs slowly, intending it to be a distraction, rested her hands on the arm rests and waited for Stirling to speak. Watching the deliberate, feline movement, Stirling noticed the light from the corridor had cast a vague line down the centre of Helen's face, leaving half of her in shade. Which was how he remembered her nature. Light and shade.

'It's a long drive to Shrewsbury, Helen. You ought to have left some time ago?' he offered as a neutral opener.

Helen watched him, thinking it might as well be three miles between them, rather than three feet. Deciding to be friendly she gave him a thin smile. 'I don't have so far to go. I work there, it doesn't mean I live there.'

With no interest in knowing more, Stirling waited for whatever was coming next. Somehow, he didn't think it was about the progress of her enquiries. Above the silence, he could hear a keyboard being pummelled next door and a sharp burst of laughter. He waited, determined not to get drawn into a mind game.

Looking pointedly at the mobile now on his desk, she asked, 'Anyone I know?'

Some protective instinct caused Stirling to move the phone closer to him, drawing another smile from her. 'Helen. We're here to work. Whatever we had was a long time ago. I thought that hatchet was buried.' He spoke evenly, but firmly, seeking to avoid an argument. Keep it professional, he thought to himself, recalling Helen's temper and how aggressive she could be.

'And, the answer is?' she pressed.

'The answer, Helen, is it's none of your damned business!' Pointing in the direction of the incident room next door, he added, 'And just so you don't need to ask any questions in there, they have no connection to the service, either.' He could hear anger lacing his voice.

Helen's smile broadened at having provoked him. 'Dougie, what you do is your business. I just wouldn't want to see a colleague hurt the way you hurt me.'

Stirling felt his hackles rising. 'That's a pretty lopsided view of how things really were Helen. In future, report in through your line manager and we'll keep out of each other's way. You're a good detective Helen, but I won't have any personal issues getting in the way of work. If that's a problem, drop your work off next door and return to work at Shrewsbury in the morning.' Stirling's voice was cold, angry that she could still provoke him so easily. But Helen had always been able to get under his skin.

Amused that she had goaded him into losing his temper, Helen answered, 'No, I'm happy to stay. It's a nice break from divisional work and you're right. We mustn't let past differences get in the way. I mean, it wouldn't look good if someone thought you'd side-lined me for personal reasons now, would it?'

Even with her soft, honeyed accent, it sounded poisonous. Stirling was considering his response to the implied threat when the door to the incident room opened and a burst of laughter filled the corridor. A familiar voice fired a witty crack back into the room as they took the few steps to his doorway. Looking at the papers in his hands, Heal was half way across the room before he realised Stirling was still at his desk, and a half second more when he noticed a pair of legs in the arc thrown by the desk lamp.

Looking with surprise from Stirling, to Williams, and back to Stirling, Heal knew he had stumbled into something and stood there awkwardly, unsure if he should remain or retreat. Mid-way between the door and the desk, he held out the sheaf of papers by way of an unnecessary explanation, hoping to be told what to do.

'Sorry boss. I've got more stuff for you to read in the morning. I didn't realise you were still here … or that you had company.'

Heal looked down at Williams who ignored him and continued to stare at Stirling, enjoying the unease of both men.

Glad of the diversion, Stirling forced a smile up to him. 'Thanks Geordie, DC Williams was just leaving. She's late in from enquiries.' Putting on a professional smile, Stirling turned to

Helen, 'Thanks for the update Helen, we'll see you in the morning.'

Picking up her briefcase, Helen stood and still ignoring Heal, looked coldly at Stirling. 'Thank you, Detective Chief Inspector. Bright and early!' and left.

Stirling listened until he could no longer hear her shoes on the stairs before turning to Heal. Putting the papers on top of the pile Stirling had been chipping away at, Heal asked, 'Sorry boss. Did I interrupt something?'

'No, Geordie. Helen and I worked on a murder inquiry a few years ago, we were just catching up.'

Heal looked at Stirling thoughtfully but said nothing. When he had entered the room the tension was palpable, and he was nobody's fool. Instead, he pointed at the papers. 'There's a document there you might want to have a look at.'

Reaching forward, he rifled through the papers until he found the action sheet he wanted and pulled it out, handing it to Stirling who began to skim read it as Heal talked.

'Someone with a business in the square near Pemberton's place, says he'd worked with him in the past. Says Pemberton was a charmer, back in the day, well known for stepping out with the ladies.'

Stirling smiled at the old-fashioned term.

'He's made a statement which is being typed into HOLMES now, but all the info you need is written up in the action sheet there. The statement's not the best, the officer could have got more detail down to be honest. I'll have a word with him in the morning.'

Looking at the action report, Stirling noted its reference number, the action instruction, the subject's details at the top of the page and details of the officer completing the enquiry at the bottom. It wasn't a name he recognised and would be one of the attached officers. Reading down, he saw the action had been raised from a call made to the incident room from the subject himself.

The enquiry officer's scrawled summary continued to mid-way down the reverse.

Holding it up, Stirling said, 'Well, at least he's put a fair summary down for us to work from. Okay, thanks Geordie.' Looking up at the clock Stirling added, 'Shut the room down by eleven Geordie. I need everyone fresh for tomorrow.'

'Will do boss.' Heal turned to leave and hesitated. 'Um, is there a problem with DC Williams? I've not met her until now, but I've heard some of the team talking, a few tales ...' Heal left the question hanging.

Choosing his words, Stirling replied, 'DC Williams is a first-class detective Geordie, so we should make the best use of her skills but, keep her busy and make sure she reports in through her supervisor. Not direct to me.' He paused, unable to say what he wanted to, but hoped Heal could read the sub-text. 'You get my drift?'

'I think so, consider it done.'

Walking back into the incident room Heal wasn't at all sure he understood, completely. He re-ran the scene he'd stumbled into as he tried to recall some long-forgotten gossip about Williams and Stirling. He would talk to Bill Edwards in the morning who would know how to handle it, but one thing was firm in Heal's mind. Stirling was the best SIO he'd ever worked for and he would do his best to protect him.

CRuda

Day 4: Thursday - 9.55 a.m.

Turning from Barbourne Road into St Martin's Square, Stirling drove slowly around the service road, checking off the building numbers until he found the address he was searching for. Parking nearby, he got out and looked around the square for any sign of the media. There were none. The Square had soon resumed its usual, quiet pace.

The address he was visiting was located diagonally across the square from Pemberton's apartment. Stirling considered walking over to check it but decided there was no need. It had been secured with a new lock and an alarm linked direct to the city's main police station half a mile away. There was no next of kin to begin a discussion with about its handover or disposal. Not that he would be releasing it anytime soon.

A strong sun was climbing above the church into a clear sky. Overnight showers had freshened the air and the heavy scent of an early lilac in a garden nearby switched on an eddying breeze, bringing with it memories of a childhood garden and a woman's laughter. The church clock was about to chime 10am, the time of his appointment with the surveyor.

Stirling turned and walked across a stoned forecourt with three cars squeezed into it. Two well used Mercedes estates, one with mud spattered along its flanks and the rear filled with a surveyor's site equipment. Nearby, a BMW saloon polished to reflect the owner's ego. Tucked away modestly in a corner was a small two door car suitable for city driving.

Reaching the glossy, black painted door, Stirling studied a vertical assembly of polished brass business plates, set in a descending order of apparent age and all edged with the verdigris of polish smudged onto the red brick. The cleaner took pride in their work. The plates advised the interested of a dozen or so businesses registered to the address, all relating to property and its associated professions. Birds of a feather flock together, thought Stirling, pushing open the door and stepping into a quiet reception hall similar to the one across the square. On a small table sat a telephone and a list of the businesses in the building with their extension numbers.

Stirling was still scanning the list when a heavy tread on the stairs above made him look up to see an overweight man descending. As he stepped off the bottom tread, the man grimaced at some discomfort in his leg and extended his hand to Stirling.

'David Jones. Detective Chief Inspector Stirling, is it?' he asked in a deep, mellifluous voice and a wheeze that signalled poor health.

'Thank you for making time to meet me, Mr Jones.' Stirling showed his warrant card which Jones barely glanced at.

Jones wore what Stirling would describe as middle-class "county professional". A green tie with a horse motif upon a checked shirt stretched over an ample stomach, and mustard yellow braces suspending dark green corduroy trousers on polished brown brogue shoes. In his sixties with a full head of grey hair, Jones's high colour and jowly cheeks suggested a lifestyle too indulgent for his own good.

Jones waved away Stirling's thanks. 'Always a pleasure to help our boys in blue. My office is on the first floor.' Jones held out an arm to indicate the way and led them up a staircase wide enough to allow them to talk as they climbed its shallow treads. Stirling asked how long his business had been in the building.

'Nigh on thirty years now. My business owns the building and I use the first floor. We rent the rest out to other businesses. Several more businesses are registered here for Companies Act requirements. We have an accountant in the building, you see. We couldn't possibly accommodate all the businesses on those plates down there.'

Stirling got the impression Jones had been watching him from above. 'I noticed that all of the businesses are in the property sector, broadly speaking. Your own business as a chartered surveyor, a commercial property company, a land management company and an architect too?'

Jones turned his head to appraise Stirling as they walked along a carpeted corridor. 'Very observant of you, Chief Inspector. We didn't set out with that intention, but it's fallen that way as the years have gone by. As offices became vacant, we turned to professionals we knew and trusted to deal with. It's very practical, sometimes. Much easier to walk down the corridor to speak with someone engaged in the same, or a similar project, rather than driving to God knows where. The traffic never improves, does it?'

Jones ushered Stirling into a room of similar proportions and style to Pemberton's lounge. The desk was sited close to the window allowing Jones to monitor movement around the square and to see people approaching his offices. No doubt, it was how Jones had known he was downstairs before he could use the telephone. Pretending to admire the view from the window, Stirling saw that Jones would have had a ringside seat of the previous day's activity. Listening to his laboured breathing from the effort of climbing the stairs and watching him sit heavily in a deep upholstered chair, Stirling concluded that David Jones was badly overweight and almost certainly suffering an underlying chronic medical condition.

'Please, do sit down,' said Jones wheezily, pointing to two chairs of similar design to his own arranged in front of his desk, the arms scuffed through long use. 'Someone will bring us tea in a moment, or do you prefer coffee?'

Stirling said tea would be fine and whilst Jones picked up his desk phone and murmured instructions to someone, he glanced around the office. The furniture echoed his first impression of Jones, his old school charm reflected in the antique desk, a large mantel clock ticking slowly over a redundant fireplace and other items of furniture arranged around the room. However, economic prudence had dictated the walls be papered in paper easily refreshed with a dull emulsion paint. Currently a bland magnolia.

Listening to Jones's professional manner, Stirling wasn't sure if it was a practised habit of many years in doing business, or if he was a genuinely pleasant man. As they waited for the tea to arrive, Jones told Stirling about the effect that Pemberton's "shocking death" and the "terrible commotion" had caused in the square before bringing them to business. The tea was taking longer than expected.

'So, how might I help you? I gave a statement to one of your chaps yesterday, I'm not sure how I can add anything more.' Stirling noticed the conditional "might" and ignored the patronising "one of your chaps", putting it down to a generational style.

'I would like to understand your relationship with Michael Pemberton, and as much as you can tell me about his professional dealings. His personal life too, if possible. I need to build a picture of the man and who his enemies might have been.'

At the mention of Pemberton's private life and enemies, Stirling noticed something register on Jones's face before he re-set his expression to impassive. Jones said nothing for several long seconds, staring at him thoughtfully. He was about to speak when a knock at the door announced the arrival of a woman carrying a tray.

Jones watched the woman silently set a cup and saucer on the desk in front of each man. She gave Stirling a fleeting, nervous smile when he looked up and said thank you. Stirling's practiced eye swiftly took in a small, delicately built woman, dressed plainly in a matching brown skirt and cardigan with a blouse buttoned to the neck. Her hair, pulled back tightly into a bun, had once been a rich auburn but was now streaked with grey and had lost its vigour. Stirling first thought her to be in her early fifties but, close up, realised she was quite a bit younger, the many years of artificial light and sedentary work having rendered her pale and fragile. Putting his saucer on the desk with a trembling hand, Stirling saw there was no wedding band on her finger, or rings of any type. Stirling wondered where she had been when he arrived. He had not noticed a secretary's office on the way to Jones's office.

'Thank you, Jenny,' Jones said, with an air that implied immediate dismissal. Jenny retreated from the room, closing the door so softly that Stirling barely heard it.

'So, where were we?' Jones resumed. 'Ah yes, background. Simply put, there was no business relationship. Our paths might cross from time to time if we found ourselves representing the interests of various clients in a development, but we never worked together in a shared venture.'

'You're a chartered surveyor?'

'Yes, and Pemberton is ... sorry, *was* an architect. A damned good one too, I should say. As a younger man, he was very much in demand and considered quite avant-garde. For these parts anyway, where people are generally predisposed to tradition. Different now, of course, with so many television programmes fuelling a demand for modern design.'

Stirling suspected Jones was playing a well-worn theme. To avoid digression, he asked, 'We understand Pemberton hadn't worked much in recent years?'

Jones shifted in his seat and reached forward to stir his tea slowly. Stirling thought he was delaying, considering his answer.

'I don't believe so. But, as I said, we weren't in each other's pockets. You'll need to make your own enquiries, Chief Inspector.' Jones leant back in his chair to sip at his tea, cradling the saucer under the cup as he observed Stirling with watery eyes over its rim.

'I appreciate that sir, but why do *you* believe he hadn't been working. I understand he was involved in a development that got into difficulties?'

Jones slowly replaced the cup and saucer on his desk and leant back in his chair to rest his hands on the arm supports.

'You've heard correctly, Chief Inspector. He'd been successful for many years designing the sort of homes only wealthy people can buy, and paid excellent commissions too. He often project managed them, if asked to, which returns a nice fee on top. Some clients like that as it provides them with the flexibility of changing design features as they go along without losing the integrity of the original commission.

'He got involved in a very significant development about four years ago, perhaps longer. Time flies as you get older! Something went wrong amongst the investors and a huge amount of money was lost. The project foundered before building started and Pemberton lost out heavily.'

'How come? As the architect, Mr Pemberton would not have been exposed in the same way as the investors or the development company, surely?'

'In the normal run of these things, you're right. However, Pemberton invested very heavily in the project himself and overreached himself. When the chickens came home to roost, he was left high and dry. Sorry, I'm mixing my metaphors.' Jones smiled self-indulgently across the desk. Stirling returned a complicit smile to massage the man's ego.

Jones gave some detail about how the contractual arrangements would usually work. The gossip was that Pemberton had invested far more than he possessed, borrowing heavily in anticipation of high returns and had been avoiding his creditors ever since.

'And where was this investment to have been?' asked Stirling.

Jones looked at Stirling and exclaimed, 'But it was where he was found!'

Stirling masked his surprise well, but possibly not well enough. Should he have known that? Was it deep within HOLMES, yet to be revealed to him? There had been no mention of it in Jones's previous interview suggesting that either the investigator had not asked enough questions, or Jones had been economic in his assistance, hoping the police would join the dots together for themselves. Stirling suspected the latter. Thinking of the location, the offshore investment scheme and this information, it was all too obvious now.

'We had some understanding of that, but you'll understand we must corroborate our information,' Stirling replied smoothly. 'Can you help me with who the investors and contractors were? It would be very helpful.'

Stirling was pandering to Jones's vanity as the other man looked at him suspiciously, wondering if Stirling had truly known. The clock ticked loudly in the silence.

'Not really. Word was that the investors sat behind a development company, probably created specifically for the project. I don't know who they were, but they certainly weren't from around here. That sort of thing leaks out generally. People like to talk about their projects and ambitions. As for the site contractors, a local company went to the wall as a direct consequence. They'd started clearing the ground when things went belly up.'

Opening a drawer, Jones rummaged around for a moment and handed a business card to Stirling. 'The mobile number might still be relevant. He's still working but on a much smaller scale now. It takes a long time to recover from bankruptcy. And from losing everything you've spent your life working for! Pemberton was not a popular man afterwards. He drew in people he knew to invest and, as people do, they needed someone to blame for their own poor judgement.'

Looking at the details on the card, Stirling recognised the company as having been a big name locally some years ago. 'So, Mr Pemberton was a victim of the development's collapse too?'

Jones frowned heavily as the muscles in his jaw tensed. With heavy cynicism, he answered, 'The word *victim* is not one that people usually apply to Pemberton, Chief Inspector. Pemberton was an extremely charming man, particularly around the ladies, and could be *very* persuasive in drawing people into schemes they might later regret.'

'I see. And was he ever married?'

Jones gave a short, derisive laugh, 'I'm absolutely confident he was never married. It would have got in the way of his lifestyle. Few women would have tolerated his numerous affairs.'

Stirling said nothing, allowing silence to fill the space, hoping for more. Jones obliged, appearing to have shed his initial reluctance to speak, now that they were talking of Pemberton's personal life.

'You need to understand that Pemberton was an extremely attractive man, when younger, with a *very* strong interest in women, *lots* of them. I'm not claiming any specific knowledge, but he was something of a local legend for his many liaisons.'

'I see, so there were some unhappy husbands?'

'Cuckolds, you mean! Yes, quite a few, I'm sure. You see, Pemberton enjoyed the chase and the conquest but soon lost interest and moved on to another. Women adored him, though, especially those who were bored, their husbands too busy building careers and businesses.'

Jones paused and pursed his lips, weighing his words. 'I believe some women discovered his tastes a little, *different*, to their own, but he had an uncanny nose for an opportunity. He offered them some excitement in otherwise tedious marriages, I suppose. As I said, he was exceptionally persuasive and charming, and women often persuade themselves that they alone are the one that can change a man's spots. Don't you find?'

Stirling wasn't sure if the question was rhetorical or somehow aimed at him. 'We've identified the body through fingerprints. Do you know of any family, or someone who does?'

Jones made a show of considering the question, leaning back in his chair and turning to gaze out of the window before swivelling back to face Stirling. He leaned forward, resting his fleshy arms on the desk.

'No, I don't think so. He was in his late fifties, I'd say. I'm not even certain if he was from the county, originally. I never heard him discuss any relatives but if anything comes to mind, how would I contact you?'

Stirling reached into an inside pocket and withdrew a silver business card holder. Selecting a card, he passed it over to Jones who studied its detail and put it to one side on the desk.

Stirling persisted. 'Do you know of any women in his life, particularly in recent years?'

'Not recently, no. Even though he was a Casanova, he tended to be discreet. People gossiped, of course, it's what people do, but much of it was speculation in the absence of fact and the married women weren't going to blab. He was a bit of a social fixer too.'

There was an insinuation in Jones's voice. 'Meaning?'

Jones hesitated, his eyes drifting out of the window in the direction of Pemberton's home. 'Pemberton loved parties. They suited his personality and when the husbands got drunk, their wives became easy prey to his smooth chat up lines. I'm talking some years ago, now. There were some riotous parties over there ...' he pointed across the square. '... and there used to be some chatter about drugs, the stuff that only wealthy people could afford ...' Jones brought his gaze back to Stirling, '... but people like to gossip, do they not, Chief Inspector?'

'Yes, but where there's smoke there's usually fire. And in past years, who could throw some light onto Pemberton's private life?'

Jones pondered the question. He knows some of the women in Pemberton's past, thought Stirling. But both men knew how sensitive the situation would be for any woman who had once been involved with Pemberton and was now quietly getting on with her life.

Jones pulled a writing pad towards him. Picking up an expensive fountain pen, he began to write in a precise, flowing script. Putting down the pen, Jones tore the page from the pad, folded it meticulously and held it out across the desk towards

Stirling, pulling it away as Stirling reached forward to take it from him.

'Chief Inspector. Three women who, to the best of my knowledge, are no longer with husbands or have any long-term partners who *might* speak to you. However, you did *not* get this information from me and I trust you will respect how delicate the situation is for them, even now. Pemberton trampled through a lot of lives with complete indifference to the harm he caused. You will, undoubtedly, open old wounds.'

Jones held the piece of paper out again, allowing Stirling to take it. Looking at the names and approximate addresses, he saw they were all within a few miles of the city.

'Thank you. I can assure you we'll tread carefully. I'll have an experienced female detective contact them. What about close friends or associates? There must be someone we could talk to?'

'None that I know of. Pemberton burnt a lot of bridges behind him. He was utterly cavalier in his relationships and, inevitably, he lost people's trust. Now, Chief Inspector...' Jones stood up, '... I have other appointments, so I really must bid you good day. If anything comes to mind, I have your card.' Jones pointed to the card on his desk.

Unsure if he could count on his help again, Stirling pressed Jones, 'You said something about some women's tastes not meeting his. What did you mean by that?' Stirling was thinking of the suitcase in the apartment.

Jones pointed to the paper in Stirling's hand. 'You might learn more by speaking to them.' He was not going to be drawn.

'One last thing, sir. I'm sorry to ask but I need to understand your own position in my investigation. Were you ever affected by Pemberton's philandering?'

Jones's eyes slipped away briefly and returned to hold Stirling's gaze, too firmly, a tiny muscle flickering at the corner of his eye. 'No, Chief Inspector.'

There was a cold finality to the answer that said the meeting had ended. Stirling shook his hand and said he would find his own way out.

Pausing at a window near the top of the stairs, Stirling realised there was a clear line of sight across to Pemberton's building.

Sitting in his car outside Jones's office, Stirling considered calling Ayesha to meet for an early lunch but knew he could not spare the time. He replayed the meeting, making notes whilst it was still fresh in his mind. Jones had begun by claiming he knew little about Pemberton but obviously knew more than he had put in his statement the day before. Stirling was certain he knew more still, but none of it suitable for a statement as it was all hearsay. Jones had lied in answer to his last question, or was not entirely truthful. He might have good reason not to discuss something personal, but it meant Stirling could not trust him completely. He would like to know more about David Jones. Selecting the telephone function on the console he made four calls before switching on the engine and drove round the square, heading for HQ.

*

Standing back from the window out of sight, thumbs hooked in his waistband, Jones watched Stirling in his car below. The glare of sunshine across the windscreen made it difficult to see what he was doing clearly, but he could make out a notebook.

Had Stirling looked up at the building he would not have seen Jones watching him, but he might have noticed his secretary standing at a window on the floor above, fiddling nervously with a button on her cardigan as she watched Stirling anxiously, wondering why he didn't just go. Looking across the square she could see Pemberton's apartment and felt the fear return.

Hearing the car below start, she watched it travel slowly around the square. By pressing her face to the glass, she watched it turn into the Barbourne and out of sight. Turning away from the window, she chewed on a finger distractedly until she was startled by the telephone ringing. Glancing again at the building in the far corner, she went to her desk and hesitantly put her hand on the receiver, its shrill tone fraying her nerves further.

Taking a deep breath to calm herself she answered, 'David? … yes … yes … coming.'

*

12.09 p.m.
Stirling decided he should try and catch up with Dave Pearson. Even though they had spoken by telephone each day, he knew the old man would appreciate a personal briefing and his vast experience was always worth listening to.

He found Pearson at his desk munching on a sandwich as he worked through a pile of papers, reminding Stirling of his doubts at taking the next rank. He already felt too removed from hands on investigative work. Looking pleased to see Stirling and waving a half-eaten sandwich towards a seat, Pearson told him to close the door to avoid interruption.

'All sorted? Culprit in the cells and a signed, hand-written confession?' he asked mordantly.

Stirling smiled at Pearson's world-weary humour. 'Sorry, not yet. I thought I should drop in and catch up with you.'

Stirling talked as Pearson listened. The few questions he asked were incisive and to the point. With over thirty years' investigative experience, not much got past him, if anything at all. They agreed on solutions to some of the resourcing difficulties that plagued all investigations and Pearson agreed the next tranche of funding Stirling would need signing off by Tanner.

'There was a time, Doug, when we were expected to just get on with the job and it cost what it cost. Not playing fast and loose and getting by with as few people as we can spare. If only the public knew.'

'Probably better they don't,' Stirling answered flatly.

He knew the old man wasn't complaining, just stating the facts. For Stirling's part, he was either given the tools to do the job or the investigation took longer. He couldn't make bricks without straw. Discussion turned to Tanner's position and he asked when McDonald was expected back.

'Monday, so if it was wrapped up by then it would be helpful,' said Pearson, 'But I know it won't be, so we'll have to weather the storm.'

Stirling agreed. Three and a half days would not be long enough. 'We're going flat out Dave, but I can only follow the evidence. I'll keep you posted.' He got up to leave.

'I know. Thanks Doug.'

As Stirling left, Pearson returned his attention to the papers on his desk, his free hand searching vaguely for the remaining sandwich.

Walking across the car park, Stirling noticed a car travelling slowly towards him as the driver searched for an empty space. As it drew closer it slowed down, preparing to stop. Sunlight across the windscreen made it difficult to see who was at the wheel. Thinking it was someone he knew wishing to speak with him, Stirling waited for the car to draw alongside. The driver's window slid down to reveal Ballard's round face peering up at him. Stirling's immediate reaction was to walk away but his pride would not let him back down.

'Chief Inspector,' said Ballard, looking up at Stirling smugly.

Forcing himself to stay calm and resisting a temptation to drag Ballard through the window, he answered, '*Detective* Chief Inspector, the last time I checked Ballard. But you're trying to change that, aren't you?'

Ballard ignored the question. 'I was surprised to learn of your appointment as SIO to a murder investigation, considering my investigation has yet to submit its findings. Mind you, Mr McDonald returns soon and I'm sure he'll have a view on the matter. Especially if no arrest has been made by then.'

Ballard's pudgy face was impassive, but his eyes darted maliciously across Stirling's face, willing him to react. Deep in his coat pockets, Stirling balled his fists as he sifted the responses he wanted to give.

'You should have completed your investigation long ago Ballard, not least of all for the sake of that poor girl's family. You should give that some thought, instead of pursuing your own ambition.'

Ballard smiled up at him coldly. 'A good investigation doesn't rush to conclusions, as you should know. I'll make my report when I'm ready to, and not before. Mr McDonald has expressed his complete confidence in me.'

Stirling bent down and leant an elbow on the open window edge, causing Ballard to flinch with concern. Staring hard into his eyes, Stirling spoke with a quiet, cold fury.

'Ballard, you're incompetent but sadly, you're too arrogant to understand your own limitations, which makes you an even greater liability. Don't make the mistake of thinking other people don't know that. If you think you've got McDonald in your pocket, then you're an even bigger fool than I took you for. The moment McDonald thinks you're likely to crap on his CV, he'll drop you like a hot brick.'

Stirling reached into the car to put his hand on Ballard's shoulder and gripped it tightly, taking some pleasure in seeing him flinch with alarm. In a low, menacing tone, he continued, 'And remember this too, Ballard ... when McDonald's left here to go and fuck up another force, the poor bastards, you'll still be here. And so will I, together with all the other people who detest you for the arrogant, vainglorious shit that you are!'

Stirling gave Ballard's shoulder another hard squeeze, finding only soft flesh where he had expected muscle as he squirmed with discomfort under his grip. Stirling stood up and walked away.

As he thought about how Ballard had flinched, Stirling felt better than he had for a long time. It would give him something to think about and even if it made him more of a threat, he hadn't been able to resist wiping the smug look from his face.

1.35 p.m.

Driving back to the MCU, Stirling's temporary pleasure at Ballard's discomfort had quickly given way to a simmering rage at the cack-handed way in which he and McDonald had handled their end of the IPCC investigation. By the time he swung into the rear yard, he was in a filthy temper. Slamming the car door behind him, Stirling took the stairs two at a time and went straight to his office. Throwing his jacket over the top of the filing cabinet he turned towards the door to see Edwards appear.

'I saw you pull in and recognise that face. Who's upset you?' Edwards stood in the doorway, preventing Stirling from leaving. Jerking his thumb in the direction of the incident room he said, 'If I'm right, I'd rather you didn't take it in there.'

Edwards stood resolutely in the doorway. Stirling knew he was right. Motioning him to shut the door, Stirling sat down and recounted what had happened with Ballard. Edwards began laughing.

Grumpily, Stirling demanded, 'What's so bloody amusing?'

'Sounds to me as though he was left with more to think about than you. He'll get found out, mark my words.'

'Easy for you to say Bill, it's not your career at risk. He's determined to screw me over because of that review last year.'

Edwards pulled a shrug, raising both hands, 'Okay, it's not my career, but you just need to be patient and get on with the job here. We've made some progress whilst you were out, and I'd like to know what you got from Jones.'

Stirling heard his stomach complain of hunger. 'Have you eaten yet?'

Sitting in the snug of the Crow's Nest with unexceptional sandwiches and soft drinks, Edwards explained the results of the cell site analysis of Pemberton's phone.

'I've set some initial parameters to identify when he arrived at the site, and where he was during the days before. Or where his phone was, anyway. We've got limited analytical support, so I've had to make the best use of his time.'

Stirling agreed, adding, 'And where the phone went to after the attack.'

'Not very far. It stopped registering very close to the scene, possibly no further than the top of the track. Perhaps our murderer was aware of tracking and disabled it as they left the scene.' Edwards shrugged, 'But, we know the phone arrived there shortly before eight on Good Friday morning and was switched off about an hour after arrival. The precise time's in the print out and has been added to the sequence of events timeline. It's registering with the local mast throughout that time with no calls in or out. Long enough to kill him and set fire to the car.'

Taking a hungry bite out of his sandwich, Stirling considered the time frame and Pemberton's damaged body. Peeling open the remaining half, he inspected the content dubiously.

'But not a huge amount of time either, Bill. If he died soon after arriving, although we don't know that, it's a long time to spend alone down there with a body. Not many people could do that once the heat and passion of the moment has passed, and then calmly set about destroying the evidence whilst covered in his blood. Was that a heat of the moment loss of control, or recklessness? Or was it a calculated, premeditated killing? As remote as it is down there, they couldn't have been certain of not being disturbed.'

'There would have been a hell of a lot of blood, certainly during the initial blows. Less as his heart weakened and stopped. It could have been a joint enterprise with someone keeping watch from further up the track?' Edwards suggested, unconvinced with his own theory. There were any number of options to consider. 'I'll chase SOCO and see what they've found under all that soot.' Edwards jotted a reminder into his day book.

The two men resumed eating silently, the only noise a low murmur of conversation and an occasional burst of laughter from the bar next door where the local pensioners would be playing cribbage. Stirling broke the silence. 'What about calls to and from Pemberton's phone in the days before?'

'The analyst has almost completed a schedule, sifting out his regular calls to identify anything different in the day or so before he died. He's done the initial analysis and is now working back three months as you instructed. Once we've cleared that we'll be guided by any intel.'

Edwards looked at Stirling for his approval. They couldn't afford to start a fishing expedition and must rely on intelligence to inform their research. Stirling described the meeting with Jones and the possibility of a financial motive to the murder.

'Perhaps there was dirty money in play?' Edwards countered. 'The violence was extreme, the sort of thing you might associate with east European organised crime groups.'

The prospect of investigating an east European OCG would be a daunting prospect. Stirling related Jones's information that Pemberton might have been involved in drug supply, probably cocaine.

Edwards chewed at his top lip as he considered the possibility. 'Interesting. Once made, those contacts are always there to return to. Remember what the SOCO was talking about at the scene? I checked it out. He wasn't quite right about where they're from, but we do have some problems with OCGs from outside the region trying to muscle in and causing the local dealers difficulties. They can't match the violence.'

As Edwards described the tit for tat violence, Stirling found himself looking at a faded picture hanging askew on the wall behind Edwards of a hunting scene with horses and hounds chasing across a wintry landscape, reminding Stirling of a quote: "the unspeakable in pursuit of the uneatable." It seemed comparable to what Edwards was describing.

Stirling picked up the conversation. 'But if Pemberton was involved in drug dealing, it ought to have shown up in our Intel research. Which doesn't exclude his involvement, only that he wasn't on the radar. Toxicology will reveal if he was a user himself but that's days away, at best. Call the Drug Squad and see what their snouts can turn up. Even the most befuddled of our informant druggies should remember a white middle-aged bloke in an old Jag!'

'Okay, but we're not short of people with a motive to harm Pemberton. Numerous cheated husbands, scorned lovers, people who've lost a lot of money and now, a possible drugs angle.'

Stirling nodded pensively. 'And we've no idea who was in the car with him. It could have been someone known to him or a pick-up through online dating, or a street pick-up, male or female. His browsing history might identify if he visited dating websites but if he limited his use to his mobile, we'd better take HTCU's advice on that. We've got the data from the telephone masts covering the scene which will identify all mobile phones checking in and out during the key times on Good Friday morning. Extract the data between six that morning until an hour after his phone stopped pinging. Once we've identified the scale of that, we'll decide how to finesse the research.'

Stirling knew only too well what a significant task that would be on already hard-pressed analysts. Better to wait and see if a specific phone was of interest first.

Noting down the actions, Edwards murmured sombrely, 'Not that it was a good Friday for Pemberton, mind.'

'No, it wasn't. Croft mentioned Kuwait and the Caymans. If any of the money was dirty and Pemberton was siphoning it off, that will throw up even more lines of enquiry. And there might be bank accounts we haven't discovered yet.' He paused pensively. 'I think we might have a runner, Bill.' Stirling was using the term to describe a complex, long running investigation.

'But Pemberton's lifestyle doesn't suggest he had a lot of money,' Edwards countered.

'No, but if he had skimmed off money, he might have lost control of it, or access to it. Or perhaps it was nicked back off him? Pemberton was a playboy architect, and an ageing one at that. If he'd started mixing it with the big boys, he wouldn't have stood a chance. There's any number of possibilities.'

Stirling pushed aside the remains of his lunch, wishing he had a good pint of bitter to wash it down with. He remembered something else. 'What are we doing with the info I got from Jones?'

'Geordie's fast tracking it through the system. Croft's team is liaising with Companies House at London about Fairway but he's already warning it's probably a shell company with some placemen to front it up, with the real players beyond sight. Geordie says he's making progress on the land ownership too.'

'And who's contacting the women?'

'Helen. She'll deal with them sensitively, but she won't take no for an answer, either. I expect to hear from her this afternoon.'

'Okay. What about the site contractor Jones mentioned, Cole & Son?'

'Terence Cole. Terry to his mates. He was known to us many years ago. Typical builder type, a handful when he was young but settled down as he got his business going. The "Son" is William Cole, better known as Billy with some convictions for assaults. Looks like street fighting mainly, but he was in front of the Crown Court last year, indicted on a section eighteen GBH, reduced to a section twenty after some plea bargaining and mitigation. He got a suspended sentence. It involved a female. Geordie's contacting the officer in the case and Croft is digging into the company to see what he can find.'

Stirling leant forward, interested. 'Billy might be interesting to talk to. A lot of money lost, the business bankrupted, and he has a record for violence.'

'And it'll be interesting to find out if there's any connection between the female in that case and Pemberton. Old man Cole lives near Malvern. We could nip down there this afternoon if you like?'

'Okay, but call ahead. We can't afford a wasted journey. And I'd like the telephone profiling on my desk when we get back, or as much as we've got anyway. Things are starting to move Bill.'

'We've got a hell of a lot of investigative lines in play Doug, especially for the size of the team we've got. I think we're going to struggle.'

Stirling gave him a fatalistic shrug. 'Bricks and straw, Bill. We prioritise, follow the intelligence and apply a good dose of investigative nous. We can only do the best job possible with the tools they give us. And document everything, or the review will do our legs!'

3.05 p.m.
They travelled in Edwards's car, leaving Stirling free to think. Near the showground east of Malvern, Cole's home was at the end of a long drive with untidy paddocks either side in which a few. ponies grazed. Although large, the house was modest in its design and faced north. Stirling suspected there would be a large rear garden to exploit the sun. The long ridge of the Malvern Hills filling most of the western horizon provided a dramatic back drop.

In front of the house, three cars were parked on a gravelled drive. An ageing estate and a newish black Range Rover Vogue sat close to the front door, both neatly reverse parked. Nearby, a scruffy four-wheel drive pick-up sat askew to the others, a ripple of stones under each tyre indicating it had been stopped in a hurry. To one side of the house and set further back was a large outbuilding with wide garage doors and living space above.

'He didn't lose all of his money then,' observed Edwards ironically. Croft had called them on the way over to say that Cole's business had filed for bankruptcy three years ago.

Alerted by the crunching of gravel, they were met at the front door by Terence Cole. Short and stocky with broad shoulders and hands like shovels, Cole's ruddy, weathered complexion told of a man who had worked outdoors all his life. Light blue eyes confidently, but warily met and held each man's gaze as he shook their hands firmly.

Cole led them to the rear of the house to the kitchen where they made small talk as they waited for the kettle to boil. No one else came to join them. Cole confirmed Stirling's expectation that he had built the house himself. Sat at a long kitchen table covered at one end in a clutter of papers, car keys and random items dropped in passing over several days, Stirling could see he had been right. Glass doors led to a south facing lawn.

As Cole told them how he built his business over thirty years, starting with a second hand JCB digger, slowly building his name and reputation through sheer hard work, Stirling quickly took a liking to him and his frank honesty. Cole had grown his business until he had many heavy plant units out on building sites around the region, surviving three recessions along the way through a dogged determination not to fail. When they began to discuss his involvement at The Wern, Cole's ebullient pride turned regretful.

With an eye to retirement, he had invested heavily in it, both personally and through his business. Anticipating a healthy return on the investment, he had reduced his other commitments to concentrate on it, disposing of machinery to realise cash for the investment. When the project failed, it coincided with a downturn in the building sector with little new work available. He'd held out for as long as possible but with much of his remaining machinery secured against commercial loans and unable to service the debt, the business had collapsed.

He still owned a couple of machines which were not in the company name and he was using these for small building projects through personal recommendation. Although business was picking up, Cole said he had neither the will nor the energy to rebuild the business. The worry had made his wife ill and they were comfortable enough for him to give it up. The house was in his wife's name, so it had been safe from the creditors and he didn't miss the stress. Stirling was struck by Cole's apparent resignation to his fate, and said so.

Cole looked at them steadily. 'I had enough experience to see the risk, Mr Stirling. There's always risk in the building trade, but what I hadn't expected was to be shafted by people I had never met. Most of it was being handled by Pemberton and I'd worked with him before, very successfully too. But, I made the mistake of trusting Pemberton without making some checks of my own. I'm old fashioned you see, Irish background. If I give my word and shake hands on a deal, it's a matter of honour that I keep my end of it. Even if at a loss. You must always think of the next job. This time, though, the other money was coming from people I didn't know but I trusted him, see? He's dead now, so I've accepted my money's lost.'

Stirling could imagine Cole stood in the mud of a building site, rain running down the back of his neck as he negotiated a hard deal before spitting into his palm and shaking on the agreement. Any difficulties on the site he would have handled himself and looking at the large, raw boned hands resting on the table, Stirling could imagine how that would have turned out. Cole dodged a question from Edwards about how much of his own money he had lost.

'It was a lot of money, that's all I'm prepared to say. All paid into the company registered for the development. What hurts the most, though, is the loss of my business and thirty years of hard work, but we'll get by.' Cole held his hands open as if to say, "what can you do?".

Cole confirmed it had been his team that cleared the ground ready for building work, with some stops and starts as funds were held up, until the project finally collapsed. Cole gave them information of his movements throughout the Easter weekend which Stirling knew would prove to be the truth.

'Your son, Billy. He worked with you in the business?' asked Edwards.

At the mention of his son's name Cole stiffened, his shoulders hunching slightly with an instinctive reflex.

'Yes, Billy worked in the business until it folded, but he works for himself now unless I need help. Why?' Cole's tone had taken on a wary edge. The question was almost a challenge as he held Edwards's gaze steadily.

'Did he have an axe to grind with Pemberton, Mr Cole? I'd ask him myself but he's not here. He was in bother with the law recently.'

Cole stared at Edwards before answering, the back of his neck reddening and the meaty fists on the table clenched tighter. Splaying his hands out flat on the table, Cole took a deep breath and got a grip of whatever was troubling him.

'Now listen here. Billy's a good lad and works hard for his living. He got into a few scrapes as a lad, but who doesn't? He works hard and used to play hard. Nothing wrong in that, but he's settled down now. As for that court case, I'll tell you this. It was six of one and half a dozen of the other, but you'll have to ask him about that. It's no business of mine.'

Cole wouldn't be drawn on the matter any further, other than to say that it had no connection to Pemberton and should never have gone to court. Giving them Billy's mobile number, Cole explained his son lived over the garage to the side but was out for the day. Stirling thought about the pick-up outside but decided not to raise it.

Asked about Pemberton's womanising, Cole said he had heard tales but couldn't tell them anything specific. When asked if they had ever socialised together, Cole laughed merrily at the thought.

'Can you imagine it now, Mr Stirling? Me! Hob-knobbing it with the likes of all them hoity-toity people with their posh accents? And all of them looking down their noses at the bloke who drove the tractor!' Cole's Irish accent strengthened as he enjoyed his own joke. 'I saw enough of that sort on the sites, patronising me with their half-arsed ideas and sneering behind their hands at the little bloke with dirty hands and muddy boots, never guessing I was worth more than most of them.'

Asked about the surveyor, David Jones, Cole said he wasn't involved. 'Pemberton was the project manager to start with which wasn't unusual. It meant another fee for him and allowed him to control the other trades too, often with a percentage from them as well to oil the wheels. For a big job like that though, he'd have needed a professional site manager, but we never got that far.'

Cole could not tell them anything about the history of the land, only that there had been a farm cottage or house which had already been demolished before he got involved.

After telling him Billy would be contacted soon, they left, with Cole watching their departure from the front door. As they drove away, Edwards looked in the rear-view mirror to see Cole striding towards the garage annexe.

'I think Billy might have been at home all along,' said Edwards, and explained what was happening behind them. 'D'you want to go back?'

'No, let them both stew a bit. Send Little and Large over to see Billy later. We've got enough to get on with.'

4.34 p.m.
Sitting down with Heal and Edwards in his office, Stirling worked through the information now flowing into the incident room.

Smoke damage to the car's interior had rendered any DNA that might have been left by the offender irretrievable. Surfaces which could have yielded fingerprints appeared to have been wiped down before the fire was started. Some blood spray was visible but as it was the victim's, it was of limited benefit until they had a suspect to talk to.

The vehicle had been identified using the chassis numbers against registration documents in Pemberton's study, which confirmed he had owned the car for over twenty years. House to house with neighbours was almost complete, confirming information that the car had appeared a few days before he died.

A female cousin from the south had made contact after seeing media coverage, agreeing to do the formal identification despite having been warned of his condition. Heal had arranged with the mortuary for the eyes to be covered and that was taking place now. She had last seen Pemberton at a family wedding some months ago, and there was no other family. Heal had made sure she was legitimate and was arranging for a Family Liaison Officer to be assigned from the cousin's local force.

Croft had confirmed the Fairway project was a shell company to shield the bigger investors from view. Considerable sums of money had regularly passed through Pemberton's business account before the development collapsed, with significant payments channelled through a legal firm in Worcester which Croft was following up. Turning to his personal finances, Pemberton had enjoyed a high income for many years with large dividends paid from his business account. Once the development failed he had struggled financially, incurring overdraft fees and with no regular income apart from some infrequent, large cash deposits. Croft was arranging for Pemberton's business accountant to be interviewed.

The Hi-Tech Crime Unit was still analysing Pemberton's computer but apart from project plans and building designs, nothing of interest had been found, so far. An encrypted file might be of interest, once they got into it. Details of clients and businesses were being put into HOLMES to see if there were any matching "hits" with information already in the system.

Cell site analysis was still being worked on, but the early indications were that Pemberton had travelled no further than the Worcester area in the days leading up to his death, with nothing obvious to follow up on urgently. Calls to and from his phone had been grouped and were being investigated by the outside team. As subscribers were identified and their names attributed to phone numbers, they were going onto HOLMES and cross-referenced to all other data.

'Geordie, I want to see the subscriber details for his phone calls in the week before he died to see if there's anything staring us in the face. I can't wait for the teams to work their way through it.'

Heal leaned forward and held out a photocopied list of Pemberton's calls. 'I thought you'd ask for that!' Heal smiled, pleased with his anticipation.

Stirling put it down to read later. 'So, house to house is complete?'

Reading from his notes, Heal answered, 'All but one. A woman called Frances Greening who lives below Pemberton's flat. A neighbour who's looking after her cat says she's travelling abroad and expected to return sometime this week. She's been away since at least a week before the murder so, apart from whatever she can say about his lifestyle, I'm not expecting much more.'

Edwards intervened. 'The neighbour will have Greening's mobile number in case of a problem with the cat. Find out when exactly she's back Geordie. We know precious little about our man's private life, which is interesting in its own way.'

Seeing them waiting for him to expand, Edwards continued, 'If he'd been popular, there would be more interest. People who knew him telling us what a lovely chap he was and the media hyper-ventilating about a crazed killer on the loose. Angie Baines told me earlier that social media is quiet and even the local press seems to be sitting on its hands waiting to see what we turn up. By the way, they haven't connected you to the investigation. Yet.'

Once he was satisfied everything was going as well as could be expected, Heal and Edwards left. Picking up the action sheet Heal had given him, Stirling scanned through the single page of telephone numbers to and from Pemberton's mobile. Subscriber names were written alongside most of them, but some remained unattributed. One of the unattributed numbers had called Pemberton the evening before he died. Stirling thought about making a "Mickey Mouse" call, pretending to be a wrong number enquiry to see who answered. But, if it was connected to the murder it might spook them and he could lose evidence. Heal had asked for subscriber details but telephone companies could be slow to respond, and some were just uncooperative.

Using his desk phone which automatically withheld the number, Stirling began punching in the number when the outer door from the stairs opened and Helen Williams walked past, followed by a young female detective. Williams glanced in at Stirling but said nothing as she walked on towards the incident room. The younger officer called out a cheery 'Hello sir' as she followed. Getting the better of his impatience, Stirling put the phone down.

Ten minutes later Heal was knocking at his door again. 'Sorry to bother you, boss, but Helen's back from interviewing a couple of the women Jones gave you the names of?'

'And?' demanded Stirling.

'I think you should hear what they've told her, boss. It's a bit sensitive and you'll need to set a policy on how we manage the women. She's got some more names to contact and it could have some bearing on why our chap was topped.'

Stirling had wanted to keep Helen at arm's length and already he was being asked to meet with her, with no good reason he could think of to avoid it. 'Where's Bill?'

'Next door, shall I bring him in too?'

'It'll be too crowded in here. We'll meet in the kitchen over a brew. Call me when you're ready but ask Bill to see me first please.'

A swell of chatter and noise flowed into the corridor as Heal returned to the incident room and receded as the door closed behind him. Stirling was contemplating a meeting with Helen in the company of others when noise from the incident room spilled into the corridor again and Edwards was at his door. Stirling waved him in and to shut the door.

'Helen's got some interesting info I believe?'

Closing the door Edwards answered, 'I can deal with it if you like, but I think you should hear it first hand. And about Helen, I spoke with Geordie this morning and told him as much as he needs to know. He'll keep an eye on things and if any of our usual suspects show too much interest in her, or her in them, he'll give some discreet advice.'

Stirling grunted. 'Okay. It might save someone a divorce. Who's the officer working with her?'

'She's from division, young in service but keen and very bright. She'll learn a lot through working with Helen and the team here. Helen's professional Doug, I doubt she'll cause any problems.'

Stirling was not so certain. 'I hope you're right.'

Edwards was almost out of the door when a thought occurred to him and he turned back to Stirling. 'Pemberton formally identified this afternoon. By the distant cousin? She was a bit shaken up but okay otherwise and her home force has supplied the FLO.'

5.37 p.m.

Sat around the chipped and stained table, Helen described the meetings with two of the women named by David Jones. Unused to being in the company of senior detectives, the younger officer sat quietly at her side, watching and listening intently.

They had met the women in their homes and had an appointment for the third that evening. None of them had been surprised to be contacted, Jones had forewarned them. Even though they were uncomfortable talking about their experiences, they had agreed to help so far as they could but were frightened of the information "getting into the papers." Helen had assured them their statements would be treated discreetly, and once she had established that neither of them had spoken with Pemberton for over a year, it was unlikely they would have to give evidence. The women were not friends but knew each other a little through their extended social circles, and because their association with Pemberton had led to messy divorces.

'They describe Pemberton as a manipulative, dangerous bastard. My words, but the message was clear,' Helen explained. 'He was emotionally callous and when he grew tired of them, or they wanted more from him than he was prepared to give, like a permanent relationship, he moved on to someone else.'

Helen looked across the table at each of the men as if Pemberton's conduct was an indictment of them too. Looking at Stirling she continued. 'You might want to consider a policy decision about how we treat them and to protect their identities. They've given us more names who might give us yet more again. Which means a lot of cheated husbands and partners to trace, interview and eliminate.'

'What have you learnt about Pemberton beyond his womanising, Helen,' asked Stirling. 'What you've described could be the behaviour of many men.'

Stirling regretted his words as soon they left his mouth as he saw Helen's eyebrows rise and her eyes light up with cold amusement. He sensed Heal's and Edwards's discomfort either side of him.

Helen looked at him coolly, her mouth pursing as she considered and dismissed a tart reply. 'Pemberton was a social gad-fly, very personable, charming and attractive, both physically and intellectually, they say.' At her side, the younger officer nodded in agreement. 'He earned well and spent his money on them freely, flattering them with gifts and always drove nice cars. He's owned the Jag for donkey's years. But Pemberton liked forbidden fruit ... other men's wives in the main and the younger the better, which was not a problem until he got older and the women he lusted after became less accessible. After all, not all women are attracted to older men.'

Helen paused to allow her words to hang in the air. Heal and Edwards assumed the thinly veiled barb was aimed at Stirling, but all three men studiously ignored it. At Helen's side, the young officer sensed the undercurrents in her colleague's briefing but couldn't fathom out what was going on.

Helen continued, 'But, Pemberton had a darker side.'

Thinking of the suitcase in the apartment, Stirling knew what was coming.

'He liked his women to be submissive. Not just how they acted around him, although that was part of it, but sexually submissive, as in BDSM.'

At Helen's side, the officer frowned at the acronym. 'I'm sorry, I'm aware of S and M, but BDSM?'

Stirling looked at Williams with a faint smile, 'Perhaps you should explain, Helen?'

Out of the corner of his eye he saw Edwards lean back and fold his arms. However uncomfortable it was for anyone else, he was enjoying the sparring between Stirling and Helen.

Helen's nostrils flared in annoyance. Forcing a patient smile towards her colleague, she explained, 'The term is used differently but essentially it means the same thing. Bondage, Discipline, Submission, and Masochism. Alternatively, Bondage, Discipline, Sadism and Masochism,' adding sharply, 'You'll find it quickly enough on the internet if you want to know more.'

The young woman blinked rapidly and blushed, keenly aware of the senior men around the table and put her head down to scribble a note.

Embarrassed for the young woman's discomfort, Stirling moved things on. 'Do they say if it was consensual?'

'Completely. They were besotted with him and wanted to please him. He was a charmer and, they say, a satisfying lover. In the context of an illicit relationship, I think they enjoyed the excitement of something a bit kinky. But they both know of other women who didn't like his tastes and of other affairs that ended acrimoniously. These two ended up divorced, losing everything. Their security, their home and their friendships. One of them is still estranged from her children, all these years on. There's a lot of pain and anger.'

'How long ago was this?' asked Edwards.

Williams looked to her young partner who answered confidently, pleased to contribute, 'Eight and ten years ago, respectively. The lady we're seeing this evening was more recent.'

Edwards frowned as he asked, 'I thought Jones said Pemberton was discreet about his relationships? How did these women get caught out?'

'Pemberton was, but they were careless. When their partners found out and things got messy, Pemberton stepped aside and found someone else. As I said, a bastard.'

'And the other women, Helen?' asked Edwards, keen to keep the meeting on track.

'Most of them live within the area but are in relationships so we'll need to be careful.'

Once various points of detail had been clarified, everyone turned to Stirling to hear his decision. 'As far as possible Helen, try and work backwards. One of the women might know who his latest love interest was and save us a lot of time. The more time that's passed, the more likely passions and anger have cooled. If a jealous partner didn't kill him on discovery many years ago, they're unlikely to have done it now. Unless, of course, something's happened recently to provoke them.'

'Helen, you and ...' he looked to the young woman.

'Lesley, sir.'

'... Lesley, have sole responsibility for this line of enquiry to be sure we're consistent in our dealings with them and to avoid any overlaps. It'll give us a consistent understanding of the information they give too. If any safety issues arise, such as dangerous partners, we'll do risk assessments as they emerge. They'll have thought their secret died with Pemberton and will be frightened when we make contact. Geordie, create a secure account in HOLMES specific to this leg of the investigation with access limited to designated staff on a strictly "need to know" basis.'

Helen intervened. 'They say Pemberton liked to take intimate photographs and are concerned about where they might be. He wouldn't give them up at the time. Were any recovered at the apartment?'

Edwards explained the ongoing search of the computer at HTCU. The meeting broke up and Stirling walked back to his office followed by Edwards who closed the door and sat down with an amused expression on his face.

'Hell. That was a bit edgy,' remarked Edwards, grinning.

'Just a bit!'

Becoming serious, Edwards asked, 'D'you think Helen's the right person to be dealing with these women? Only, she doesn't appear to have much ...' he searched for the right word.

'Empathy? Compassion?' Stirling offered. 'Helen will be brilliant with those women. She'll empathise with them, coax and encourage them and if necessary, she'll be tough as well to get their help. But she'll hold you and me to account for their welfare too, so make sure the risk assessments are watertight. It'll be quite an experience for young Lesley, so keep an eye on her? She might be someone we want to consider here in the future.'

Once Edwards had left, Stirling picked up the list of telephone numbers from his desk. He thought again about calling the number. Something about Pemberton's lifestyle in recent years was bugging him. The funds in his bank accounts suggested a modest standard of living with little visible income. So how had he supported himself? And how would someone used to an extravagant lifestyle have adjusted to that?

7.39 p.m.

Slipping the keys back into his pocket, Stirling stood looking around the lounge of Pemberton's apartment. Without SOCOs and search officers crowding the room, it looked bigger. Remnants of evening sunshine lay across the shabby carpet as the sun slipped west.

Going to the window, Stirling looked across the green to Jones's building, off to the left a little but clearly visible. The frontages of the buildings on the other side of the square were already in shadow. Although some distance away, Jones had a clear view of the various comings and goings to the building, unless outside office hours or in darkness. The curtain tie backs appeared to have been permanently fastened. If Pemberton was not in the habit of closing them, it was possible that with the lights on inside, Jones and anyone else in that building could have seen something of the interior too.

Putting his back to the window, Stirling examined the room. Had he missed anything? The forensic examination and evidence search had been thorough, but inconsequential items could become significant as the story developed. In the redundant fireplace, a tired arrangement of artificial flowers pollinated with dust sat in front of the blanking panel. A woman's touch, perhaps? The style of its faded contents said it had been there for many years. On the mantelpiece above lay a collection of pocket turn outs, loose coins and other small items he could associate with a man living alone, uncaring of tidiness. To the right of the fireplace a dozen or so paintings had been assembled according to their dimensions. Moving over to look at them more closely, Stirling saw they were all originals. Some had been executed with pen and ink whilst others, the landscapes, had been painted in watercolours and acrylics. The use of colour and proportions was good, and care had been taken in framing them, suggesting they had held some personal value. All were dusty, the mounts faded with age. An indecipherable scrawl in the bottom right corner of each claimed the same authorship.

Further along the wall a smaller collection of modern, ready-made plastic frames contained abstract paintings with splashes of paint, brush daubs and savage lines in harshly contrasting colours that seemed to have an innate skill but expressed something Stirling did not understand. At their centre, in contrast, was what appeared to be a Celtic styled symbol printed in black ink. None were signed. Stepping back and tilting his head each way to try and understand them, Stirling concluded that Pemberton's taste in art was eclectic.

Sitting at Pemberton's desk, Stirling pushed the swivel chair around with his feet to study the room, trying to see it as Pemberton had used it as he schemed his affairs, personal and professional.

Pulling open desk drawers, he studied their contents without expecting to find anything of interest. The evidence search had been thorough. Running his eyes along the shelves above he saw only professional and trade books and journals packed along their length until, at the far end of one shelf, a difference in material caught his eye. Standing up, Stirling could see a wooden edge, barely distinguishable from the books it was packed in amongst. Levering it out with his finger, he found it was a book sized frame containing a black and white photograph.

The search team would have opened every book to check for any loose contents and might have dismissed this as irrelevant.

Sitting at the desk, Stirling studied a photo of a cottage against a backdrop of fields with a low, stone walled fore garden planted up with flowers and roses in the full bloom of summer. At the centre of the building, a gabled porch over which roses scrambled from either side was set between diamond latticed windows, with similar windows above for the bedrooms. Recessed within the open fronted porch was a door hidden in shadow cast by the gable roof and other short shadows in the garden told Stirling the sun was high when the picture was taken.

It was only when he peered more closely that Stirling noticed a figure standing in the shadow of the porch, leaning against the door frame and looking out towards the camera. Despite switching on the desk lamp, he could not make out the face except that it was a woman standing with one hand leaning on the frame. The other hung loosely at her side with a cigarette between her fingers and one bare foot hooked casually behind an ankle. The shadow was darkest across her shoulders making her hair and face indistinct, but sunlight falling across her breasts and a triangle of pubic hair made clear she was naked.

Turning the frame over, Stirling prised open the retaining clips and removed the photograph, holding it at the card edges. Written on the reverse in a neat, sloping script was a faded message: *"Happy days my darling. Truly in love with you, forever! X"*

Turning the photo over, Stirling studied the picture again, wondering if it was significant. After replacing it in the frame, he looked for something to put it in. Pulling open a filing cabinet drawer he saw a collection of used brown envelopes, all addressed to Pemberton. Lifting one out and sliding the frame inside, Stirling recognised the sender's address. Rifling amongst the other envelopes he found many of them were from the same sender: James & James LLP, Solicitors, Worcester. Ayesha's practice.

Putting the envelope on the desk, Stirling continued to survey the room. The suitcase had been discovered in here, so Pemberton could have hidden the photographs in here too, or elsewhere in the apartment. A man who enjoyed taking photographs of naked, bound women would enjoy reminiscing on his exploits. Stirling decided to get the Task Force back to do a PolSA search of the apartment, checking all floorboards and voids, anywhere that might contain hidden items.

Picking up the envelope, Stirling returned to the lounge for one last look around. The room had become dark as nightfall cloaked the square. He was about to leave when a noise from below made him stop. Standing still to listen, he noticed how the floorboards creaked softly as he adjusted his weight. Hearing nothing more, he moved towards the door.

After setting the alarm, Stirling was attaching the Police sign forbidding entry when a brief movement on the stairs below caught his attention. Stepping over to the bannister, he looked down to see a woman in her thirties standing at the foot of the stairs looking up at him with concern. She was dressed for the outdoors in patch pocket trousers, a fleece sweater and walking shoes

Stirling called down politely, 'Good evening.'

'And just who might you be?' she challenged confidently, but a waver in her voice revealed some anxiety.

Walking down the stairs Stirling began to reach inside his jacket pocket to pull out his warrant card, causing the woman to step backwards towards an open door off the reception hall.

Stirling stood still. 'I'm Detective Chief Inspector Stirling, police. I have a warrant card in my pocket, may I show it to you?'

The woman nodded, edging into the open door as she looked at the man filling the centre of the stairway. Stirling held out his warrant card at arms' length so that she could see it clearly. Squinting between his face and the photograph, she nodded cautiously.

'Would you be Mrs Greening, the lady who's been on holiday?'

The woman frowned up at him, how did he know that? 'Yes, why?'

Stirling walked down and held out his hand. Greening glanced around the hallway, aware she was alone with a man who said he was a policeman. Taking Stirling's hand, she shook it firmly and withdrew it immediately to step back inside her doorway, one hand ready to slam it shut.

Gesturing upwards, he asked, 'Are you aware Mr Pemberton died recently?'

'Yes, I heard, but I don't know anything. I've been away for two weeks.'

Greening sounded defensive, but Stirling thought it was probably just nerves.

'I've only just got back and heard someone walking around up there so I was worried, considering he's dead.'

Stirling smiled reassuringly and asked, 'Could you spare me a few minutes please, Mrs Greening. I'm sure you're tired after travelling but I would be very grateful.'

Greening struggled for a moment between the forthright answer her tired body wanted to give and her principles of community. She stood aside and beckoned him forward. 'Very well, come in, but I'm knackered, so this had better not take long.'

Following Greening inside and stepping around a large backpack thrown carelessly against the wall, Stirling had a feeling Mrs Greening didn't suffer fools gladly.

*

8.37 p.m.

Over the next thirty minutes Stirling confirmed his first impression of Mrs Greening as being a determined, independent minded and opinionated woman. She frankly described having separated from her husband ten years ago because he "hadn't got enough about him" having decided that life was too short to be held back by a "low achiever." Stirling had nodded in agreement, wondering to himself how Mr Greening was faring since being released from his wife's high expectations. A happier man, probably.

Greening worked as a freelance contractor in media marketing which gave her the freedom to travel extensively, so far as time and funds allowed, and had just returned from walking with friends in the Lake District. She was delighted when Stirling described his own favourite mountain walks there and the shared interest softened her demeanour a little.

She had learnt of Pemberton's death from the neighbour looking after her cat who had been keen to break the news. Stirling was surprised at Greening's apparent lack of concern that a close neighbour had been brutally killed, but waited to see what she had to say first.

In her mid-thirties, Greening was a sturdily built woman with dark hair cut ruthlessly short. When Stirling showed an interest in her travels, Greening became quite animated, her hands gesticulating decisively when emphasising a point, or when giving an opinion on something. When he spoke, she listened attentively whilst perching on the edge of the seat, hands pressed tightly between her thighs and frowning with concentration to follow his lips in case she might miss a syllable.

As they talked, Stirling surveyed the room discreetly. On the lounge walls and the surfaces of Scandinavian self-assembly furniture were many photographs, all testifying to the range of Greening's travels. In many of them, she frowned earnestly at the camera in front of familiar landmarks around the world, but with the appearance of authenticating her attendance rather than capturing any perceivable pleasure of the moment. She often seemed to be alone and where she was in company, it was with a disparate looking collection of individuals, possibly gathered together from a nearby hostel.

Although determined to fill her life with experiences, there was a driven urgency about Greening's nature and Stirling sensed a woman who was unhappy with the hand life had dealt her. He thought that living with her would be a restless experience, but liked her clear-eyed forthrightness.

Greening had moved into the ground floor apartment nine years ago, after separating from her "useless husband" and had got to know Pemberton only a little as they crossed paths in the hallway. She knew he lived alone but had never visited his apartment. Had Pemberton ever been in here? "Not likely!" she replied, emphatically.

She worked from home a couple of days each week, often on a laptop at a table set in the bay window for the natural light and from where she could see the comings and goings around the square. Greening had become accustomed to seeing women arriving and leaving with Pemberton, usually just for a few hours during the daytime, sometimes staying overnight. Some had come and gone alone and had tended to avoid speaking if she met them in the entrance. They were usually attractive women, well dressed with nice hair. As she said this, Greening had unconsciously put a hand to her own bandsaw cut fringe. Those that had spoken "sounded posh." None of it was any of her business, but she thought Pemberton was a "snake."

Although away for several weeks of the year, Greening had noticed that over the last couple of years Pemberton was at home more and when she saw him, he seemed diminished somehow. She paused as she searched for the word, " ... lost his mojo. He didn't seem to have the same confidence about him. He'd go unshaven for days!" Clearly, a sin.

Stirling nodded his understanding, thinking Mrs Greening would be highly attuned to any man without the requisite degree of "mojo." Greening confirmed what he already knew about the Jaguar car, but she had no idea where it was kept during the winter.

'So, overall, a good neighbour? No concerns?' Stirling asked.

Greening's mouth set more firmly as her gaze shifted around the room before returning to look at him. She appeared to want to say something but was uncertain. Greening replaced her hands between her thighs as she chewed her bottom lip in concentration.

Stirling asked smoothly, 'May I call you Frances? Thank you. Any information you have will be treated discreetly, Frances. Even small details can have a significant bearing on a murder enquiry.' He sat back in his chair comfortably to indicate he was in no hurry to leave, leaving the silence to press down on her conscience.

'Well, it could be very noisy up there, if you understand me, Chief Inspector?'

Affecting incomprehension, he replied, 'I'm not sure I do, Frances?'

Greening drew a deep breath and launched herself into it. 'These old buildings don't have any insulation between the floors like modern homes do and my bedroom is right below his. When he had women visiting there was often a lot of ... *noise* ... above my bedroom and it was quite clearly, well, you know ...'

Greening tilted forward on her seat, looking at him with a pained expression, silently imploring his understanding to avoid having to say it. Stirling frowned and shook his head vaguely.

Greening's voice rose in exasperation at his apparent stupidity. 'Shagging! Fucking! Whatever you want to call it! But if that wasn't bad enough there were a lot of other noises, besides. Slapping noises, spanking, whatever that kind of people do to each other! And the noises the women made ... well, it was disgusting!' Greening's face twisted with distaste at the memory and she squirmed awkwardly with the embarrassment of discussing it.

With an expression of concerned surprise, Stirling answered, 'Oh! I'm sorry Frances, I understand what you mean now. So, did this happen every time a woman visited, the slapping noises?'

'No. Sometimes it was quiet up there and I just heard music or talking. If the same woman came in and I knew what to expect, I found a reason to go out for a few hours, but I couldn't always if I had a deadline to meet, so I'd turn my music up. It wasn't nice, listening to that sort of thing, but if they were coming back for more, what business was it of mine? It was far too embarrassing to complain about to him and he knew I could hear it all. He'd have a smug look on his face if we passed each other soon after one of his "sessions". He didn't care and seemed to enjoy my embarrassment.'

'You had no reason to be concerned for the safety of the women?'

Pulling her mouth about in thought, Greening shook her head. 'Never. Whenever I saw them with him he was very attentive, opening the car door, quite the gentleman really. They seemed happy enough in his company.'

'And when did you last see any women visiting him, Frances?'

'There were a lot of women in the years after I moved in, but they got less and none that I've seen for a year or more. But I've been away a lot over the last year for several weeks at a time. The benefits of self-employment,' she added smugly.

Apart from his female callers, the only thing of interest Greening could think of was a disturbance about two years before when a man had come into the building twice and had banged on Pemberton's door for a long time shouting aggressively, using "terrible language" and something to do with money. She'd called the police the second time because she was frightened, but he left before they arrived. Greening couldn't give a description because it was dark, and she'd only seen his back as he walked off down the path. The man drove off in a pickup truck and was heavily built.

As they shook hands at the open door, Stirling felt something rubbing against his leg. Looking down, he saw a grey tom cat staring up at him with bleak yellow eyes as it twined itself between his legs, mewing for attention.

'There you are, you wastrel!' exclaimed Greening. 'I was wondering where you'd got to.' Bending down, she scooped the cat up into her arms and with a curt goodnight to Stirling, closed the door leaving him staring at the door number.

9.17 p.m.

Sitting in the car outside, Stirling contemplated what to do next. There seemed little point in returning to the MCU. He called Edwards and told him about the conversation with Greening, arranging for an officer to visit her the following day. Edwards mentioned Pemberton's cousin had called to say she had a photo of him from the wedding, which reminded Stirling of the photograph in Pemberton's study.

Describing it to Edwards, he said, 'It's probably irrelevant Bill but check with the search team and see if anyone remembers if it was stored that way prior to the search, or if someone put it there?'

'Okay. Nothing locally so far with the drugs angle so our people have pushed it up to the National Crime Agency to see what they might have.'

Stirling ended the call and checked the time. Ayesha would be awake and was only a mile away. He looked down at the envelope on the passenger seat and read the sender's address again. At the thought of talking with Ayesha and the possible pleasure of her warm body against his, Stirling pushed aside his concern. Telling himself he was being too cautious, he scrolled through his contacts for her number. Finding the number, he was about to push the button when professional integrity nagged again at his conscience. What if? He couldn't side step the possibility of professional compromise and didn't he have enough problems already? If he had any doubt at all, he should stay away.

After some moments thought, he sighed with regret and sent a text explaining he was busy and drove home.

*

Stirling did not see the woman standing deep in the shadows of a garden nearby. She had been walking towards the building when she spotted Stirling opening the porch door. Ducking through a gateway, she watched from the shadows as he talked on his phone, desperate to run away but too frightened to move in case he saw her. Anxiously, she waited until the car started and crouched low as he drove past the garden and out of the square.

After waiting a few minutes to be sure he was not returning, the woman stepped out onto the footpath and after glancing around the square, walked to the building. At the gateway, she gave another long look down the square and up at the windows of the building, then stepped on to the grass to muffle her footsteps. Pulling some keys from her pocket, she selected one and inserted it into the external porch door. The worn key turned easily.

Stepping into the hallway, she stood perfectly still to listen before moving stealthily up the stairs, hugging the wall to avoid flexing the old stair treads and remembering to step over the tread that had always creaked.

Ignoring the police notice forbidding entry, she was about to slip her key into the lock when she realised with a shock it had been changed. Dizzy from shallow breathing, she brought a hand to her mouth and bit it hard to stifle a cry of fear and frustration. Fleetingly, she thought of trying to force it open but knew it was too strong, and the sign said it was alarmed.

Feeling hot tears of frustration on her cheeks, she felt another wave of dizziness and nausea. Leaning against the wall, she forced herself to breath regularly and then froze as a door opened below. Pressing herself harder still into the wall to be out of sight to anyone who might glance up, she looked about frantically for a means of escape, but knew the only way out was down the stairs. Had the policeman returned?

Someone walked across the hallway below into the porch. The slap of a letterbox closing, slippers scuffing across the carpet, a woman's voice speaking firmly to a cat, a door slammed shut to cut the voice off mid-sentence. Seconds later, music filtered through the building and pans clattered.

Taking care to remember the creaking tread, she moved lightly down the edge of the staircase, sliding her shoulders against the wall for balance and hurried out of the building. Turning left out of the gate, she walked quickly towards Barbourne stopping only to retch violently into the gutter.

CR 80

Day 5: Friday - 7.32 a.m.

Edwards stopped abruptly as he saw Stirling at his desk, reading a document on the screen, the "Out" tray piled high and the "In" tray almost empty.

'Hell, Doug. Have you been home?' he asked.

Stirling ignored the question. 'I came in early to clear the backlog.' He held out an action sheet stapled to a clutch of papers. 'I found this waiting for me.'

Taking the papers from him, Edwards thought Stirling looked tired and wondered how early, "early" had been. Turning the pages over he saw a collection of papers which included a Land Registry document detailing the history of title transfers of the land where Pemberton's body had been found. Putting down the battered, tan coloured briefcase he had carried since he was a young detective, Edwards slouched into the chair.

Tapping a page, he said, 'So, Fairway Development Ltd., the company Pemberton was a shareholder in, bought the land from a local company ...' he squinted to read the small print without his glasses, '... Martin Estates Ltd., five years ago, and Martin's owned it for some twenty years before that.'

'Before Martin's bought the land, it was part of the local manor estate which was broken up to pay death duties. And before then, I expect it was let to generations of tenant farmers paying their dues to the estate.'

Looking back to the papers Edwards put his finger on a line. 'There's a reference here to James and James Solicitors in Worcester who handled the purchase from Martins to Fairway. I'll raise an action to see what they can tell us about the people behind the Fairway scheme.'

Stirling described the empty envelopes he had seen in the apartment the previous evening.

'But is Martin Estates relevant?' asked Edwards, still reading through the pages.

'Probably not, but feed it into Croft.'

Edwards looked up from the papers, curious when Stirling walked over to close the office door and went back to stand behind his desk and leant on the window ledge. Stirling looked uncomfortable.

'I need to take you into my confidence Bill and declare an interest in James and James solicitors. I leave it to your judgement what you tell Geordie, if you need to, but I don't want this in the system unless it becomes absolutely necessary.'

Edwards waited, expressionless, unsure what was coming.

'I have a friend who's worked at James's for about four years. I need you to keep a close eye on our enquiries there so that I don't compromise anything.'

'A *friend*?' asked Edwards. Stirling was notoriously private, but he needed more information.

Taking a piece of paper from a pocket, Stirling handed it to Edwards who unfolded it, read the name and looked back at Stirling, waiting for a fuller explanation.

Uncomfortable at having to discuss his private life, Stirling explained, 'A *very* good friend, Bill. For a few weeks now, someone I like very much. I think it highly improbable but, if there's the *slightest* possibility she's part of anything dodgy, I'll need to know so I can step away from the investigation. Meanwhile, I'll keep away from her until we know more.'

Handing the note back, Edwards knew Stirling would have wrestled with the decision overnight and now understood the early start. 'Okay. I'll speak to Croft and meet you later.'

Alone again, Stirling turned to lean on the window ledge and stared down into the yard where team members were beginning to arrive, running for cover from another heavy shower.

He wondered if there had been any dishonesty in the solicitors' dealings with Fairway and of any possible implications for Ayesha. He couldn't believe she would knowingly involve herself in dishonesty, but could she have been drawn into something unwittingly?

11.03 a.m.

It had been easier for Edwards and Stirling to travel to meet Croft in the CID building at HQ, a long Cotswold stone coloured building that accommodated many of the specialist investigative teams, including the ECU. They sat around Croft's desk as he took them through documents and registers he had accessed through the professional services the ECU subscribed to.

As Croft explained some technical details to Edwards, Stirling's gaze wandered out of the window to the line of high trees bounding the far car park. The last time he had stood looking at them was when he took the call from Inspector James, asking him to attend the bridge. The trees were stark then, black against a dull sky and bending under the weight of the incoming storm. Now, almost in full leaf, they swayed gently under a south westerly breeze that was bringing high white clouds up from the Atlantic. Above the tree tops, the resident colony of crows dipped and wheeled above their rebuilt nests, complaining loudly at their neighbours. A buzzard hovered above the nests looking for easy pickings until it was mobbed by three crows and glided away. Stirling tried to remember if it was a "horde" or a "murder" of crows. Murder seemed appropriate.

Croft's glasses reflected the light as he looked at them across the table. 'Fairway was a shell company to shield the main shareholders from public view. Not uncommon, I should say. The share certificate recovered from Pemberton's place represents his shareholding, far beyond his means to absorb the loss of. But, there was much more money invested.

'From what we can discern, which is still incomplete, other money came through a complex mix of individuals. All offshore, the Isle of Man, the Channel Islands and further afield. It's going to take a while to unwind and there'll need to be a very good argument for me to stop other work to do this.'

Croft looked across to Stirling, his sharp blue eyes enhanced through the rimless glasses. Stirling knew the ECU was under pressure from Chief Officers to trace and confiscate the assets of career criminals. But he needed Croft's help.

Seeing no immediate answer forthcoming, Croft continued. 'Fairway, as a company entity, secured a sizeable loan for the development at The Wern.'

'Sizeable?' asked Edwards.

'About twenty million,' Croft answered unemotionally. Big numbers were the ECU's bread and butter.

Shocked by the figure, Edwards swore. 'But I thought money was put in by individual shareholders?'

'And so it was, which would have paid for initial development costs, professional fees and the like, but the company entity borrowed in its own name. My guess is the loan was predicated on a projected valuation of the development, once completed. This was not a traditional, plot by plot, freehold housing development but an extensive complex with a range of shared amenities and facilities with high annual service charges and, most importantly, with the leasehold retained by the company. That would have made it extremely valuable. Whether it was worth that value though, I can't say.'

Stirling wondered again how planning permissions could have been gained for such a development in a rural location. It probably hadn't. Perhaps the "loss leader" had been to show a site apparently under development, to draw in and persuade prospective investors. Public officials were often slow to react to public concern and with the site so far from view, how long would it have been before any planning officers had got to hear about it?

Stirling looked at Croft. 'The fraudsters used a sprat to catch a mackerel.'

Croft smiled humourlessly at Stirling. 'I think you've got it sir. I strongly suspect there's been a significant fraud based on a grossly inflated valuation. After the global recession and the sub-prime loan scandals in the States, things are much more difficult for criminals. But, mortgage fraud is still possible with insider knowledge and, most importantly, what we describe as "enabling agents". Bent solicitors, architects, surveyors and the like who collude to ease the paperwork through the usual system of checks and balances.'

Croft paused to allow the information to sink in. 'We've got a couple of cases on the anvil with the Economic Crime Directorate at the City of London Police, and the Serious Fraud Office. There might be some overlap with this case.'

Stirling remembered a colleague from years back who now worked in the ECD at the City of London Police, CoLP to its friends. Based in discreet offices near Bishopsgate, close to the heartbeat of the UK's financial services sector, CoLP held "lead force" status for UK policing's response to economic crime and fraud. With the exponential growth in fraud, much of it enabled by the internet and based safely offshore, CoLP had developed a large team of specialists to help combat the drain on the national economy through fraud. Almost two hundred billion a year at the last count, and rising.

'So, where's the money gone?' asked Edwards, slightly puzzled.

'I can't tell you at present, but there's a name here that features in the cases we've sent to CoLP and the SFO. He's a senior partner at a firm in Worcester, James and James, they're near to the cathedral.'

Stirling mentioned the envelopes in Pemberton's study, feeling Edwards's eyes on him.

Croft nodded. 'They're a long-established practice in the city which has expanded over the last decade, broadening its range of services and taking a lot of work away from the smaller firms, some of which they've absorbed into the practice. Consequently, they're not well liked amongst the local lawyers. The person we're interested in is a senior partner named Elias Parry, Percy to his pals. He may have had more going on than we were aware of and his lifestyle would certainly suggest that. He drives a Bentley convertible and lives in a swank house outside the city.'

Edwards broke in. 'If Pemberton swindled money from professional fraudsters, usually OCG's themselves, then it might be motive enough for someone to kill him.'

Croft continued. 'Large amounts of money left Pemberton's account to Fairway when the company was in formation but, on the face of it, he appears to have lost it all. Unless you can find another account in his name, or under his control, they're not necessarily one and the same, signposting us to something off shore, he seems to have been broke. He doesn't appear to have been living the high life. Personally? I think Pemberton was duped into the scheme, but others might not have seen it that way if he'd drawn them into the project.'

Stirling sat back, fingers steepled in front of his mouth as he considered the complexities of this leg of the investigation. It needed to be pursued but he was concerned at the resources it would consume.

'Pemberton was living modestly in recent years,' Stirling said, thoughtfully, 'which is not to say he didn't swindle the money and was double-crossed by someone else. Or perhaps he took the money and lost control of it, or couldn't access it. You're sure your people didn't miss anything during the evidence search?'

Croft prickled and looked Stirling steadily in the eye, feeling the competence of his team was in question. Replying firmly, he said,

'Sir, between the evidence search and our research here, we've not missed anything. But, we *are* still waiting for the results of the search of his computer.'

It was a polite rebuke and seeing Croft's irritation, Edwards intervened. 'Anything they've got will be passed directly to you.'

The meeting was wrapping up when Croft held out a buff coloured folder. 'You asked me to research Martin Estates, sir?'

Thumbing the pages of the file, Stirling asked, 'Anything in here relevant to the murder d'you think.'

'I couldn't say, sir. It's your investigation.' Croft was still smarting from the inference his team could have been less than thorough. 'A local property company which operated for some twenty years before being wound up soon after the land sale to Fairway, together with the disposal of all of its other assets. All submissions to Companies House appear to be in order.'

Thanking Croft for his work they stepped out of the meeting room. Once the door had closed, Stirling turned to Edwards with a twinkle in his eye. 'He got a bit prickly at the end. Was it something I said?'

Edwards looked at Stirling and shook his head.

'Go down to HTCU Bill and put a flea in someone's ear please. We need to know if there's anything on Pemberton's computer, or not. I'll wait in the car.'

As Stirling walked under the photographs lining the walls of the stairwell, he was acutely aware of the searching gaze of every Detective Chief Superintendent of the last fifty years on his back.

Enjoying the warm sunshine and with classical music playing quietly on the radio, Stirling sat in his car reading through the file Croft had given him.

Martin Estates had been a significant property holding company with land and commercial assets around the region and further afield, London included. The sale of The Wern had realised one and a half million pounds, give or take a few thousand. Tracking the company's value, year on year, all of its assets had been steadily disposed of until being fully wound up five years ago.

Drumming his fingers on the steering wheel, wondering what was keeping Edwards, Stirling was curious why the holdings had been disposed of. Over the long term, property and land rarely lost its value and, meanwhile, there were leases to be traded and rents to be collected. Stirling looked for the names of the company directors, finding one only, a Katrina Martin with a private address near Pershore. The company's registered address had been in Sansome Walk, close to the city centre where many of the city's accountancy practices were based.

Stirling's mobile began to ring. It was Edwards.

'Doug, come up to the HTCU. You need to see this.'

11.55 a.m.

Bound at the ankles and with each wrist tied to the chair's ladder-back, the woman sat looking sightlessly towards the camera, a black cloth blindfold masking her eyes and her mouth gagged tightly with a thin band of material. Sitting naked on the rattan seat, her knees twisted to one side, she might have been trying to shield herself from the camera's cold eye.

Stirling estimated the woman to be in her late twenties with a supple body and no excess weight. A tight lower belly and small, firm breasts inferred she had not yet borne a child. The next image on the screen showed the same woman with her head cast down to one side in an attitude of submission. It was impossible to know if it reflected the woman's emotional state, or a pose struck for the benefit of whoever had been behind the camera.

Stirling had joined Edwards in the HTCU's cramped office where they were squeezed around one of three desks in a room designed for two people. On the walls were racks of shelves on which sat seized computers and hard drives in polythene evidence bags, all bearing exhibit labels. At another desk sat a woman engrossed in reviewing child pornography, categorising the content according to legal designations of unlawfulness. And awfulness. Not for the first time did Stirling wonder how they could do this work, day in, day out, and many of them with children of their own. Nothing would ever erase what they were required to look at and some suffered "burn out" after two or three years, sometimes sooner.

Not all of them coped though. The HTCU had briefly been under Stirling's command some years ago when an officer had suffered a nervous breakdown. Whilst reviewing child pornography he had seen terrible images of a female child with features strikingly similar to his daughter, of a similar age. Once he had made the emotional connection, transposing the images of abuse and cruelty to his daughter, it had left him unable to hold his daughter.

Returning his thoughts to the screen, Stirling studied the background in the images, trying to work out if they were taken in Pemberton's home. His thoughts were interrupted by the unit's Detective Sergeant, Dan Billing, an energetic officer who Stirling had worked with before and liked for his energy and professionalism.

'I'm sorry it's taken longer than we would have liked, but some of the files are protected by encryption software which took a while to penetrate. We couldn't start until yesterday because of an FBI case we're assisting with.'

Knowing Billing's enthusiasm would be less succinct than Stirling needed, Edwards summarised the key points.

'Dan's told me that there's been some occasional deletions of the browsing history, but we've recovered a lot of it from the hard drive. Business wise, there are technical drawings and files relating to correspondence with planning departments and the like. We'll get all that put into the HOLMES system in due course and cross-matched to whatever we already have. There's a consistent browsing history of websites and blogs relating to sado-masochism and BDSM. Nothing yet on dating websites, but there's more research to be done. Buried in a sub-file was this cache of photographs, almost all in black and white with a few in colour, which might relate to some of the women Helen's interviewing.'

Pointing at a photograph Stirling commented, 'I'm sure that's Pemberton's lounge, Bill.'

Bending in to examine the picture closely, Edwards replied guardedly, 'Possibly.' He had too much experience to make assessments without checking first.

'The use of black and white is a bit dated, don't you think?' suggested Billing.

Edwards gave a shrug, 'Artistic preference, perhaps. Not that I'd call that art!'

They spent the next few minutes scrolling through images that had been taken over many years, counting over twenty women dating across as many years, with further analysis of the hard drive to be done. The women were either naked or wearing items of underwear, stockings, bodices and suspenders featuring prominently. There was nothing to help date the photos other than the changing hair styles in the pictures.

Pointing to an image of a woman naked and bound by her wrists to the head of what was unmistakeably Pemberton's bed, Stirling asked, 'How many years since you saw a woman with that hair style, Bill?' Billing was too young to include in the question.

Edwards studied the woman. 'Ten, fifteen years, possibly longer?'

Billing cut in, 'They're all scans of original wet film prints, so the digital date stamp is of no use to us in dating them accurately.'

Billing fiddled with the mouse to reveal the content data of the pictures, all created digitally five years before. Stirling wondered why Pemberton had decided to digitise his archive of photos. Would someone who had kept images like these, together with whatever nostalgic value he placed on them, have destroyed the originals? Unlikely, he thought. Could they have had some commercial value?

Billing continued, 'Some were taken more recently, in the last five years. See?' Billing scrolled rapidly until he found the picture he wanted. 'Many of the older ones are a bit grainy, being a scanned copy of an old photo, but some were taken in recent years with a digital camera although, not an expensive one. Consequently, the resolution is better.'

Absorbed in the technical aspects of the images, Billing's professional interest was dulling his sensitivity to the women's humiliation. But he saw worse each day. As Edwards discussed some evidential process with Billing, Stirling scrolled though the images on the screen, curious as to whether they had all submitted willingly. It was hard to know. One image in colour was of a woman in her early thirties with fair, short bobbed hair, sat naked on the same chair and in a pose similar to the first black and white picture he had seen. Her hands were bound behind the seat back and each ankle and leg had been tied tightly to the chair so that her legs were forced open to expose her vagina. A thin leather strap drawn tightly across her nipples and around the rear of the chair cut deep into the flesh of her breasts. Over the black gag in her mouth, the woman's eyes blazed furiously at the camera, her cheeks damp with tears. Partially visible at the rear of her thigh and buttock were fresh weal marks where she had been struck with something thin. Stirling thought of the riding crop in the suitcase.

'She doesn't look happy,' Edwards remarked quietly.

'Perhaps the camera wasn't supposed to be part of the deal.'

'Perhaps pain and degradation wasn't part of the deal either!' Edwards said bluntly.

Stirling turned to Edwards. 'Most of these women are probably still alive, Bill. We should try and trace as many as we can. Respecting their privacy and dignity will be tricky.'

Edwards frowned. 'To what purpose, we've got enough on our plate already, haven't we?'

Staring down at the screen, Stirling answered, 'One, to eliminate them as suspects from our investigation and two, to be sure they survived. The more we learn about Pemberton, the more concerned I am for the women he knew.'

Stirling looked at Billing. 'Dan, I'll need an evidence file in due course but for now, I just need a working file.' He explained the enquiries Helen had started. 'We'll limit their embarrassment as far as we can so create a file with a cropped image of their face, where it's available, with any explicit images collated behind. We can rely on Helen's discretion as to what she reveals to the women, if we locate them.'

Edwards told Billing about the meeting with Croft, describing what the ECU needed. They were about to leave the room when Stirling turned back to the screen.

'Dan, put up the images of the women in his car please.'

A number of the pictures had been taken of women in various poses inside and across Pemberton's Jaguar, most of them in a countryside setting. Stirling scrolled through the images until he stopped at one with a woman lying in the boot of the Jaguar. Naked, her hands and feet bound, she looked terrified as she peered up from the well of the boot, her eyes squinting, possibly against the light. But there was no mistaking her fear as she reached her hands up pleadingly towards the camera, her mouth frozen in movement. She had been speaking when the picture was taken. Under her, a wide, dark stain had spread across the carpeting.

Behind him, Edwards muttered, 'I hope she survived that.'

Resting his fists on the desk, Stirling studied the fear in the young woman's face. Looking at Billing, he said, 'Get the proofs over to us quickly.'

12.35 p.m.
They walked back to the car deep in thought. Edwards was the first to speak as they fastened their seat belts.

'What makes a woman let herself be subjected to that kind of treatment? It can't be love. Can it?' He sounded both angry and sad.

Stirling was surprised at the question. 'Come on Bill, you're not naive. We see the very worst of human behaviour, their weakness, their cruelty. Some people just enjoy hurting others and, strangely, some like being hurt. Or if not hurt, then the psychology of the sub' and dom' game playing.'

Reflecting on the images, Stirling asked, 'Did you notice that in many of the images there were no apparent signs of injury, particularly the older ones? The poses were voyeuristic, as if he was spying on them, watching. They might have been the prelude to something more physical taking place and some were marked from being slapped or whipped. Think of the stuff we seized from his apartment. I might be wrong, but I think Pemberton was essentially a voyeur to begin with and his tastes developed into something more sadistic. Perhaps his exploitative nature developed into a contempt for women in general?'

'Frances Greening described noises consistent with that.' Edwards added.

'Yes. If sex is involved, which is usually the case, and consensual, there's a power play in relationships like that by at least one of those involved, if not both. Giving, controlling and withholding. If Pemberton had a naturally cruel streak, moving from fantasy to experimentation would have been a short step. Did things get out of control as he became more abusive?'

'Well, I never met any women like that, and it's no way to treat a woman either!' replied Edwards huffily.

Stirling laughed softly, putting a hand on his friend's shoulder. 'Bill, you've been a one-woman man, all your life! If it was consensual then, with certain exceptions, it's not a crime.'

'But *was* it consensual? Some of them look frightened, Doug, even allowing for the pain.' Edwards was genuinely affronted on the women's behalf.

Stirling thought back to the images. He was right. 'Pemberton was a skilful and charming manipulator, Bill.'

'A bloody scoundrel, more like!' Edwards blurted out heatedly.

It was a side to his colleague's personality Stirling had not seen for a while. Edwards was very traditional in his views of how to treat a woman, and unforgiving of those who dealt with them poorly.

'I agree, but if we apply professional experience, we could imagine some women, bored in their relationships, being flattered by Pemberton's seduction. Excited by something a bit different from a dutiful and unsatisfying conjugal fumble each weekend. But, I *am* concerned about whether any of them came to serious harm, or worse. Either by misadventure or through a loss of self-control on Pemberton's part, or simply sadistic intent. Which is another possible motive for his murder. Have any females who Pemberton was associated with been missing for a long time? Pull the force's misper records for the last twenty years and see if we've got any women missing who could have been associated with him.'

Stirling paused. 'It puts a new emphasis on Helen's enquiries in tracing as many of those women as we can, if only to be sure they're alive and well. If we can't, we might have something much more complex on our hands.'

Edwards was inspecting the far end of the car park as he considered the new hypothesis. 'Because it wasn't complex enough already, was it!' he muttered, gloomily.

Stirling smiled at the fatalistic sarcasm and pressed the auto start.

1.16 p.m.

Carrying food bought hastily from a service station on the way, Stirling and Edwards entered the incident room to see Geordie Heal look up and express relief at their return. Under pressure because information from the enquiry teams was arriving faster

264

than the room could keep pace with, Heal was filtering everything as it arrived to make sure anything important was seen sooner, rather than later.

Rummaging amongst a pile of papers, he pulled out an enlarged photograph and handed it to Stirling.

'Pemberton's cousin, who did the ID yesterday? She's emailed a picture of him taken at the wedding a few months back. It's not the best photo but better than anything we had before,' Heal waiting as the two SIOs stood together studying it.

The original snapshot had not been the best quality to start with, and enlargement had diffused the pixilation. Sitting in an armchair, his arm draped casually over the side, Pemberton smiled up to the camera looking slightly surprised, as if he had turned at his name being called. Clean shaven with a strong chin, Stirling saw a man in his late fifties who was ageing well with blonde hair which had greyed significantly, combed back to sit on the collar. Even in a photograph there was a tangible arrogance about Pemberton. The flash from the camera had reddened his eyes, giving him a sinister appearance.

Searching the image for detail, Stirling recognised the shirt from Pemberton's wardrobe, cufflinks he had seen on the mantelpiece and a signet ring with an engraved black stone on the small finger of Pemberton's left hand. The design of the signet ring was obscured by the angle of Pemberton's hand so that only an outer edge was visible. A pair of stockinged legs next to Pemberton suggested he had been accompanied by a female.

'Geordie, find out who the legs belong to. She might be of interest to us. And check if that ring was amongst his personal effects. I don't remember it, do you Bill?'

Edwards shook his head. 'I'd have to check the crime scene pics.'

'Anything else Geordie?' asked Stirling.

Heal's eyes flitted left and right, indicating the people about them. 'Can we go through to your office?'

Sat in Stirling's office with the door closed, Heal rattled through a series of updates as Stirling and Edwards munched on sandwiches past their sell by date, but too hungry to throw them away. So far, none of Heal's updates appeared to have been worth removing themselves from the hearing of others.

The psychological profile report had been emailed through that morning. Holding a copy of the report in front of him, Geordie paraphrased the summary: "... the injuries might have been inspired by revenge ... or a ritualised but unstructured satanic killing with a belief that the eyes retain the last image they see, i.e. the identity of their killer ... or a criminally motivated killing using extreme violence as a warning to others."

Through a mouthful of cheese and pickle, Edwards responded scornfully, 'Bloody hell! We'll be charged a thousand quid for that bollocks, only to tell us what we've worked out for ourselves.'

Stirling said nothing. It was a necessary box ticked in the process. If nothing else, it confirmed their own assessment and might prevent a sharp defence lawyer from striping them in court if they hadn't covered it. And it might yet prove useful, *if* he found the killer.

Heal smirked in sympathy before continuing, 'Helen called me. They've spoken with two more women and although they were reluctant to speak, she's gained their confidence and they're giving her some useful info. They've got names for twelve or more women who the witnesses either know for a fact, or had heard gossip about being associated with Pemberton in the past. One name has cropped up three times though. Does the name Katrina Martin ring a bell with either of you?'

Stirling frowned, 'Yes, she was the sole director of Martin Estates, the company that sold The Wern to Fairway.' Turning to Edwards he explained. 'The file Croft gave me? I was reading it when you called me up to the HTCU.'

Unconcerned, Edwards looked at Heal. 'I'm still not sure why you needed to bring us in here, Geordie?'

'The last of the telephone subscriber info came in this morning. The call to Pemberton the night before he died came from Martin's mobile phone.' Heal watched them as the information sank in.

Edwards spoke first. 'Have I got this right? Katrina Martin, said to have been a former lover of Pemberton, who sold The Wern to Fairway which Pemberton had a shareholding in, called him the evening before he died?'

'Well, a call was made to his mobile, from her mobile phone. Shall I get Helen to go and see her?' asked Heal.

Stirling wondered if they had seen Katrina Martin amongst the photographs that morning. Both men were waiting for Stirling's decision. Aware of the heavy silence in the room he looked at them. 'I'd like to give that some thought. I'll let you know.'

Heal and Edwards left. Stirling stood up to stretch off his muscles, his shoulders and back tight from sitting around too much. The innate detective in him wanted to confront Katrina Martin himself. But, if she proved to be a suspect, he needed to justify the decision against delegating the interview to an experienced, operational detective. He accepted the view that interview skills are perishable and, as senior officers become increasingly desk bound, they lost their edge in interview technique. But old habits die hard. Stirling still trusted his skills and instincts and enjoyed the intellectual challenge in interviewing wily characters.

Staring down into the car park, the solution presented itself as Stirling watched a car drive in and Helen Williams got out with her young partner. Watching them walk towards the building, he realised he could compromise.

3.06 p.m.

Looking at the large houses, Helen said cynically 'Life's a struggle down here then, I see?'

They were travelling slowly along the curving road of the private estate as they searched for Martin's home. None of the large executive homes had numbers, only names at the end of long, screened driveways.

Edwards had expressed concern when told of his plan, but Stirling had assured him it would be okay and anyway, it was only for the one job. Helen's partner was set to work making telephone enquiries with the remaining women they had names for and they had set off in Stirling's car.

Helen was as surprised as Edwards. The atmosphere in the car had been awkward to begin with but as they discussed her enquiries with the women, the mood had relaxed as professional interest took over. Each of the women she had met so far had got to know Pemberton ten or more years ago through social circles, flattered by his charm and aware of his reputation as a lover. One had been in a suffocating marriage and had enjoyed the distraction with no regrets to this day. She had enjoyed the excitement and the sex was so different to anything she had previously experienced it had, she said, "been an awakening".

Another had been engaged to a man who was going places but once her fling with Pemberton was discovered, the engagement had foundered. She was still bitter. A subsequent marriage on the rebound was a disaster and she knew she had lost her chance of happiness for the sake of a one-sided, coercive relationship which Pemberton had ended as soon as things got difficult. Both women knew he had taken photographs but at the time were so besotted with him, they hadn't objected. Neither of them had seen the photos, hoping they would never see the light of day. Helen would revisit them if any of the photographs resembled a younger version of the women.

Stirling asked if the sex and bondage had been consensual.

Helen answered, 'Completely! They got a lot of excitement out of it, at the time. Understandably, they're embarrassed talking about it now.'

Over the intervening years they had seen Pemberton infrequently at social events, but the women had kept their distance. He was often in the company of a woman and, if alone, the conclusion usually drawn was that he was seeing someone who could not be seen out with him.

Helen pointed ahead. 'It's the one at the furthest end set back from the others, next to the fields.'

Heavily screened by mature landscaping and a line of evergreen trees, the house was barely visible from the service road. As they turned into the drive behind the trees, a large house came fully into view. What took Stirling's eye was the quality of its design, a simplicity of style that understated its scale. He couldn't fix a precise decade on it by brick type, or architectural trend, the usual characteristics which defined a building. At its centre was a wide, recessed porch entrance with an oak door and windows either side to allow a view out, and light in. Above the porch, slightly offset, a large window gave a glimpse of stairs up to an open landing. Five to six bedrooms, he guessed.

Two cars were parked to one side of the porch. Nearest to the door, a silver Mercedes sports saloon less than a year old which he anticipated would belong to the house. Next to it, a shabby red, VW Polo, ten years old.

Parking on the far side of the porch, they got out and walked to the door. Helen reached for the heavy door knocker but changed her mind when she noticed a door bell button and pushed it.

Turning to Stirling, she said, 'Just in case the back of the house is in the next county!'

Stirling smiled at the acidic humour. It took two more long pushes on the door bell before the door flew open and a woman rushed out, barging between them with her head down, sobbing as she half ran to the red VW. Turning from the woman's departing back, wondering what they had stumbled into, Stirling looked through the open door.

Halfway up a wide, curling flight of stairs a woman stood, half turned towards them, looking down at Stirling intensely with her hand resting on the handrail, one foot on the tread above the other.

Stirling could not be sure if she was going up or coming down the stairs.

Behind him, a car door slammed and an engine started. Turning to the noise, he watched the VW lurch forward, front wheels spinning until they found traction and speed forward to slew round the line of trees and disappear from view. Beyond the trees, he could hear the car straining through its gears as it accelerated towards the main road half a mile away.

Stirling and Helen looked at each other across the space where the woman had pushed them aside. Under her breath, Helen said, 'I've got the number.'

Looking through the open doorway again, Stirling saw the woman had remained on the stair, motionless, looking down at them coldly with no indication she intended to speak. Unsure of what they had interrupted, Stirling stepped over the threshold into the wide hallway and went to the foot of the stairs. Behind him, Helen's heels on the tiled floor told him she was close by. Stirling was surprised why the woman had not walked down to meet them when he realised he had not explained who they were.

'Mrs Martin?' he asked.

The woman looked at him for some seconds before demanding in an educated voice, 'And you are?'

With the woman above him, Stirling felt at a disadvantage but felt that that might be her intention. 'I'm sorry Mrs Martin. We were caught off guard by ...' he gestured to the door, '... the lady's departure. Did we call at an inconvenient time?'

Looking over his head to the door, she stared for a moment before looking back down at him. 'A friend. We quarrelled and she got upset. You still haven't said who you are.' The voice was cold, challenging.

Holding out his warrant card, Stirling answered, 'Sorry, we've got off to a poor start. I'm Detective Chief Inspector Stirling and this is Detective Constable Helen Williams. We would like a few minutes of your time, please.'

Another silence. 'About *what*, Chief Inspector?' The woman's eyes had not left his and she seemed not to have noticed Helen.

'I'm investigating the murder of Michael Pemberton, Mrs Martin, who I believe you knew. You are Mrs Martin?'

Stirling was not sure what to make of Martin's cold, detached demeanour. Whether it was her usual manner, or she was masking some other emotion as she decided whether to be helpful, he could not tell. Dressed in a cream sweater dress that hugged her figure, the hemline above the knee, Stirling guessed Mrs Martin to be in her early fifties but would easily pass for several years younger. Standing barefoot with her foot still one step above the other, Mrs Martin appeared undecided whether to walk down to meet them, or to turn and flee. The knuckles of her hand were white with pressure as she gripped the handrail.

Martin began to step down to them, drawing her hand slowly down the rail and moving with a practiced elegance as she held Stirling's gaze. Watching her fluid movement, Stirling thought it likely that Martin worked hard at keeping mortality at bay. Reaching the bottom of the stairs, Martin remained on the first tread so that her eyes were almost level with his to look him directly in the eye. Hard, pale blue eyes only reinforced her cold demeanour.

Stirling held Martin's gaze. Fascinated by her intensity, he noticed her jaw muscles clenching and nostrils flare slightly with some primal instinct. At the notch of her throat, a soft pulse beat quickly. Anger, or fear? At the corners of her eyes and ear lobes, despite light make up, fine lines betrayed her age and the faint perioral lines of her upper lip suggested a woman used to disappointment. Or expressing disapproval. Martin had still not acknowledged Helen's presence. Stirling had a feeling he had seen Martin somewhere before but could not think where.

Something shuttered in Martin's eyes and she turned to Helen. 'Do shut the door, will you?'

Stepping past them, Martin headed towards a door at the rear of the hall, calling over her shoulder, 'We'll talk in the kitchen.'

Stirling raised his eyes in a question mark to Helen who scowled at Martin's back and muttered under her breath, 'Bitch!'

An attempt at making small talk was rebuffed, so they waited for Martin to invite them to sit whilst looking appreciatively around a high value kitchen into which Stirling could have fitted his own into three times over, and swallow most of his annual salary. Fitted out in cream and granite work tops set on a black porcelain tiled floor, the room could have graced a celebrity fashion shoot.

To Stirling's practical eye it looked recently fitted and was clinically spotless. Looking at Martin, he thought clinical to be the operative word. He wondered if the woman who had left in a hurry was the cleaner, but Martin had said a "friend". Women like Martin did not confuse friends with their cleaners.

Martin stood with her back to them, leaning her hands on the worktop as she waited for the kettle to boil, her face hidden from view. Watching the tension in her shoulders, Stirling felt an inner conversation was going on and decided to try and break the ice again.

'We should have called ahead, Mrs Martin, but we were already in the area so I decided to call on the off chance of catching you in.'

Helen raised her eyebrows and pulled a face at him that said, "Really?"

Martin turned and pointed at an island unit around which six high stools in chrome and white leather were arranged. 'Take a seat, Mr Stirling. I'll be with you as soon as I've made your coffee.' Without inviting a reply, she returned to preparing the drinks.

With practised habit, Stirling and Helen arranged themselves so that Martin would sit between them and they could work off each other's eye contact. With only the kettle for background noise,

Stirling watched Martin moving about the kitchen with a slow, deliberate grace as she collected mugs and coffee makings. Martin was an attractive woman and there was no doubt in his mind she was aware of her appeal and would use it to her own purpose. The feeling that they had met somewhere before returned to puzzle him. He was certain Martin was not amongst the photographs.

Placing their drinks in front of them, Katrina Martin took the seat they had intended for her opposite Stirling, with Helen to her left. Looking at Stirling, Martin straightened back her shoulders so that her breasts pressed forward through the soft wool dress. At her side, Helen gave Stirling a discreet upward roll of her eyes.

'So, Chief Inspector, why do you think I can help you?' asked Martin.

'I'm leading the investigation into the murder of Michael Pemberton, an architect who was found murdered on land once owned by your company, Martin Estates. I'm hoping you can tell us something about him and how you knew him?'

'I sold the land to a development company, Chief Inspector.'

'Yes, Fairway Development.' Stirling looked at Martin with a faint smile, hoping to project something friendlier than he felt. He wanted her to believe they already had a lot of information to avoid having to draw information out slowly.

Martin stared at him appraisingly. 'My company owned the land for many years, it was agricultural land but the old farm buildings were derelict and not commercially viable. I'm not interested in agricultural land management so I decided to sell it, along with other assets as part of a process of winding up my business. I'd lost interest in the business and wanted to liquidate the assets to invest in something requiring less of my time.'

Martin sat with both hands wrapped around a glass of water, her manicured nails polished to a shine. There were no rings on her fingers to suggest a partner and whatever emotions she had been fighting with, she had overcome and was now calm and composed.

Determined not to be side-lined any longer, Helen asked, 'And Mr Pemberton? Where did he fit into the sale?'

Martin turned towards Helen with a slight frown as if she had forgotten her presence. 'Michael introduced Fairway to me. He was part of it, but I don't know to what extent. He and I had known each other for many years.'

Martin gestured about her, 'He designed this house. He was an outstanding architect which is how I first met him. When we moved up from London we bought this plot and he designed it to our specifications. Over the years, we occasionally saw each other at social functions, but that was the extent of our friendship.'

Martin had directed her answer to Stirling. Helen persisted, 'We, Mrs Martin?'

Martin looked at Helen, puzzled for a moment before answering, 'Oh, my husband and me. We parted company many years ago. Not amicably, sadly. We met in London where we both worked in the financial sector. He was quite a few years older than me and already a wealthy man when we met. I had a good job too, so we were very fortunate, I suppose. We moved up here to start a family and he commuted to London each week but, ...' Martin's eyes drifted over Stirling's shoulder, '... things didn't work out as we'd hoped. He got tired of the commute and didn't take to the slower pace of life up here. Things became difficult, so we parted. He was French, rather volatile and *very* controlling. He went back to Paris and, so far as I know, he's still there. We've not spoken for many years and we don't correspond. It was not a happy marriage.'

'Just for the record, Mrs Martin, can we have his full name please?' asked Stirling.

'Why? What could he possibly have to do with Michael's death? I haven't seen or spoken to him for over fifteen years.'

Smiling pleasantly, he said, 'Procedure, I'm afraid Mrs Martin. Saves us coming back.'

After Helen had noted down Gérard Martin's details, Stirling changed tack. 'What was your involvement with Fairway development?'

'None, whatsoever. I was tidying up my holdings and, quite frankly, I was glad to get rid of the land and the property and thought good luck to them, which they swiftly ran out of.' Martin smiled with cold amusement. 'It was to be some sort of luxury development, overpriced and with high margins anticipated in a rising market, but it went bankrupt. I heard Michael lost a lot of his own money, as did others. I believe the contractor lost his business too.'

'You know Mr Cole then?' Seeing Martin's surprise at Cole's name he added, 'We're talking to a lot of people.'

Stiffening slightly on the bar stool, Martin replied stonily, 'Well, I don't know Mr Cole *socially*, of course, but I used to see him here as he was the main contractor for this development. I had nothing to do with him though. Michael was the project manager and he dealt with the trades people.'

'What was at The Wern before, Mrs Martin?'

Martin's gaze flickered away for a moment. 'Derelict farm buildings. I leased the land to local farmers, but it simply wasn't viable to spend a lot of money on the building and, as I said, I was selling up.'

'What sort of a character was Pemberton? What was he like, to know?' asked Helen.

Looking from Helen to Stirling and back again, Martin hesitated. Something registered in the pale blue eyes and a red flush crept up the back of her neck. Martin raised a hand to stroke at it, pulling her hand down when she noticed Stirling watching.

'He was a charming man, very good looking but with a certain reputation. I believe he had many relationships over the years, but it was none of my business. I was married when I met him so it was of no concern to me, but others used to get very agitated about his many affairs.'

'Affairs with married women?' asked Helen.

'That was the gossip, but it was none of my business. I'm sure he made many enemies over the years through his philandering. Men's egos don't take kindly to other men screwing their wives and partners, do they, Chief Inspector?' She looked at him with a cold stare before returning to Helen with a note of complicity, 'Male pride and vanity, the bane of our lives. And always inclined to blame the woman first!'

Helen would not be drawn, asking flatly, 'Did you have an affair with him?'

Martin stared at Helen. When she answered, the controlled, unemotional voice had hardened. 'Absolutely not!'

She's lying, thought Stirling, and wondered which of them should introduce the photographs. Timing was key. Despite Helen's apparently relaxed demeanour, he knew she was watching Martin like a hawk to see how she would respond to her next question.

'I understand this is a delicate subject, and it happened a long time ago, but how close were you and Mr Pemberton?'

'Pemberton was employed as our architect. I occasionally saw him at social events and that is all!'

The atmosphere around the table had become taut and Stirling was concerned they would lose the conversation. If Martin demanded they leave, the moment would be lost.

Helen put her hand on Martin's arm, a gesture of female empathy and softened her voice. 'A search of Pemberton's apartment has revealed many photographs ... intimate photographs.'

Drawing her arm away, Martin stared at Helen and asked aloofly, 'Really? And what does that have to do with *me*?'

'We're still discovering images. If there are any of you amongst them it would be better to discuss it now, rather than have us return.'

As Martin continued her denials, Stirling interjected. 'This is very sensitive so perhaps I should leave you to discuss it with Helen, privately? I should warn you that we have witness information that you were one of a number of women linked romantically to Pemberton, some years ago. We know he had particular tastes, in the bedroom, which would be difficult to discuss with me here.'

Martin remained resolute. 'Chief Inspector. Whatever people have told you, it's vicious gossip amongst women who have too much time on their hands and not enough to think about. I know such rumours have been bandied about over the years, but they are completely false. Now, if that is all, I have much to do?'

Martin slid from her stool and stood looking at them, making it clear she wished to end the meeting. Helen looked across to Stirling, waiting for her cue. He gave her the slightest of nods.

Calmly, Helen asked, 'Why did you telephone Michael Pemberton shortly before he died?'

Startled, Martin looked at them both, replying forcefully, 'But, I didn't!'

Helen looked down to her notebook and read out a telephone number. 'Is that your mobile number?'

Martin's eyebrows knitted with concern. Shaking her head, she said, 'Yes, but I *didn't* call him!'

Listening to the exchange, Stirling heard a slip in Martin's polished accent. She seemed genuinely surprised by the information.

'Does anyone else have access to your mobile phone?' asked Helen, instinctively scenting the chase. For the first time since they had arrived, Martin's poise had slipped.

'No, no-one.' Martin looked nervous but even now as she looked beyond them, Stirling could see her calculating something.

Helen pressed on, enjoying the shift in control as Martin, struggling to recover her composure, put a hand on the edge of the island to steady herself. 'So, please account for the call to his mobile shortly before he died?'

Shaking her head blankly, Martin asked, 'What time was this?'

'Nine twenty-seven, last Thursday evening. The call lasted for over two minutes, which suggests a conversation took place.'

Martin digested the information for some moments and began to regain her composure. 'I *was* at home that evening, but I must have been messing with my phone, like we all do. Perhaps I pressed the number without realising it, but I did *not* call him intentionally, *nor* did I speak with him. I haven't spoken to him for over two years,' adding with some force, 'I would not have *wanted* to speak with him.'

'Why not?' Helen had picked up on the emotional emphasis in Martin's reply.

Martin opened her mouth to reply but checked the impulse and instead, breathed deeply to calm herself and answered crisply, 'Because I had no *need* to speak with him.'

Stirling cut in, 'You'll understand that we must eliminate people from our investigation. May I have your permission to examine your phone records please, to help eliminate you from our investigation? Helen has a form for you to sign giving specific information as to what we can search.' Stirling smiled, making it sound like a perfectly reasonable request.

Martin looked away towards the garden as she thought about it. 'Yes, I will help, of course. Now, Chief Inspector, if there is nothing else, I must get on. If you wish to speak with me again, do *not* turn up unannounced.'

Martin began to walk towards the door, looking at them to follow. Stirling pointed to the work surface where Helen had placed a document.

'The form, Mrs Martin? It won't take long,' and smiled again.

With an impatient huff, Martin returned to the island and stood next to Helen who began to write down the information, slowly. Stirling walked over to a wide bank of bi-fold doors leading to the garden. A stone terrace and flight of steps led down to a long garden with views beyond over open fields.

Pointing to something in the distance Stirling asked, 'You have a lovely view here Mrs Martin. Is that Bredon Hill over there?'

He knew full well it was, but was stalling for time. With unconcealed irritation, Martin walked over to stand near him and followed his gaze towards the squat outline of Bredon Hill some miles away.

'Yes, it is. We're... I'm very fortunate to live here.'

Stirling watched Martin's reflection in the glass as she stood looking fixedly across the landscape, arms wrapped around herself protectively. Older than him by some fifteen years, Stirling thought the silver threads amongst the fine hair at her temples added something to her appeal.

Striking a friendly note, he asked, 'So, are you a Londoner originally, or were you coming home when you moved up here?'

Martin continued to stare out of the window for some moments before looking down and her shoulders dipped. When she lifted her head to look out to the garden again, Stirling saw Katrina Martin's eyes were moist with suppressed tears. Had she responded to his kinder tone, perhaps? For the first time, Stirling sensed a vulnerability in Martin.

'I grew up in the county, if that's what you mean. We came here to start a family.'

There was a sad finality to Martin's voice that forestalled any further enquiry. Sensing some personal tragedy, Stirling changed the conversation quickly.

'I'm a keen gardener.' He pointed to the furthest edge of the garden. 'While you go through the paperwork with Helen, may I look round your garden please? You have some wonderful flowering shrubs over there.'

Martin frowned up at Stirling, her eyes sharp and questioning. Unsure yet if she was a suspect or a witness and determined to try and win her round, if only a little, Stirling smiled innocently.

Responding reluctantly to his smile, Martin gave an impatient sigh and unlocked the door.

'Oh, just for the record, please give Helen details of where you were last weekend between, say, 6pm Thursday and 6am Monday morning? Thanks.'

With a sly wink to Helen as Martin walked away from him, Stirling stepped out of the door. He could rely on Helen to probe Martin's affair with Pemberton.

Stepping down the flight of steps onto the lawn, Stirling sauntered down to the far end of the garden hoping the delaying ploy might get Martin to talk.

Moving slowly along a border planted up for year-round colour and interest, Stirling reviewed the conversation. Martin had struggled to explain the call to Pemberton and appeared to have been genuinely surprised. She was lying about the affair with Pemberton but he wasn't sure why. Pride, reputation? It wasn't enough to make her a suspect. Something else intrigued him. When Katrina Martin became agitated, her polished accent had slipped with the intonation and inflection flattening, suggesting to Stirling she was not originally from a middle-class home.

Stirling took his time walking around the garden, stopping occasionally to appreciate some of the shrubs now coming into bloom. He rarely had time for gardening and even then, it was usually a swift maintenance operation. He was enjoying the distraction.

Reaching the garden boundary where it met the fields, a large summerhouse set back in a secluded corner came into view. Painted in a light blue with a cream gable and checked curtains at its windows, the whole thing had settled slightly and faded out gently under the suns of successive summers, giving it a rustic, neglected charm. Looking up to the house to see if he was being waited for, Stirling saw the summer house was screened from the house by trees. With a little envy, Stirling thought the shabby little building looking out across the countryside was perfect. On its veranda decking, garden chairs were arranged around a low table.

Walking back to the house, Stirling spotted an open space through a gap in a tightly clipped yew hedge. Next to a pile of grass cuttings and rotting vegetation, a rusted garden brazier stood on a bare patch of earth with burnt debris inside. Glancing up to the house and seeing the door was still open but with neither woman in sight, Stirling stepped through the gap and went to the brazier. Amongst the ashes were metal buttons and a belt buckle, all of which could have been part of a woman's fashion garment. Picking up the buckle, he turned it over in his hand. Damaged first by fire and then exposed to the elements, it was badly corroded. Dropping it back in, he knew the ash could not have been there for many days or the recent rains would have washed them out through the mesh base. More ash had been swept by the wind into the edges of what he could now see was a redundant vegetable plot.

Stepping back through the gap onto the lawn, Stirling saw Martin and Helen on the terrace waiting for him to appear. Stirling walked unhurriedly up the garden to them.

'You have a lovely garden Mrs Martin. Are you the gardener?'

Looking over his head as he climbed the steps, she said, 'No, I have a man who comes in to do it for me. I've completed the form Chief Inspector. Is that all now?'

'I was admiring your summer house, Mrs Martin. It's a beautiful spot, tucked out of the way down there.' Stirling swept his hand across the landscape. 'It must be wonderful relaxing down there with that view.'

Martin looked past Stirling in the direction of the summer house and answered dismissively, 'Yes. It was used a lot but not now.'

'Oh? With the chairs out, I thought it must still be in use.'

Irritated, Martin snapped, 'The gardener puts them out. Just how is this *relevant,* Chief Inspector?'

Helen watched closely, trying to work out where Stirling was going with the questions.

'I noticed you've been burning something. In the brazier?' He offered her a puzzled half smile, making no move to leave.

Martin looked from him to the garden and back again. 'Some old clothes I didn't want to give to charity as they were too sentimental. Old bank statements, the usual sort of thing.'

Noticing Stirling's eyes glance over her own clothes she added impatiently, 'They weren't expensive clothes.'

Unsure himself where the conversation was leading, Stirling changed tack and stood looking up at the building and across its width.

'It's a lovely home Mrs Martin, but it must be lonely living here on your own?'

The question seemed to catch Martin off guard and both detectives watched as she fought away some emotion. With a wavering voice, she replied. 'That's none of your business. Now, if you have no further questions of relevance to your investigation I *insist* you leave my home!'

*

Standing at the window above the porch, Katrina Martin hugged herself tightly as she watched the car disappear, trying vainly to control her breathing and the cold, sickening churn in her stomach. Unable to fight down the nausea any longer, she ran to the bathroom and fell on her knees to vomit into the toilet, producing nothing but foul, hot bile.

After washing out her mouth and splashing cold water on her face, she leant heavily on the sink sucking air in through her nostrils and waited for the spasms to subside. Looking in the mirror, Martin turned her face each way to study the greying hair and the fine lines in her skin, wondering if a man could find her attractive still. She had aged so quickly in recent months.

The phone call had warned her the police might want to talk to her, but she had expected a telephone call first. Not for a moment had she thought *he* would arrive at her door. Unexpectedly face to face with Stirling, the shock had rocked her habitual self-control. And why on earth had she let him in, here, into her home? Their home? Curiosity? Yes, in part. The last person to speak with Cassie. She had recognised him immediately. Confused, her first thought had been to run away until her usual, steely self-control had re-asserted itself. Watching Stirling from above she had seen that he, too, was momentarily uncertain, giving her an advantage. But as the conversation played out, he had wrested that from her with ease.

After Cassie died she had desperately wanted to meet Stirling but they said he had refused to meet her. And now he was here, pretending not to know. Was he playing a cruel game to torment her, or an elaborate plan to trick her? She had imagined meeting him with scenarios alternating between a desire to attack him for not saving her daughter, and a need to talk with him, to know how Cassie had looked, what had she said and had she given him a message for her? And did he let her fall as the pictures suggested? She didn't believe it, really, but needed to hear it from him. She thought back to seeing him in the café with the beautiful young Asian woman, suddenly realising he looked like the man in the photographs, but uncertain.

Something, though, about Stirling's manner had surprised her. Beneath the professional, watchful manner there was a warmth, a kindness even. At one point, when they were stood close together, she'd had to fight away a strong urge to confide everything about Pemberton. But she couldn't bring herself to talk about it and as the memories swam back into view, she doubled over the sink to retch emptily.

Wiping her mouth clean, Martin looked at her figure in the mirror, as slender now as when she was twenty. The weight had fallen away through the stress and anxiety, but she took no pleasure in it. She had kept herself sane only by exercising each day to the point of near physical collapse.

The call to Pemberton's phone had caught her by surprise. Thinking back to that evening, she had quickly worked out what had happened, creating a new anxiety.

Tired, she walked to her bedroom and lay across the bed, staring at the ceiling as she calculated her options. She could sit tight and see what happened. Or might there be some advantage in calling that awful man, Ballard, to complain about Stirling? Would attack be the better means of defence, her instinctive reaction to any threat?

She needed to think clearly, but was desperate for sleep to quieten her mind, to close out the images and her imaginings. She had not slept properly since Cassie died.

Rolling onto her side, Katrina Martin pulled a pillow tight into her stomach and curled herself around it. Hollowed out, and no longer able to cry, she surrendered to a fresh tide of regretful grief, groaning out her loss to the empty house.

So many mistakes. Too many regrets. Such unendurable pain.

*

As they drove towards the main road, Helen asked, 'What did you make of her?'

'Very self controlled, and probably controlling too. You?'

'You mean, apart from being a cold, calculating bitch?'

'You said it, not me!'

'And what was all that crap about looking round her garden?' she demanded.

'But I like gardening!' he answered with a low laugh 'It was only to see if she might open up if I was out of the room. Did she?'

'No. She's lying about Pemberton, but why lie about it now he's dead? While you were outside communing with nature I tried, but she wouldn't budge. Interestingly, she didn't ask who told us. Perhaps she was tipped off like some of the others.'

'You've heard the expression, "Deny! Deny! Deny!" She's a successful businesswoman with some standing in the community. So, pride and reputation, perhaps?'

'Possibly,' Helen shook her head. 'No, it's something else. Is she in those photos?'

'I don't think so. They're putting together a working file for you. I didn't see anyone that looked like her this morning, but some are blindfolded and taken years ago. People change but if she'd been there, I think I'd have recognised her younger self.'

'I bet you would have,' Helen said with heavy sarcasm. 'And pushing her tits out for you wasn't very subtle, was it?'

Stirling smiled at the barbed remark. 'I think Mrs Martin's capable of using every trick at her disposal to get her own way. I doubt it's relevant but for the sake of completeness, we should trace her ex for elimination.'

'Why? If Pemberton was having it off with his wife fifteen years ago, it's a long time to wait for revenge? Anyway, I thought extra-marital affairs were a national sport in France!'

Stirling laughed at the pithy sarcasm, 'I agree a lot of time has passed, but it's a loose thread.'

'I know, I know. You don't like loose threads!' Helen knew Stirling's mantra well enough.

'No, I don't. I'll get Geordie to do the phone analysis for her lines as a high priority. She's hiding something but whether it's the affair or something else, I don't know. Why call Pemberton the night before if she hadn't spoken to him in over a year?'

'I'm surprised you didn't bring her in on suspicion. We could have, couldn't we?'

Stirling changed gear and concentrated on a bend in the road ahead, preparing to overtake a lorry. Pulling back into lane he replied, 'At a stretch, yes. But we need more to talk to Martin about than a random phone call and we'd be rushing our fences.

I'd like to know the answers to any questions we ask her. She can afford an expensive lawyer so let's see what her phones tell us first.'

Drumming his fingers on the wheel, Stirling felt a fresh wave of impatience tightening his nerves. 'What parameters did you agree with her for the phone record?'

'Six months, up to today, her mobile and landline. I've got the number of the Merc' and I'll find out who the Golf belongs to.'

Stirling nodded his satisfaction, 'Good work, thanks for your help Helen. I appreciate it.'

Selecting gear for another overtake, Stirling saw Helen give a small smile of pleasure.

4.45 p.m.
Back at the MCU, Helen went in search of Heal. Stirling found Edwards as he had left him earlier that day, still ploughing through the reports, witness statements and actions the incident room was producing tirelessly. Not for the first time was Stirling grateful to have such a capable deputy alongside him.

Edwards looked up as Stirling entered, tiredness etched around his eyes. Glad of a break from reading, he pushed himself back from the desk and stretched as they caught up with the day's progress.

The search officer had confirmed he put the photograph of the cottage and naked woman back as he had found it, believing it was irrelevant. The search video footage confirmed his account.

'It's an old picture, perhaps it didn't mean anything to Pemberton any longer?' suggested Edwards. Seeing a non-committal shrug for reply he continued.

'Billy Cole has been seen by Cooke and Banner. Plenty of brawn but none too bright and as for business acumen, he's certainly not a chip off the old block. He's a jobbing builder and unlikely to be as successful as Dad. There was no love lost between him and Pemberton after the business went bump, but they don't think he's up to murder. His alibi's a bit flaky but we don't have anything more to put to him at present. Says he went to the apartment a couple of times after he'd had a few beers but plays down the account given by Greening. Pemberton wasn't in, or wouldn't answer. I can't see Billy doing Pemberton in with a knife. If he was responsible he'd have gone off like a bottle of pop and used his bare hands in hot blood, or a blunt instrument. So, Billy's not eliminated completely, but we've nothing more to put to him for the moment. The details are in their report.'

Edwards scanned his book, checking off the items as he went. 'We covered the psychological profiling this morning. Croft hasn't got back to me yet with anything more on the lawyer at James and James, it'll take a few days.' Seeing Stirling's reaction, he added, 'As soon as I hear anything I'll let you know.'

Mention of the solicitors' firm caused Stirling to frown. He still needed to make an excuse to Ayesha about not seeing her for a few days. He asked about the signet ring in the picture. Edwards confirmed it was not amongst the personal effects removed at the PM and on checking the scene photos, it was not on his finger. Either he had not been wearing it, or it was removed with the other personal items before the fire was started. It had not been recovered from his home.

'So, for the present, I suggest we work on the basis it was removed by the killer along with his wallet and phone.' Edwards paused, 'If they expected the body to be destroyed by the fire, they might have thought it could lead to his identification?'

'Possibly, but rings are often difficult to remove, which meant spending more time handling the warm body of someone you've just murdered, your hands sticky and slippy with blood. That's calm, cold blooded work. Perhaps the ring meant something to him, or to the killer? Or was it personal to them both?'

Edwards's thinking had gone in a different direction. 'Or simpler than that, it looked valuable? We can't rule out that Pemberton was unlucky with someone who decided to turn him over in a remote spot and things got out of hand. An old guy with an expensive looking car and a reputation for splashing his money about. We know he was keen on women but who's to say he wasn't bi-sexual and took a man or a rent boy down there? It was a vicious attack and would have taken some strength.'

Edwards was warming to his theory. 'What if someone, a boy he'd abused when they were a child say, finally got their revenge? If he wasn't the original abuser, Pemberton might have represented all that had gone wrong in someone's childhood. Historic child abuse is surfacing in the media all the time. And then there's the suggestion of his involvement in drug dealing? Croft said there were some irregular but large cash deposits into his personal account. If he was desperate for money then perhaps he'd gone back to his old ways and was doing some occasional, high value dealing? If someone thought he was worth a few quid, we know how bizarre the imaginations of our druggie pond life can get, especially if they're desperate for a fix.'

Stirling shook his head in frustration. It felt as though they were going around in circles with one hypothesis leading remorselessly to another, and all of them bringing him full circle back to the first. Leaning back in his chair, Edwards exhaled a long sigh, rubbed his eyes with the heels of his hands and looked wearily at Stirling.

'We need some luck, Doug. We're piling up theories without eliminating any!'

'I know, but we make our own luck. Raise an action on the ring as outstanding property. If we recover it from a suspect, it ties them into Pemberton.'

Noting down the instruction, Edwards continued his summary. Forensic odontology confirmed Pemberton's teeth matched his dental records, so ID was complete and Angie Baines was aware. HTCU was still working through the browsing history and hard drive. Billing had sent a working file of all the images recovered so far with access limited strictly to them, Heal and Helen.

Pushing a file of proof copies across the desk, Edwards tapped the cover. 'Twenty-three women but Dan's still unlocking files. Each woman has been given a unique reference. As Helen identifies them, we'll cross reference husbands, partners, etcetera to eliminate them from the murder. I don't think we should assume they're all local women, married or otherwise. Pemberton might have used prostitutes. Some specialise in that sort of stuff.'

Stirling knew it was a fair point and deserved to be followed up but neither of them thought it would result in anything.

'Can the cousin tell us who the legs belonged to?' asked Stirling.

'Slight problem there. We can't get hold of her on the number she gave us, but we're chasing it up with her FLO.' Edwards shrugged a frustrated apology.

Stirling described the meeting with Martin and of the telephone analysis on her phone that Heal was now actioning as a priority. Picking up the photo album, Stirling was about to leave when Edward's tiredness caught his attention again.

'Perhaps you should get away earlier this evening Bill and catch up with Ellen and the family? It's been a tough week.'

Pointing at the remaining work, Edwards answered resignedly, 'I'll see how it goes. You too, Doug?'

'Perhaps. Tell Geordie I need a copy of the photo of the cottage.'

'Any particular reason?' asked Edwards.

'I'm not sure for the moment,' replied Stirling and left.

Suppressing a yawn, Edwards reached for the telephone.

Back in his office, Stirling placed the bundle of photographs in front of him and sat looking at the cover without opening it. He felt like a peeping tom looking at them alone, intruding on the women's dignity, even though they were unknown to him.

Had they consented to the photos being taken or, once incapacitated, were they taken without permission? But it would have made for a short-lived relationship and would not have benefitted Pemberton. On balance, he thought there must have been some degree of consent but, once blindfolded, were some of them even aware? Remembering the image of the angry young woman, not all of them were happy with their indignity being frozen for Pemberton's lasting enjoyment.

Bill's suggestion of prostitutes had some merit. Most of the women in the photos were attractive, looked well-nourished and healthy. Stirling thought back to his experience of working in vice in a busy city district for some months. The women, and girls, were usually poorly educated and having crossed into that world, or forced into it, were unable to break out a cycle of drug dependency, gratuitous violence, easy money and tended to age quickly. And if Pemberton had used prostitutes, their pimps, usually violent criminals, might have thought him an easy target.

Stirling continued to turn the pages, looking for anything which might point to the identity of the women and where they were taken. The distinctive bed frame, no doubt bought for purpose, made it clear that many were taken in Pemberton's apartment, verifying Frances Greening's description of the "goings on" above her.

The women were all white, which probably reflected Pemberton's social network, and ranged in age from early-twenties to mid-forties. Although some were of a heavier build with the tell-tale traces of maternity, Pemberton had obviously preferred slim women. How had he gained their trust to submit to bondage? Even though many were married, their wedding bands visible and with everything to lose if their infidelity was discovered, Stirling could not believe he would have gone unreported if he was forcing women into acts of submissive bondage.

Helen said the women she spoke with had enjoyed the excitement of something different. Perhaps many of the liaisons were brief, intense, with Pemberton exploiting the first reckless excitement of illicit love, with the photographs sustaining his fantasies and reminiscences afterwards? Over thirty years, the photos might represent just a small number of women amongst his numerous relationships, many of whom might have rejected his predilections.

Another set of images had been taken in a countryside setting and more again in woodland. One series showed a woman with her hands tied around a tree looking over her shoulder to the camera in reducing stages of undress until naked, her vulnerability exposed by different camera angles. As the sequence progressed, there was a reducing confidence in the woman's eyes until, Stirling thought, there was uncertainty and fear. Items of clothing lay on the ground around her, some torn. Naked, she bore a growing number of welts and marks across her buttocks and thighs, their spread widening as the pictures advanced and her face no longer visible as she pressed herself into the distinctive bark pattern. In the corner of two pictures, a man's bare leg and foot could be seen. Stirling thought of the tripod in Pemberton's study. At some point a gag had been applied. To stifle her cries? Were there more images of Pemberton copulating with the woman as he acted out a rape fantasy? Or was it simply a rape?

The same woman and others had been photographed on and inside the Jaguar, its registration plate clearly visible. Many imitated soft porn poses with the women smiling confidently, or coyly, or painfully self-consciously at the lens as they lay across the car either naked or partially clothed, some with hands bound, their legs spread immodestly.

Of concern to Stirling were the pictures of the woman lying bound in the boot of the Jaguar with the dark stain spreading over the carpeting. There could be no mistaking her fear as she pleaded to the camera. Stirling felt pity for her. Checking back through the images in the woodland, although her face was hidden from the camera, Stirling was reasonably certain she was amongst the women tied to the tree, the weals across her bottom telling their own story. Had it ended safely for her, and for all of the other women? Or was there another dimension to Pemberton's murder? It was clear that Pemberton had taken pleasure in causing fear and in inflicting pain. How far had he taken his fetish, and was he always in control? If any of the women had threatened to reveal him, how might he have reacted?

Feeling he was missing something, Stirling went back through the photos to find the pictures of the Jaguar in the foreground with countryside behind. An idea began to form.

Stirling found Heal talking with Edwards. Beyond them, in the far corner, Helen sat with her back to them talking quietly on the telephone, the only other noise being a steady drumbeat of keyboards. Both men looked up as Stirling entered the room and walked towards them. A shadow flitted across Heal's features as he steeled himself for more work on top of an already heavy burden.

'Geordie, is that copy of the cottage photograph ready?' he demanded, too brusquely.

Heal went to his desk and returned with an envelope, handing it to Stirling. 'I've had both sides copied to A4 size, boss.'

Examining the picture as he walked back to his office Stirling called over his shoulder, 'Get yourselves home this evening, both of you!'

As the door closed, Heal and Edwards looked at each other and with a lift of their eyebrows, resumed their conversation.

Back in his office, Stirling studied the copy. The woman in the doorway was no clearer. Putting the cottage at the centre of his desk, he positioned photographs of the Jaguar car around it, shuffling the arrangement before standing back to regard them, arms folded. A text interrupted his thinking. It was Ayesha asking if he was free to speak. Needing to stay in this train of thought, Stirling replied he would call later.

Sensing a presence, Stirling looked up to see Helen leaning on the door frame watching him, her briefcase in one hand.

'Dirty pictures, Dougie? Not your style, surely?'

It was intended to irritate, and did. Helen had always been able to push his buttons, effortlessly. Stirling motioned her in.

'I need a woman's point of view. Have you looked through these yet?'

Helen ambled in, put down her briefcase and came to stand close to him.

Helen turned the pages. 'I'm not sure what you're looking for, but even allowing for the beatings, as far as S and M goes, it's pretty tame stuff. There's much more graphic stuff freely available on the internet, and it's not limited to the sex industry either. People upload their own pictures. They don't seem to understand it's there forever. Many of these women here appear to start off happy enough, though some look frightened. Some of them might have become unwilling victims. Hard to know without talking with them.'

'I agree, but that's not my point. I'm trying to understand the relationship between these women and Pemberton. He seems to have been a controlling man with an easy charm but, to my mind, the way a lot of the pictures have been framed, there's a level of voyeurism with a conscious construction of the pictures and settings.'

Helen tilted her head as she looked at the pictures. 'Perhaps he was just imitating the lads' mags of the day?' she suggested. 'But why black and white? Wouldn't colour be more gratifying if he was wanking himself off to them later?' Her tone was humourless, objective.

'Perhaps he fancied himself as an artist? Black and white does show human emotion in starker relief. More defined.'

Turning the pages back and forth, she murmured, 'Possibly. But there might be more brutal stuff we haven't found yet. These were all taken some years ago.'

Stirling agreed with her, 'But my concern is whether this was early ideation and experimentation before he moved from fantasy to realisation as he gained confidence. Look at this one for example.' He pointed to the woman in the boot of the car. 'She's frightened. What was going on there, a punishment for some fantasised transgression? Or did she think something sinister was about to happen? How long had he kept her in there and what happened next? She's either pee'd herself through fear or was in there a long time, or both.'

Helen answered, 'Pemberton was very proud of his car so that would have really pissed him off, no pun intended. He was a nasty piece of work.'

Spoken with a cold, flat anger, Helen was too used to meeting women who had suffered abuse at the hands of cruel, coercive men. 'What was that word you used, idea something?'

'Ideation? Sorry, negotiator-speak. It's a psychological term describing the shift from having an idea to planning how it could happen. Amongst negotiators it refers to a shift from having suicidal thoughts to actually imagining how they'll do it.'

Stirling had become aware that Helen was uncomfortably close to him, her perfume and body scent evoking memories he needed to keep at bay. Stirling began to speak but halted as he heard a huskiness in his voice.

Helen had noticed it instinctively. Containing a smile, she turned her body slightly and leant forward, ostensibly to study a picture but allowing him to see down her blouse. Helen shifted sideways until her hip and thigh pressed against his. With her scent in his nostrils and the warmth of her body against his, Stirling felt his pulse quickening and a primitive stirring. Turning her head to look at him, she gave him an astute smile, increasingly confident of her continuing appeal to him.

The door to the incident room opened and Stirling heard men's voices talking together as they drew closer to his door. He stepped aside to put some space between them just as Edwards and Heal appeared at his doorway. Both men had their coats on and were on their way home. Seeing Helen stood next to him behind his desk, Stirling could see each man guessing at what they had interrupted.

Taking everything in at a glance and ignoring Helen, Edwards said smoothly. 'We're going over the road for a swift one before heading home, Doug. Fancy joining us?' He was offering an escape route.

'Thanks Bill, I'll be over in a few minutes.'

With a steady look at each of them Edwards left, followed by an untypically silent Heal. Realising the moment was lost, Helen moved round to the other side of the desk and sat without waiting to be invited. Happier with a desk between them, Stirling sat down too as Helen eyed him with a vague smile on her lips.

Clearing his throat, he asked, 'You came to see me, to start with?'

Still smiling, she replied, 'Three more of Pemberton's past lovers have returned my calls.' Stirling remembered her sat in the corner of the office speaking quietly into the telephone. 'They're reluctant, but will talk to me, in strict confidence. A couple of them were aware of his tastes through tittle tattle but because he was discreet, with his looks and his money, and well-endowed too, apparently, they were curious.'

Helen broke off for a moment, waiting for a reaction but seeing none, continued. 'But, there's a new twist. The one I talked to a few minutes ago is very frightened. Pemberton had threatened to publish photographs of her, unless she gave him money.'

'Blackmail would explain why he digitised the older photos. The Fairway debacle left him broken financially. He must have got desperate.'

'She won't discuss it on the telephone so we're meeting in the morning before she starts work. That's what I came to tell you. Lesley's got the day off for a prior engagement so d'you want to be there?'

'It depends on what else I've got to do here, I'll let you know. Didn't any of the women you've already spoken to mentioned blackmail?'

'No, but they were embarrassed and frightened. I'll contact them again.'

Helen left and Stirling listened for the corridor door to close before letting out a sigh of tension, until he heard it open again and Helen reappeared to lean on the doorframe. Stirling tensed, preparing to reject any attempt to draw him into something he would regret.

'I forgot to say. The Merc' is registered to Martin at her home address, bought recently from the local dealership in Worcester. The Golf is registered to a Carol Evans at Danes Green, Worcester. I'll make some enquiries there tomorrow.'

Stirling considered the world of difference between Danes Green, a large post-war social housing estate on the west side of the city and Martin's executive home with twelve or so miles and the River Severn between. For years, Danes Green had been a by-word amongst local coppers for anti-social behaviour, casual vandalism and home to many petty criminals. It had settled down as the resident population had aged, but it was not one of the city's better postcodes.

'Martin doesn't strike me as someone who'd have friends on Danes Green.' he replied.

'The cleaner, maybe?' she suggested.

Stirling shook his head. 'She said a friend and they'd quarrelled.'

'Okay, I'll look into it.'

Helen gave Stirling a lingering look, hoping for something more, but seeing him pulling papers towards him and deep in thought, she left again.

6.37 p.m.

When he was certain of being alone, Stirling put his feet up on the desk and closed his eyes to think. Helen's musky, sharp spiced perfume lingered over the room, a metaphor for her temperament and personality.

Helen was still very desirable, certainly, but he did not have the energy to revisit the relationship. Apart from a mutual physical desire, they had had too little in common and too many differences in their respective temperaments for it ever to be successful. Consequently, the relationship had blown its stormy course out within a few months. But there was a predatory streak to Helen's nature and he would need to remain careful in her company. Not that he was particularly seeking a long-term commitment to anyone. Work was his mistress, when the likes of Ballard and McDonald allowed him to get on with it.

Which brought his mind back to the investigation. There were too many lines of enquiry. He needed to suspend some and invest the team's efforts in those which looked the most promising. But which could he afford to put aside, and at what cost if he made the wrong choices?

Thinking of the Fairway scheme brought Stirling to the possibility of Ayesha's unwitting involvement. He should call and make an excuse for not being able to see her for a few days. Stirling wanted to confide in her but after working through the pros and cons, he decided that professional integrity must override his personal feelings. And if Ayesha was innocent, he should not burden her with inappropriately gained information.

Reluctantly, Stirling picked up his mobile.

Putting the phone down five minutes later, Stirling wondered what more he could have said. Ayesha had been waspy, to say the least.

With hindsight, he realised his explanations for not seeing each other for several days were vague, imprecise, and he would have sounded evasive. Ayesha had ended the conversation tersely with a barbed invitation to call her tomorrow, if he could bother to spare her the time.

With a frustrated sigh and swearing to the empty room, Stirling wondered if he should end it before he got too involved. It would certainly make life simpler all round, and it would be kinder to Ayesha too.

Stirling remembered the invitation to join his colleagues at the "Twigs". Deciding he would be poor company, he lifted a report from the pile and set to work.

ᆭ ᆬ

Day 6: Saturday - 7.35 a.m.

Standing at the centre of the clearing and turning in a slow circle, Stirling reacquainted himself with the topography of The Wern. Scorched stone and burnt debris marked where the Jaguar had stood. The south westerly breeze was warm but dark edged clouds heralded more rain. He could smell the moisture on the wind.

The track from the main road would not have changed so the buildings had to have been close to where he was standing, but their presence had been completely erased. Walking back and forth across the hard-standing, Stirling began to think his imagination had got the better of him before reminding himself that however much the site had been levelled, the landscape around it would have remained the same. He returned to the centre.

Opening the folder under his arm, Stirling pulled out two photographs of the Jaguar and held one in each hand at arm's length. Ignoring the naked woman draped over the car in each, he turned slowly, seeking out features that were unlikely to have altered as he tried to replicate the angle from where the photo had been taken. Stirling stopped, took a few steps back and aligned the photographs to the horizon above him.

'Gotcha!' he heard himself shout, surprised at how easily noise carried across the low-lying ground. Looking from the photograph to the horizon and back again, the photos were consistent with the lie of the land above him. There was the line of the field wall tracking uphill from left to right to the copse of trees at the top edge of the field. Even allowing for the growth of the trees since, the similarity was unmistakable.

Stirling's self-satisfied grin disappeared quickly as he realised the discovery created another puzzle. The pictures were taken years before Fairway acquired the site and with it, Pemberton's involvement. Stirling took out the photo of the cottage and began the exercise again. Unable to make a clear match, he took out a picture of the Jaguar and scrutinised the reflections in the car's side windows which had caught his attention the previous evening. Holding a photograph in each outstretched hand, Stirling turned until both the cottage and the Jaguar aligned to their respective horizons. Looking from one to the other repeatedly, he worked out where, approximately, the Jaguar had been parked.

Walking across the clearing, Stirling stood looking at the area where the cottage had been. "Found you," he thought to himself, and then stared at the naked woman in the shadow of the porch. "But, who are you?"

The sound of a car made Stirling turn to see Edwards travelling downhill, bouncing carelessly in and out of the ruts. Later than hoped for, but it was early when he had called Bill away from his breakfast. Standing still so that he would not lose the spot, Stirling waited for Edwards to park and walk over to him.

'Sorry to drag you away from your cornflakes Bill, but I've made a discovery and wanted you to see it.'

Edwards smiled thinly, hoping the early morning call was worth the quarrel it had caused with his wife. 'Okay. So, what have you got?' he asked patiently, noticing the photos in Stirling's hands and the satisfied look on his face.

'There was something about the photos with the Jag that was bugging me. The more I looked at them, the more the background seemed familiar. And the picture of the cottage? That was nagging me too. The message on the back meant it was a significant relationship, to one of them at least.'

'Hang on, we don't know for certain it was written for him, do we?' questioned Edwards irritably.

Stirling realised he had not considered that possibility. Was he making a presumptuous leap of faith? 'It's a fair point Bill, but I think the coincidences are too great. Look!' Holding out the picture of the cottage, Stirling pointed to the line of ground above them. 'Look at the background behind the cottage.'

Edwards moved closer and looked along the length of Stirling's arm to the photo of the cottage, lifted his eyes to the contours of the land and grunted, 'Okay.'

'Now, look the other way Bill. What d'you see?' Stirling held out the photograph of the Jaguar with the naked woman bent over the bonnet, exposing herself.

'A bit soon after breakfast to be looking at this kind of stuff,' Edwards mumbled grumpily.

Despite his manner, Stirling saw Edwards was smiling as he studied the landscape behind the car. Several moments passed as Edwards looked from one photograph to the other and up to the land behind.

Uncertainly, Edwards said, 'Both correspond with the landscape?'

'Yes, but what else can you see, Bill? In the side windows of the car!' Stirling asked impatiently, thinking it was abundantly clear. And his arms were aching.

Bending in close enough to look, Edwards muttered gruffly, 'We're standing dangerously close together. People might talk!'

'We're alone,' answered Stirling sarcastically.

'That's what bothers me!'

Edwards studied the photo of the car, turning his head between the cottage image and the car. Standing up, he let out a long-held breath and gave Stirling a slow smile, nodding appreciatively at his friend's deduction.

'The cottage is reflected in the car's windows. The cottage was here and the car over there, give or take a few yards. Bloody good detective work Doug. I'm impressed!'

Edwards didn't hand out many bouquets and from one seasoned detective to another, it meant a lot. Stirling allowed himself a loud laugh of relief 'Which means Pemberton knew this site, *years* before Fairway!'

Reaching inside the folder, Stirling took out a photograph of a woman tied to the tree and held it out. 'What d'you see in that picture?' he demanded.

Looking at the naked woman, Edwards grimaced. 'Must I?'

Shaking his head pityingly, he studied her fear. He knew it was not the woman Stirling was asking him to look at and looked around the landscape, not sure what he was searching for. With a shake of his head, gave the photograph back to Stirling.

Stirling looked at him with surprise. 'No?' He pointed to a feature in the background, barely discernible amongst the trees. 'What d'you think that is?'

Edwards could see something set in a stone wall behind the trees, beyond which was the merest glimpse of an open field. 'An opening of some sort.'

'Exactly, but not something you'd expect to see in this part of the country. It's a squeeze gate, made of stone. Just big enough to allow someone to step through sideways, but too small for livestock to escape through. And I'll bet you a fiver it's in that wood up there, where it's probably been for a couple of hundred years, if not longer.'

Following Stirling's gaze uphill, Edwards looked up at the copse a few hundred yards away. Stuffing his hands in his pockets and looking uphill, he said, 'Keep your money. You might be right but unless you insist, I've got my best shoes on and I don't have time for a nature ramble this morning. I've got a statement to prepare urgently.'

Edwards went to speak again but seeing Stirling absorbed in shuffling through the photos, he gave no more explanation. 'D'you want me to get a photographer down here to you?'

Stirling looked up at the sky, feeling some light flecks of rain on his face. 'No. If it is up there, it's not going anywhere.' Pointing to the woods he added, 'I'll have a quick look round. If I can't find it, we'll get the TF back here to do another search.'

'Okay, let me know and I'll sort it out.' Edwards was preparing to leave when Stirling put a hand on his arm.

'Bill, I think Pemberton's death was linked to this place, somehow. But what the link is, I'm not sure.'

Edwards looked around them and back to Stirling, giving him a jaundiced eye. 'Perhaps, Doug, perhaps.' He pointed at the photos in Stirling's hand. 'Equally, now we know he was familiar with the place, what if he just didn't want to be seen? It might have been Pemberton who dictated the terms of the meeting, precisely because of its remoteness.'

Tapping the photos, he added, 'All those prove is that Pemberton knew this place, which is useful. But, beyond that it could be nothing more than coincidental.'

Edwards gave him a long, questioning look, 'You didn't join me and Geordie at the pub last night.'

'No, I worked until late,' replied Stirling, absorbed in looking at the photos and the site.

Edwards gave Stirling a sceptical look. 'Okay, I'll see you back at the office.'

As Edwards drove up the track, Stirling pulled on wellington boots and then started up the slope of the field towards the copse. Enjoying the fresh air and exercise, he kept a steady rhythm to get his lungs open.

Reaching the stone perimeter wall, mildly out of breath but feeling better for it, Stirling stopped to look back down to where the cottage had stood a hundred yards away and across to where the track rose towards the main road. Edwards's car was already out of sight. Listening hard for the car, all he could hear was morning birdsong over the land which had supported the farm for generations. The peace of the place must have been a mixed blessing, he thought. Isolated, but isolating too. Had the tenant families who worked this soil appreciated its beauty and quietude, or had the daily, back breaking toil made it an adversary to wrest a living from, each season presenting its perennial tasks and difficulties?

Ignoring the scars of the groundworks below, to Stirling's eye it was idyllically remote with towns only a few miles away when needed. Perfectly remote too for Pemberton's activities. An ordnance survey map of the area had shown no public footpaths for a mile in any direction.

Stirling turned back to the lichen crusted stone wall enclosing the copse which disappeared for yards at a time under overgrown brambles which had crawled out from the wood behind. He found the squeeze gate about fifty yards along, its stone flanks mossy from overhanging trees. Partially hidden by overgrowth, passage through it was possible as some of the brambles had been knocked back. Stepping sideways through the gate, Stirling noticed recently trodden down grass and put it down to one of the dog handlers entering the wood during the scene search.

Using the photograph to guide him, Stirling worked his way deeper into the copse, bending frequently under low growing branches and stepping around mounds of overgrown brambles that grasped at his trousers. Striving for light, fern fronds were uncurling from the ground and where sunlight dappled a few open spaces, bluebells tolled their light scent into the breeze. Looking back to check the gate's location, Stirling swore loudly as he stumbled over a tree root and almost fell headlong into a high growth of bramble and low growing holly.

Most of the trees were typical of coppicing, beech, birch and some ash. The multiple growths at their base showed the copse had once been managed, but not for many years now. Growing some distance from the gate, singular and proud, was the gnarled oak he was looking for.

Holding out the photograph, Stirling worked his way around the tree until the squeeze gate in the boundary wall aligned and then checked the distinctive bark pattern. Fighting for light amongst the changing canopies of its neighbours, the oak had strained and twisted as it grew, creating ridges and corrugations as unique as a fingerprint to match the patterns in the photograph. Even allowing for the years of growth since, there was a consistency between the photo and the tree in front of him.

Using the photograph to guide him, Stirling put his hand where the face of the young woman in the car boot had pressed herself into the bark, trying to sense her presence, imagining what she and others might have endured here. Had it all been consensual? Looking around the copse, removed from any external view, he was struck by how lonely it was.

Mindful of the possibility of latent evidence, Stirling searched around the base of the trunk but found nothing. If it had not been taken away, over the years hemp or sisal ropes would have perished. He was not sure if it mattered anyway, until he reminded himself he had yet to account for all the women. Looking around at the unkempt vegetation, Stirling speculated on what the ground might contain and felt a cold shiver across his shoulders, as if there was a presence about the place.

Not inclined to superstition, Stirling dismissed the sensation and put it down to the changing air temperature as a shadow swept through the wood and a freshening wind stirred the tree canopy above. Rain began to patter onto the leaves and splash to the ground around him.

Working his way back to the squeeze gate, Stirling took a last look at the oak and walked down the field to his car.

*

8.28 a.m.

Emerging from the shelter of his camouflaged hide, the poacher crept to the edge of the wood. Staying behind cover, he watched the man reach his car and moments later, drive away up the track. After a few scrapes with the law over the years, Osmand knew a copper when he saw one.

After a luckless night poaching for the roe deer that strayed this way from the big estate, Osmand had fallen asleep in the hide he had built inside a high growth of bramble and holly. Woken by the noise of car tyres on the stone below and men's voices carried on the air, he had watched the two men talking together. When one of them had driven away and the other started to walk uphill, Osmand had not been unduly concerned. Retreating into the hide, he doubted the copper would enter the wood.

He had arrived quicker than he had expected, though, and without any panting. He was physically fit and looked strong built. Barely breathing, concerned at being discovered with a rifle, Osmand had watched through the tangle of camouflage netting and foliage as the copper entered the wood. When he almost fell onto his hide he'd thought the game was up.

Watching the car disappearing up the far track, Osmand's low cunning worked through what he must do. Thinking the copper might come back with search dogs, he dismantled the hide, scattering the bed of sweet smelling fir branches widely. Standing back to assess his handiwork, the poacher grunted his satisfaction. It would take another countryman to notice the tell-tale traces.

With the rifle over one arm and carrying his traps, Osmand walked over to the oak tree and stood looking at it. It took him back to when he was teenager, roaming wild all summer long, his parents only too happy he was out of their way. He could disappear for days on end and there would be no alarm, only the risk of a cuffed ear if he returned empty handed.

Leaning one hand against the old oak, Osmand put his coarsened hand over the tortured bark and remembered when people used to come up from the farm below, smiling slyly at the memory before a troubled look creased his features. Why did the copper have photos? With a final glance down to where the farm had once stood, Osmand worked his way out of the wood in the opposite direction until he reached an indistinct track. Standing in the shade of the treeline, he searched for movement in each direction until certain no one would see him leaving.

Whistling tunelessly, Osmand sauntered down the puddled track to where he had hidden his Land Rover under branches the previous evening. Looking at the brightening sky, he sniffed the air. The rain would pass by soon.

*

9.03 a.m.

Driving around the island over the motorway and signalling left onto Pershore Lane and HQ, Stirling glanced across to the bridge railings and saw a sad collection of withered flowers, fading with the memory of a girl's life. Stirling felt his high spirits dip as he was reminded of his vain effort to save the girl.

Driving past the rugby stadium and seeing the match day signs out, he was reminded there was a home game that afternoon which he would have gone to. On recent form, he might have expected a win but remembered it was the local derby against Gloucester. Maybe not then.

Once past the club entrance Stirling looked across the fields at the biscuit coloured HQ building standing proudly on its hilltop pedestal, the tall aerial mast incongruous with the graceful architecture of the mansion house. Swinging left into the drive, he turned his mind towards his next meeting. Believing the key to Pemberton's secrets lay inside his computer, he had called ahead to Billing to confirm he was in the office. The hands-free rang loudly and he frowned when he saw it was Helen calling him.

Intending to keep some distance between them after the previous evening, he answered simply, 'Stirling.'

'Dougie? It's Helen.' She had anticipated a friendlier tone.

'Did you see the witness?'

Helen paused to absorb the business-like manner. 'I've just left her. She has an interesting story to tell which I think you should hear, but not over an open line. I'm off to see someone else now. Can we meet?'

Unable to think of a good reason not to, Stirling reluctantly agreed to meet later.

9.16 a.m.

Flicking through the bundle of papers, Stirling sat across the desk from Dan Billing. With advance warning to say Stirling was on his way, Billing had scurried around to bring the information he and his team had pulled out of the computer into a comprehensive file.

Tapping the file, Stirling looked at Billing. 'Tell me what I've got here, succinctly.'

Clearing his throat, Dan reached across to point at the schedule of contents. There's a shitload of … sorry sir. There's a large amount of data on the hard drive. It's a modern system ...'

Stirling smiled at the correction. He and Billing were half a generation apart but as a young officer, he had been just as inappropriate in his choice of language around senior officers, usually through an abundance of energy and enthusiasm. Rattling out a description of gigabytes, terabytes and a stream of barely comprehensible techno-speak, but not wishing to dampen the young man's enthusiasm, Stirling assumed the appearance of absorbed interest, nodding where it seemed appropriate to when Billing emphasised some point. In summary, Billing had created a file broken down into the core themes of the hard drive's data.

Itemising them on his fingers, Billing explained, 'The report's broken down into images and anything else of a visual, sexual nature. Discernible patterns of browsing. Bank accounts, but not their content, obviously. Personal and professional contacts. A schedule of past architectural projects of which there's very little in the last five years, but there's a stash of older projects which he'd archived....'

As the list grew, Stirling was already thinking about the impact so much additional data would have on the investigation and what to concentrate on first. None of this could be analysed in a few hours and distilled into actionable information. Stirling realised Dan had stopped speaking and was waiting for an answer to a question he had not heard.

'Sorry Dan, I was thinking about how to deal with all this. What was that?'

Dan smiled patiently, quite used to senior officers losing concentration when he talked data. 'I was saying there's a file we haven't accessed yet because it's been uploaded to a cloud-based database and encrypted differently. We're having to be extremely careful to avoid corrupting whatever's in it. I've contacted the NCA's national cyber team and hope to crack it soon, but it could be a few days.' Seeing the look on Stirling's face he added, 'Sorry, but those are the challenges of Hi Tech crime investigation. I'll get it to you ASAP.'

Stirling was disappointed, but knew Billing would work hard to get him what he needed as quickly as he could. Meanwhile, there was more than enough to get on with.

Stirling carried the file back to his car and thumbed through it whilst he made some calls. The first was to Edwards to arrange a PolSA search of the copse and to tell him of his meeting with Billing.

With only two days until McDonald's return, he called Pearson next. Stirling didn't envy Tanner's position but owed her for supporting him. Six days in and with no suspect in view, a detection before McDonald got back seemed highly unlikely.

The last call was to Ayesha who was about to leave for a visit to her parents at Leicester. The conversation was stilted, both still unhappy with the other after the previous evening's spat and too proud to apologise. Listening to the cool edge in her voice, Stirling could understand her anger, confused by the hot and cold nature of his attention. She knew he was avoiding her and inferred as much before changing the subject, leaving the accusation hanging between them. He should have lied better the previous evening, he thought. It would have been easier, and kinder. When Ayesha asked when they would next see each other, uncomfortable with lying to her, Stirling had fudged an answer. The conversation ended with Ayesha telling him coldly not to bother and had ended the call abruptly.

Stirling replayed the conversation and wondered if his thoughts about ending the relationship had insinuated an indifference into his tone. Ayesha was acutely perceptive. Resigned to the fact that the relationship was fatally harmed, Stirling resolved to contact Croft and see how soon he could complete his enquiries of James solicitors. Ayesha deserved an honest explanation, at the very least.

With time to kill, Stirling began skimming through Billing's report again. Scanning the columns of professional contacts, he wondered how many were current. Pemberton had not been working in recent years and the volume could bog the enquiry down. He would need to filter and prioritise them. Some names he recognised as having been spoken to, or were actioned to be seen. David Jones, Chartered Surveyor, was there, along with his email address, office and personal numbers. Passing on, Stirling stopped and returned to Jones's details to check the telephone numbers again. Tapping a forefinger on the steering wheel, Stirling considered a possibility.

Scrolling through his contacts on the car phone, he called Heal and asked for some research to be done.

A text from Helen had arrived as he was talking to Heal. Locking the file safely in the boot, Stirling began the short drive into Worcester.

10.48 a.m.
From their vantage point, Stirling looked around the wide square balcony of the city's former library which now served as a café. A few doors down from the Shire Hall where he and Ayesha had first met, the building's red facade and ornate brickwork boasted

Victorian confidence, civic pride and days of Empire. Now, it was home to the city's art gallery and museum. Helen was half way through her breakfast when he arrived and had coffee waiting for him.

'Unusual place to meet?' said Stirling.

'It's close to the home of the last victim and I needed to eat after an early start,' Helen explained without apology, annoyed at his brevity on the telephone.

She had taken a table in a corner where they could talk without being overheard and allowed Stirling to watch the room, a detective's trait. Stirling sipped at his coffee as he waited for Helen to finish eating, his thoughts wandering as he watched people and families on the mosaic stairs rising from the entrance below. Outside, noisy teenagers were heading into the city centre to enjoy the last weekend of the Easter break. The noise of cutlery on china and a plate being pushed aside brought his attention back to Helen.

Keeping her voice down, Helen said, 'Pemberton was definitely blackmailing his former mistresses. I've spoken with two victims this morning and both are frightened about what might get into the media. I've explained the measures the court would take to protect them but since he's dead, it's unlikely to get that far.'

'But, they could be witnesses in the defence of another blackmail victim, *if* that was the motive for his murder,' replied Stirling.

Helen nodded. 'We're talking about serious sums of money over the last few years. These are reasonably wealthy women, well, one *was* until he milked her dry. He had about twenty-five thousand from the first one I met this morning but from the second, over two hundred thousand.'

Helen paused when she saw the dismay on Stirling's face, and shook his head. 'I know. She's broke and living in a small flat round the back of here in the Arboretum. She used to live in a big house near the private golf course at Bransford, but lost it when she defaulted on her mortgage.'

Stirling turned his head instinctively in the direction of the Arboretum behind the old library, a collection of narrow streets of terraced houses with a growing migrant community. Although unsurprised that Pemberton had been a blackmailer, the scale of his menace had surprised him.

'How on earth did he take her for that much?' he asked, slightly incredulous.

'Usual story, a combination of charm, flattery, vague promises of "settling down together" and finally, naked threats. It's a sad story. They first had an affair about fifteen years ago, but she had since become divorced which was nothing to do with him, well, not directly. She was married with young kids then, but a bored housewife with an indifferent husband who showed her no affection, either emotional or physical. She was easily seduced by the discreet attentions of a racy lover and says the experience showed her there was another life available. She got divorced and was enjoying her life completely until Pemberton got in touch.

'Her kids had left home and she was lonely with empty nest syndrome, and the creeping anxieties of getting older. When he contacted her, she was flattered by the attention and let him back into her bed, wanting to believe he cared for her. The sex was pretty conventional second time round, she says. I suspect it was a means to an end. I doubt his tastes would have altered.

'He began tapping her for money, small amounts to start with but getting larger, until his big "project" landed. When that story began to wear thin he started threatening to expose her with the pictures he'd taken of her during their affair, threatening to publish them on the internet. She was terrified her children would see them and destroy her family. She absolutely lives for her kids and once she'd made a few payments, it was impossible to stop. He wasn't above physical abuse, which shouldn't surprise us after those photographs. He knocked her about a couple of times when she threatened to report him.'

'But how did she lose her home?'

Helen sighed and shook her head. 'On the promise of a good return on making an investment in Fairway, he persuaded her to re-mortgage her home. When she couldn't keep up the repayments, it was repossessed.'

Stirling groaned, despairing of the foolishness of people with their money. He had seen it too many times.

'It's bloody sad Dougie, I really feel for her. She's a lovely woman and has lost everything. Now she's terrified that even though he's dead, it could all still come out because of our investigation.' Seeing Stirling about to speak, she cut in, 'I know, loose threads! She's given an alibi which I'm confident will stand up and I'd be amazed if she's our murderer, or even involved in it with another. Her spirit's broken.'

Saddened, Stirling said, 'All for some photographs when she was in love.'

Running a hand through his hair, Stirling slouched back in his chair and looked around the café, busier now with people going about their humdrum routines and blissfully unaware of the viciousness of their neighbours.

Stirling looked at Helen. With a note of despair, he said, 'This job's getting ever more convoluted. I don't know if I'm looking for a random attacker, an unknown lover, the victim of a sexual assault, a criminal creditor, a vicious drug dealer, a co-conspirator in fraud and now, a victim of blackmail. Not to mention an avenging cuckold of which there's a good few to choose between!'

'Keeps it interesting though!' Helen retorted with irony.

Giving a resigned sigh and knowing the answer he asked, 'And all the payments were in cash?' Money trails might prove helpful.

'Yes,'

Watching Stirling pondering the new turn, Helen wondered if she could bring the conversation round to another subject but seeing him frowning in concentration, she decided against it. 'I've got another woman to see now and then I'll go back to the MCU to write up my report.'

'The photos of the women are all from some years ago. Do we know when his most recent relationship was?'

'The woman I've just told you about last saw him about eighteen months ago. He stopped answering her calls when the money ran out.'

Even though the nearest occupied table was some feet away Stirling lowered his voice to tell her of Billing's discovery of another encrypted file. Leaning forward to listen, Helen recognised the after-shave Stirling often wore and resisted an urge to reach over and put a hand to his cheek. Glancing at her watch, Helen began to gather her things together and stood.

'I've got to go, next appointment in thirty minutes.' Looking out of the high window she pulled a face, 'Worcester traffic on a Saturday morning, wonderful!'

Their eyes met and held, both aware of the underlying tension. One wanting to unpack it, the other determined not to.

'Where are you going now?' Stirling asked, determined to keep things business like.

'Over the river, to St John's. While I'm over there I'll nip over to Danes Green and see if I can find the Golf we saw at Martin's house yesterday.'

As they moved towards the stairs leading down to the main entrance, Stirling asked about the progress of enquiries to locate Martin's husband. Tight on staff, he had asked Helen to speak with a DI in Special Branch who owed him a favour. Helen said he had not got back to her yet.

Stirling stepped aside too late as two children, squealing with excitement, came bundling up the mosaic steps and barged into his legs, followed closely by a harassed young mother who offered a weary smile of apology as she passed.

Catching up with Helen on the pavement, he said, 'I forgot to say that trying to find someone in France called Martin is a bit like looking for a Smith in the UK. And it's pronounced Mar-tan. Not the anglicised style of Mar-tin.'

Helen laughed lightly and put a hand on his arm, leaving it there as she moved closer to him to say, 'Dougie, you spoil me with all the easy enquiries.'

It was said humorously but the touch on his arm and the way she held his gaze conveyed something else. Turning from him, Helen walked away as Stirling watched, admiring the movement of her hips and the shape of her legs until she turned out of sight.

He chided himself, "Leave it. You can't go back". But the memories persisted.

*

11.58 a.m.

Parked across the road, Helen checked the house number against the PNC print out for the VW Golf. Right address, but no car in the tight driveway.

Looking down the street of solid, terraced and semi-detached homes, the functional regularity of a 1950's council estate reminded Helen of home. Originally built in utilitarian pre-cast concrete, many houses on the estate had since been given a facelift of brick facades but without managing to shake off their working-class roots. Thatcher's policy of "right to buy" had introduced a confusion of individuality. Some homes had been improved well, but with aspiration and imagination constrained by tight budgets, to Helen's eye there was an air of suppressed ambition.

The house she was visiting sat at the centre of a terraced row, its front door offset to the left, a lounge window to the right and above, two bedroom windows bordered each side by faux, Provencal style window shutters; the peeling yellow paint implied a romantic whim incompatible with its plain neighbours. Many of the front gardens in the street had been converted into parking bays for vehicles which crowded up to front doors and windows, with white trades vans over represented.

Getting out of her car, Helen gave a quiet prayer of thanks she had escaped an estate like this, constantly in competition for space with her parents and three noisy siblings. The day she joined the Service was the day she had gained her freedom, determined never to return.

Not expecting a reply, Helen knocked and waited, taking in the detail of the house for clues about the owner. Around a small front lawn, a border of neatly kept shrubs and flowers suggested a pride in their garden. Getting no reply, she stepped onto the lawn to look through the lounge window. On an estate like this, she knew hawk eyed neighbours would be watching her every move, but she had not built a reputation for getting results through timidity. A small front room was over filled with a three-piece suite and a modest sized TV in the corner nearest the window. Set above a dated gas fire hung an oval, bamboo framed mirror that would have been out of fashion fifteen years ago. On the far wall above the settee were several painted landscapes and some framed family photographs. The light from the window on the glass obscured whatever was inside them. An open door from the lounge gave a narrow view through to a small dining room at the rear where a table and chairs sat below a window with the curtains drawn closed. If the front garden was any indicator, the rear garden would be small but well kept. The overall impression was of a cramped but tidily kept home.

Helen was about to cross the pavement towards her car when a man's voice called out. 'Need any help, love?'

Turning in the direction of the voice, she saw a man in his sixties standing in the front door of the neighbouring house, reluctant to venture out fully but too curious to miss the chance of finding out more.

Pointing at the house and giving him her most trustful smile, Helen answered, 'I was trying to contact the lady,'

'She's out!' he barked across the lawns.

"No shit, Einstein" she thought. Keeping her smile in place, Helen answered politely, 'I noticed. What time does she usually get back?'

Eying Helen up and down with open suspicion, and something she knew would be unsavoury, he looked past her. He had been nosing out of the window long enough to associate the car with her.

'Who's asking?' he demanded.

Ducking the question, she answered, 'I'm Helen.'

The man stepped out of his door to glance sideways to his neighbour's house then stared at Helen distrustfully, one hand held across his chest with yellowed fingers cupping a thin cigarette. His other hand scratched idly at the contents of unwashed, ill-fitting trousers. He hadn't shaved for several days and Helen doubted he had bathed for longer still. She didn't need to get close to him to know how he would smell. Twelve years of interviewing witnesses and suspects had stamped the odour onto her memory so indelibly, she could taste it.

Taking a heavy draw on the thin cigarette, he narrowed his eyes against the smoke and light ash. 'Who are you then, social services? Or a copper?' His jaw jutted aggressively.

Helen considered going to speak with him but didn't want to be drawn into explanations. 'No. I'll come back another time.' Without allowing him time to bark another question at her she walked to her car.

*

Taff Morgan stared after the car until it disappeared before returning indoors. Kicking the scuffed front door shut behind him with his heel, he slumped back into the stained armchair that allowed him to watch both the street and a television that was rarely switched off. Scratching at his crotch through habit, he sucked the last life out of the roll up and squinted against the smoke as he thought about the good-looking woman.

Blowing smoke up to the yellowed ceiling, he spat a stray strand of tobacco onto the dirty carpet and declared to the empty room, 'Fucking copper!'

*

Three miles away, two women walked arm in arm along a wide promenade next to the river, both wrapped in coats against the cool air. High above them, the ornate limestone tower of the cathedral stood pinned onto a light blue sky with white clouds fleeing before a cool breeze.

A black balustraded railing separated walkers from the river, dirty brown and swollen by heavy rains which had fallen several days ago in the Welsh mountains. Driven inland by storms, seagulls wheeled, screamed and swooped to steal bread thrown by children and strollers to the clamouring ducks below.

An observant passer-by might have noticed the two women were only two or three years apart in age. The older, well dressed woman in her early fifties was only slightly shorter than her companion who looked the older of the two with greying hair that had once been blonde falling evenly onto her shoulders, brown eyes staring ahead and indifferent to people strolling past. Where the older woman's coat was warm and of this season's styling, her companion's coat gave little protection against the thin wind. Pulling it tighter around her she shivered into the older woman's side.

Walking in silence, they stopped to watch a family feeding swans which had nudged up to the river's edge, waiting for small hands to throw bread. Watching a small girl totter ungainly to the balustrade with bread clutched tightly in a dimpled fist, the woman with greying hair began to weep, drawing an impatient rebuke from her smart companion. Fishing about in a pocket of the thin coat and mumbling apologies, she drew out a damp tissue and wiped ineffectually at her nose.

'For God's sake, pull yourself together!' hissed the smart woman. 'I thought this would do you good, to get out of the house and some fresh air.'

The younger woman nodded compliantly, as she was used to doing, allowing herself to be tugged forwards by their linked arms to leave the family behind. As her companion talked, she said little, agreeing where she was expected to and trying hard to remember what she was being told. Seeing her confusion, the smart woman stopped abruptly and grabbed her by both arms to force attention on her, speaking forcefully before darting a look around to see if anyone was watching.

An old man sitting on a wooden bench nearby enjoying the sunshine watched the women curiously through rheumy eyes, a black Labrador dog alert at his feet. Giving him a cold stare, the smart woman pulled her companion's arm back into hers and led her past the old man.

Watching them pass by and continue down the river walk, the old man speculated idly on the relationship between the two women. Reaching down, he scratched the dog's head and remarked, 'I wouldn't want to cross that'un Sam.'

The dog's ears pricked and looked up at him with intelligent eyes, wagging a reply and whimpering softly as he watched the children playing.

*

12.16 p.m.
Stirling had enjoyed getting out of the office and returned to the MCU reluctantly. Everyone was busy. Heal was answering queries from his team, fielding calls from the enquiry teams and badgering people to do what needed to be done. Stirling tapped on the

window of Edwards's office as he went past. Edwards raised a hand and returned to the papers on his desk.

Half an hour later, a tap at the door made Stirling look up to see Heal in the doorway with his notebook, interested to know more about Stirling's visit to the scene that morning. Every good detective was greedy for information. Stirling described what he had found, the search now being carried out by the TF and described the file Billing had given him, which would be with him soon to which Heal groaned theatrically.

'Anything back from the cousin yet Geordie?'

'Aye, boss. She's a bit vague but remembers the ring because she asked him about it a few years ago. All she can tell us is it was a signet ring with some kind of design on it, sort of circular like, and ...' he paused to decipher his own writing, '... thought it was to do with some sort of club he was a member of.' Geordie looked up and shrugged his shoulders. 'Sorry, best she can do. The Mason's, perhaps?'

'I hope not!' Stirling replied. 'We've got enough to think about without the bloody Masons as well!'

Stirling had strong opinions about fairness. As a young officer, he had watched with scorn as incompetent officers were promoted over the heads of colleagues of proven ability because of who they knew. Only after some high-profile scandals nationally had exposed perceptions of inappropriate influence had the Service discouraged membership of secretive associations. Stirling thought of Ballard's smug face. Who could know?

'Okay, let's not make assumptions Geordie. So far as we can see, Pemberton's ring had a circular form to the design. The masonic symbol is unlike that so unless we receive firm information to say we should, I'm not unpacking any links to the Masons. What about the legs in the picture?'

'She says Pemberton arrived on his own. They belong to another guest he happened to be sitting next to.'

Stirling swore softly. If Pemberton had taken his current squeeze to the wedding, it would have brought them closer to his recent private life. Heal confirmed that apart from the call from Martin's mobile to Pemberton the evening before he died, there had been no calls between their phones in the six months of collected data. Cell site analysis put Martin's mobile phone within the mast footprint for her home when the call was made, and for much of the following day. The analysis showed Pemberton's phone receiving the call in St Martin's Square, where it remained until he left for the crime scene about seven thirty the next morning. Stirling asked about the analysis for the crime scene.

'There's a couple of overlapping masts covering The Wern. Intel has triangulated the data and we've a schedule of all mobile phones passing through the footprint, but none stopped there. They've sliced the data and we can see Pemberton's phone entering the cell at 7.44 a.m. There were no calls to or from his phone, but it continues to shake hands with the mast until...' frowning, Heal searched the heavily printed sheet of data in his hand, '... 9.07 a.m. when it went dead close to the scene. It's not been switched on since, not a peep. If they'd switched it on only to find they were locked out, it would have registered on the provider's network. We'll get immediate notice if it's switched on.'

To cover their tracks, the killer needed only to destroy the phone and dispose of it in several pieces. Was it an attempt to delay identification, or had they only wanted the SIM card? With a SIM card reader, the content could be read without it registering on the network. Stirling thought of the women Pemberton had been blackmailing.

'How many other phones were inside the mast at The Wern between the relevant times that morning? Someone might have walked down to meet him there.'

'With the main road running nearby, a little under two hundred! None were registering alongside his phone between him arriving and his mobile leaving the site.'

'Are we certain? There can't be any foul up on this.' Stirling knew this was crucial.

'Certain. I had them run the data twice. That made me popular!' Heal remarked jovially. 'We can see Osmand travelling through the cell about the time he says he found the body, but there's nothing more of interest until the patrol get there later that morning. Pemberton was the only person down there with a mobile switched on.'

'Okay, but raise an action to input into HOLMES all mobile phones passing through the mast between 7.30a.m. and 9.30 a.m. in case one of them cross matches with other data collected from elsewhere. We can't exclude someone arriving on foot.'

Once Heal had noted down the action, Stirling asked, 'What about the drugs angle, anything flagged against him at region or the NCA?' Stirling was referring to the national system of "flagging" by law enforcement agencies to register an interest in someone without revealing their hand, to avoid so-called "blue on blue" operations; where one agency blunders unwittingly into another's investigation. There was no interest in Pemberton for drugs and Stirling was pleased to agree Heal's proposal to suspend the line of enquiry.

'Thanks Geordie. After the team briefing on Monday morning, I want you, Bill, Croft and Billing to meet with me at ten when we'll hypothecate every line of enquiry with the aim of shutting down or suspending a few. Helen too, she's leading an important leg of the investigation.'

Geordie gathered up his papers and left, grinning to himself. As office manager, he had one of the best jobs in the force, involved in key decision making but able to keep a finger in the operational pie.

A glance at the clock above the door confirmed what Stirling's stomach had been telling him for some time. Heading for the door he decided to grab some lunch from the local supermarket.

1.52 p.m.
Walking to the kitchen with a packet of sandwiches in his hand, Stirling decided to see if Edwards was still at his desk to chat through the meeting with Heal. Seeing the chair empty, he stood in the doorway listening in the direction of the kitchen for Edwards's voice when something on the desk tweaked his professional curiosity.

A witness statement lay ready for signing but it was the evidential standard photograph albums next to it which had caught his eye. Interested to know what Edwards was working on, Stirling went to the desk. Pulling open the sandwich wrapper, he took a hungry bite as he rotated one of the albums to face him and opened it half way through.

With a sickening lurch in his gut, Stirling found himself looking into the sightless eyes which had been haunting him.

Unprepared, Stirling stepped away, the bread in his mouth a wad of damp cardboard. Swallowing with difficulty, he stared at the album lying open on the desk. His first reaction was to walk away but felt compelled to look. Was it as he remembered? Might the photographs assuage the guilt he felt?

Stepping forward, Stirling began to look through the albums from the beginning. The photographs were sequenced to show the overall scene for context, the girl's body covered by a medic's blanket, getting ever closer and more detailed. Seeing the girl's disfigured head and broken body again took Stirling back to the scene. He could sense the cold wind and rain on the back of his neck and his hands.

The last album documented the post mortem. Stirling had attended too many to linger over these and rippled the edges under his thumb disinterestedly until a brief glimpse of a detail made him stop and turn back the pages. Pulling open the first album of the scene, he found the picture he was seeking and studied the detail again.

Someone clearing their throat made Stirling look round to see Edwards stood in the doorway and looking uncomfortable. 'Sorry, Doug. I should have put those out of sight. I gave Ballard a hand over report on the day but got an email from him yesterday demanding my witness statement by Monday. I was using the albums to be sure I'd covered everything.'

Waving away his concern, Stirling asked, 'D'you see anything in these pictures of interest to our investigation?'

Coming to stand beside Stirling, Edwards looked at the albums now arranged side by side and frowned, unable to understand how there could possibly be any link between the two investigations. 'Sorry, you'd better explain what's bothering you.'

Stirling put his finger on a photo of the girl lay under the bridge with her abdomen revealed. 'The mark by her waistline, Bill. From above it looked like road oil or something off the road surface, and I wasn't in any mood to stand there staring at her. But in the post mortem photos I can see what it is!'

Edwards cast his mind back to the examination, still confused how the girl could be linked to Pemberton's death. 'She had a tattoo. What of it?'

Seeing his confusion Stirling said impatiently, 'Bill, it's the same Celtic design as the picture in Pemberton's lounge! Is that important to us?'

Perplexed, Edwards bent to stare again at the images but saw nothing remarkable, other than to remind him of many heated arguments with his teenage daughter, badgering him and Ellen for their permission to have a tattoo like "all of her friends had."

Answering cautiously, he said, 'I don't remember the picture in the apartment, but I'll take your word for it. I can look through the scene photos. But, you do know that Celtic designs have been very popular as tattoos for years now, don't you? Personally, I wouldn't get too excited about it.'

Stirling stared hard at the picture. Was he reading too much into it? Picking up a sheet of paper from the desk, Stirling drew the picture in Pemberton's apartment and put it alongside the photos. 'That's hanging on the lounge wall. It's essentially the same symbol, with that same variation in style.'

Taking it from him to study it more closely, Edwards saw a pattern which reminded him vaguely of the Chinese symbol of Yin and Yang, sometimes sexualised to represent soixante-neuf. This pattern had a similar, third element, all within a circle delicately embellished with three bramble roses. Handing the drawing back with an unconvinced pull of his mouth, Edwards related the difficulties with their daughter.

'Every tattoo shop has a range of Celtic designs Doug. It was probably just a pretty design that she liked. I'll keep an open mind for the moment, but I'll need some persuading that it's got anything to do with our case.'

'Okay, but they're remarkably similar.' Stirling left, his hunger forgotten.

He was half way down the corridor when a thought checked him and he went back. Edwards looked up from signing his statement, a question mark on his face.

'Bill, I've been kept completely in the dark by Ballard, he's treated me little better than a suspect! I avoided the news coverage because of the way they were portraying me.' He pointed at the photos albums. 'I know nothing about her, who was she? What was her name?'

Edwards shared Stirling's contempt for Ballard's incompetence. 'I've no idea. She hadn't been identified when I handed over to Ballard and I've had nothing to do with it since. I've been busy ever since with other investigations and two jury trials.'

Edwards examined the album covers. 'Her name's not on here either, just the operational name for Ballard's investigation. I've had the same treatment as you, Doug. He sees me as your mate and considers me a threat. Which I would be, given half a chance.'

A cold smile formed as Edwards savoured the possibility of puncturing Ballard's pompous bubble. 'I had a couple of phone calls to clarify some detail, but that's it. It was just another sad death amongst the many we deal with and I was extremely busy, anyway. To tell you the truth, I was only too glad not to have to work for the prat.'

Stirling was leaving again when Edwards called him back and held out his lunch. As Stirling took it from him, Edwards tapped the albums.

'I know you're under pressure to get a result, but we should avoid clutching at straws. The tattoo? It's a coincidence.'

3.23 p.m.
Only one of the scene photos of Pemberton's apartment showed the collection of paintings in the lounge and the design he needed to view was obscured by the camera flash bouncing off the glass. He could have got it brought into the MCU but had taken the chance to escape the office.

Alone again in the apartment, Stirling looked around the lounge as he waited for SOCO to arrive. He could pick out the changes caused by the PolSA search which had checked every loose floorboard, cavity and anywhere that might conceal evidence with nothing of interest discovered other than a Victorian farthing. What Pemberton had done with the original photographs remained a mystery. Stirling was surprised they still did not know where the Jaguar was stored. Perhaps he had garaged it with someone he knew?

Standing in front of the abstract oil paintings, Stirling wondered if he was being fanciful in interpreting an anger or violence in the raw lines and brush strokes. Moving closer to the Celtic symbol he saw that what he had first thought to be a print was hand drawn, faint pencil marks visible amongst the black ink. With no signatures on any of the abstract paintings or the symbol, they were so dissimilar that it was impossible to know if they had been done by one or more people.

Edwards was right to be sceptical, but a niggling instinct was driving Stirling to know more about it. It was a loose thread. He would need to find out who the girl was too and wondered how he might avoid speaking directly to Ballard.

Pulling out his mobile, Stirling photographed the symbol and called Jaz Cooke who he knew was working alone. Mick Banner had requested time off to go to the rugby match to witness the local side's relegation. Banner defined loyalty.

After a brief conversation, Stirling sent the photo to Cooke as a knock at the door announced the arrival of two SOCOs. Still not entirely sure of his reasoning but staying true to his instincts, Stirling instructed them to photograph the pictures in-situ and then seize and bag each one separately.

Ignoring their questioning looks, he left them to it.

4.32 p.m.
Stirling was pulling into the yard at the MCU when Croft rang with information of Pemberton's finances which he had emailed across, but wanted to give him the headlines.

'Regarding Pemberton's personal accounts, as we thought, he was broke. But there have been occasional, significant deposits during the last five years. All cash, so no transfer details from other banks but they *might* correspond with the extorted monies DC Williams has talked to me about when we compare the dates.

'City of London Police confirm a senior partner at James solicitors features in a criminal enterprise that's defrauded several banks over the past ten years and hundreds of private investors in investment scams similar to the Fairway development. Many of the victims are retirees and ex-pats who have lost their life savings. Because there are several UK police services involved and some overseas law enforcement agencies too, CoLP will lead and coordinate the investigation. Consequently, I'll be submitting our evidence to them in the next few days. The SFO is involved too.'

An alarm bell rang in Stirling's mind as Croft described sending papers to London. 'How much are we talking about? Does it mean I've lost control of that element of my investigation?'

'Impossible to say. Millions in sterling, large Euro and dollar losses too, plus dirty money being washed through the various investment schemes, I'm told. Information gathered by us remains available to you, but the wider UK investigation must proceed.'

'So, where does Pemberton fit in? His lifestyle doesn't suggest he was a player in an international investment scam.'

'I suspect Pemberton was an associate of our local solicitor and got drawn into something he didn't understand on the promise of big returns and got skinned himself. I'm told the main players are career criminals who specialise in these kinds of scams. As we know, fraud gives high returns with low risk and is often sited offshore. They've operated a series of "boiler room" investment frauds with different wrappers, but all with the same generic scam.'

'The local firm of lawyers is James and James?'

'Correct.'

'So, is the whole firm bent?'

'No, not at all. Only one name has appeared consistently in the transactions we've seen and is referenced in the investigations. The chap I named previously, Parry?'

Stirling was about to breathe a sigh of relief as Croft added, 'However, if Parry transacted matters under the umbrella of the partnership's good name to lend credibility, I can't exclude the possibility that someone else in the practice might have been involved. Alternatively, the partners might have derived some financial benefit through their annual company dividends. I think it's unlikely, but I can't exclude it for the moment.'

Ending the call, Stirling thought through the consequences for Ayesha. If she was implicated in a large-scale fraud, if only by unwitting association, he would have to consider the risk to his professional reputation and, by implication, to the force itself. Stirling was struggling to think Ayesha could knowingly be involved in anything dishonest but, in the cold light of day, just how well did he truly know her?

5.00 p.m.

Reading through Croft's report, Stirling decided that without any intelligence to the contrary, he could rule out a revenge killing by an Organised Crime Group, an OCG. The injuries were inconsistent with a contract killing and Pemberton had clearly not been a "controlling mind" in the fraud Croft described. But, had someone drawn into the scam by Pemberton taken their own brutal revenge?

He thought back to Greening's account of the disturbances at Pemberton's house. Cole had admitted going to Pemberton's home, but had he told the complete truth? Running through the men they had discussed in team briefings, two, possibly three characters known to the enquiry came straight to mind, Osmand and Billy Cole amongst them. Smiling at the prospect of a combative interview, Stirling wondered which of them he would like to talk to. Anything to get away from this desk, he thought. He was contemplating the pros and cons of each option when his phone rang.

'Helen?'

'Hi. I've tried the Danes Green address twice but there's no one there so I'll try again tomorrow.'

'Okay, what about the other woman you were going to see, similar story?'

'Yes, but different again. Her name's Valerie Downing. She's a much stronger personality than the others I've met and he would not have got very far threatening her! She's not in the least shy in talking about what the two of them got up to, quite the opposite in fact. If she was a sub with Pemberton, she's a committed dom now with her own network.' Stirling heard Helen give a low chuckle, 'She has a *very* low opinion of men and the boot is very much on the other foot, literally!'

Helen continued, 'She did lose a lot of money to him, though. She loaned him a large chunk of money as a straightforward loan to help him with Fairway and he strung her along with excuses until she accepted the money was lost. She's wealthy enough to be philosophical about the loss and her alibi's strong. I've got her statement.'

'Anything else?' He was impatient to press on.

Irritated at Stirling's impatience, Helen added sharply, 'The reason I'm calling you is because Downing knows Katrina Martin through their extended social circles. She says many years ago, Martin and Pemberton were *definitely* involved, soon after Martin moved up from London. Martin's husband worked away in London a lot. The interesting thing is, Downing confirms Pemberton didn't gossip about other women, but he would sometimes mention Martin. Pillow talk you might say, but he had a strong dislike for Martin.'

'Why?'

'She never found out but there was definitely bad feeling between them. Downing says that once when she was at his place … *playing* … Downing pushed him to tell her and he lost his temper and treated her quite badly. She thought she was getting what he wanted to do to Martin.'

'And she gave him money, after that?'

'It was a long time ago. She has an appetite for risk, physical or financial, which is why she's a wealthy woman. The loan was about four years ago and she got taken in by his patter about the potential return on investment.'

'Okay. I know you've had a long day, but are you free this evening?'

6.43 p.m.

For a moment, Helen had felt her heart lift. Thinking Stirling was about to suggest something social, she had forced herself to keep her voice neutral when he explained what he had in mind.

Leaving Stirling's car on a hotel car park to the east of the city, Helen drove them towards Pershore. Stirling had intended taking Edwards to see Osmand but thought an experienced female detective alongside might help. It would also allow them time to talk about Downing and the other women. With Cooke busy on the enquiry Stirling had given him, he had sent another pair of detectives to find Billy Cole to have another look at him. Stirling was quietly hoping the evening would deliver the breakthrough he desperately needed.

Travelling in the opposite direction from Evesham and the Cotswolds was a steady file of cars full of families and day trippers returning from their holidays and days out. It reminded Stirling that it was less than a week since he had been walking with Ayesha. It seemed more like a month. A clean evening sky invited recreation rather than looking for a murderer. Helen was talking about Downing's relationship with Pemberton.

Watching the road ahead for the junction they needed, Stirling asked, 'So, there's no jealous husband in the background?'

'No. She was a liberated divorcee and happy to be seen out on Pemberton's arm. She knew about his reputation and that it wouldn't last, so she enjoyed it for what it was. As far as she was concerned it was mainly about the sex. She's very candid. Says it opened her mind to something she'd been curious about for some time but might not have experienced otherwise. She's got her own network of devotees now through the internet.' Williams looked across at Stirling with an amused expression. 'A woman who enjoys exercising control through sex.'

Continuing to watch the road ahead, Stirling murmured flatly, 'No change there then.'

Stirling returned to the conversation. 'Each to their own Helen, but it's an interesting dynamic. What interests me is that Pemberton seems to have treated some women differently to others. Did it depend on their strength of character, or the absence of it?'

'I'm not sure,' she said. 'We're not psychologists and people are infinitely variable in their needs and motivations, and their flaws too of course ...'

Stirling cut in, 'Not professionally, no. But we shouldn't underestimate the real-world experience we get in dealing with society's damaged goods every day. We meet and deal with people at every level of society and all character types from the "mad and bad" to the simply inadequate, and all shades in between. With all the mental health problems in our communities it's almost always in dynamic, fluid situations. An eminent professor of psychology friend of mine once told me it was experience most psychologists and psychiatrists would love to have. So much of their work takes place in either secure or controlled environments.'

Helen glanced at Stirling appraisingly as he continued, 'We might not be able to apply fancy clinical labels to all the behaviours we encounter but, more often than not, we learn how to respond appropriately.' Stirling touched the old scar on his shoulder, adding, 'The hard way, sometimes.'

Stirling pointed out a turning ahead. Helen slowed to wait for a gap in the oncoming traffic and turned into a country lane skirting the west of Pershore. Free of the heavy traffic, she took the car up through the gears quickly, handling the car confidently through the long sweeping bends.

With a straight stretch of road ahead, Helen returned to their conversation. 'That's you talking with your negotiator hat on. What I was going to say is the whole sub-dom dynamic *is* complex. I've done some reading over the last few days to be sure I understood it better. In BDSM they speak of the "gift." The sub *gifts* power to the dom, surrendering control in a mutual exchange of pleasure. I think we have that dynamic in *some* of the relationships with Pemberton. I don't believe all of them understood what they were getting involved in but, for the most part, they say it was in the context of a mutually affectionate and stimulating relationship. Well, to begin with, anyway. He rewarded them with attention and care for their "gift" of submission and sexual satisfaction. Mutually so, for the most part. For some it filled an emotional gap in their lives, or at that particular moment in their lives. It's complex but perhaps it taps into something primal. Giving to receive, creating mutual dependency.'

Stirling was reminded of the negotiator's strategy of creating dependency within hostage situations, the so-called "Stockholm Syndrome" before replying, 'Sexual relationships can be fascinatingly complex. Even boring ones, I suppose.'

Hoping to draw him into an intimate conversation, Helen smiled complicitly. 'Well, no one could ever accuse you of boring sex, Dougie.'

Stirling ignored the remark. 'We'll need to be careful with our language around BDSM in team meetings. What people do privately and consensually is their own affair.'

Ignoring the rebuff, Helen replied, 'I agree, and think how it contrasts with sexual violence against women that we usually encounter. Remember the rape I worked on a few years ago? He kept her in his home for three days, raping her repeatedly, and other degradations. That had nothing to do with mutual pleasure and everything to do with sadistic, self-gratification. She'll spend the rest of her life looking over her shoulder and fearful.'

Stirling could hear an angry edge to Helen's voice as he recalled the case. It was a terrifying ordeal for the young woman who was lucky to survive. Helen had spent a huge amount of time supporting the victim all the way to trial, many months later.

Stirling broke the thoughtful silence that had fallen. 'The photographs suggest a developing sadistic streak in Pemberton and I'm concerned whether all the women he knew made it home safely. If Pemberton *was* bitter with Martin, it couldn't just have been because she wouldn't submit to his fetish, surely? He'd have been rebuffed by many women over the years. I think something else happened, either personal or professional.'

Checking a print out of the last police contact with him, Stirling directed Helen for the last mile to the village where Osmand lived. He had decided it would be a knock on the door. Although not a suspect, for the moment, even as a witness he wanted to catch Osmand off guard.

7.32 p.m.

There was no answer at Osmand's address. Some door knocking at the neighbours' homes gleaned the reluctantly given information that Osmand would most likely be drinking in the village, on the promise that Stirling would not divulge who had told him, because Osmand was "a nasty bastard".

The village had two pubs. Stirling doubted the gastro-pub with a car park stuffed with Range Rovers and other expensive marques was the sort of place where Osmand would feel at home, or would be made welcome. Instead, he settled for the second pub looking much as it must have done fifty years ago, hunched quietly at the edge of the road leading out of the village, trying to avoid the attentions of prosperity. Prominent amongst a collection of older cars and pickups parked outside was Osmand's battered Land Rover. Stopping to peer into the cab as they walked past, Stirling saw the butt of a shotgun stowed behind the driver's seat. An unattended firearm would be useful leverage.

Ducking his head to enter the low door to the bar, Stirling stood with Helen at his side and scanned the room quickly, looking for Osmand. The room stretched left and right with a wood clad bar opposite the door, a hammered copper surface dimly reflecting the bar's poor lighting. There was a fusty, tired feeling to the room. Between the door and the bar, a path worn across dark flag stones marked the passage of thirst as villagers and farm hands through the generations had found their way there at the end of long working days. A low ceiling was supported by dark beams onto which tarnished horse brasses had been nailed randomly without care for regularity or alignment, harking back to a bygone era. On the walls hung obsolete horse bits, bridles and other reminders of the village's lost rural purpose.

The sullen atmosphere of the room was matched by the low, murmured conversations of a dozen men still in working clothes who sat at tables around the bar playing dominoes or cribbage, passing the time of day with men they had known all of their lives. And all of their indiscretions too.

Unburdened by heavy custom, the landlord leant with his arms folded on the bar, his head bent over a newspaper spread across the bar. Unshaven and overweight with greasy thinning hair combed back from a shrewd face, the landlord continued reading until the dying conversation got his attention. Following the collective gaze of his regulars, he joined them in staring at the smartly dressed couple at the door.

Wearing a suit and tie, with Helen in black jeans and white blouse, Stirling knew they looked out of place. Most would assume they were a couple looking for the other pub, but it would be a matter of moments before shrewd, country instinct moved past that assumption. Stirling was searching the room for anyone who might present a threat. He saw no one that troubled him, but neither could he see anyone fitting Osmand's description.

A movement at the furthest end of the room where the bar counter returned around a pillar caught his attention. Osmand was stood where he could watch the room, resting meaty hands on the bar edge as he stared across the room at him. Nursing his beer, Osmand had not bothered to look up when the door opened until he felt the silence. Looking lazily across the room, he had recognised the man immediately. Their eyes met and held across the room, each instinctively judging the other for size and strength.

Walking towards Osmand, Stirling gave each of the other men a curt nod that said he had no interest in them, and they had no business with him. Helen followed, and all conversation stopped as everyone tracked their progress towards the village rogue, each sensing the altered atmosphere and anticipating what might follow.

Stirling had done this many times over the years. Usually, there was no problem but sometimes it could go spectacularly wrong. Getting closer, he took in Osmand's appearance. Dressed in a check patterned wool shirt with the sleeves rolled above his elbows and dirty jeans tucked into builder's boots, even allowing for his beer gut, there was no mistaking Osmand's physical bulk and strength. There was a brooding surliness about his hard features that spoke of a rough life and a bullying demeanour as he watched Stirling from under heavy brows.

As Stirling neared, Osmand stepped away from the bar to leave his hands and boots free to swing if needed, his eyes darting around the room to see where his support would come from. Hunching his shoulders, he moved one foot behind the other for balance and lowered his jaw as he measured the detective's capability. Stirling recognised Osmand was intuitively weighing his options and would obey his instincts with little regard to the consequences.

Stopping a yard in front of Osmand and loud enough for the others to hear, Stirling gave him a tight smile and said, 'Hello Jim.'

Behind him, chair legs scraping on flagstones told Stirling that some men were leaving. Or preparing to join the sport. Unable to take his eyes from Osmand, he would have to rely on Helen to watch his back. Putting her back to Stirling, Helen glared at two well-built men in their twenties who had risen to their feet and fancied having a go. Holding her warrant card out with one hand, she fixed them with a hard stare and motioned them to sit again. The older of the two men sat immediately but the other stood glaring aggressively, only sitting reluctantly when his friend tugged at his jacket sleeve and muttered something to him.

Hearing the silence fall behind him and seeing Osmand's attention shift back to him, Stirling began to introduce himself, 'I'm Detective Chief Inspector ...'

'I know who you are,' Osmand interrupted aggressively, loud enough for the room to hear.

Aware that everyone in the bar was now watching, and waiting, deciding on which side to take, Stirling lowered his voice so that only Osmand could hear.

'Jim, we can do this at the police station if you prefer, but if you make me fight you out of here, I'll have the local law all over you like a rash.' Jerking a thumb over his shoulder, he added, 'And anyone I decide to associate with you.'

Osmand stared at him mulishly, hesitating. Stirling knew he must dominate the situation quickly and smiled a challenge. 'Jim, I'll let you into a secret. I've had a really shit few weeks, so a bar fight will suit me just fine! Work off a little tension. So, either make a start, or we could sit down and have a quiet chat over a beer?'

Osmand remembered the detective's fitness up the hill that morning and now, close up, knew instinctively that Stirling would be a hard fight. Osmand was used to men being frightened of him, but this man had no fear.

Noticing Osmand's eyes roving across the bar behind him, Stirling realised Osmand's reputation amongst the locals hung in the balance and gestured to an alcove with an empty table nearby.

Puffing his chest out, Osmand jutted his chin towards the room and growled, 'Pint of bitter then, if you're buying. We'll talk back here, away from them nosey bastards,' and stepped towards the alcove.

The landlord, who had been hovering at the other end of the bar with one hand on the telephone, came over to serve their drinks before Osmand changed his mind. After handing Stirling his change, he began to busy himself nearby, intending to eavesdrop the conversation. Leaning over the bar, Stirling suggested quietly he should return to his paper. The landlord stared at him stubbornly and muttered it was his pub and he'd stand where he liked. Pointing to dirty shelving and stale sandwiches smiling from under a grubby plastic cover, Stirling asked him when he had last had his kitchens inspected by environmental services. Taking the hint, the landlord grudgingly shuffled off and with a long, baleful glare at Stirling, returned to his paper.

Steering Osmand into a seat where he could not be distracted by the regulars, Stirling took a chair with a view of the room over Osmand's shoulder. Taking a sip of his beer, he was surprised to find it tasted better than expected.

They quickly eliminated Osmand as the man who had visited Pemberton's apartment. He had no idea where the dead man had lived, less still money to invest in property. He rented his home, having taken it over when his Mother died.

His account of discovering the body remained consistent but watching his features as they talked, Stirling saw an amusement playing at the corners of Osmand's mouth and something shifting behind the cunning eyes.

Osmand struggled to keep himself from leering at Helen's breasts but Stirling knew she would ignore it for so long as it served to keep his attention, or needed to put him in his place. To keep him talking, and to stroke his ego, Stirling asked Osmand about his lifestyle, treating his poaching lightly as a countryman's legitimate pursuit whilst avoiding the contentious issue of taking deer. Slowly, Osmand relaxed and his usual boastful nature returned.

Helen asked how often he visited The Wern. Osmand lifted the glass to his lips and sipped at his beer slowly as he pretended to think, slipping his eyes to take another surreptitious glance down her cleavage. She guessed Osmand's age to be about thirty-five but a lifetime's exposure to all weathers and hard physical work gave him the look of a man ten years older. Ignoring his sliding eyes, she stared at him unwaveringly as she waited for his answer.

Setting his glass down, Osmand replied, 'I'm across there a couple of times a week, usually. There was a small farm there once, but it's not been a working farm since I was a kid. It was more a cottage with some outbuildings. When I was 'bout fifteen or sixteen, there was a chap living there for a time. Had a fancy car like the one I found the body in. He'd have women with him sometimes. I'd see him outside the house with 'em.'

Seeing the officers waiting for him to continue, Osmand went on. 'Well, sometimes, in the nice weather, summer like, he'd bring the women up into the wood above the cottage. They'd be, well ... you know.' He smiled crudely.

Helen persevered, 'What did you see Jim?'

'They'd be screwing!' Osmand exclaimed, thinking it obvious what he meant.

'And was there anything *different* about what they were doing, the sex?'

Osmand shifted in his seat, glancing uncertainly between the two detectives.

Helen gave him a sympathetic shrug and smiled indulgently. 'Come on Jim, you were a young lad. Naturally, you'd have been curious.'

Picking up his glass again Osmand raised it to take a sip but set it back on the table. Glancing over his shoulder to be sure no one could hear, Osmand bent forward to speak more quietly.

'The bloke was posh with longish blonde hair. Dressed smart, too.' He looked at Stirling, 'He'd tie the women up against that tree you was looking at this morning. The big oak.'

As he watched Stirling's surprise, Osmand gave a cunning grin. Recognising he had Stirling at a disadvantage for the first time, he added, 'You didn't have a clue I was there, did you? You almost fell on top of me.'

Recalling the pricking sensation down his spine and the sense of a presence, Stirling understood. He realised too that Osmand probably had a firearm with him. Stirling decided to massage Osmand's ego. 'I'm impressed Jim, you had the drop on me. Okay, go on.'

Osmand sat looking at him smugly, thinking how much he would enjoy telling the story later to the men in the bar. With his confidence returning, he replied, 'He'd bring different women up there. There was three or four over a couple of years, dark haired mostly but one was blonde ...' he gave Stirling a vulgar wink, '... real blonde, if you know what I mean, not a stitch on.'

Warming to his subject, Osmand began to drop his guard and as Helen drew him methodically through his story, Stirling watched and listened, trying to divine the truth behind the tale. How he gestured freely to describe some aspects of his story or tightened and frowned if asked something that might lead to talking about his own conduct.

Enjoying himself, Osmand continued. 'He'd tie 'em 'gainst that old oak and whip 'em for a while with a riding crop and different things until they'd beg him to stop, then he'd fuck ...' Osmand checked himself, looking at Helen who ignored the obscenity, '... well, you know what I mean. Funny thing was though, after, he'd make a real fuss of 'em, talking nice like and they'd go back down to the cottage. He'd leave the ropes and stuff on the tree but they went. Took 'em when he left, I reckons.'

Deciding to take a punt, Helen asked, 'And the photographs?'

Osmand frowned as he cast his mind back. 'Yeah, he'd have a camera with him sometimes, taking pictures.'

'Did the women seem to be agreeing to being treated like that?' asked Helen.

Seeing Osmand's puzzled expression, as if the idea had never occurred to him, she added, 'Do you think the man with the blonde hair had the women's permission to hurt them?'

Osmand sat looking into his empty glass for a few moments as if the answer might lie amongst its frothy dregs. 'Dunno. Seemed like they was playing a game, I thought. Mind you ...' Osmand smirked, '... they yelped when he was laying the crop on. It was usually the same. He'd smack 'em and then he'd screw 'em up 'gainst the tree. One of 'em used to cry a lot, a little dark haired piece.'

'Did any of the women appear to be completely unwilling to be there, they might have tried to stop him tying them up, perhaps?'

'Not as I remember, not when I were there,' he answered, lifting his glass to drain the dregs and set it back on the table with a questioning look at Stirling.

Calling the landlord across, Stirling ordered more drinks and watched Osmand discreetly whilst he waited. Looking at the sheen of sweat on the man's upper lip and easing himself into a more comfortable position as he talked to Helen's chest, Stirling suspected Osmand had become aroused at reliving what he had seen in the wood. After the landlord had drifted away, Stirling put the fresh beers on the table and picked up the conversation.

' .... school holidays and weekends, I was always out roaming. I'd bring rabbits and pigeon home for me and Mum and sell some to the neighbours. My old man was a bastard who drank anything he earned, so I did what I could. After a couple of years, the bloke stopped bringing women up to the wood and there was just one woman who was there a lot, the blonde I said about just now, a real looker. Looked like they was living together.'

'You said the blonde woman came into the woods with him?' asked Stirling. He couldn't remember a blonde woman in the photos with the tree.

'Yeah, to start with, he done the same with her like he done with the others, but then they'd be down the cottage all the time, weekends and evenings too. Then her lived on her own for a few months and then her was gone too. About then I started working on a farm round here, so I didn't get across there much. It were empty for years before being flattened.'

Stirling thought of the chill sensation he had felt in the copse earlier that day. Was it because Osmand was watching him, or had it been something more preternatural? Why and how had the blonde woman disappeared?

'Anything different about her from the others, Jim?' asked Helen, knowing Stirling would want to explore this.

Taking a gulp of his beer, Osmand thought hard as he wiped his mouth with the back of his hand. 'Can't think of anything. A bit skinny, long blonde hair ...' Osmand smirked at something. 'I'd go down to the cottage in the evenings if they was there and peek through the windows to see what they was doing, but it'd be ordinary stuff like reading and listening to music.'

Stirling spoke. 'This morning, you saw me holding some photographs. We have photos of women, taken down by the cottage, with a car?'

Osmand nodded. 'I'd watch him from the wood doing the same sort of stuff down there with 'em.'

'What type of car was it Jim?' asked Stirling.

'It was an old Jag like the one I found the bloke in.'

They talked on for several more minutes but Osmand couldn't offer any more useful information. He looked pointedly at his empty glass, but Stirling had no intention of buying him more beer. Instead, he gave him a time to be at home the next morning to make a statement of what he had told them.

Relieved that the meeting was over, Osmand was lifting himself out of his chair when Stirling reached over and put a hand on his shoulder, holding him firmly in place. Osmand had not told them everything.

'One more thing Jim.'

Osmand's heavy eyebrows knitted, suspicious that Stirling was about to renege on their agreement to talk there and not at the station.

'You said the man would bring them up into the wood?'

Osmand looked at Stirling belligerently. 'Yeah, so what?'

'Which means, you were already there. Waiting.'

Osmand's neck flushed red as his eyes flashed between the two detectives watching him impassively. 'I already told you that!' His tone was defensive.

'So, why were you there, Jim?'

'I told you! I'd be rabbiting. You didn't see me, did you?' Osmand had blurted out the words too loudly so that ears pricked up in the bar behind him.

Stirling looked at Osmand and saw his innate cunning scuttling about behind his eyes as he recovered from the initial surprise.

'So, all the times these people were in the woods having sex, and the rest, no one ever saw you? You just happened to be there already and watched it all without ever being seen?'

'Yeah. So what?'

Stirling eyed him shrewdly. 'Tell me Jim. Why would you need a hide for rabbiting? They're usually hunted from dawn to dusk.'

A silence hung over the table as the detectives waited him out. Over Osmand's shoulder Stirling saw one of the men in the bar nudge his companion and lean over to speak quietly. Both men looked in his direction. At the bar, the landlord feigned disinterest but was alert to the changed mood in the corner.

Osmand sat back and folded his arms defensively across his barrel chest. 'Okay. I'd poach deer up there if one strayed in from the big estate. There! I've told you now but there ain't no evidence, so you can't do nothing 'bout it. I'd watch, and they didn't know I was there. I wasn't breaking any laws, 'cept for trespassing perhaps.'

Stirling felt Osmand was being too defensive. 'Had you ever spoken with the dead man in the car, Michael Pemberton, before? He was an architect.'

'Ain't much call for architects round here, 'cept down the other pub perhaps. I saw a picture of him in the paper, but I couldn't see much in the dark when I found him, and I weren't hanging about. But I reckon he'd be the same bloke. Why else would you be asking so many questions 'bout him?'

'So why haven't you mentioned this before?' asked Stirling.

Osmand replied pugnaciously, 'Because you didn't ask me right out. I don't talk to coppers 'less I must. Look! I rang in when I found his body, what more d'you want?'

Leaning forward over the table to look Osmand directly in the eyes, Stirling spoke slowly, 'When you make that statement tomorrow, make sure you leave nothing out. I'll be talking with your local bobby who's going to be keeping a close eye on you. You can start by putting that shotgun in your cab in a secure firearms cabinet. Now! Understand?'

Osmand stared back defiantly but knew he was at a disadvantage. Wanting the conversation to end quickly, he nodded sullenly.

9.05 p.m.

Daylight was fading beyond the far horizon as they drove out of the village with nightfall trailing close behind them. A gnawing hunger reminded Stirling he had not eaten properly all day.

'Interesting character,' said Stirling.

'He's a cruel, lecherous brute,' replied Helen. 'I wanted to punch his ugly face.'

'Me too. He's not told us everything, either. I'm sure of it.'

'Like what?'

'I think more went on in that wood than he's told us.'

They drove on in silence. Stirling was troubled about the blonde woman Osmand described. If he was telling the truth about that, he thought he had been, why had Pemberton's behaviour altered with her? Did she leave, or was she still there? Had Pemberton's sadism got the better of his self-control and, if so, might there be others? Stirling sent Pearson a text arranging a telephone call the next morning and called Edwards to find out if Billy Cole had been found.

Terry Cole had been spoken to again and they were confident he was in the clear. He knew roughly where Pemberton's home was but had never been there. Billy Cole was proving hard to find and the team would make an early start in the morning. Edwards said he would be at home the next day catching up with his family and dropped a heavy hint that he would like to be left undisturbed.

Which reminded Stirling that Helen had started early that morning and had a long journey home. Anticipating Stirling would tell her to take the day off too, Helen told him she had already made appointments for the morning. Rather than expect her to make a long journey home, only to return early the next morning, Stirling agreed the cost of a budget hotel.

Turning into the car park where they had left Stirling's car, Helen pointed to the brightly lit signage of a national chain of turnkey hotels. This one was bolted onto a large pub and restaurant.

'This'll be fine, I've used one of these before. Fancy a quick drink and something to eat?'

Stirling hesitated. A small voice chattering in his head warned caution, but the thought of food silenced it.

Cʒ ʘ

Day 7: Sunday - 5.39 a.m.

A dull pain kicking at the inside of Stirling's skull roused him from a drug like sleep. His tongue was dry and felt too big for his mouth.

Lifting himself up on one elbow, he looked around the darkness of an unfamiliar room. Shaking his head to clear the pain, he tried to remember where he was. A movement made him look behind him. Stifling a groan, he registered the warmth of Helen beside him.

From the car park, dull light sneaked past the edges of the lightweight curtains to outline Helen's body. The cover had slipped away to show her back, naked to the cleft of her cheeks. Listening to Helen's steady breathing, he glanced around for his clothes. Seeing them lying where he had dropped them on the floor, he considered slipping away quietly but decided against a coward's departure.

Taking care not to wake her, Stirling lay again and cursed himself for his stupidity. Pressing his hands to his eyes against the pain and trying to clear the fog from his memory, he pieced together the evening.

Waiting for Helen to join him in the restaurant from her shower and a change of clothes, he had made some calls and looked over the menu. Like any experienced detective, Helen kept a "grab and go" bag of essentials in her car in case of being sent somewhere at short notice. Dressed in a tailored blue shirt and tight jeans, Helen drew admiring glances as she walked over to him, smiling with a genuine pleasure that she had him to herself.

Released from driving and happy to use her own money, Helen had chosen a decent bottle of wine and conversation had flowed easily as they relaxed into each other's company again. There had been laughter as they replayed the confrontation with Osmand, speculating on how it might have turned out if there had been a fight. Preoccupied with Osmand in front of him, Stirling had not known how Helen had faced down the two men behind him and was impressed with her gritty nerve. The landlord's reaction at being told to bugger off back to his paper had caused more laughter.

Helen had been witty and serious, as required. When the conversation had edged its way cautiously to the girl's death and the repercussions for Stirling, she had known instinctively what to say with a sincere empathy. Lubricated by the alcohol and Helen's insight, Stirling had surrendered to his need to confide in someone who understood the complexities of the job, and who knew him well.

He had drunk more wine than would allow him to drive home and, if he was honest with himself, had discarded the idea half way through dinner. A taxi home would have been expensive but by then he was already entertaining the possibility. A possibility implicit in the warmth of Helen's dark eyes, in the touch of her hand as she became increasingly tactile, resting her hand on his arm in laughter as they relaxed in the bar, the occasional long, meaningful gaze. But if Helen's flirting was obvious, there was no seduction. He would not blame that on her. Her circumspect references to him seeing someone else had been replied to obliquely. Stirling was not even sure himself if there was anyone else in his life any longer.

Walking Helen to her room, simple want and need had overwhelmed any residual caution. Opening the door, Helen had stepped aside and waited, leaving the final decision to Stirling. He had crossed the threshold without hesitation.

From either side of the bed they had watched each other undress, holding the moment before joining to couple immediately and urgently in a reunion of lust and desire, in a release of sexual tension and of past hurts. It had not been lovemaking but hard, physical, self-gratifying sex. To satisfy and be satisfied, until they had collapsed entwined, sweating and slipping against each other, panting for air in the too warm room.

Physically sated, his eyes heavy with wine, Stirling had soon fallen into a dreamless, unstirring sleep.

In the cold light of a regretful dawn, Stirling was angry with himself for allowing his familiar weakness to overcome his better judgement, believing Helen would reassert her claim on him as tenaciously as she had previously.

Feeling him stir, Helen pushed backwards to reassure herself Stirling was still there, moving against him. Feeling him responding, she turned and opened sleepy eyes. Seeing him watching her, she opened her eyes wide, alert for any sign of regret and reached down to hold him before his attention wandered.

As Helen pressed herself to him and he smelt the warm scent of her body, Stirling felt the primitive urge stirring and knew he would not leave.

Murmuring huskily through sleep and desire, Helen kissed him. 'Morning Dougie. You're still very reliable.'

Pushing at his chest until he lay on his back, Helen straddled him and watched intently as he gave way to his need and arched under her. Helen smiled with satisfaction as she controlled their movement, controlling him and determined to erase the other woman.

*

7.05 a.m.
After he had left, Helen dozed in and out of sleep but was fully awake now. Stretching out languidly, she smiled as her body reminded her of their sex. It had been as good as she remembered.

She had been pleasantly surprised at how easy it had been to entice Stirling back into her bed. Caressing him and sitting astride his back, she had massaged the taut muscles in his shoulders until he had fallen asleep. Watching him sleeping, she had reminded herself of the fine detail of his features, how the dark wavy hair fell forward over his brow, the dark mole on his left cheek. Noticing the first, fine silver lines in his hair, Helen imagined Stirling lying beside her, older and greyer.

The evening had revealed they still enjoyed each other's humour and company, and still found each other physically appealing. But emotionally? Of that she was not certain. Things had got very acrimonious last time, so she had taken care to be funny and relaxed, deftly steering the conversation away from anything that might awaken past differences. Talking about the girl's death had been the tipping point, letting Stirling unburden himself to someone who knew about managing painful experiences. But, more than that, Helen understood men.

Knowing he valued discretion and prepared to play a long game, she had agreed the night could not get in the way of work. Helen wondered if she wanted to be in a steady relationship with Stirling. With too many broken relationships behind her and mortality slowly eroding her looks and her figure, it would be good to have some certainty of the future. The more she thought of a future with Stirling in it, the better the idea seemed.

The pretty Asian woman someone had gossiped of seeing Stirling out with would have to give way.

*

8.00 a.m.
Stirling had driven home to change his suit, but able to smell Helen on him still, had showered again. Running the water as hot as he could stand it, he had scrubbed his body hard, as if he might wash

the regret from him and had stood under the shower for a long time reflecting on the night.

The red wine hangover was growing in intensity. Forcing down a slice of toast that stuck wilfully to the inside of his dry mouth, he had still managed to be in the office before anyone else.

Seeing the two detectives searching for Billy Cole walk past his office, Stirling called them back and tasked them additionally with taking a statement from Osmand, making sure they understood what needed to be covered. The officers were about to leave when Stirling gave them a final, irritable instruction.

'And tell Terry Cole from me that if Billy doesn't present himself for interview today, he'll be arrested on suspicion of murder. That should concentrate their minds!'

Watching the grinning detectives leave, Stirling felt a stab of envy as he remembered how much simpler and fun the job was as an operational DC or DS; still part of the office banter, pursuing criminals and suspects with none of the stresses and tedium that went with senior rank. Sipping at a strong coffee, trying to clear the cotton wool from his brain, Stirling returned to working through the latest batch of reports Heal had left for him.

Jaz Cooke telephoned to say he would be continuing with the action Stirling had given him the day before. Ending the call, Stirling sat thinking about the information Cooke had given him. It was some minutes later when he realised his thinking had strayed back to Helen and grunted with disappointment that, once again, he had allowed his physical needs to overcome his better judgement.

Guiltily, he thought of Ayesha. He had failed to call her the previous evening. With a quiet groan at the pain behind his forehead, Stirling forced himself back to work.

8.27 a.m.

When his mobile rang, Stirling was surprised to see it was Pearson. Reminding Pearson good humouredly that he would have been calling him later, he heard a heavy silence at the other end.

Pearson replied brusquely, 'There's been a development. Where are you?'

Irrationally, Stirling thought of Helen. Had she made some form of complaint? 'I'm at the MCU. Why?'

'I'll be there in half an hour. Steph Tanner will be with me.'

Before he could ask what was bringing him and Tanner to the MCU on a Sunday morning, the phone went dead. Concerned, Stirling swiftly ran through the events of the last forty-eight hours, trying to identify a problem he had overlooked or could be unaware of. Calling Heal into his office, he told him of the imminent visit, but they could not think of any "developments" to warrant a visit from both the temporary Detective Chief Superintendent and the Assistant Chief Constable, early on a Sunday morning. Experience told them it couldn't be good and Heal beetled off to make sure everything was ready for scrutiny.

Reluctantly, Stirling called Edwards on his mobile to avoid having to speak to Ellen. Edwards answered immediately. He couldn't think of a problem either and despite Stirling's protests, insisted he would come in straight away. Although Ellen would have his guts for garters the next time she saw him, Stirling was pleased. Their combined knowledge could field the toughest questions Tanner or Pearson might throw at them and if for reasons not yet known, he was to be removed from the investigation, Edwards could pick up the reins immediately.

Stirling knew that Tanner only lived a few miles away and tried at reassure himself that with a few hours free, she was simply taking the opportunity to put her face about and, now that it was a week old, to catch up with the investigation ahead of McDonald's return the next day.

But every instinct told him otherwise.

8.59 a.m.

Out of courtesy, Stirling had offered his desk to Tanner where she now sat, notebook open in front of her with Pearson to one side and Stirling and Edwards sat opposite her. Stirling was reminded of the headmistress's study. Dressed casually in a light blue sweater, the arms tugged up above her elbows and faded blue jeans, to an outsider Tanner would look nothing like the popular image of a senior police officer.

As Stirling gave them a headline summary of events over the weekend, he was acutely aware of Tanner's scrutiny and Pearson's half hooded eyes watching him impassively from the side-line. As improbable as his concern had been, their inclusion of Edwards in the meeting ruled out anything to do with Helen. Stirling was impatient to know what the problem was.

Looking at the three men under her command, Tanner saw the better part of seventy years of investigative experience and knew her own position was more secure for it. Pearson knew what the problem was. She expected him to protect his officers' interests as far as he could but, ultimately, he was a company man and would do whatever was best for the service and the public.

The other two were out of the same mould. They knew something was wrong, but were showing a cool, professional calm as they waited for her to open the subject. Tanner thought Stirling looked tense, tired too. He had been working long hours, certainly, but she knew of his reputation with women. Thinking there was a slightly dishevelled look about him this morning, she wondered who Stirling had been losing sleep with.

Stirling finished his briefing. Resting her elbows on the arms of the chair, Tanner held the silence for a few moments before explaining their visit.

'Late yesterday evening, a call was received from a witness in your investigation complaining of unprofessional conduct. The caller demanded to speak with Chief Inspector Ballard.'

Tanner watched to see if anything registered on the men's faces. At the mention of Ballard's name, Stirling's eyes had narrowed warily. A brief, puzzled frown had crossed Edwards's features before continuing to stare at her impassively.

Tanner continued. 'The caller was referred to the on-call professional standards officer and soon after, I was contacted as the on-call Chief Officer.' Pointing to Pearson, she continued, 'We've agreed you should have the chance to explain your actions, Stirling, before I decide on next steps.'

Seeing Stirling and Edwards look at each other questioningly and return to looking at her, Tanner was about to speak again when Stirling interrupted.

'I accept responsibility for anything that has been done poorly, or seems to have been, but I'd like to know what *exactly* the problem is?' Tanner's slow-fuse reveal was annoying him, and he'd like her to get to the point. His head hurt more than ever.

Fixing Stirling with a hard stare, Tanner replied stonily, 'Good. Because it's you that's been complained of!'

Tanner saw from Stirling's quizzical expression that he had expected it to be someone on the team, not himself. 'The caller was Mrs Katrina Martin who you visited recently. Ring any bells?'

Stirling glanced at Pearson but saw no help there, only an unblinking stare as he waited for the story to unfold. Still no clearer, Stirling answered, 'I went to interview her on Friday afternoon with DC Helen Williams, but you haven't explained what the complaint is about?'

Studying his features, Tanner wondered if it was truly possible that Stirling did not understand, or if he was lying skilfully. She looked at Pearson and gave him a slight nod.

Looking at him steadily, Pearson said, 'Katrina Martin is the mother of Cassie Martin.'

Seeing Stirling's frowning incomprehension, he said quietly, 'The girl who died at the bridge?'

Stirling felt the room tilt under him as he stared at Pearson, stunned. Tanner was scrutinising him bleakly as he absorbed the information, made the connections, and then the growing realisation of the implications.

At his side, Edwards had exclaimed loudly, 'What?'

Assuring both men the information was accurate, Tanner described Martin's complaint of incompetence, insensitivity, of gross intrusion into family grief, and all by the man who may well be responsible for her daughter's death. Martin had screamed abuse at the duty officer, stating her lawyer would be lodging a formal complaint on Monday morning with the intention of seeking punitive damages from the force. The media was mentioned several times.

Tanner said she had spoken to the Chief Constable who had "expressed concern" - a euphemism Stirling knew to mean "is bloody furious" at the prospect of more damaging media coverage. Unstated, but understood by all, was the "concern" the Chief and Tanner would share for their own reputations.

Although Tanner's manner was calm and professional as she detailed the several elements of Martin's complaint, her underlying anger and bewilderment at his actions was plain. When she finished speaking, Stirling knew he was facing the isolation of another suspension from duty.

Shaking his head in confusion, Stirling could not fathom how he had stumbled unwittingly, and so spectacularly badly, into Martin's home without any forewarning from the incident room. The hammering in his brain beat in time with his pulse and clouded his thinking as he tried to marshal his thoughts into something coherent. At the same time, a cold nausea dragged at his stomach as a muddle of images wheeled though his mind's eye: the girl falling away from him, Katrina Martin's hesitation on the stairs, dark grey eyes, Martin stood close to him, her fragrance, the girl's smile. Why had she not said something? Screamed at him? Anything would have been more comprehensible than this. How had she kept herself so composed, and why?

Stirling was conscious the others were waiting for him to respond. Tanner and Pearson for a rational explanation. Edwards unwilling to say anything until he knew what line Stirling was going to take. Pearson had quickly recognised that Stirling was genuinely shocked at the news, but cold professionalism required him to remain neutral. If Stirling had truly not known, as the SIO, should he have? If there were gaps in his investigation, Stirling remained accountable.

Breaking the tense silence, Pearson asked, 'How is it possible that you went to see Mrs Martin without knowing she was the mother of the girl who died at the bridge? It seems a crass, indefensible decision.'

Stirling heard the cold formality in Pearson's voice and accepted there could be no favours after such a foul up.

Shaking his head in bafflement, his hands open in appeal, Stirling answered, 'Dave, I had absolutely *no* idea.'

With the shock subsiding and knowing he was professionally wounded, Stirling looked at Tanner and repeated with rising anger, 'I had *no* idea. None!'

Edwards interjected, 'Surely our Intel cell would have made the connection, if it was there to be made?'

Tanner leant forward to stare into Stirling's face, her mouth set in a firm line. 'Stirling, you're a DCI. Why the *hell* did you go there anyway and not send one of your officers? Even without the connection between the girl and Katrina Martin, it looks heavy handed!'

With her decision to appoint Stirling unravelling, Tanner watched him hawkishly, ready to swoop on any weakness. Stirling knew that however loyal Tanner had been, she would move against him quickly to protect the service first and within that, her own position. And he wouldn't blame her either. He knew at the time he should have delegated it to one of the outside teams. He thought of his meeting with Osmand which they didn't know about.

Realising an honest answer would seal his fate, Stirling groped amongst the fog in his head to locate the answer Tanner needed. 'It was a judgement call, and my decision to make. Considering what we now know, I can see it looks heavy handed but without that knowledge, it was a reasonable decision. I understood the complex background to the ownership of the land, the fraudulent business arrangements and of the alleged relationship between Mrs Martin and the murder victim, and I took a highly experienced female investigator with me too.'

Stirling re-iterated Croft's report, the interlinking factors relating to the land where Pemberton's body was found and the phone call from Martin's mobile. As he recounted the facts, Stirling felt his confidence returning, and his anger too.

Looking from Tanner to Pearson, he continued hotly, 'What I don't understand is why we weren't aware of the connection between Cassie Martin and this investigation in the first place?' He shook his head, still confused. 'Something's out of place. Do you *really* think I would be so callous as to go there if I'd known of the relationship? *Honestly*? For God's sake!'

Aware he was fighting for his professional survival, Stirling's pent up anger spilt over. 'From the start, I offered to meet the parents of the child to help them understand what happened, how she died and that I did as much as could be done. But Ballard's been determined to keep me in the dark and out of the way!'

Feeling Edwards's restraining hand on his forearm, Stirling looked at him and saw the slight shake of his head and a message in his eyes to say, "calm down." Suddenly aware of how he must appear to Tanner, Stirling settled back into his chair and shut up as he wrestled his anger and breathing under control. He had to keep Tanner's confidence until they found out where the problem lay.

Tanner waited for Stirling to get his anger under control. 'In the confidence of this room, the Deputy returns from leave tomorrow and will be hopping mad when he hears of this. I'm concerned for the reputation of the force and how we've responded to the Martin family which, so far, seems to have been very poorly done. We don't need another media shit storm about Cassie Martin's death.'

Pearson coughed lightly to gain Tanner's attention. All three faces turned to him as he leaned back in his chair, his hands folded in his lap and hooded eyes turned to Tanner. This was not the worst crisis he'd faced, not by a long way.

'Something you need to be aware of, Ma'am. On my way here, I received a snippet of information. Ballard knows about Mrs Martin's call last night, so we should assume if he's not already contacted the Deputy, he will this morning.'

Rare for Tanner, she swore a quiet obscenity and turned back to Stirling. 'Well? The shit's already hit the fan so, any last requests before I formally remove you from command of this investigation?'

'Ma'am, can I make a suggestion?'

All heads turned to Edwards. Still struggling to think of a good reason why he should not be fired from his own investigation, Stirling wondered what Edwards was about to say, hoping he would not make matters worse still.

'As Doug said, something's not right. I can't believe we'd have failed to make the connection to Mrs Martin *if* the information was in the force intelligence system. I accept the possibility of human error in the Intel cell here, but can we check, please? Another hour will make no difference, surely?'

Edwards had made the request sound utterly reasonable. Momentarily helpless, Stirling watched Tanner weighing her options before looking at Pearson who gave a barely perceptible nod. The silence was so intense that all Stirling could hear was the wall clock ticking down his career.

Tanner was inclined to cut her losses, being seen to distance herself from Stirling quickly. How soon she acted would tell its own story later. Leaning back in her chair, she studied Stirling, experience telling her to act decisively.

With a glance up to the clock, Tanner pointed her forefinger at Stirling. 'You have exactly one hour to review your intel process and report back to me with an explanation. And remember, I'll be having it independently reviewed tomorrow, so no tricks!'

Turning her attention to Edwards, she added, 'And if this *was* avoidable, you'll be leading the investigation until I can get a fresh SIO in here. You're tainted by this as well!'

As the two men rose to leave Tanner said, 'I'll make some calls and see what damage limitation I can put in place. I don't trust that fucking weasel Ballard one inch.'

Seeing their surprise, Tanner added quickly, 'You didn't hear me say that.'

09.27 a.m.

The moment Stirling and Edwards entered the incident room, Heal jumped up from his desk and began a pantomime of rapid gesturing movements for Stirling and Edwards to join him as he walked to the far corner of the room where they were unlikely to be overheard.

Thinking he was about to offer one of his many amusing anecdotes, Stirling began testily, 'Geordie, I haven't got time to piss about, I need ...'

Raising both hands to stall him, Heal said in a low voice, 'Boss, listen! I've had a call from a mate.' Seeing the irritation on both men's faces, Heal glanced cautiously towards the main door, 'Ask no questions and be told no lies, let's just say us Geordie's stick together.'

Sternly, Edwards said, 'Geordie, get to the bloody point!'

Speaking directly to Stirling, Heal continued hastily, 'Just after you went in there I had a call from a pal telling me about Katrina Martin's call last night. I couldn't understand how we'd have missed the connection, so I called in one of our Intel guys to review everything we've got in the system. He's already made a start and I've been helping.'

In the tension of the moment Heal's broad accent had filled so that he might have just got in from a long, boisterous night out on Newcastle's Quayside.

Edwards cut across him, 'That's all well and good Geordie, but we're reviewing our own work. If anyone's screwed up they might be tempted to cover their tracks.'

Grinning widely Heal added, 'Aye, well, I knew you'd say that, so I've got a DS from force intelligence coming in to independently oversee the review. She lives nearby and owes me a favour, so she'll be here soon. In fact, here she is.'

Heal inclined his head towards the far door where Stirling saw a Detective Sergeant he recognised from the Force Intelligence Bureau looking across the room at Heal with a faint look of irritation. It was not how she had planned to spend her Sunday morning.

Heal had excelled himself this morning, thought Stirling. 'Good anticipation Geordie, but either the witnesses in Ballard's investigation were in the force Intel' system, or they weren't! Behind every entry there's a digital footprint stating when it was entered, any subsequent amendments and who by. Why didn't we see them when we were inputting our own witness names, Katrina Martin chief amongst them?'

Edwards stood to one side, arms folded and tugging at his chin thoughtfully. Looking between Stirling and Heal, he asked, 'PSD investigations are always ring-fenced with strict protocols for access to protect their sources and investigations.'

Stirling replied quickly, urgency driving his thinking, 'But there should still be flags on the system to indicate someone is of interest to another investigation to avoid "blue on blue." Has that happened here?'

Heal and Edwards considered Stirling's suggestion. Each understood the national protocols of "flagging" to allow discreet, third party conversations to take place through formal firewalls. Particularly if confidential sources, informants, were in use.

Thinking aloud, Edwards replied, 'But Ballard's inexperienced. And arrogant, which might have stopped him asking for advice, or ignoring any advice offered to him. It's possible he's kept his investigation completely firewalled without observing basic protocols on the force Intel database.'

'That would be against good practice policy!' Heal blurted out, amazed such an elementary mistake was possible.

'Yes, but as Bill said, Ballard's arrogant and ambitious. He would cut corners without even knowing he had. With the Deputy behind him he probably thinks he's bomb proof, when in fact he's holding a grenade with the pin out.' Stirling paused as something occurred to him. 'If Ballard has screwed up, the shit will stick to the Deputy too.'

Heal started chortling delightedly. 'So, it's not all bad then, eh?'

Edwards and Stirling looked at each other and were silent. Heal saw only the potential for damaging a disliked senior officer, but they understood the politics.

With a glance to where the intelligence officer was waiting patiently for them to finish talking, Stirling explained, 'Geordie, we must tread carefully. The Deputy is supposed to be giving oversight to Ballard, and the IPCC's involved too. If Ballard's screwed up, they're compromised as well. If Ballard called the Deputy last night about Martin's complaint they're ahead of us which makes them more dangerous than ever. The only advantage we've got, for the moment, is they don't yet know what might have happened.'

Stirling wasn't thinking just about himself. Steph Tanner could catch some stray bullets too.

Following Stirling's line of thinking, Edwards added, 'Ballard will use Martin's complaint to his advantage. I'd bet a safe fiver he'll be speaking with McDonald again today to agree what they'll do tomorrow morning.'

Explaining Tanner's ultimatum, Stirling said urgently, 'Geordie, I *have* to know what happened. We've got less than an hour before I lose my job!'

Heal was turning to leave when Stirling added to them both, 'See how many of the team can come in if we need them. I may need to move quickly today.'

10.23 a.m.
Looking at the Detective Sergeant, Tanner asked, 'You're absolutely certain?'

They were crowded into Stirling's office with the addition of Heal and the DS from FIB. The meeting was already underway when Stirling realised Heal was behind him, and too late to eject him without embarrassment. For his part, Heal had decided he wasn't missing out on this and pressed himself into the corner behind Stirling to remain inconspicuous as he followed the interaction between the senior officers. Tanner was looking keenly at the young Detective Sergeant from the FIB.

'No doubt at all, Ma'am. I've quickly reviewed the data in the Intel cell's work here and cross-checked it against the force's database. DCI Stirling's team could not possibly have been aware of the relationship between Cassandra Martin and Katrina Martin as neither has been flagged from the PSD investigation. Consequently, this investigation was blind. By contrast, for example, information about both Osmand's and William Cole's previous convictions were revealed in the usual way as we'd expect.'

The young Detective Sergeant spoke confidently. Unfazed by the four senior officers present, for common understanding she described the national "flagging" protocols, what should have been done and what appeared not to have been done, giving her best interpretation of Ballard's failure.

Several questions and answers later, Tanner thanked the two Detective Sergeants and asked them to leave. She considered asking Edwards to leave too, but decided against it. It was his calm, common sense which had stopped her acting hastily. The discussion that followed was frank as they discussed the impending political fallout amongst the chief officer team. There was a tacit understanding of the remaining risk to Tanner herself, but the three men were experienced enough to talk around it.

Deadpan, Pearson summarised the overriding issue. 'There's still a high risk of serious reputational harm to the force.' Seeing Tanner's silent question mark for elaboration, he continued. 'We're going to look like a parade of clowns. Two investigations working in parallel, in the same force, the one blindsided by the other? That's going to be difficult to explain away. Martin's lawyer will be expensive which means toxic for us. We'll need to get our media strategy prepared today.'

As the conversation passed back and forth around him, Stirling slouched down into his seat, fingers knitted under his chin as he sifted and distilled information from the many lines of investigation. A plan was emerging in his mind. Sooner than he would have preferred, but it might just work.

Sharp with irritation, Tanner's voice cut through his thinking. 'Are you with us?'

Stirling saw everyone waiting for the answer to a question he had not heard. Pearson was fuming at him quietly.

Wishing the pain in his head would improve, Stirling answered, 'Sorry, I was thinking.'

'And so are we, but your contribution would be *most* appreciated!' Tanner snapped sarcastically.

Sarcasm from Tanner was unusual, but it was a measure of her concern and the pressure she was under. Pulling himself up in his seat, Stirling began to speak quietly, but firmly. Still mustering his thoughts as he addressed his words to Tanner, he knew she would need some persuasion to agree to what he was about to say.

'I propose a course of action which is high risk and requires us to act quickly in moving against Katrina Martin. Today! So, you'll need to think about what that will look like tomorrow morning, apparently attacking a grieving mother who has just made a formal complaint. And I'll need to pull people in from their rest day, so there'll be a cost too.'

Stirling paused to watch Tanner's reaction, expecting her to rebuff immediately anything that would look like attacking a complainant. Instead, she waited for him to continue. Tanner wasn't short on nerve.

'There are many potential motives for Pemberton's murder but I'm increasingly certain his private life caught up with him. In fact, I think it's possible there's another body waiting to be discovered, a female we haven't accounted for yet. He *might* have died because of his business dealings, but I think it unlikely. Katrina Martin was the mother of Cassie Martin. We now know that a tattoo on Cassie Martin's body is extremely similar to an image in Pemberton's apartment which describes his sexual tastes.'

Seeing the puzzled looks on the faces of the other three, Stirling told them about Cooke's telephone call earlier. Cooke had spent much of the previous day trekking around the city visiting tattoo studios with the photograph sent from Stirling's phone of the symbol in Pemberton's apartment. Eventually, he had found a tattoo artist who had the design and knew what it represented.

'The symbol represents BDSM fetishism and although the drawing in Pemberton's apartment is an artistic, stylised version, there's no doubt in my mind they're the same. You can look through the photo's later.'

Stirling watched as Tanner drew another strand to the mind map in her journal, the same process he used. Stirling hoped it might be another nail in Ballard's coffin. Now that he had their attention, Stirling continued unhurriedly, making sure to pull in every strand of supporting information to support his case.

'What if there *was* an association between Pemberton and Cassie Martin? We know Cassie was pregnant. There are images in his computer that we still haven't accessed because of encryption. Might they be of Cassie? I expect to get them later today.'

At his side, Edwards shifted slightly but kept a straight face. Both knew there was no expectation of that when they had entered the room.

'If so, it places greater significance on the call from Martin's mobile to Pemberton the evening before he died. I would prefer to be acting on this after more work, but we could legitimately act now. Consider this. She owned the land at The Wern which she sold to Pemberton's investment concern. We're certain she had an affair with him years ago, which she adamantly refuses to discuss. Why? We've been told Pemberton disliked Martin intensely. Why? A call is made to Pemberton from her phone the night before he died. Why? There were burnt clothes in the garden when I went there for which she gave an unconvincing explanation. Why? The tattoo on Cassie's body is the same as the one in his home. Why would a girl of sixteen have such a tattoo?'

Stirling paused, but there were no questions. He continued, 'Martin is a wealthy woman and we know Pemberton had been extorting money from other women with threats of publishing intimate photos of them online. I can't imagine him missing the opportunity to milk her too, can you? And if Pemberton had compromising, sexualised photographs of Cassie, with the risk of lifelong damage to Cassie through uploads to social media, how far might Martin have gone to protect her child? What might any parent do in such circumstances? Or any of us in this room, for that matter?'

Tanner stopped writing to look at Stirling thoughtfully. He knew she had a teenage daughter from her previous marriage and in the corner of his eye, he saw Edwards nodding thoughtfully, thinking no doubt about Ellen and his two girls.

Stirling continued, pressing the point, 'And don't you think it strange, extraordinarily strange, that she recognised me at her home but said nothing? Instead, she's waited over twenty-four hours before making a complaint! I turned up unannounced so there was no time for her to develop a strategy of how to respond to me. Some urgent, overriding need took over. As Cassie's mother, how on *earth* did she manage to contain her emotions? Unless, of course, she had to!' Stirling spread his hands in echo of the question.

Stirling looked at Tanner for comment who was pushing her pen through her fingers onto the desk, then rotating it to repeat the motion as she considered his argument.

It was Pearson who spoke. 'Do any of the tattooists remember someone of the girl's description having it done?'

'Not yet, but Jaz Cooke is out there looking.'

In reply to another question from Pearson, Stirling gave them his and Helen's assessment of Martin's detached, calculating personality before continuing.

'Martin spent well over a day thinking about this and has decided to take the initiative by turning us back in on ourselves. If we don't act now, today, we'll be too busy infighting and defending ourselves from the media. Martin's lawyer will portray her sympathetically as the grieving mother treated poorly by a bumbling police service. The spotlight will shift from her possible involvement in Pemberton's murder, lost in a smoke screen of accusations and recrimination. We *must* go on the front foot to regain control of the investigation.'

'So, what do you suggest we do?' asked Pearson, quietly encouraging Stirling to press his argument.

'We shake the tree and see what falls! We have more than enough circumstantial information to make an arrest and any gaps in our knowledge will fill as we search her home, examine her car forensically and test her story under caution in interview. It's high risk, but we're facing criticism anyway. This is not the time for politically correct timidity!'

Seeing Tanner arch an eyebrow at this last comment and Pearson's frown, Stirling thought he might have over-stepped the emphasis. The room fell silent as Tanner and Pearson digested the proposal. Stirling knew that moving against the grieving mother of a child who had died in constructive police custody would have been difficult enough before, but immediately after she had lodged a formal complaint would appear retaliatory and was extremely high risk, both politically and professionally. If they got it wrong, everyone would be damaged by the fall out, not least of all Tanner.

Playing devil's advocate, Tanner countered, 'We'll be heavily criticised for arresting her from her home. Why not make an appointment to interview her tomorrow with her lawyer present?'

'Because we'll lose what little advantage we still have and, if it's there, any recoverable forensic evidence. But, as difficult as our circumstances appear to be, I'm afraid that's still not the worst of it.'

Tanner's eyes narrowed as she wondered how things could be any worse than they already were. Aware of the pregnant silence, Stirling weighed his next words.

'Pemberton's murder was avoidable!' He waited to see if they understood. Tanner looked curious whilst Pearson nodded his head sagely. The old man had got it straight away.

Stirling continued, 'If Pemberton *was* the cause of Cassie taking her own life, Ballard's narrow focus in pursuing me, rather than leading an open-minded search for the truth, created a vacuum into which Martin may have stepped to deliver her own brand of justice for her daughter. If I'm right, that's going to be extremely difficult for the force to explain away.'

In considering cause, effect and consequence, Stirling was ahead of them. As Tanner sat reassessing the additional burden, Pearson smiled at him with paternal pride at Stirling's acuity.

Tanner leant forward with a new resolve. 'Okay, let's hear your plan.'

11.02 a.m.

After a brief discussion of who would do what, Tanner and Pearson agreed to provide the top cover Stirling would need to lead the investigation and Martin's arrest without interference from above, in case McDonald belatedly tried to intervene.

Pearson would work with Angie Baines in preparing media options for the different possible outcomes following Martin's arrest. Tanner would brief the Chief. Tanner had quickly agreed the cost of pulling in the team on a rest day, pragmatically accepting it was insignificant when put against the negative media coverage if they didn't close out the enquiry quickly.

Tanner would not contact the IPCC, saying it was for McDonald to explain any cock ups which had happened on his watch. Tanner made a passing reference about contacting McDonald later in the day but Stirling had read the sub-text: it would be the last thing she did and only when she knew what she had from Martin's arrest, and the Deputy could do nothing until the morning.

Stirling sat in the incident room with Edwards, Heal and the DS from FIB who he had held back in case of need. She had not been best pleased but, professionally, had decided to get on with it.

He had demanded from HTCU the remaining images from Pemberton's computer with an expectation they would be with him later that day. Unreasonable, certainly, but he didn't care. He was not going down without a fight and if that meant others must feel the heat, then so be it. Watching him, Edwards could see an energy about Stirling he had not seen for a long time. Despite the pressure, Stirling was enjoying the quick-time decision making. Finally, he ordered everyone to meet for a briefing at midday with the intention of making an arrest as soon as possible that afternoon.

In case Martin was absent, Stirling had despatched a Detective Sergeant to the on-call magistrate to lay information for a search warrant. Now, sat alone at a desk in the corner of the incident room, Stirling pondered on how much information Ballard held which could be helpful to his own investigation, and how to access it, legitimately. The last thing he wanted was to speak to Ballard, but he was struggling to think of how to avoid it when an idea came to him.

Impatiently, Stirling pulled out his phone and called Billing who answered straight away. After a brief but very prescriptive conversation, Stirling ended the call, thinking wryly how much you can get done when you take responsibility for a junior officer breaching procedure.

Pocketing his phone, Stirling called over to Edwards, 'Dan will be here with whatever he's got within the hour, and with Cassie Martin's laptop.'

Edwards looked at him surprised and walked over.

'It occurred to me that Ballard *might* have been just competent enough to seize any computers she owned, which he did. Or someone did for him. A laptop. But, here's the rub. It's been sat on a shelf in Dan's office ever since waiting for Ballard to instruct him on what to do with it. Dan sent him an initial analysis of the content, broken down into generic categories, but nothing more was requested. HTCU's got more work than it can cope with, plus our murder and the FBI referrals, so it's been sat there gathering dust. A request from Dan to Ballard for a decision was not replied to. Can you believe it?'

'But he's had that for what, six, seven weeks? What the *hell* has he been doing?' asked Edwards, incredulously.

Stirling shook his head in disbelief. The laptop might contain information explaining why Cassie had been on the bridge in the first place: her browsing history, contacts, emails, social media messaging. It was hard to understand how Ballard had been so incompetent, but Stirling could guess at Ballard's mindset. Driven by naked ambition and seeking revenge, he had decided to paint Stirling as responsible for Cassie's death and had tilted his efforts and limited resources in that direction, whilst ignoring basic investigative good practice. All compounded by poor supervision from the Deputy who had limited investigative experience himself and was far too busy to check the detail.

12.51 p.m.

Placing the small, expensive laptop on the desk, Dan Billing looked at Stirling uncertainly.

'This is a bit irregular sir. This was seized in another investigation and I have no authority from the SIO, Mr Ballard, for anyone else to examine it.'

Looking at the faces of Edwards and Heal for support, Billing saw only hard, uncompromising stares which made him more nervous.

In reply, Stirling told him firmly, 'And *this* SIO is giving you a direct order to show me the content. Now! I haven't got time for niceties Dan and you're free of any responsibility if there's any criticism later.'

Accepting he had no choice, Billing explained that the hard drive had been unlocked and copied by someone else in his team, so he had not yet examined it himself. He reassured them that as it was quite new with relatively little data stored on it, so the examination would be relatively easy.

'You're the specialist Dan, I'm happy to be advised on what we should look for first. Call me if you find anything.'

Seeing Stirling's determination and no sympathy from the others, Billing took refuge in what he was good at. A few minutes later he had scanned through Cassie Martin's online profiles and called Stirling and Edwards back across.

'From what I can see, she seems to have been a private individual. Typically, a young woman of her age might have well over a hundred friends on social media but there are fifty at most, which surprises me. And no obvious adult family members.'

All of Cassie's contacts were young females of about her own age who lived locally, and many attended the same college. Pemberton did not feature in her contacts list. Billing confirmed no mobile phone had been submitted by Ballard for examination and Edwards confirmed that none had been located at the bridge.

The photo file had less than a hundred pictures in it; local landscapes, some selfies with friends, and old family snapshots in some of which Katrina Martin stared unemotionally to the camera. The family pictures with Martin had been taken inside her home or in the garden during the summer, with the summerhouse visible in the background. In three photographs, another woman with greying blonde hair and a few years older than Martin sat looking beyond the garden towards the fields, her face in profile as if uncomfortable with the camera's stare.

The only pictures discernibly different from the others were five, fading colour photographs. A graininess about the images indicated they had been scanned. The photographs were of a garden party at Martin's home. Judging by the fashions, the hairstyles and the immature landscaping in the background, Stirling estimated they were taken on a fine day, fifteen or more years ago with some fifty people present, sitting or standing in groups around the garden and chatting as they held drinks and plates. Stirling picked out Martin easily, younger and strikingly attractive but even then, there was a restrained, self-awareness in the tight lipped, sidelong look to the camera that said, "must you?". In one photograph a tall, good looking man a few years older than Martin who he thought must be Gérard Martin stood with a possessive arm draped around her shoulders. Martin looked uncomfortable under her husband's arm.

'Interesting, there are no boys as friends.' said Billing thoughtfully, referring to Cassie's contacts. 'Even if she was gay I would expect there to be some lads amongst her peer group.'

'And we know she was pregnant,' commented Edwards quietly over his shoulder.

Billing looked up to Edwards. 'Oh, I didn't know that. I need some time to look through it in more detail and her browsing history. I'll give you a shout if I find anything useful.'

As they began to move away, Billing called them back. Reaching into his briefcase, he pulled out an evidence wallet of images. 'Sorry, almost forgot. We retrieved the stuff cached on his cloud account. They're sort of similar but … well, you'll see.' Billing returned to his research.

Around them, investigators were slowly filing into the room, many bantering noisily at the prospect of overtime but others looking sullen after a difficult conversation with partners and another lost family day. Moving to a corner where they could look at the photographs away from prying eyes, Stirling opened the album of black and white photos and began to turn the pages, stopping at a frightened young face staring at them.

'Oh, dear God!' exclaimed Edwards and turned away.

Stirling felt a cold twist in his bowel as he looked once more into Cassie Martin's frightened eyes.

1.15 p.m.

Heal had worked his way around the room talking to the team in small groups to explain what was going on behind the scenes. Slowly, the banter had subsided to be replaced by a sombre determination.

Stood discreetly in one corner was Pearson, lending his authority to the briefing without intending to speak. His presence was enough. Edwards summarised the preceding twenty-four hours, omitting Ballard's apparent errors. It would be unprofessional to slate a senior officer in an open meeting, and most had heard something of it from Heal.

As Stirling rose to speak, a door opened behind him and all eyes travelled over his shoulder to follow Tanner as she went to stand next to Pearson. If anyone had doubted the seriousness of the situation before, they couldn't now.

Stirling resumed, 'Our aim is to arrest Mrs Katrina Martin on suspicion of the murder of Michael Pemberton. We have information that her daughter, Cassandra Martin, known as Cassie and not quite seventeen, was in an intimate but abusive relationship with Pemberton, a man over thirty-five years her senior when she died in an apparent suicide earlier this year. A Coroner's inquest has yet to decide that, so be careful with your terminology outside this room.'

With everyone assigned roles and responsibilities, the briefing broke up without the usual chatter and banter but instead, a low murmur of professional determination.

2.30 p.m.

Stirling had not anticipated any difficulties at Martin's home. He could search it once Martin was in custody, but if she was not at home he would need to gain access quickly. By force if necessary. The Magistrate had readily granted a search warrant once he had listened to the information, given on oath.

With Helen appointed as the arresting and escort officer, Stirling had parked well out of the way. Once he knew they were on their way to Worcester police station where Helen would book Martin into custody, he drove to the house.

Parking next to the Mercedes sports saloon, Stirling entered the house to find Edwards in the hallway checking off arrangements with the forensic and search coordinators. A truck would arrive soon to lift Martin's car, sheeted over, and take it to HQ where a SOCO team was on standby.

Stirling swept a critical, appraising eye over the search arrangements. He could not afford any mistakes. A SOCO officer was already making her way through the house creating a video record of the house before the search began. An Exhibits Officer was setting up a small table in the hallway where anything seized for evidence or examination would be recorded, with a SOCO nearby to photograph items in-situ before removal. Outside the front door, the search team leader was sectoring the building amongst four teams of paired officers, prioritising anything linking Katrina or Cassie Martin to Pemberton and any financial dealings. It occurred to Stirling he could have added contact details for Gérard Martin too, but they would keep an eye out for that as they went along. Stirling was concerned whether he had been advised of his daughter's death. He had a right to know.

Checking the time, Stirling estimated it would be early evening before an interview could take place. By the time Martin had been booked into custody, waited for her lawyer to arrive followed by private consultation - almost certainly lengthy - and before an interview could begin, carry out the disclosure process requiring him to give Martin almost everything he held to which he wanted answers, Stirling estimated he had at least three to four hours. God bless the British criminal justice system, he thought. For once, it might play to his advantage.

Once the videoing had finished, the search began in earnest. Pulling on examination gloves, Stirling followed them in. With little to do whilst the search was proceeding, he drifted through to the kitchen. It looked as sterile now as the last time he had been there. Moving through to the lounge he took time to walk round it, looking for anything that might give insight into the lives of Katrina and Cassandra Martin.

Above an antique walnut sideboard could be seen a faint outline and an empty fixing indicating a large picture had hung there until recently. A painting, or family portrait perhaps, prompting Stirling to look around the room for any family photographs on display, but there were none. In a self-consciously middle-class home like this, he would have expected to see them dotted around in expensive frames, or arranged as a collection. Were the memories of happier days too painful now? For a mother to put away the memories of a loved child so soon after their loss would need a particularly unemotional nature, he thought. But when Stirling thought of the photographs and painful memories he had locked away, was he so different?

Beyond the lounge was a study with doors leading to the terrace. Situated at an oblique angle at the corner of the house, he had not noticed it from the terrace previously. Standing behind a modern desk positioned to look out to the countryside, Stirling imagined Martin sitting here plotting her revenge. Had Cassie worked in here too? Lifting the lid of a high spec' laptop, the screen illuminated immediately with a screen save picture of Martin holding Cassie wearing school uniform when she was about six years old. Cassie's dark grey eyes laughed into the camera, sparkling with the carefree joy of childhood, unmatched by Martin's faint smile. Stirling found himself wondering what kind of a mother Martin had been to Cassie. Looking at the background in the photo he could see a wooden panel fence. It had not been taken in the garden to this house. More in hope than expectation, he tapped a key to see if it was unlocked. A password was required and with no further pictures appearing on time lapse, he closed the lid. Martin would most likely have removed anything incriminating and whatever HTCU might recover, it would be some days away and of no use to him this evening. A quick check of the desk drawers revealed nothing of interest.

Standing at the door to the terrace, Stirling thought of Cassie the child, full of promise and endless possibilities, especially from a home like this. With a deep sadness, he recalled the images he had seen earlier. He called Billing who said there was nothing more of interest on Cassie's laptop and advised they look for whatever she had used previously.

Standing at the brazier to examine the contents again, Stirling could see some ash remained, but the buckle and metal remnants had been removed, leaving him to wonder if they could have been important. Helen called to say Martin was booked into custody and waiting for her brief to arrive.

'She's very calm and controlled, I think she was prepared to be arrested. No questions, no protests.' Helen said a solicitor was on his way and mentioned a firm in Birmingham he had never heard of.

'How did you get on with your ladies this morning, before we re-assigned you to this?'

'I met three at one of their homes. Word's getting around and I sense some sisterly support is developing. They don't have anyone else to talk to so it's probably a good thing. All of them were contacted by Pemberton to lend him money and if they refused, he threatened to publish pictures of them, giving them sample copies to reinforce the threat. They paid as much as their means allowed, but nothing like the amount Downing paid, for example. None of them strike me as being a murderer. But the terrified young woman in the boot of the car? I haven't identified her yet and none of the women recognises anyone of that description.'

Helen had been too busy to chase up enquiries of the French authorities by Special Branch, so Stirling said he would follow it up. There was a long silence at the other end of the phone.

'Dougie, is everything okay?' Helen asked, concerned that he had still not mentioned their night together and there was no complicit warmth in his voice.

Pre-occupied with the search and everything else in play, Stirling had spoken more business-like than he had intended, but it was symptomatic of how he felt. Helen wanted reassurance that the previous evening had been a welcome development, a new start and that he had no regrets. He had many, but could not start unpacking it now.

'Yes, everything's fine Helen but I'm really busy here with the search. Catch up later, okay?'

Pressing the phone to her chest, Helen watched the line of cars filing up Castle Street past the police station and thought through the conversation, analysing Stirling's cool manner.

"Careful Douglas. Be nice or I'll make you pay for it" she thought to herself.

3.26 p.m.

Sitting on the corner of Cassie's bed, Stirling realised he knew no more about Cassandra Martin now than he did after their fleeting encounter at the bridge. As a participant in her death, he felt a trespasser in so personal a part of her life.

Cassie's bedroom was fitted out with modern furniture and expensive soft furnishings, as he could have expected in a home of this value. But instead of the usual array of keepsakes, cosmetics and fashion accessories typical of a teenage girl's bedroom, he saw little that said a young woman once lived here. Opening wardrobes and drawers, very few clothes remained. He remembered Martin's explanation for the fire in the brazier, the choke in her voice as she had talked of burning inexpensive clothes. Cassie's? Katrina Martin was a cold fish, no doubt, but why had she cleared out so much of her child's life so quickly, and so efficiently?

In Stirling's experience, grieving parents struggling with the pain of a lost child endlessly deferred clearing out their bedroom. Instead, they preserved it as it was left, a shrine to heartbreak to be visited, the child's existence proven in the layered accretions of childhood; the favoured soft toy, cheap sports trophies recalling the triumphs and despairs of weekends spent in rain and draughty gymnasiums. Profound love invested vicariously in each keepsake once treasured by the lost child, hoping against all rational reason that if the room could be kept as it was left, it would be familiar when the child returned.

Kneeling to open a bedside cabinet, Stirling caught a faint drift of scent from the bed linen. Lifting the pillow, Stirling could smell a woman's perfume. Not an expensive perfume such as Martin would wear, or a cheap girl's scent either, but reminiscent of one worn by someone he had once known. The recollection teased at his memory, but the face would not come. Seeing a small collection of bottles on the dressing table, Stirling went over and removed each of the caps. None matched the scent on the pillow. Replacing the last of the bottles, he cast an eye over the dressing table and noticed small torn pieces of card tucked into the gap between the mirror and its frame, where photographs held there had been removed carelessly. Or snatched out hurriedly.

Returning to the bed, Stirling pulled back the quilt. The bottom sheet had been slept on recently, but who would Martin have allowed to sleep in Cassie's bed, if not herself? With several bedrooms to choose from, surely this would have been too personal a space?

With a final look round, Stirling checked each of the other bedrooms, all perfectly furnished and ready for use but empty in every sense. Two detectives had started to search the master bedroom which occupied most of the rear of the house. Sliding doors led to a balcony with seating overlooking the garden. Expensively furnished in creams and whites with not a hint of intimacy, to Stirling's mind it matched Martin's personality perfectly. Looking at the king size bed and remembering Martin's athletic figure, he speculated on what sort of lover she would be. Emotionally sterile, he suspected, like being captured by a python in a slow, cold eyed, and smothering embrace.

On the dressing table were two silver frames with photographs of Martin with Cassie taken when Cassie was young. It struck him that the few pictures he had seen so far were limited to Cassie's childhood and none from her teenage years.

Nothing of interest had been discovered so far. Leaving them to it, Stirling began making his way to the stairs, unsure if he was surprised or not. His expectations had been low but something else was becoming clearer. The house was like a show home and as devoid of warmth and welcome as its owner appeared to be. What was it like for Cassie growing up here? If devoid of both maternal warmth and homeliness, Stirling was beginning to see more of the frail, frightened girl on the bridge parapet.

If her own mother was incapable of showing love, had Cassie become susceptible to affection offered by others?

Half way down the stairs, Stirling paused at the landing window to watch the Mercedes being sheeted over on the back of a recovery wagon and driven away.

Stirling was becoming concerned if he would have anything substantial to put to Martin other than his suspicions. Tanner and Pearson had supported his high-risk plan, but could he deliver it? Finding Edwards in the kitchen talking to a SOCO, he led him out onto the terrace for some air and described the bedroom searches.

'How's it going down here?'

Edwards pulled a face and shook his head, 'Not much better. The files and laptop in the study might reveal a link to Pemberton, but not in time for an interview this evening.'

They were discussing the interview planned for that evening when a woman's voice called out to them from inside the kitchen. Stepping back inside the doors, a SOCO officer at the far side of the kitchen was pointing at something on the work surface in front of her.

'I need a decision on whether you want this seized collectively or treated separately?'

Walking across the room, Stirling saw her gloved hand was resting on a wooden knife block designed to slant eight, black handled knives towards the user. Laid out on a wooden chopping board next to it, the SOCO had arranged the eight professional chef's knives in order of size. The polished blades cast corresponding shards of bright light across the tiles behind. They all looked unforgivingly sharp. Stirling wasn't sure what he was being asked to decide as the SOCOs had been instructed to seize all potential weapons.

Seeing his questioning look, the SOCO selected a paring knife with a narrow five-inch blade and held it by the edges between her thumb and forefinger so he could inspect its profile.

Pointing to the blade tip, she explained, 'The blade tip is damaged with about a millimetre broken off, perhaps two. I was at the post mortem. The pathologist estimated a knife of about this length and width with a single cutting edge was used. It might have been damaged through normal kitchen use but if it *was* used on the victim, it might have been damaged during the attack.'

Reaching out a gloved hand, Stirling took the knife from her and felt the perfectly balanced weight of it in his hand as he held the blade up to the light and studied the broken tip. Barely noticeable at a casual glance, Stirling knew that magnified many thousands of times under a high-resolution camera, the broken tip would reveal a profile as ragged and as unique as an alpine ridge. And if he could locate the piece that had broken off, the corresponding edge would provide a perfect mechanical fit, reuniting the pieces. Analysis of their metallurgical composition could also prove they were once forged from the same material.

Taking Stirling's wrist to avoid touching the knife, Edwards squinted in concentration as he rotated the knife under the lamp above them. 'Are you thinking what I'm thinking?' he asked quietly.

As they examined the blade, the SOCO spoke again. 'If it's the murder weapon and it's been used regularly since, then between other contamination and the dish washer, the chances of recovering any DNA are pretty much zero. But, if it was washed poorly and has sat unused, it's *possible* there's trace DNA. On both the knife and inside the sheath of the block itself.'

Stirling thought of the wounds to Pemberton's skull and how the blade tip might have lodged severely enough to need levering free. 'If we locate the tip, we should get a mechanical fit.'

Handing the knife back to the SOCO he instructed, 'Seize it all, the block and the knives, but I want the examination of this knife expedited as a high priority for finger prints, DNA and then high-resolution magnification. I know it can't all be done today but I need the results as fast as we can possibly achieve.'

As the SOCO began to label and secure the knives, Stirling turned to Edwards. 'We've still got Pemberton's body at the mortuary.'

Edwards knew where the conversation was going. 'We'll need X-rays and possibly some specialist imaging to find a tiny fragment of metal like that in the body.'

'True, but we'd concentrate initially on the wound sites where the knife struck bone.'

Stirling was drumming his fingers on the marble worktop as he thought through the logistics of getting the examination done quickly. Seeing Edwards studying the block thoughtfully, Stirling knew he would be applying a devil's advocate assessment to the find.

Thinking aloud, not expecting a reply, Edwards said, 'You'd have to be frighteningly cold blooded to return the murder weapon into daily use and prepare your food with it.'

'You haven't met Katrina Martin properly yet, have you?' Stirling replied. 'If she's responsible, perhaps she took some macabre satisfaction in using it? She's highly intelligent and would have calculated we might discover a connection between Pemberton and Cassie and would come calling at some point. A missing knife would arouse more attention than one hidden in plain sight. How many times have you and I seen murderers keep some sort of trophy as a souvenir, Bill? Is Martin any different?' Stirling had long concluded it was impossible to underestimate human callousness.

'Bill, call the Pathologist, and the hospital. See how quickly we can get the various scans done. It's *got* to be today. If necessary, I'll get Tanner to call the Director of Services at Worcester Hospital. Whatever it takes!'

Edwards walked out of the room, mobile phone in hand and scrolling through the contacts.

'And to hell with the cost, Bill. The PACE clock is ticking!' Stirling called after him.

Edwards held up his free hand in acknowledgement as he passed through the door.

4.45 p.m.

Leaving the building, Stirling saw he had two missed calls on his mobile and leant on his car as he returned the last call. It was one of the officers looking for Billy Cole.

'We found Billy, and we've eliminated him. He went to Pemberton's place more times than was reported. His account ties in with the incident logs and Greening's description. Pemberton encouraged him to put all the money he had into Fairway. About a year ago, he heard Pemberton had some money, the money he was extorting from the women, probably, and went there to get his money back. He's not very bright and wasn't subtle in his demands, but we can account for him during the time band of the murder. He spent the night and morning with some friends and we've got their statements. His alibi checks out.'

The next person Stirling called was Cooke who was still wearing out shoe leather tracking down tattoo shops in and around the city, not made any easier as some were closed for Sunday. Nothing so far, but he would call back if he got something.

5.40 p.m.

Driving past the cathedral and turning left into Deansway, Stirling caught a glimpse of Ayesha's offices and felt a sharp pang of guilt.

Preoccupied with the investigation, Stirling had forgotten about Ayesha completely and was struggling to remember what day of the week it was, and when they had last spoken or exchanged messages. Yesterday morning?

He thought about their last, taut conversation. He doubted Ayesha would wish to make contact with him and with the pressures of the investigation, the absence of a relationship would be a blessing of sorts. It would be kinder to let Ayesha move on and find someone better to build a relationship with. His occasional self-destructiveness would only hurt her in the long run.

Absorbed in thinking through the last two days and the discovery of the knife, Stirling braked suddenly by the Glovers

Needle as a family darted across the road towards the riverside car parks, glowering at him as they towed fractious children beside them.

Turning alongside the river on North Quay and on under the railway viaduct, Stirling glanced across the racecourse. Only two weeks earlier it had been submerged by its near perennial flooding from the river, leaving the grandstand marooned like an angular hulk upon a sea of dirty brown water. The course was now lush green and had been prepared in readiness for the next meeting, its white running rails bright against the grass. Swinging left from Castle Street into Loves Grove, he turned into the secure yard of the police station. A modern building with the Magistrates Court next door, it was a considerable improvement on the old nick in Deansway. Stirling was about to get out of the car when the car phone rang loudly.

'Any progress Jaz?'

'Yes, boss. The last tattooist on my list! The chap remembers doing the tattoo, about six months ago.'

'Why does he remember it so well?'

'Because it was a young woman who brought a hand drawing with her. It wasn't one he was familiar with, so he did some internet research to get a base pattern while they waited. He's not your typical rock and roll tattooist, a nice bloke and a bit shy. He liked the girl which, together with the meaning of the symbol, is why he remembers them.'

Stirling's ears pricked up. 'They? Them?'

'Yeah, there was an older guy with her who did most of the talking and watched it being done. The tattooist thought the relationship looked a bit strange, but it wasn't his place to judge, and the bloke was paying. I've shown him photos of Cassie and Pemberton and he's sure it was them. I've got his statement.'

Remembering how young Cassie appeared Stirling asked, 'He couldn't have thought she was eighteen, surely?'

'I did ask, but because the older guy was with her he didn't ask any questions.'

5.59 p.m.

Stirling settled himself into the station conference room which would not be needed until the following day. Located high in a glass turreted corner at the south corner of the station, it gave a commanding view east, south and west over the nearby cityscape.

Dominating the foreground opposite was the former Victorian hospital infirmary which now served as the city's university campus. Over the rooftops he could see the cathedral tower, its four turrets defined against the skyline and nearby, the elegant spire of the Glovers Needle he had just driven past. As he scanned the rooftops, reflecting on the day and contemplating the evening ahead, the cathedral's bourdon bell began to toll out the hour, its sonorous chime rolling over the city to fall into its streets and passages.

A firm knock at the door announced the arrival of the two detectives he had brought in to interview Martin. Already experienced investigators, they had attended an advanced suspect interviewing programme, an intensive programme. Stirling had worked with them before and would trust them to interview the wiliest criminal liar. Over the next half hour, they planned the interview strategy and agreed key points of information and evidence to be covered with Martin, if she chose to answer any questions at all.

Stirling was explaining Cassie's tattoo and the knife at Martin's home when Helen knocked on the door and joined them. She described Martin's composure to the two detectives. Martin had given the Custody Sergeant a lawyer's business card, asking for him to be contacted immediately. The lawyer was a senior partner of a firm in Birmingham with a reputation for high end criminal defence work.

Helen added, 'She's possibly the coldest, most controlled woman I've ever met.'

'Nevertheless, she can't evade the facts' said Stirling. 'I think she's keeping a lid on a lot of stress and anger which you might be able to tap into, *if* you can get her talking. When Helen and I first met her, there was a lot of emotion bubbling below the surface and she had to work hard to control it. I now know it was because I was the last person to speak to her daughter, but I didn't know about the connection. Expect them to use that against us and how to deal with it.'

Tapping the crime scene photos of Pemberton's mutilated body open on the table, he said, 'Once that attack began, there was *no* control, it was a frenzy. If she lost it once, she might again. See if you can get her to lose some of that glacial composure and say something she'll regret.'

The interviewers left to complete their preparation, leaving Stirling and Helen alone for the first time since they had parted company that morning. There was a heavy silence as each waited for the other to initiate the conversation which must come. Stirling crossed the room to check the door was shut and returned to stand at the table opposite Helen.

'Helen, last night …'

Smiling, Helen interrupted him. '… was wonderful Dougie. Better than I remembered. I'm looking forward to the next time.'

Watching the amusement in Helen's dark eyes, Stirling was unsure if she was conceding it was a pleasant one-night stand and was baiting him, or expected confirmation of something more binding between them. With the investigation at a critical point, Stirling was torn between his preference for an honest conversation, or to defer it until they could talk properly. Knowing Helen's mercurial temperament only too well, he decided to avoid a confrontation.

'It was Helen, but we must focus on the job at hand. Can we not talk about it right now, please?'

Stirling tried a smile, but realised Helen was disappointed as she stiffened in her seat and the smile died in her eyes. He had seen that sudden mood shift before.

Moving swiftly to avoid a bitter comment, he continued, 'Let's see how the next day or so goes? It's going to be a long night and I'll be here until the finish, whatever happens. You could get away home, if you'd like to?' He tried not to sound too encouraging of her departure.

'I've got to make up my notes then I'm going to try and locate the Evans woman at Danes Green. If she's Martin's cleaner, or friend, she might have some background stuff on Martin which could be useful.'

Helen gave him a long, cool look as she closed the door. Stirling watched the door close and sat thinking. He wanted to let Helen down gently and knew he had only deferred a confrontation.

*

6.43 p.m.

Sitting in an empty office writing up her notes, Helen fought down tears of wounded pride and some sadness. Although determined not to let Stirling upset her, Helen felt torn between an urge to fight for him, to see off the young pretender to his affections, or to treat their night together as an entertaining and satisfying liaison on the journey to her next relationship.

Unlike many of the men in her life, Helen had never fully shaken Stirling from her heart. There was something obscured about his personality that was frustrating and fascinating in equal measure, so that she never felt she completely knew him. But his insight to her own flaws had moderated the more turbulent days of their relationship.

The sex had always been extremely satisfying, reckless sometimes. Helen smiled at a memory of somewhere they had coupled, quickly and urgently, the risk heightening their arousal. The previous night had been a happy coincidence of time and place when Stirling had needed an understanding ear. Yes, the sex had been good, but he was a man, so no emotional engagement was needed for that.

Looking back, the heat of their relationship had made it seem they were together for longer than a few months. Helen knew herself well enough to accept that the reason it ended so abruptly was her own fault. Her quick temper, sharp jealousy and even sharper tongue often got the better of her, but it was her nature and she couldn't always control that. As she considered her personal life, and where it was not going, she knew she wanted Stirling in her life again. On any terms, if necessary, but on her terms eventually. In her heart, Helen knew he didn't feel the same way, but a stubborn pride would not allow her to give him up easily.

Shaking her shoulders to be free of the distraction, she decided to wait it out. He had succumbed once, he might again.

*

8.02 p.m.
Walking away from Carol Evans's home, Helen recognised the man's voice calling to her.

'Back again then, are you?'

Slipping on her professional smile, Helen turned to the voice. The scruffy neighbour was leaning against the frame of his front door again, half in shadow below the flat concrete porch cover and still scratching at his crotch as he drew deeply on the roll-up cigarette cupped in his hand.

He gestured at the house with the cupped hand, 'She went out, about half an hour ago.'

'Any idea when she might be back?' Helen called across the gardens brightly, reluctant to walk down the footpath to him.

With an apathetic shrug, he said he had no idea. Resigning herself to speak with him, Helen walked down a weed infested concrete footpath to him. He was still wearing the same clothes as the previous day, and for several days or weeks before that too, she suspected. She knew he would smell of stale sweat, cheap tobacco and unwashed clothes.

'You're a copper,' he accused, as Helen drew closer and when she held out her warrant card, added contemptuously, 'I bloody knew it! I can spot you lot a mile off.'

'So, what's your name then, just so I know who I'm speaking with?' Helen asked, keeping her smile in place but wondering if she could spare time for a nosey neighbour, and a smelly one at that.

'Dai Morgan, but most people round here call me Taff,' he replied proudly. Taking a long pull on his cigarette, he began to cough. Hacking up a heavy gobbet of phlegm, Morgan turned his head and spat it onto a bed of weeds.

Helen closed her mind to Morgan's crudeness. She had spotted an opportunity to strike a rapport. Slipping into the lilting cadence she quickly relapsed into when she visited her family, and emphasising her accent, Helen asked, 'So then Dai, which part of God's country are you from then?'

Hearing her accent properly for the first time, Morgan straightened up and looked at Helen with new interest. 'Cardiff, Butetown. Haven't lived there since I was a kid though. You?'

Exaggerating the syllables, she answered, 'Sandfields, Port Talbot. Dad worked at the steel works. Mind you, that was when we had a steel industry worth talking about.'

Smiling widely to expose broken, nicotine stained teeth, Morgan stepped aside and beckoned her in, 'Come in love, always happy to help one of our own, even if she's a copper!' and laughed at his own joke.

Steeling herself against yet another smelly house and smiling more cheerfully than she felt, Helen stepped through the door. As Morgan shuffled about the shambles of his kitchen, sloshing milk into half clean mugs proudly emblazoned with the Welsh dragon, Helen saw loneliness and self-neglect everywhere.

Keeping up a light banter with him, Morgan wasted no time in telling Helen he had lived alone for over ten years since his wife had "buggered off with my best mate" and that his kids never visited, even though they lived nearby. Looking at him critically as he busied himself between the kettle and a grimy looking fridge, she wondered what sort of man could have lost everyone so completely. An unpleasant man, she concluded. Smiling indulgently, Helen nudged him along with sympathetic responses whenever Morgan paused to wheeze for breath and take a heavy drag on a fresh roll-up he had made whilst the kettle boiled. Helen didn't miss him ogling her body furtively whenever he thought she wasn't looking, dragging his eyes from her chest to answer her questions. Looking at his dirty skin and grimy fingernails, Helen's flesh crawled at the thought of his hands on her.

Following Morgan through to the front room where a television flickered silently in the corner, Helen could feel the soles of her shoes sticking on the grimy carpet as she went to sit on a worn settee, shiny from long use. Perching on the edge of the settee, Helen felt her own body heat returning to her as it failed to penetrate the accumulated grime of many years. She closed her mind to the thought of the variety of fluids spilt on it. At the window, grubby half-closed curtains gave Morgan a view of the street.

Morgan knew the woman next door, Carol Evans, not a Welsh Evans mind you, English, but never mind. She'd lived there all her life, growing up there as a kid and took the place on after her Mother died, like you could in those days before "bloody Thatcher" sold off the nation's council houses, another attack on the "working class". Helen wondered how well acquainted Morgan and hard work had ever been; he sounded like a man who talked a good fight.

Morgan knew she'd bought it off the council years ago. Not that you'd know it to look at. She hadn't done much to it except for fitting some shutters to the windows. Said it reminded her of somewhere she'd been to on holiday. Evans lived alone, had been a "real good looker" once but had let herself go, he thought, nothing personal like, but that's how it looked to him. She kept herself to herself, no regular visitors or he'd have noticed - which Helen believed - and when she had visitors it was usually family. She didn't talk to him much, she'd never liked him for some reason he'd never understood. Helen understood why a woman living alone would avoid Dai Morgan.

Asked if Evans worked, Morgan said she worked at the Cathedral, something to do with the shop there. He knew she liked art when she was young, had been good too, he'd heard. Had some of her paintings in her front room, not that he'd ever been in there, he added. Too quickly, thought Helen.

'So, all in all, a pleasant woman, Dai?' Helen summarised, wishing to escape the smelly, smoke laden house.

'Oh yes, nice woman. Not like her sister, mind. Now then, there's a hard-faced bitch, I can tell you,' Morgan said contemptuously.

'Sister?'

'Lives in a big fancy house somewhere over the other side of the river. Out in the country. You don't see her round here much though, not with her bloody airs and graces and all the time looking down her nose thinking she's better than us. Which makes you laugh since she was brought up here. Next door.'

Trying not to show too much interest, Helen asked casually, 'Really? So, who's she then, Dai?'

'She was Katy Evans when she was growing up next door. Their Mother died when they were still teenagers so, being the eldest, Katy looked after Carol, who still lives there. She was tough mind, even then. Katy, I mean. But Carol was a quiet, sensitive sort. Losing her Mum so young knocked her badly. Like I said, Carol was an arty type, but Katy was sharp, really brainy, got to hand that to her. She did well at school and went off to London as soon as she could and when she came back years later, she'd got herself a rich husband. French bloke but I never met him. By then she was calling herself Katrina. Bloody cold woman though, the Ice Queen I call her.'

'So, Katrina is Katy, Carol Evans's sister?' Helen's pulse had quickened as she listened to Morgan's biography of his neighbours and thought of the woman who had pushed past them at Martin's home. Was it important to the investigation? Probably not, but interesting all the same.

'One and the same. Katy's daughter used to visit Carol sometimes. Nice kid, bit skinny for a girl but some of them are though, aren't they? Half starving themselves to death. You'd have thought she was a boy unless you was close to her. Looked a lot younger than she was too, underdeveloped. No tits at all really … sorry.' Morgan glanced compulsively at Helen's breasts before continuing. 'But she and Carol seemed to get on well and she'd stay next door some weekends.'

Morgan fell silent and stared at the television. Helen was thinking she could leave when Morgan spoke again, 'Terrible what happened to her though.'

Helen waited for him to explain.

Jerking his thumb in the vague direction of the city Morgan said, 'The girl who fell off the motorway bridge a few weeks back? Or the copper pushed her, if you believe the papers. All bollocks I expect but the pictures didn't look good, did they? The poor kid was only sixteen.'

'You're saying the girl on the bridge was Carol Evans's niece? You sure of that, Dai?'

Distracted by a half-naked dancer on the television, Morgan nodded.

8.42 p.m.

Sat in her car, Helen ran through Morgan's information trying to work out if it was materially important. When Evans pushed between them at Martin's home she was distressed. Martin said they had been arguing, describing the woman, her sister, as a "friend" which was an unusual thing to say. Why?

Martin would not be the last woman to make something of herself and to consciously turn her back on humble beginnings. And why not, thought Helen, looking down the row of functionally designed houses. Had she not done the same thing and turned her back on estate life with its circular, incestuous gossip? Cassie's visits to a kind natured Aunt and probably to a more relaxed home than her own were understandable. Katrina Martin did not appear to ooze maternal warmth.

After a long day, Helen felt a sudden, deep tiredness. With over an hour's drive ahead and only an empty house waiting for her, she considered texting Stirling to ask if she could stay with him, longing to be beside him. But she knew it would only push him into a corner and reluctantly dismissed the notion. Helen called Stirling to tell him of her meeting with Morgan but got his voicemail.

Leaving a summary of Morgan's information, Helen began the long drive home.

*

8.56 p.m.

Martin's confession surprised Stirling.

Sat in the monitoring suite watching via the CCTV camera fixed high in a corner of the interview room, it was against the run of play up to that point. For an hour, Martin had fenced with the two interviewers, answering their questions in the calm, emotionless voice he now knew to expect of her. He would have liked nothing better than to be in there himself.

Fixed to the wall at the end of the table, the digital clock of the twin deck recorder marked the passage of the interview. Surprisingly, for a Sunday evening, the solicitor was dressed immaculately in a dark suit, starched white shirt with a scarlet silk tie and black shoes polished to a high shine. He was good, and so he should be for the fee he was undoubtedly charging Martin. Particularly for attendance on a Sunday evening. Except for a few wealthy career criminals who could pay a retainer fee for their lawyer to be available twenty-four-seven, it was a rare occurrence, and he did not believe Martin to be a career criminal.

That Martin had chosen to answer questions had been a pleasing surprise. Her lawyer sat at her side making notes, occasionally placing a cautionary hand on his client's forearm and leaning in to whisper in Martin's ear, causing her to nod, then sit erect and frame her reply.

Watching her, Stirling thought Martin was a study in self-control as she paused to consider a question, replying in her carefully enunciated, middle-class tone. Analysing Martin's manner as much as her answers, he thought there was a conscious condescension about her, leaving him to wonder why. Most wealthy, middle-class people he had met over the years were consciously self-deprecating, whereas Martin appeared to wear her social status as a badge of honour.

The interview had started in the usual way with background information of her circumstances, with Martin giving only what she estimated they knew already. Married once only, to Cassandra's father, a wealthy French national named Gérard Martin who she had met when they were both working in London's financial sector. Moving back to her home county to start a family, he had continued to work in London and the marriage became strained soon after she fell pregnant with Cassandra. She insisted they use her full name. They had separated some months after Cassandra was born. She and her husband had not been in touch for many years. Financially independent, she had raised Cassandra on her own without seeking his assistance and she had discouraged his involvement in their child's upbringing. It was a tempestuous relationship and she had not wanted the emotional stress around her daughter. As far as she knew, he returned to France soon after they broke up. Over the years, she had heard snippets of information from past colleagues that he had gone to travel the world, with Indonesia being referenced once. Gérard was a keen mountaineer and liked all manner of outdoor pursuits, and he was wealthy enough to retire young. She had not remarried, not that it was any business of the Police, and most certainly had not been in a relationship with Michael Pemberton.

Stirling sensed an internal tension ebbing and flowing in Martin whenever Pemberton's name was raised. She repeatedly denied an intimate association with the architect, dismissing the information Helen had gleaned as malicious gossip and lies, predicated on some historic misinterpretation of their friendship. She knew that amongst the "county women" she was unpopular. She did not like them or their pretensions and had never courted their friendships. Yes, Pemberton had been an attractive man when younger but other than business, there was never anything between them.

With a keen professional eye, Stirling admired the quiet efficiency of the interviewers as they slowly pegged out the ground around Martin, making sure there were no misunderstandings or unresolved information, allowing them to challenge any contradictions later, if needed.

The officers described Pemberton's blackmailing of past lovers with the compromising photographs, and of the ongoing research of his bank accounts. Martin had fallen quiet when they explained how each of her bank accounts would be researched for significant withdrawals or transfers which correlated to similar sums arriving in Pemberton's accounts, which could indicate motive for his death. Martin had inclined her head towards her lawyer and a whispered conversation followed with him appearing to confirm the Police had the powers to do so for a serious crime investigation. Straightening to face the two officers, Martin had stared up into the lens of the CCTV camera. She knew the red light indicated she was being monitored. Stirling could feel the intensity of her stare as if she was in front of him.

Turning back to the officers, for the first time she had answered 'No comment.'

In the monitoring room, it felt like a significant moment and Stirling had turned to say something to Bill Edwards, forgetting he was at the hospital where Pemberton's body was being scanned. Stirling thought it just as well it was a Sunday evening. Wheeling a mutilated corpse through hospital corridors from the mortuary to X-ray would have been tricky at any other time.

Further questions on the same theme met with a similar response, neither admitting nor denying that Pemberton had been blackmailing her. To do so would be to acknowledge a relationship with Pemberton.

The interviewers turned to the telephone call from her mobile to Pemberton the night before he died, which she explained away as she had when Stirling and Helen had visited her. When the forensic examination of her car was raised, Martin seemed confident it would reveal no connection between her and Pemberton's death. Too confident a rebuttal, thought Stirling, making a note to research car valet companies and migrant hand wash spots. Stirling was becoming concerned the interview would not provide anything substantive to support a charge of murder and began to worry if he could make a case for her overnight detention. The lawyer would make strong representations to the Custody Officer for Martin to be released on bail. Chief amongst them, their insensitive and intolerable handling of a grieving mother.

The lead interviewer reached down to an unremarkable bag he had carried into the room and put on the floor at his feet, showing no interest in it until now. If Martin had noticed the bag, or been curious, she had long since forgotten about it. Lifting out a small brown plastic box with a clear plastic pane on one side, the detective put it on the table in front of him with the viewing pane towards him. Martin stared at the box. Absorbed in his notes, it took the lawyer some seconds to notice a hiatus in conversation and only looked up in time to see the detective turn the box to face Martin, revealing the knife secured inside.

'Do you recognise this knife, Mrs Martin?' he asked, quietly.

Now alert, the lawyer sat forward and began to protest about pre-interview disclosure, to which the detective calmly raised a hand and silenced him momentarily as he continued smoothly, raising his voice above the lawyer's.

'This knife was seized from a knife block in *your* kitchen following your arrest today. You can see the point of the knife is broken off. As we speak, an X-ray examination of Michael Pemberton's body is taking place to be followed by a physical examination. If the tip to this knife blade is found in his body, we will be *very* interested to hear your explanation as to how that could be?'

As the detective spoke, Martin stared at the knife intently, gripping her hands together in her lap. The lawyer leant in to whisper urgently in Martin's ear before demanding a break for private consultation.

Ashen faced, Martin watched silently as the interview recordings were sealed and the detectives gathered up their papers and the box and left the room. Switching off the camera, Stirling was pleased he had pulled the knife back from forensics for a short while.

When the interview resumed twenty minutes later, the lawyer said his client wished to make a statement. Martin sat with her head bowed, a tissue clutched in one hand. She had been weeping and her defiance had shrunk.

In a faltering voice, Martin began to speak and stopped, the words appearing to stick in her throat. With a deep breath, she pulled herself upright to face the interviewers.

'I killed Michael Pemberton. I was grieving for the death of my daughter Cassandra. Nobody could understand why she had decided to die in such an awful way, what had driven her to select such a bleak, awful place. She was only sixteen! The police investigation was incompetent, and that awful man Ballard seemed unable, or unwilling to give me any information or explanations. He left me in the dark about what was happening. I had to ask for information, *all* the time. When I found out Cassandra had been visiting Pemberton at his home and what he had been doing to ...'

Martin's voice choked. She clutched the tissue to her mouth to suppress a dry retch at some recollection. The lawyer handed over another tissue and Martin wiped her mouth and eyes. In the monitoring room, Stirling sensed the production of the knife and the acceptance of confession had triggered a cathartic, emotional impact on Martin's usually impenetrable nature. He thought of the images of Cassie's humiliations. How much did Martin know, or could guess at?

Martin continued, her voice ragged with anger and emotion. 'What that perverted bastard had been doing to her! The poor child … she must have been so frightened, and so terribly alone. Cassandra was still a child really, naïve and very inexperienced. I was too protective when she was growing up, I can see that now.'

Martin looked at the two detectives who sat listening patiently, using the silence to draw her on. Martin admitted to having had an affair with Pemberton when she met him as the architect to her home. It was, she said, a brief fling which she regretted and had already ended before her husband, Gérard, moved up from London. Pemberton had contacted her out of the blue about three years ago asking for money. She knew about the collapse of the Fairway development but had no financial interest in it as the sale of the land had transacted some years earlier. She refused to pay him, but he had threatened to publish embarrassing photographs he had taken when they were together. Martin would not elaborate on their content. She gave Pemberton two large sums of money in exchange for the photographs which she destroyed. Giving details of the sums and the approximate dates, she said they would see the withdrawals from her personal account. Realising he might have other copies she had told him forcefully that if he threatened her again she would contact the police and complain of blackmail, whatever the consequences. She had not heard from him since.

After her daughter died, she became frustrated at the slow pace of the police enquiry. Desperate to understand why Cassandra had wanted to end her life and to discover who the father of the baby was, she had made her own enquiries amongst Cassandra's friends. She assumed there must have been a boyfriend at college, or something similar, and needed to know. Cassandra's friends said she had become secretive, cutting herself off even from them. They knew she was seeing someone, but no one had met him or knew who he was. Some had speculated whether she was gay and too embarrassed to discuss it.

A week or so before Pemberton died, she received an anonymous phone call from a woman who withheld her telephone number and refused to give her name. A woman in her forties, telling her that Cassandra had been visiting Pemberton. Martin had thought it an absurd claim and the caller was playing a cruel game. She knew she was disliked by many women. But the idea had played on her mind and the next day she had searched Cassandra's bedroom and found letters from Pemberton hidden under a wardrobe. The letters responded to letters Cassandra had sent to him. Martin broke down. She would not discuss their content in detail and had destroyed them in disgust as they increasingly inferred sexual activity. Knowing Pemberton's perverted tastes, the thought of Cassandra having experienced that had been extremely distressing.

Watching remotely, Stirling could understand Martin's revulsion. For the first time, he felt some sympathy for her; the sincerity of her distress was all too evident. She did not know how or when Cassandra had met Pemberton. She believed Pemberton discovered she was Cassandra's mother and knew how much pain he could cause. Martin was certain Pemberton intended her to discover the relationship with her daughter.

She had called Pemberton asking him to meet her at The Wern, choosing the location because it was isolated and they both knew it. She didn't want him at her home and she certainly would not go to his apartment where he had seduced Cassandra. Martin denied planning to harm or murder him. She just needed to look him in the eye and know the truth. If he confessed, she had intended to inform the police.

The knife was for self-protection and, if necessary, to frighten him into telling the truth. She was sat in the front passenger seat when he arrogantly intimated what he and Cassandra had been doing together, smirking as he said it. Stunned when he showed no contrition and then disgusted when he claimed Cassandra was an enthusiastic participant, Pemberton had mockingly pointed out that as Cassandra was sixteen, the legal age of consent, there was nothing Martin could do about it.

It was in response to his smirking arrogance that she had lost control. Martin claimed she had little recollection of the attack, only becoming aware when physical exhaustion prevented her from stabbing him and she realised he was no longer moving. She had panicked and set about covering her tracks.

Step by step, Martin answered the detective's questions about how she had sought to prevent or delay his identification, downplaying her actions as amateurish. Having seen on television how people set fire to cars to destroy evidence, she took a rag from the boot and stuffed it down the fuel cap with a stick to soak up the petrol and set fire to the rag. Putting her bloodied clothing in a plastic bag from the boot of her car, the Mercedes, once the car was burning, she drove home wearing as little clothing as she dared. Using the back lanes, she saw few cars and because her home is screened by trees, no one saw her in her underwear.

She had planned to wash the clothes but thought it better to burn them, using the garden brazier DCI Stirling had seen. The car was valeted inside and out that day by a migrant hand wash operation in Pershore, paying them extra in cash for a thorough clean. Noting the location of the car wash, Stirling considered the chances of getting any cooperation to be remote. Some of the workers might be illegal and if not, informed by experience in their own countries, were likely to be deeply suspicious of the police.

So, how was the rag lit, Stirling wondered? Martin had said somewhere she was not a smoker, so was unlikely to have had a lighter or matches with her. Unless planned? Using the message system between the monitoring room and the interviewers, Stirling typed in a prompt and the interviewer presented the question. Martin paused for a long time before saying the ignition key was still in the ignition, so she had switched it on to heat the cigar lighter until the coil was hot enough to ignite the rag, then threw the lighter away nearby.

If true, Stirling believed it would have been discovered during the fingertip search. Making a note to check the scene photographs of the car interior and the cigar lighter fitting, Stirling was sceptical. Martin's explanation seemed improbable, and was it even possible? She would have risked self-immolation by lighting the rag so closely, as the petrol vapours exploded into flame. Martin's description of her "amateurish" endeavours at concealment sounded calm and clinical. Nor did they correspond with a spontaneous, frenzied attack.

'Pemberton's mobile phone and wallet were missing. Can you explain that?' asked the lead interviewer.

'I took them. I thought he might have photographs of Cassandra on the mobile which would bring the police to my door.'

'And what did you do with it?' The questioning was patient but relentless, quietly drawing Martin down a route intended to cover all the points that only a culprit could know, but taking care not to fracture the atmosphere.

Martin looked at him blankly for a moment. 'Oh, I couldn't get it to work. He had a password, so I destroyed it soon after leaving there. I know you people can follow mobile phones, so I took it apart and threw the pieces out of the window as I drove home. I burnt the wallet and the SIM card with my clothes.'

Making another note, Stirling thought of the cost and logistics of carrying out a search of the hedgerows along the route to Martin's home to prove or disprove her story. He had not seen anything resembling the remnants of a wallet in the brazier.

'Did you take your mobile to the scene?'

Stirling understood the significance of the question, as did Martin's lawyer who straightened up, uncertain if he would need to intervene. If Martin had deliberately left her mobile at home, it undermined her account of an unpremeditated attack and taking a knife solely for her own protection. She could not admit to leaving it at home to avoid tracking.

Martin seemed to have recognised the implications of her answer and looked flustered for a moment before answering, 'No. I forgot it. I left in a hurry.'

But you remembered to take a knife, Stirling thought coldly. We'll see what a jury makes of that. When asked how she had retrieved Pemberton's wallet, Martin explained he had always used the glove box for personal items which is where she took it from, together with some vehicle documents.

The interview continued for several minutes, when the investigator asked unexpectedly why she had removed Pemberton's signet ring. Martin was surprised at the question and hesitated, clearly uncertain what to say. Stirling had seen the reaction before, when Helen had asked her about the telephone call to Pemberton.

'You've told us you went back into the car to switch on the ignition for the lighter, and you took his mobile phone and wallet. Tell us about the signet ring?'

Martin began to speak, stumbled and hesitated. 'Um, yes, from his finger but I don't remember it clearly. He wore one on his small finger.'

'Why did you take it from him?'

Martin put her head into her hands. 'I don't know! I don't know why. I threw it away with the phone.'

The lawyer had been sitting back, one leg crossed casually over the other as he made notes of the interview. With a cold, professional smile he held up a hand to interrupt the questions. Speaking in a smooth, measured tone, he addressed the interviewers.

'A psychologist might explain it to us all in due course, officer. Naturally, I will be seeking a full psychological assessment of Mrs Martin's state of mind at the time of this offence following the impact of her daughter's tragic death in … *questionable* circumstances, exacerbated by an *incompetent* police investigation which kept Mrs Martin in the dark.'

Exuding reasonableness, he continued, 'In the face of extraordinary provocation, with some understanding of what Cassandra, who was little more than a child, had suffered at the hands of that vile man, Mrs Martin may have suffered some momentary loss of reason and self-control. Faced with Pemberton's malicious taunts, she reacted as many grieving parents might wish to do. The man was clearly a depraved, predatory character, and a grasping blackmailer too! As regrettable as any death is, I suspect that any right-minded jury might consider his death a benefit to society, with him no longer able to prey on vulnerable women. Children too, it seems.'

So, there we have it, thought Stirling. Katrina Martin's defence would be manslaughter on the grounds of diminished responsibility.

9.58 p.m.

The lawyer had called for a break in the interview to allow his client to recover her composure and for him to take further instructions.

Stirling and the interviewing officers were discussing next moves when Edwards returned from the hospital. Stirling summarised the interview and asked about the examination. Something in Edwards's demeanour concerned him.

Edwards shook his head with a regretful look. 'Sorry, bad news. We don't have it.'

Stirling's good humour dissolved. If they did not have the knife tip, did it undermine Martin's confession? She had given detail that only someone who was there could have told them. He turned to ask Edwards a question and saw he was grinning broadly.

'But, the good news is, we can see where it is!'

There was a loud burst of laughter as the tension in the room evaporated and Edwards stood looking pleased with himself.

Stirling swore softly. 'Hell, Bill, don't do that to me!'

'Just keeping you on your toes, Doug,' replied Edwards, enjoying the moment. To successfully blag Stirling was a rare achievement.

Edwards turned slightly and pointed to the back of his head. 'It's deep in the base of the skull, here, probably during one of the downward strikes when he was bent away from her. Now he knows where he's aiming for, the pathologist wants to make a fresh start in the morning to remove it without risking any damage to the fragment and with SOCO there to photograph the detail. Once we've got it, I'm confident we'll get a physical match.'

After the tension and tiredness of a long day, the laughter and good-natured banter that followed was a welcome relief.

10.57 p.m.
Edwards and the interviewers left to prepare for Martin to be charged with murder and her detention overnight, ready for the City Magistrates Court the next morning.

Stirling made a conference call to Tanner and Pearson. Talking them through the evening's events, he felt satisfaction that his judgement had been vindicated, but the force still had heavy weather ahead of it and Tanner was edgy.

A press conference would be held late the next morning after the court appearance. Asked if the Deputy was yet aware of developments, Tanner said it was best left until the morning when all the facts were known. Strangely enough, though, she would be calling the Chief as they had talked earlier, and she ought to explain the latest developments. The politics of command, Stirling thought, but admired Tanner's canniness. He would have given good money to be present when McDonald's problems were laid out for him. And, by implication, Ballard's too.

Ending the call, Stirling sat on the edge of the desk and looked across the now darkened and silhouetted roofscape. A half-moon hanging over the racecourse was disappearing behind clouds that were filling the sky quickly. Seeing his reflection in the window, Stirling saw how tired he looked. It had been a short night followed by a long day. Pressing his fingers into his eyes until patterns danced, he tried to rub away his tiredness to no effect. Now the chase was ending, Stirling could feel a weariness settling into his limbs.

He had not heard from Helen and assumed she had booked herself off duty through Heal. Thinking of Helen made the link to Ayesha. He had not had chance to call her, but he could have sent a message. Staring at himself in the window, Stirling wondered if he was being deliberately careless, or just felt guilty for last night. He certainly felt guilty.

Deciding it was too late to call, and too tired for an argument, Stirling resigned himself to it being the end of their relationship.

Picking up his jacket, he went downstairs to the custody centre to check everything was in place before heading home.

11.52 p.m.

Driving slowly to unwind, the rhythmic beat of the wiper blades teased his fatigue, seeking to lure him into sleep. Stirling opened a window slightly and breathed in the cool air, forcing his concentration onto the road ahead as the headlights probed the sinuous bends and glanced off large puddles already forming at the edges.

Reviewing the interview, he felt a growing sense of unease. Something about Martin's account didn't hang together. Thinking of Martin brought Cassie to mind, haunting him from the changing shadows at the edges of the roadside so that by the time he reached home, a despondent gloom had settled on his mood.

Turning into the drive, he was surprised to see Ayesha's car parked in the far corner. Switching off the engine, he sat looking across expecting her to get out, but the car seemed empty. Ayesha had no keys to the house, so where was she? Listening to the rain pelting the car roof, Stirling looked around to see where she was sheltering. It was almost midnight, why would Ayesha be here? If she drove out here to confront him, surely, she would not have waited this late before going home? As Stirling considered the remoteness of the cottage and Ayesha alone in her car, he felt a growing concern for her safety.

Pushing his car door shut softly and tugging his collar up against the rain, he went over to confirm the car was empty and locked. Putting a hand on the cold engine grill, he estimated the car had been parked for at least an hour.

Finding the front door locked, Stirling made his way stealthily around the building to the rear, checking each window as he went. The most likely place for a burglar to force entry was the rear kitchen door, but it was secure. Peering through the kitchen window, Stirling could see a soft glow from the table lamp in the lounge casting shadows across the floor. Had he left the light on that morning?

Checking the garage on the way, Stirling returned to the front door and slipped his key into the lock. Bunching his fist, he pushed the door open and stepped aside, ready to punch an intruder bursting out of the darkness inside. The door opened with a low squeak of the hinge he should have oiled weeks ago. Closing the door softly, he listened for movement. Silence.

Uncertain of what to expect and keeping his fists clenched, Stirling cast a swift look around the lounge. Seeing it was empty, he swiftly crossed the room to the kitchen in case an intruder was slipping out of the rear doors, but they were locked. Standing still to listen, Stirling was increasingly concerned for Ayesha's safety.

Feeling his heartbeat in his chest, Stirling's eyes raked the kitchen looking for anything missing, or out of place, his gaze falling on an empty slot in the knife block. He disliked knives lying about and always returned them to the block after use. For a moment, he was in Martin's kitchen with the damaged knife, thinking of Pemberton's ruined face. Was Ayesha upstairs, alone with an intruder and frightened?

Anxious now, Stirling started across the room when a note lying on the table next to a discarded towel caught his eye. Picking up the note, he tilted the paper to the light from the lounge lamp to read the message: "So sorry."

Frowning at the words and trying to understand its message, Stirling looked at the knife block again and felt aa sudden fear tighten in his gut. Alarmed, he ran through the lounge and bounded up the stairs, flicking the light switch on as he went.

On seeing Ayesha's still form body outlined under the cover, Stirling crossed the bedroom and crouched at the bedside, fearing what he would find.

Confused, and believing he was too late, he gently pulled aside the hair that had fallen across Ayesha's peaceful face cradled in a palm, her other hand lying flat to the pillow beside her. Watching her regular breathing, he realised she was fast asleep. There was no blood and looking around, he could see no knife either.

Releasing a long, pent up breath, Stirling sat back on his heels and felt a strong tremor of relief as his fear left him. But how the hell had she got in? As anxiety turned to anger, he reached out to shake her roughly awake but stopped himself, deciding to let her sleep.

Stirling was almost out of the room when he heard the bedclothes stirring behind him. Turning, he saw Ayesha half sat up, resting her weight on one arm as she pulled hair from her eyes. The sheet fell away to her waist revealing her breasts as she blinked against the brightness of the landing light silhouetting Stirling's frame in the doorway.

'Douglas? Is that you?' she asked, her mind drugged with the heaviness of first sleep.

Unable to see his features, Ayesha held a hand up to shield her eyes and tried to rub away the sleep with the other.

Still groggy, she mumbled, 'Douglas? I tried to stay awake, but I was so tired.'

She reached over to switch on a bedside lamp. Seeing his angry face, Ayesha drew her knees up reflexively and wrapped her arms around them protectively.

Striding back to the bedside, the tension and stresses of the day coupled with his relief that she was unharmed burst in Stirling's voice more forcefully than intended. 'What the *hell* are you doing here, and how did you get in?' he demanded angrily.

Shocked, Ayesha gulped with anxiety and answered falteringly, 'There was a spare key on a hook by the door when I was here … last weekend. I'm sorry, I shouldn't have taken it … I was going to surprise you during the week with dinner …' Her voice trailed away as Stirling reached the bed. Instinctively, she leant back into the pillows and half turned from him.

Incredulous that she had taken a key without his permission and ignored his privacy so lightly, he bellowed, 'You did *what*?'

The strains of all the difficult weeks, their irritations with each other in recent days and his fear when he entered the bedroom all collided in an eruption of hot anger. Venting his frustrations at their difficult conversations, her barbed comments on the telephone and, to cap it all, entering his home uninvited, Stirling's hot temper grew with every utterance. Somewhere, though, through the mist of his anger, he registered Ayesha looking up at him in shock and incomprehension. Stopping mid-sentence, realising suddenly how he must appear to her, he stepped back from the bed and wrestled his temper under control.

With the light outlining the power of his body, Ayesha was bewildered and frightened by Stirling's hot, emotional outburst. Watching him with mute, detached fascination, she saw a side to his personality she had not perceived previously. Where was the funny, relaxed and thoughtful man she had grown fond of, so quickly? As her thoughts scrambled to assimilate his fury, her fear and amazement, she saw Stirling falter and step away from the bed. A heavily charged silence filled the space between them.

Fully awake now, Ayesha's own temper and frustrations bubbled up into the void between them. 'I should not have been so difficult with you on the phone, and because you'd not contacted me since, I came here to say sorry, personally! Was that *so* bad? But I waited so long, I came to bed thinking, *stupidly*, you'd be happy to find me in your bed!'

The more she thought about Stirling's failure to understand her good intentions, of his misdirected anger and now livid with herself for swallowing her pride to even come here, Ayesha felt her own temper gathering strength. Pulling the sheet around her body she swung her legs out of bed and stood up to face him, intending to leave.

Eyes blazing, she spat at him, 'But I shouldn't have bothered, should I? You bad tempered, ungrateful *bastard*!'

Stirling's anger had dissolved completely. Understanding the offence he had caused, he wanted Ayesha to understand what had brought him upstairs, so concerned for her safety. Adopting a softer tone and appealing for her understanding, he gestured towards the door. 'I'm sorry Ayesha, but the note, I thought you'd ... you'd done something foolish.'

Clutching the sheet tightly, her hair falling over her bare shoulders, Ayesha looked at him in confusion, struggling to comprehend what he was talking about.

'Note? What note?' she demanded hotly.

Gesturing to the stairs, he explained, 'On the kitchen table, you left a note. I thought ...'

Following the direction of his arm Ayesha frowned as she tried to clear away the fog and confusion of their heated exchanges. A sudden realisation spread over her features and taking a step towards him, she looked at him, her green eyes blazing.

'It was an *apology* you bloody fool. Together with your supper!'

It was Stirling's turn to look confused. Looking down at her, he repeated, 'Supper?'

With an exasperated exclamation, she threw aside the sheet and pushed Stirling aside and stormed out of the bedroom.

Listening to her bare feet pounding down the stairs, Stirling followed, baffled, and feeling guilty at his bad temper. He found Ayesha in the now illuminated kitchen standing next to the oak table, careless of her nakedness except for a pair of white lace knickers. Even in the bewilderment of the argument, Stirling registered how incredibly attractive they looked against her skin, emphasising the flare of her hips and the flimsy lacework leaving just enough to imagination.

Pulling back the cloth he thought had been thrown carelessly onto the table, she pointed at a cold supper of bread, pickles and a chunk of cheese.

'Your *supper*! I thought you might need something to eat when you got in, because I was *concerned* that you eat properly. More fool *me*!'

Realising how ridiculous the situation had become and looking as foolish as he felt, he replied, 'Ayesha, I'm so sorry, I completely misunderstood.'

'What the *fuck* did you think was under there together with a note saying *"Sorry"* you *stupid* man?'

Stirling's eyebrows rose in surprise at the obscenity. He had not heard Ayesha use bad language before but took it as a measure of how upset she was. And with good reason, he now realised. As Stirling struggled to find the right reply, something else dawned on Ayesha's face and her eyes narrowed as she considered something.

'You said you thought I'd done something ...' Ayesha shut her eyes to recall his words exactly, '... *foolish*?'

Stirling groaned as he saw the realisation light in her eyes and take a step towards him.

'I don't *believe* you! We have a wonderful weekend together, you disappear at the drop of a hat, send me cryptic, emotionless messages and then hear nothing from you for two days, and you thought ... you think I ... that I would ... I could ...'

Ayesha's angry disbelief was stifling her ability to speak coherently. She stepped closer and beat each accusation onto his chest with her clenched fist. 'You arrogant *bastard!* Do you *seriously* think I would harm myself because of *you*? You *vain! Arrogant!* Self-righteous, *prick!*'

As Ayesha beat his chest, Stirling caught sight of her reflection in the glass door behind, of her hair swinging in rhythm with the movement of her arm, the shape of her bottom defined by the white lace knickers. Even in the heat of their fight he could admire how desirable she was. He wanted to kiss her, but thought his timing might be off.

Ayesha had every right to be angry with him, but he needed to explain before she left. Taking her wrists in each hand, Stirling held her close to him, taking care not to hurt her.

'Ayesha. Listen! Please?' he appealed, as she fought to free herself from his grip and continued swearing at him.

Shocked at the ferocity of Ayesha's temper and language, and a hot passion he had not suspected, Stirling tried again, 'Ayesha, enough now! Listen to me? Please?'

Breathing raggedly from exertion but unable to free herself, she stopped struggling to listen, but was still determined to leave.

'I can't say how sorry I am Ayesha. The last few months have been hell for me but meeting you changed that. For the better. We'd argued, and I had no reason to expect you to be here. When I saw the knife was missing, and then the note … it sounds stupid now, but I'm so used to dealing with people's unhappiness. Something involving a knife happened today, in the investigation. I misunderstood the sentiment of your note and, stupidly, jumped to the wrong conclusion. Your car was empty and it's so remote out here, I was concerned for your safety and over reacted. When you woke up and I saw you were alright, well, all the strain of the last weeks came out. I'm sorry, I didn't intend to upset you. Or frighten you.'

'*Knife*? What knife?' she demanded. She was a lawyer, detail didn't escape her.

Letting go of her wrists, he gestured across the room. 'From the knife block.'

With a look of incredulity, Ayesha reached over to the cloth and yanked it fully off the plated food. Next to it lay a small knife.

'It was to cut the *cheese* with! You bloody *idiot*, Douglas!'

Staring at the knife and seeing Ayesha's bewilderment, Stirling groaned and felt a sinking feeling at how his hasty assumption and reaction had turned a small act of kindness into a blistering row.

He was left wondering too, what his anxiety said of his feelings for Ayesha.

Contritely, he replied, 'Ayesha, you're right, I'm an idiot. I jumped to a foolish conclusion. Worse than that, I lost my temper and I frightened you. For that I'm truly sorry. I couldn't understand how you could have got into the house and I was worried about you.'

Tentatively, Stirling stepped closer and gently pulled her to him. Hearing the conciliatory tone and that he clearly regretted his actions, Ayesha felt her own temper subsiding.

'You were worried, about me?' she asked, searching his face inquisitively. 'Explain that to me.'

Looking over her head, Stirling examined his feelings and his reaction. 'I'm not sure. All I can tell you is that when I was running up those stairs, I was frightened. If you hadn't woken up I would have come downstairs, found the supper you'd prepared and everything would have made perfect sense. You were very thoughtful, but I spoilt it. And I upset you, which I regret most of all. I think the whole thing has made me understand I care for you.'

Ayesha saw his sincerity. It was not exactly a declaration of love, but she had not been expecting one and was reassured that Stirling had expressed his feelings for her. Reaching up, Ayesha put a hand on Stirling's check and stroked it, feeling his stubble rasp under her palm. 'I'm sorry too. I shouldn't have taken the key, and I'm sorry we quarrelled.'

As the tension flowed out of their bodies, Ayesha wrapped her arms around his waist and pressed herself into him tightly. Stirling bent his head to breath in the scent of her hair and then kissed her slowly, enjoying the moist softness of her lips on his. After some moments wrapped in each other's arms, Stirling looked over Ayesha's shoulder.

Holding her away from him slightly, he asked, 'Do you have any idea just how beautiful you are when you're blazing mad?'

'I can't say the same for you!'

'No, but then again, I'm not undressed.'

Following Stirling's gaze behind her, she saw herself mirrored in the door. Thinking about how she would have looked during their fight, she demanded, 'D'you ever think of anything else?'

Looking at her admiringly, he replied, 'I'm just saying you're beautiful, that's all.' He paused and added, 'I'm not sure if hot temper does that to a woman's body or if you're just cool, but perhaps we should get you something warm to put on?'

Before she could stop herself, Ayesha instinctively followed his eyes downwards and felt hot blood rushing to her cheeks. Lifting an arm within the circle of his embrace she hit him lightly on his chest, but was able to smile at her awkwardness.

'You really are a conceited sod, Stirling,' she said, encircling his waist again and put her head on his chest. 'I've missed you Douglas. You're not the only one who's had a shitty week, you know? I needed someone to talk to, but you weren't there. Not even on the end of the phone!'

After a long silence, she added with a mixture of concern and thoughtfulness, 'We just had our first quarrel.'

'Some quarrel, too,' he said, cradling her head against his chest. Massaging her scalp with one hand, Stirling traced his fingers down her spine so that she shivered and arched under his touch.

Putting his hand on Ayesha's hip, he pulled her closer to him.

 beginsymbol end

Day 8: Monday – 6.55 a.m.

Dressed in the oversized shirt again, Ayesha sat across the corner of the table as Stirling ate hungrily, enjoying watching him eat the breakfast she had prepared while he showered and shaved. As they chatted, Ayesha drew her hand across his cheek and cupped it to her nose to smell his aftershave, wanting to keep the spicy scent with her through the day.

There had been a lot of laughter as they lay together recalling the absurdity of the quarrel, making fun of each other's bad temper and Stirling claiming never to have heard such language from a woman outside of a prison cell. Ayesha was still embarrassed. She had never been so angry with a man before, leaving her to wonder if it reflected her feelings for him. Talking quietly together, they had fallen into a deep sleep without making love, until the early alarm had given them time to begin the day with a renewed desire.

With a long kiss and a solemn promise to call her later, Stirling left Ayesha to lock up when she left for work.

7.35 a.m.

Sat in his office, Stirling considered the day ahead. Martin would be the first business of the day for the Magistrates Court at ten that morning and her appearance would be swift. He doubted her brief would advise she pursued a precious application for bail at her first appearance with many police enquiries outstanding. The Crown Prosecution Service would claim Martin could compromise or obstruct enquiries if she were released. Better to apply in a few days when the Police could be accused of dragging their feet.

Thinking about Martin's remand in custody to one of the few women's prisons in the region, Stirling wondered how she would cope. Prison, like death, is one of society's great levellers. Sharing a fetid cell and toilet for twenty-three hours a day with prostitutes, thieves, drug addicts and the socially disadvantaged from the toughest districts of Birmingham and other cities in the region would be extremely stressful. The constant noise of prisoners and prison officers shouting, the banging of steel doors and gates and the odour of prison wings came to him uninvited; disinfectant, stale bodies and sweaty socks. Like dirty homes and post mortems, once experienced a few times, it was an indelible smell that never left the memory. Prison would be a painful contrast from Martin's perfectly coordinated, magazine-shoot home.

Bringing his attention back to the day ahead, Stirling made a check list of tasks. First amongst them was to check if the cigar lighter was missing from the wreck and if so, another search of the scene would be needed. A search too of the hedgerows on Martin's route home for mobile phone parts. Getting resources for the searches would be a challenge. Working through the list of tasks and making calls, Stirling felt a creeping unease. Something didn't fit and the older he got, the more Stirling trusted his instincts. There were too many loose threads.

Loose threads led to appeals and acquittals.

11.12 a.m.
Answering his phone, Stirling heard Pearson's voice at the other end. It was the call he'd been waiting for all morning.

The morning had flown by. As the team went past his door, many had stopped to congratulate him on the previous day's success. Stirling had opened the team briefing at nine, summarised Martin's confession and made it clear there was still a lot of hard work ahead to secure a safe conviction.

Handing over to Edwards, he had left to call Pearson before he went into the Chief Officers "Monday Prayers," the weekly meeting that pump primed the executive week. Keenly aware that on the altar of public opinion, and Chief Officer's careers, he was still vulnerable to sacrifice, Stirling needed to know what the mood music was.

As Pearson talked, Stirling felt a growing sense of relief, and some absolution too. After giving him the headline information, Pearson lowered his voice. Stirling suspected his door was open as usual.

'Between you and me Doug, the shit's hit the fan in some style. The Chief's seriously grumpy. He's had to give the Police and Crime Commissioner a personal briefing. There'll be a press conference early afternoon which Tanner will front up but, behind the scenes, the Chief's got his hands firmly on the levers.'

'What about McDonald and Ballard?' asked Stirling, still not sure if he was out of danger.

'The Dep won't escape this without some shit sticking to his CV. The downside to that, though, is we'll have to suffer him for longer if he can't get a job somewhere else as a consequence! Ballard's to be suspended immediately pending a review of his investigation. I've arranged with PSD for someone in your team to have supervised access to Ballard's files to be sure that anything relevant to the murder is available to you. Let them know who your liaison officer will be.'

'What about the IPCC? Haven't they screwed up too?

'Yes. Their SIO is inexperienced with too much work on his plate and some problems in his private life. He assumed Ballard was as good as he said he was and gave him far too much free rein, letting him get on with it. Ballard took advantage of that and ran the investigation in his own dogmatic way telling the IPCC and McDonald only what they wanted to hear.'

'And what *he* wanted them to hear, too!' Stirling added, bitterly.

Pearson heard the bitterness in Stirling's voice. 'True. It's a bad do all round Doug, and no one's coming out of it very well.'

11.21 a.m.

Putting the phone down, Stirling reflected on Pearson's call. He was surprised to feel no pleasure in Ballard's fall from grace, only anger that he had failed to serve Cassie and her family better. Nothing could have returned Cassie to life, but a thorough investigation would have provided explanations and, perhaps, might have brought Pemberton to book, too. And might Pemberton have lived?

Thinking of the Martin family reminded Stirling of Helen's voicemail. He had only noticed it that morning and she was not at the morning briefing. Heal had said she was required at Shrewsbury Crown Court and would be in as soon as possible. Deleting the voicemail, Stirling was considering how best to approach Carol Evans when Bill Edwards walked in and sat down.

'Remanded in custody for a week and no application for bail,' he announced with a smile of professional satisfaction. 'Prison is going to be a shock, but I can't say I feel any pity for her.'

Stirling pulled a face. 'I'm not so sure. If Ballard had done his job properly things might have been very different.'

Edwards shrugged his shoulders, answering matter of factly, 'There's nothing you or I can do about that. We can only do our own job as well as we possibly can. McDonald knew Ballard was inexperienced … and a pompous prick too!'

It was a fair observation. Stirling told him about Pearson's call which cheered Edwards up even further. After agreeing a review of the material held at PSD, Edwards related the latest enquiry updates.

'Forensics called. The Merc' is exceptionally clean, inside and out but, an initial UV lamp inspection of the interior indicates possible blood traces inside the glove box, where the knife was put perhaps? However good the valet was, it would be unusual for the inside of a glove box to be cleaned. The satnav memory is being sent off for analysis of its journey data which should show the car going to and from the scene at the material times.'

Edwards continued. 'The cigar lighter *is* missing from the Jag's dashboard, but I doubt the TF's fingertip search would have missed it if she threw it away as described. They searched the area very thoroughly, but they're doing it again on a more limited scale for a radius of fifty metres from the car's location. I don't think she's an Olympic thrower!' he added sardonically.

Stirling smiled. 'We need to do some tests to see how easy it is to ignite a fuel-soaked rag with a cigar lighter.'

'Cassie's DNA will be compared with anything recovered from the bindings in his apartment. It doesn't take us any further forward in proving Martin's culpability, but it would corroborate the facts, and Martin's defence will want it done. We'll limit the analysis to the items we can see in the photographs.' Edwards's face showed his distaste at the memory.

Cassie's DNA would be there, Stirling was certain of that, recalling the images of her slim figure bound across the bed, her face shadowed with humiliation and the tattoo branding her as Pemberton's possession. Stirling dearly wished he had been able to arrest Pemberton and not Cassie's mother.

'What about the enquiries to trace Gérard Martin?' asked Stirling. 'He has a right to be told of his daughter's death. Martin hasn't done so by her own account.'

'I'll chase it up. We're relying on the old pal's network, though. Special Branch has a contact at the French Embassy in Knightsbridge, London. A liaison officer to UK policing but a full Colonel of the Gendarmerie so he ought to have some clout across the Channel.' Looking at his watch Edwards smiled, adding, 'I better hurry though, they'll be at lunch soon!'

Stirling relayed Helen's voicemail and described the woman they had seen at Martin's home. 'Was Evans in court this morning?'

'No, the courtroom was empty.'

'Okay, I'll see if I can find her, I'm going into the city anyway.'

1.45 p.m.

Parking near to the river, Stirling walked briskly along the Severn Way riverside path towards the cathedral, enjoying the fresh air and being able to stretch his legs after too many days in the office. The spring sunshine and a clear sky matched his mood as he thought about the argument of the night before, and their making up. With the holiday over and children back in school, there were few people about and for want of better prospects, a pair of swans sailed towards him in hope of food.

Stirling paused at the railing for a few moments to admire them and to watch the river slide by, its surface broken occasionally by tangles of branches and other debris still being carried downstream from Shropshire and beyond. Stirling turned and craned his neck back to look up at the cathedral tower high above him, its delicate carvings picked out in sharp relief by the sunlight. Even though he was not a subscriber, it was a building he never tired of looking at, always amazed at the sheer force of will, devotion and grinding labour needed to build such a beautiful monument to faith with relatively primitive tools. A faith he had struggled to understand for many years. Rubbing shoulders with death and constantly witnessing the worst of human behaviour had eroded Stirling's already shaky belief, leading him to a more existential view.

Turning away from the river, Stirling paused to study the high-water markers for the Severn's most exceptional floods. Passing under the Water Gate, he began to climb the flights of steps rising through the cathedral lawns where early blossom, plucked by the breeze, reeled and skittered around his feet before dancing across close-cut grass, confetti to the rites of spring. With his confidence growing that he would be cleared of blame in Cassie's death and the fine weather, Stirling felt a lightness of spirit he had not experienced for a long time. Drawing the clean air deep into his lungs, he took the remaining steps at a run and headed for the main entrance at the north door.

The cool, dry air settled on his neck immediately. Stirling paused to stare, smelling the dust of history in his nostrils.

His shoes echoed off the black and white tiles as he walked to the centre of the aisle and stopped to admire the vaulted ceiling high above him. Two lines of symmetrical, decorated columns processed along the nave towards the East Window far away where clusters of visitors drifted between the royal tombs of wicked King John and the young Prince Arthur. Somewhere, high up and out of sight, speakers breathed gentle choral music so that the building seemed to be weeping centuries of accumulated piety and sorrow. Dotted around the nave, solitary figures sat in contemplation of the cathedral's beauty, or knelt in prayer. Despite his own loss of faith, Stirling could understand that a troubled soul might find peace here.

Helen's message said Carol Evans worked in the cathedral but not what she did there. Seeing no one resembling the woman at Martin's home, Stirling discreetly pulled aside an elderly, white haired volunteer. Yes, Carol Evans worked in the cathedral. Where? Oh, wherever needed. 'We're all one team here,' she told him joyfully, her wrinkled face beaming up at Stirling with an inner peace he never expected to find. Today? Well, she thought she was working in the shop. No, no, that was yesterday. She was in the café today. It's in the Cloisters, you know, she explained helpfully. Thanking her warmly, he followed the direction of her arthritic finger.

Set to one side of the cloister garth, the café plied its trade from a high vaulted room, painted simply in cream. A dozen tables lined the walls on either side and an uneven stone floor worn smooth through the centuries led to a counter at the far end. Holding open the door to allow a group of elderly tourists to make their stiff exit, Stirling looked over their grey heads to the counter where Carol Evans stood below a large, round clock. Slender, with prematurely greying hair parted at the centre to frame her face, Stirling saw the resemblance to Katrina Martin straight away, although Carol would pass for the older of the sisters. Even at a distance, Evans looked life worn and there was a tangible sadness about her. Dressed simply in faded jeans and a floral print blouse, she possessed none of Martin's self-conscious poise, or visible wealth.

Stirling loitered near the door as Evans served a customer. Thinking he should return when it was quieter, he was about to leave when Evans looked down the café. When she saw Stirling, the recognition was immediate. Seeing Evans's response turn from surprise to anxiety, Stirling smiled and made his way down the aisle as casually as possible to avoid alarming her. She watched him, trancelike, until he came to stand near her.

'Carol?' he asked.

Evans nodded mutely.

'I'm sorry to arrive unannounced but we've had difficulty contacting you. Can we talk quietly somewhere, please?'

Evans stared at him, her eyes darting rapidly between his eyes, searching for the reason he was there.

Concerned at her response, Stirling put a hand gently on her arm. 'Carol, are you okay?' he asked quietly. 'I'm Detective Chief Inspector Stirling and I ...'

'I know,' she answered in a strained voice. Looking down at his hand Evans seemed surprised to see it there and stepped away. 'Um, I'm not sure. I ...' she pointed vaguely along the counter to no-one, '... I'll need to get someone to cover for me.'

Evans disappeared through a gothic archway into the kitchen. Moments later, she reappeared followed by a large woman with an upholstered bust who smiled warmly at Stirling as she shooed Carol Evans along in front of her encouragingly, telling her to 'take as long as you like with the nice gentleman.'

It occurred to Stirling the woman had mistaken him for an admirer.

Sitting together amongst rows of wooden chairs in a small side chapel, their backs turned to the inquisitive looks of tourists,

Stirling explained he wanted to be sure she was aware of Katrina's arrest and if there were any welfare issues he should be aware of.

Hesitantly, Evans confirmed she was Katrina Martin's only living relative. Her eyes frequently drifted off to some vague point in the corner of the chapel so that Stirling was not certain she was listening all of the time. Evans knew her sister was in custody. The solicitor had called her at home the previous evening and again this morning, after the court appearance. She was keeping herself busy as she did not know what else to do.

Sitting bent forward slightly as if to reduce her presence, Evans held her hands in her lap, constantly twining and untwining her fingers. Listening to her rapid, shallow breathing, Stirling was concerned she would hyper-ventilate and pass out. Taking care to explain how she would benefit from having a Family Liaison Officer so she could contact him at any time, Evans was adamant she did not need, or want a FLO. The more he saw of her restless, fidgety manner and listened to the stress in her voice, Stirling began to wonder if Carol Evans had suffered with mental health problems.

What Stirling did not know, and could not discuss with Evans, was whether she knew about Cassie's involvement with Pemberton. Martin might have said nothing to protect her daughter, even in death.

Sniffing loudly, Evans searched for a tissue in the embroidered, cloth shoulder bag she had put on the empty chair between them. Evans fumbled distractedly amongst its contents, her hands shaking so violently, that she caused the bag to fall onto the floor where its contents spilt around their feet. Dropping to her knees, Evans began to hastily scrabble the contents back into her bag, apologising profusely and unnecessarily. Slipping off his seat, Stirling crouched in the narrow space between the rows of chairs to help her.

Bent together in a parody of prayer, Evans paused in her search to look at Stirling, holding his gaze for several seconds, searching for something. Trying to lighten her embarrassment, to reassure her that he was not a threat, Stirling smiled, but saw only confusion and fear as she bit hard on her lower lip. Holding out to her the few items he had picked up, Evans snatched them from him and stuffed everything back inside the bag, still apologising.

Putting a hand on the chair to lift herself back up, Evans's hand slipped, and she stumbled forward into Stirling. Still kneeling, he caught her easily with both hands as their heads bumped together slightly, resulting in another bout of apologies and tears of embarrassment. Taking her hand, Stirling helped Evans into her chair where she stared ahead at the saint's simple altar, wiping away her tears.

Quietly, Stirling said, 'Carol, I'm truly sorry I wasn't able to save Cassie. Or did you call her Cassandra?'

It wasn't the conversation Stirling had intended to have but she clearly knew who he was, and it seemed right to try and explain. At the mention of Cassie's name, Evans bent her head and began to weep quietly. Lifting her head, she waited for him to speak again.

'I tried to help Cassie, but I only had a few minutes with her before she ... she fell. I couldn't hold on to her, as much as I tried. Her hand was wet from the rain and she was very cold. She just slipped through my fingers. I'm truly sorry, Carol.'

Evans's eyes shuttled between his and tears began to roll down her cheeks as she felt Stirling's compassion, recognising his own pain at the memory. She put a hand to her mouth to stifle a sob.

Stirling continued, 'After Cassie died I asked to meet her family, to explain how she had died, but I was prevented from doing so. I didn't know Katrina was her mum. Would you explain that when you see her, please?'

Staring at him with an empty sadness, Evans nodded mutely.

'Can I arrange for a female officer to meet you at your home later, Carol?'

Shifting to face her more comfortably, Stirling lifted his arm to rest his weight on the back of the empty chair between them. Seeing the movement towards her, Evans flinched away sharply. Surprised at her reaction, Stirling lowered his arm onto the chair back slowly and watched her fiddle with her fingers in her lap again.

'Carol? Detective Constable Helen Williams will see you at your home this evening, at seven? I won't be there. Will that be okay?'

Evans's eyes drifted away to the alter, lost in some deep thought. Turning back to him, she frowned as she tried to remember what he had asked her and then mumbled 'Yes.'

'Do you have a mobile phone number in case we need to contact you?'

Evans shook her head.

'Okay. Helen will visit you at your home then, at seven.'

Evans nodded and waited for him to speak again. Realising the conversation could be over, in a meek voice she asked, 'Can I go now, please?'

Surprised that she seemed to be asking permission, he answered, 'Yes, of course, and I'm sorry if my visit has upset you.'

Evans rose and walked to the gated chapel entrance where she stopped abruptly and turned to look back at Stirling. She was crying again, her cheeks wet with tears. Holding a hand to her mouth, Evans took a faltering step towards him and stopped. Noticing the enquiring stare of two camera laden tourists, Carol Evans gave Stirling a sad, lingering look, bent her head and walked from his sight.

To a casual observer, the man sat alone in the half gloom of the chapel looked like any other supplicant. Listening to the silence, Stirling wondered if that was the appeal. Somewhere to hear your own thoughts?

The meeting bothered him. In the soft light of the chapel, as they knelt together recovering her possessions, something of Evans's sad, life worn features had fallen away to reveal the exceptionally attractive young woman she had once been, traces of strawberry blonde hair still visible in her greying hair. Wide set, hazel green eyes above a straight nose and a full mouth that some would describe as "sensual" would have been attractive enough, but high cheek bones and a tapering jaw gave a symmetry to her features and would have turned any man's head.

When she had stumbled into him, he had caught the scent of her perfume. It was the same as that on Cassie's pillow. A cigarette lighter had fallen onto the floor too, yet she did not have the unpleasant smell of dead cigarettes on her clothes. Analysing their conversation, Stirling realised she had said very little and was extremely nervous, but as the last person to speak to her niece, and responsible for the arrest of her sister, her nervousness was understandable.

Looking around the plain chapel and its dusty stonework, Stirling wondered what life had done to Carol Evans to find her here, greyed out and fading into the fabric of this temple of spent prayers? Trailing in the wake of a successful, domineering sister? Possibly. Or mental illness? Thinking about how she had snatched her arm away, Stirling wondered what had made her so fearful. Simply because he was a man? If Pemberton had an affair with Martin, he might have met her sister and if so, was Carol Evans another victim of his blackmailing project? As a young woman, her beauty would have attracted his predatory attentions, but she was not among the photographs. If Martin had been able to demand her own back, she would surely have recovered any of her sister. Even so, Pemberton was sure to have kept digital copies for his own pleasure.

Dragging himself back from his wanderings, Stirling found himself staring up into the face of the Virgin Mary, who returned him a forgiving smile.

Feeling undeserving of forgiveness, Stirling left.

*

Slamming the cubicle door shut, Carol Evans crouched over the toilet and retched between despairing sobs.

She had recognised Stirling the moment she set eyes on him. Fearful of him and why he was there, she had been bewildered to feel a comforting presence when she was close to him and saw the reassurance in his eyes. It was the closest she had been to a man for many years. The thought made her retch again.

Pulling out more tissue paper, she wiped her mouth and stood up shakily, putting her forehead against the wall to feel the cool stone. Tasting the sourness in her mouth she bent over the toilet and spat several times.

At the sinks, she rinsed out her mouth and splashed cold water on her face to wash away her tears. Leaning heavily on the sink, Evans stared at the woman looking back at her, seeking amongst the dark spots of peeled silvering the pretty girl who had once smiled back. Studying the dull, grey hair and ageing face, she wondered again how she had let herself become this woman. She had always worn her beauty lightly, careless of her good fortune that men thought her attractive and never needing to try and get a man's attention. They were already looking.

Men were always interested in her, arriving on a conveyor belt of promise, each soon forgotten by her next romantic self-indulgence. Determinedly carefree and consciously avoiding personal responsibility, she had been far too trusting during her "wild child" years, as she had liked to describe them. Too late, she had understood that all she ever really wanted, and needed, was someone who would love her faithfully and take care of her so that she didn't have to think for herself. Even though she could be cruel, only Katy had ever looked after her.

Feeling again her fear and isolation, another crisis of emotion washed over her and she sobbed out to the empty room, 'Who will look after me now?'

A toilet flushed behind her. Frightened, Carol Evans fled from the room.

*

4.30 p.m.
To save a journey to the MCU, only to return later, Stirling found an empty office at Worcester Police Station from where he called Edwards to tell him about the meeting with Evans. Edwards would arrange for Helen to meet Evans later.

'Special Branch called,' said Edwards. 'Their contact at the French Embassy has got back to them. The official report will take a few days to reach us but our Colonel's a resourceful man. He knows where to ask the questions, or knows people who do. Using the information Katrina Martin gave Helen, date and place of birth and the French company he worked for in London, he's got the French equivalent of a national insurance number. They've got no record of him on their systems for years, no bank accounts. Well, none in his own name. No death registered, and no family identified. Either he's fallen off a mountain in Indonesia, or he's sitting on a beach sipping rum and sunning his arse somewhere.'

'What about the parent's details on Cassie's birth certificate, any information there?'

'Yes. With Ballard out of the way, PSD can't do enough to help us! Cassie's birth certificate shows Gérard and Katrina Martin as her parents with the birth registered in a nice part of London.'

'Okay, we'll let the official channels take their course. By the time they've pushed it out to their embassies around the globe, they'll probably find him. Anything else?'

'Helen believes she's now traced, or has the ID of all but one of the women in the photographs. We've no idea who the woman in the boot of the Jag is.'

"Or was" thought Stirling, recalling the abject fear on her face.

Edwards summarised the remaining work in hand, warning Stirling not to expect a result from the searches for the cigar lighter or phone soon. It would be slow, painstaking work. Edwards was about to ring off when a thought occurred to Stirling.

'Bill. Check out the availability of a cadaver dog, please. I'm considering another search at The Wern.'

7.00 p.m.

From inside his car a little way down the street, Stirling watched Helen knock at Carol Evans's front door. The driveway was empty. Stirling wondered how long they would need to wait for her to return home, which meant an uncomfortable time alone with Helen. Next door, a man opened a window and leant out to speak with Helen. A minute later she got back in the car.

'That's Morgan. Says he heard her leave about twenty minutes ago so she's either nipped out to the shops, or she's avoiding us. From what you've told me, I'd say she's keeping out of our way.'

Helen sat half turned to face him. Stirling knew there was more going on in her mind than a critique of Evans's behaviour.

'Let's give her twenty minutes,' he said. Shrugging down into his seat, Stirling folded his arms and closed his eyes as he settled down to wait. 'This is just like the old days on surveillance, Helen,' he said humorously, hoping to avoid any conversation which might lead to an argument.

7.37 p.m.

They gave Evans thirty minutes. Accepting they had a job to do, Helen had decided to wait until they were clear of the commitment before she would insist on a conversation,

Stirling drove back to the local community police station where they had left her car. With the engine running, each waited for the other to start.

'Helen, we should clear the air,' started Stirling, still not sure if Helen had hopes of rekindling their relationship.

Helen stared ahead waiting to hear what he would say.

'I should have gone home the other night. I'm sorry. I shouldn't have messed with your feelings. Or let you mess with mine, for that matter.'

Helen turned sharply towards him. 'Really? Your feelings looked perfectly fine when you were fucking me!' she snapped, the tension of the last two days spilling over.

Trying to choose his words to avoid confrontation, Stirling replied, 'Helen, I'd prefer it if we don't fall out over this. Physically, it was great and if we're honest with each other, we *both* enjoyed it. But, neither of us was seduced. I had a drink but not so much that I can't remember the conversation. You pushed all the right buttons Helen. I needed someone to talk with who understands the job, and who understands me, too. But, I should have gone home. You were good company, Helen. We had an enjoyable evening together and you're very desirable, but if you think we could make a life together, it wouldn't work. We'd fight like cat and dog and, if you're honest with yourself, you know it.'

Helen retorted, '*Don't* tell me what I think, you arrogant bastard!'

There was silence as each waited for the other to take the next step. Regretting her flash of temper, in a softer voice she said, 'I never stopped loving you Dougie. I thought Saturday night was a new start. It still could be, couldn't it? Can't we try?'

There was hurt in Helen's voice as well as a suppressed anger. Heavy tears clung at her eyelids before spilling down her cheeks. Angry at herself for crying in front of him, Helen brushed the tears away with both hands and turned to look out of the window. The only sound above the low hum of the engine was the radio playing quietly.

After some silence, without turning to him she asked, sadly, 'Why did you ask me to work with you if you knew how you felt?'

'Because I needed your help. I had no intention of ending up in your bed, but it happened. We can't change that, but we're not suited to each other for the long term. We'd end up hating each other and I really don't want that to happen.'

'We can be friends, though, see each other now and then?' Helen felt as if she was pleading and hated herself for it, but wanted something of him for herself.

Stirling shook his head and sighed, 'Helen, we'll *always* be friends, if you can allow it to be just that. But I'm not getting involved in a "friends with benefits" arrangement. It's messy and not what I want.'

Helen gave a snort of cynical laughter, 'No, you prefer to screw your way through life without ever making a commitment. And what about that woman I heard you on the phone to? You're obviously fucking her as well! What would she make of the other night, I wonder?'

Stirling replied evenly, 'Helen, our private lives are our own. I didn't intend to rake up old feelings. It happened in the moment and if you were hoping for more, I'm sorry, but it won't work. Let's part as friends?'

Helen turned back to him and seeing the firm set to his face, saw what she already knew. Reaching out, she pushed her fingers through his hair, enjoying the thick wave of it between her fingers and drew her hand slowly down his face to let it rest on his cheek. Giving a sad, regretful smile, she thought there was so much more she wanted to say, but it was pointless.

Helen got out of the car and walked away.

8.25 p.m.

Sitting in a corner of the pub well away from other diners and a group of regulars at the bar, Stirling sat with a pint of beer in one hand and a half-eaten meal pushed aside. He had lost his appetite.

After leaving Helen, he had decided to take an hour out to collect his thoughts. Something was niggling away at the back of his mind like an itch he couldn't quite reach. Resting his head on the back of the bench seat, Stirling closed his eyes to think, to knit the threads together into something that made sense. Taking a pull at his beer, he lifted the glass up to the light to study it critically and sighed at the cloudy sediment in the bottom. One thing was plain enough. The beer was poorly kept and he would avoid the place in future.

Stirling's thoughts turned again to the last moments of Cassandra Martin's life. Even with Martin's confession and everything from Ballard's investigation gone through, something was eluding him, fluttering at the edge of his mind's eye.

9.21 p.m.

Ramping the car up onto the broad path next to the railings, Stirling switched the engine off and sat looking around him. He had not returned to the bridge since Cassie's death.

In the rear-view mirror, he could see the collection of dead flowers picked out by the regular sweep of headlights whipping round the island. Laid by Cassie's friends and, presumably, her small family.

The rumble of heavy wagons thundering north and south below him echoed around the barren island, the rhythmic swooshing shattered by a long, angry blast of a lorry horn bellowing southwards.

Stirling was not sure why he had felt a need to come here. He would not stay long.

Looking down at the dead flowers, Stirling was struck by how pitifully sad they appeared. Most of the tributes were inexpensive supermarket or garage bought offerings tied onto or poked through the railing mesh to hold them in place against the wind and elements. Most of them had long since shrivelled and died. A pink teddy bear tied lopsidedly onto the mesh gave him a banal, button eyed smile through accumulating road grime. Standing out from amongst the collection of fading grief were two fresh bouquets, both tied efficiently to the mesh to stop them being blown away.

Both bouquets looked expensive but where one was ostentatiously elaborate, the other was a simple arrangement of white lilies with a single red rose at its heart. Without needing to look closer, Stirling knew the elaborate bouquet would be Katrina Martin's. The other bouquet of lilies intrigued him.

Squatting on his haunches to see it better, a car's headlights passing behind illuminated the waxiness of the blooms to show the petals were still dewy. Rubbing a petal between his fingers to feel its waxy texture, pollen from the stamens brushed against his hand leaving an orange stain. The bouquet had been freshly placed.

Tucked in amongst the lilies was a tribute card enclosed in a clear cellophane envelope. Casting a swift, guilty look around him, Stirling lifted the card out and turned it to the lighting above him to read it. Frowning, Stirling reached over and detached the card from the more elaborate bouquet and stood to get a better view under the lights. Oblivious to the roar of traffic beneath him and the constant rush of cars behind him, he tilted the cards to the light and compared the writing.

Replacing the cards inside their respective bouquets, Stirling took out his mobile phone and photographed the bouquets together, and then separately. Removing the cards again, he put them safely inside his wallet.

Resting his hands on the railings, Stirling watched the ribbon of red lights streaming north into the darkness as he thought about the cards. Across the fields, HQ sat on its pedestal a mile away with many of the office lights still on. Picking out Tanner's office, Stirling thought back to a late evening meeting that seemed weeks ago, not just seven days. Looking down to where Cassie's life had ended and feeling the cold railing under his hand, Stirling rotated the facts through his mind to align the cogs.

It began here. And here was where the answer lay.

9.42 p.m.

Waiting impatiently for Heal to answer, Stirling wondered if he had gone home. When Heal answered with a tired 'Yes boss?' Stirling gave him some brief instructions and ended the call.

As they were talking a text alert had vibrated. It was a text from Helen. Needing to get away urgently, he put his phone away to read the message later. They had said all there was to say.

10.25 p.m.

Geordie Heal was tired. The last person in the room, he was getting ready to leave for home when he saw it was Stirling calling. He had groaned loudly as it could only mean something else to do.

He had just promised his wife he was on his way home. Mrs Heal had been giving him serious earache for not being at home during the school holiday to spend time with their two energetic boys. Heal wasn't best pleased either, but the job came first and he had reminded her that the overtime paid for the nice home they were buying and the two holidays they had got used to taking the boys on each year. But he would like to see his sons more, chiding himself that they would only grow up once.

When the boss strode briskly into the room, his jaw set and looking determined, Heal's heart sank. The evening was about to get longer.

'Got it?'

'Aye boss. Over there with the other photos you asked for,' Heal replied.

Heal followed Stirling over to the desk where he had laid out copies of the photograph of the cottage alongside photographs of Pemberton's apartment. Curious to know what was bugging the boss, Heal watched him study the cottage photo before placing it face down to reveal the dedication on the rear. Taking two small cards out of his wallet, Stirling lay them side by side, next to the picture. Heal was puzzled why Stirling had floral dedication cards.

'What d'you think, Geordie?' asked Stirling. He wanted to check his own assessment.

Heal examined the three items. Both tributes had a brief dedication in similarly styled hand-writing: one to *"My darling Cassandra, forever in my heart. Mother."* The other to *"My sweet, beautiful Cassie. Together soon X."*

'Hard to say boss. There's very little space to write on these cards. The writing on the back of the photo could have been written by either hand, but ...' Heal studied them again to attempt a better interpretation, '... if I had to put my life on it, I'd say the one on the left is closest to the writing on the photo.'

'Me too,' replied Stirling and picked up the photographs of Pemberton's apartment until he found the paintings on the wall. Heal was about to ask a question when a text alert pinged on Stirling's phone and waited for him to read the message, watching Stirling's expression turn from irritation to concern, and then he swore.

'Get your coat Geordie, you're coming with me. And hurry!'

Heal wanted to protest but watching Stirling's back disappearing through the door, he snatched up his mobile and coat and ran to catch up. Thinking briefly of his long-suffering wife, he said aloud, 'Life in a blue suit, Geordie lad!'

10.43 p.m.

Gunning up through the gears, Stirling pushed the BMW hard through the bends out of town. Turning onto the dual carriageway leading south to Worcester, he drove as fast as he dared through the light traffic.

Without Helen available, Stirling instructed Heal to get a uniformed patrol with a female officer on board to meet them near to Evans's home, but out of sight to avoid scaring her off or drawing the attention of neighbours.

Stirling was annoyed at himself for not reading Helen's message straight away, her second text checking he had received the first. Dai Morgan had called her to say Evans returned home about eight fifteen and she was too far away to return. The first text was about an hour ago, so over two hours had passed, and Evans might have left again.

11.12 p.m.
After banging on the front door for the third time, Stirling stepped back to look up at the windows. The car was in the drive and a flickering light in the lounge indicated the television was on. Peering through a slim gap between the drawn curtains he could see the room was empty.

Heal returned from the rear of the house. 'There's a bedroom light on but no movement. One of the uniform's is covering the back.'

Stirling weighed his options. Evans was probably hiding upstairs, frightened. He didn't want to make her any more fearful. He could force the door but that might seem excessive, foolish too if she had gone out to see someone nearby. Seeing a movement out of the corner of his eye, Stirling caught Dai Morgan skulking in the shadow of his doorway trying to avoid being seen.

Stirling stepped across the small garden. 'Mr Morgan? Has Carol gone back out since you called us?'

Morgan flashed a look around the street and cringed, fearful someone might overhear and mark him out as a copper's nark. Shaking his head resentfully, Morgan disappeared inside.

Swearing at the man's cowardice, Stirling returned to stand at Heal's side. Nearby, a young female officer, conspicuous in a high visibility jacket, stood waiting to be given something useful to do. Stirling recognised her as the officer who had knelt at Cassie's side. Motioning her across to him, Stirling told her to call to Evans through the letterbox. A woman's voice might reassure her. After several attempts and still no answer, Stirling instructed the officer to warn Evans that if she refused to open the door, they would force it open.

Interest from the houses opposite had been growing for some minutes with curtains being drawn back and windows opened to watch and listen. Under a nearby lamp post, half a dozen local strays had collected on their bicycles to offer jeering abuse. With no one free to move them on, they were growing in confidence and their language was getting offensive.

With no answer and continued silence, Stirling felt a growing unease as he thought of the message on the tribute card. Reaching a decision, he told the officer to note the time. Her first operation with the CID and keen to impress, the officer swiftly withdrew her pocket notebook to make a note as Stirling judged the strength of the door. A wooden door fitted many years ago with a latch lock above a mortice lock, both of which would be worn. The door did not look very strong.

Turning to Heal he asked, 'D'you want to put it in, or shall I?'

Heal needed no second bidding. It had been too long since he had broken down a door and he had already sized this one up, experience telling him where to concentrate his force. After calling out one last chance to open the door and getting no reply, Stirling stood to one side and held the door handle down as Heal gave the door two heavy kicks, close to the locks. The wood splintered but held, before finally yielding under Heal's shoulder. In the background, the youths yelled sneering encouragement.

Instructing the officer to follow, Stirling and Heal entered the hallway and moved swiftly through the downstairs rooms, finding no one. Leading the way up the narrow staircase, Stirling looked inside each room briefly as he reached it. A bathroom and two small bedrooms, empty. Just one shut door remained, a line of light visible under its bottom edge. Stirling motioned the two officers behind him to step back. Although unlikely, it was possible Evans was waiting with a weapon.

Calling out Carol's name, Stirling tapped on the bedroom door.

Pushing the door open, Stirling saw two bare feet on the bed. Followed by Heal and the officer, he walked to stand at the foot of the bed. Carol Evans was very obviously dead.

Behind him there was silence followed by a sharp gasp and a gagging exclamation of revolt from the young officer. Heal ushered her from the room and a moment later Stirling heard her vomiting in the bathroom.

Moving to the side of the bed, Stirling went through the motions but knew it was futile as he held a wrist, seeking an impossible pulse. Cool already, but too soon for rigor mortis to have set in, Stirling put Carol Evans's arm gently back on the bed and went back to the foot of the bed where he could see the room and absorb detail. On the landing, Heal was encouraging the young officer and giving her tasks to keep her busy, instructing her to call for a paramedic, for SOCO and another patrol to help secure the scene.

Wearing a simple shift dress with a floral print design Stirling remembered as fashionable many years ago, Carol Evans had lain on her back, surrounding herself with photographs, a child's heavily brushed paintings and other keepsakes.

In many of the photos, a child played happily on a beach, or sat with Katrina Martin's arms around her. In others, the pretty child lay wrapped in the arms of a young Carol Evans. Picking some up by their edges, Stirling recognised Katrina Martin's home and garden with the summer house in the background. Others showed a small garden with a wooden panel fence. He did not need to look outside to know it was Carol's garden.

In some older photographs, two teenage girls stood side by side in the same small garden posing for the picture to be taken: one girl with long fair hair smiling shyly whilst her slightly shorter sister stared at the camera seriously, impatient for it to be taken.

A group of seaside snaps with the sisters in swimwear showed them to have both been good looking young women, but Carol particularly so with her tousled blonde hair and willowy figure. Even then, all those years ago, there was a sense of fragility in Carol's eyes. Quite different to those of Katrina Martin who presented a consistently direct gaze to the camera and a prepared smile. In some snaps, the sisters sat on sand mats with Cassie playing between them. In the background were signs written in French. Stirling wondered if they were taken on a timer function or if someone else had been there. Had Gérard returned? Pemberton?

To one side of the bed a roll of silver duct tape and a pair of scissors lay where they had been thrown. Moving back to the side of the bed, Stirling looked at the clear polythene bag Carol Evans had pulled over her head before sealing it around her neck with clumsily applied tape to prevent its easy removal. Inside, her face was obscured partially with a grisly mask of blood. A blood vessel had ruptured as her body fought for air. Apart from one hand at her throat, the fingers curled in a dying clutch, Stirling was concerned there were no signs of life's instinctive struggle against death. Death by asphyxiation would have been frightening and the urge to tear the bag off overwhelming.

Slipping on examination gloves, he picked up an empty glass on the bedside table and could smell whisky. Looking around the floor, his eyes settled on a tablet container. He lifted it to read the label; a sleeping medication prescribed for Evans, and empty. Resting his elbows on his knees, Stirling studied her head in profile. The pills alone might have been enough, only toxicology would say, but the sedative in quantity and enough whisky would have rendered her unable to tear off the bag. Carol Evans had been determined to die.

Putting the pill container back where he had found it, Stirling was standing up when he noticed two white envelopes propped up behind the bedside light. A fountain pen lay next to them. Recognising the handwriting, he picked them up to read the names on the front of each. The first was addressed to "Katy." Stirling was surprised to see the second letter was addressed to him. Holding it up to the light he could make out the outline of a piece of paper inside and something more solid. Pressing the envelope between his fingers, he could feel something small and hard inside. Resisting the temptation to open it, Stirling returned the letters to where they had been to be photographed. There would be time enough to read Carol Evans's last thoughts.

Looking down at the body, Stirling worked back through the timings. If he had read Helen's text straight away, could he have prevented this? Carol had arrived home an hour before Morgan contacted Helen. Stirling would never be completely certain, but he felt it was unlikely he would have prevented this. And if not this evening, then another.

Heal re-entered the bedroom to see Stirling in a corner speaking quietly into his mobile. Heal had been to plenty of tragedies like this over the years but working in the MCU meant he rarely got out now. As awful as this was, it was good to be involved in something operational and away from the office routine.

Heal sniffed the air uncomfortably. The odours of death were already stealing over the room as the body's muscles relaxed, releasing faecal matter and urine to seep into the mattress. There was little dignity in death, he remembered. Stirling finished his call and joined him at the bedside.

Looking down at the body Heal muttered, 'This is a sad do, boss.'

'That was the Divisional DI. I've called him out to take over from us here. It's looks like a determined suicide but it's the division's responsibility. We need a thorough investigation done independently of us. I don't want any suggestion later that we tried to cover our tracks.'

As they stood contemplating the scene, Heal pointed to the letters and commented on the handwriting. 'You might be right boss.'

C3 80

Day 9: Tuesday - 8.16 a.m.

Stirling waited for the Sergeant to finish briefing his team of dog handlers at The Wern, assessing and sectoring the area before assigning them to individual specialists. Nearby, five dog vans were parked together, their passengers barking incessantly. As his team dispersed to their vans, dressed in black coveralls with a black cap pulled firmly onto his shaven head, the Sergeant strode over to him.

'All set, Sarge?'

In the crisp style typical of the tactical specialists from the Operations Department, he rattled out his answer. 'Yes sir. I've called in an extra cadaver search dog on mutual-aid from the region to help us cover the ground. It's a big area. Because you want us to search for human remains from many years ago, I've also brought in a specialist historic human remains search dog too. If there's anything out there to be found, that is.'

The Sergeant eyed him directly. Getting his scepticism in early, thought Stirling. Was he so certain himself?

Sweeping his hand across the line of the copse at the top of the slope, the Sergeant continued. 'Based on your briefing, I'm concentrating the search up there first. It's not that big so it shouldn't take long. Then, I've sectored the ground radiating out for two hundred metres in all directions from where the cottage stood. But, I have to tell you that if anything was buried out here, the ground levelling work is likely to have redistributed any remains across the area. When we've finished here, we'll transfer to the other place.'

Stirling watched the search for a while before leaving. Driving up the track which had brought Pemberton to such a grisly end, he thought about the visit to Katrina Martin later that morning.

*

The visit to break the news of her sister's death to Katrina Martin was brief. Helen and Edwards met her in a small room surrounded on four sides by windows with corridors either side patrolled by prison officers. Busy with a court appearance, her solicitor had sent along a para-legal to provide support.

Helen explained the discovery of her sister's body the previous evening. After the initial shock, Martin's reaction had been to bolt down her emotions and to wait steely eyed for whatever they wished to discuss.

After cautioning her, Edwards handed Martin a photocopy of the letter addressed to her, explaining it had been opened with the permission of the Coroner. The original had been retained as it was required for the inquest and was relevant to Pemberton's murder. Grudgingly, Martin accepted the explanation and read the one-page letter several times.

Putting it down, she refused to answer any questions about it, saying it was too soon. With a patronising comment on the experience and skills of the young para-legal, she had insisted her solicitor be present for any further interviews.

When Edwards described the searches being conducted that day, Martin was asked if she had any information she should give them in advance. Giving Helen and Edwards a long calculating look, she had shaken her head and asked to leave the room.

*

6.54 p.m.
'Bonjour! Monsieur Martin, je présume,' Edwards muttered sardonically.

Three feet below them, a yellowed skull grinned maniacally up at them through its soil shroud, the eye sockets full of earth.

Inside the white forensic tent erected some hours before, Stirling ignored the gallows humour and studied the partially revealed skeleton with remnants of clothing adhering to the ribcage. Two SOCOs in white coveralls and rubber gloves were knelt in the tight space around the skeleton carefully removing soil and passing it up to a colleague above them who was passing it through a sieve, extracting anything that might prove important later. Another SOCO stepped forward occasionally to photograph the grave as it revealed its occupant.

Harry Robinson, Director of Forensic Services had turned out for this one. A short, stocky and highly intelligent man with a perpetually enthusiastic nature, he stood at Stirling's side chattering away animatedly, pointing out the technical aspects of the excavation. Working through the implications of the discovery for his investigation and next steps, Stirling was only half listening, answering Robinson where necessary. Catching Edwards's eye across the shallow grave, Stirling gave a discreet incline of his head towards the tent entrance.

Walking up the lawn together, Stirling watched the last of the dog handlers slamming shut the rear doors of his van as the two dogs inside barked madly. He had never understood why anyone could want to drive around all day incubating tinnitus with that constant racket in the back. With a spray of gravel, the van was gone and silence settled over the garden.

Sitting on a wrought iron bench set into the side of the garden, Edwards brushed dust from his suit as Stirling looked back down the lawn to the tent. A halogen lamp illuminating the interior was casting exaggerated, stooping figures across its walls in a macabre magic lantern show. The two men remained silent as they reflected on the discovery. Stirling was concerned that no remains had been located at either the copse or the land around where the cottage had once stood. Had they missed anything or was he looking in the wrong place? In the absence of hard information to the contrary, he would have to accept the specialist's findings.

Edwards was speculating on what had led to Gérard Martin's death, if it was him, and how her father's absence had affected Cassie Martin's life and, ultimately, her death. Once the search dog had wagged his tail enthusiastically to indicate the presence of human remains, he and Stirling had helped the search officers to push and drag the summer house from its slabbed base to reveal subsidence nearest the field boundary.

'Thoughts, Bill?'

'Plenty, but I'd like to know why you told them to concentrate the search on the summer house first?'

'When I was here with Helen last week, I took a stroll round the garden to give Helen chance to get Martin to open up about her relationship with Pemberton. She wasn't a suspect then. I was admiring the location of the summer house and noticed it had settled in the rear corner. I thought it was either poor workmanship or, more likely, subsidence caused through natural drainage from the field. When we began to think about Gérard's whereabouts, it led me to thinking.'

'Why?'

'Look around you, Bill. Everything about this small community is expensively perfect. They don't pay for shoddy work. It occurred to me that Gérard might have been put under there in a hurry after the base had been prepared, but before the summer house was erected on top. The earth would still have been soft, but only she can tell us.'

'And the ground subsided as he decomposed,' said Edwards, imagining the process over many years.

Both men fell silent again until Edwards asked, 'Gérard was a big chap, wasn't he? D'you think she could have done it on her own? Seems unlikely.'

'That's what I've been thinking. If Pemberton was involved it might have had something to do with why he hated her. Or Carol? Hard to know and we'll only have her version of events, if she talks. The other two are dead.'

Edwards pointed down the lawn to where the summerhouse now stood lopsidedly beside the tent. 'Can you imagine spending all those summers down there with Cassie as a child, and her kiddie friends too, knowing your husband was rotting away beneath you? That takes a special heartlessness.'

Stirling nodded. 'It probably explains why she's stayed here all these years in a house that's far too big for two people. She couldn't leave for fear of his discovery. By disposing of him down there, she chained herself to this place. And, ironically, to Gérard.'

'Having to live with that goes some way to explaining her nature.'

Stirling pointed at the tent. 'Once we've got as much information as we can from there, we need Martin produced for interview.'

'Okay. And I'll arrange for house to house to see who remembers him.' Edwards looked around at the setting and let out an envious sigh. 'Me and Ellen would love a garden like this.'

'With or without corpses?' asked Stirling, mordantly.

A voice calling to them from the tent disturbed their laughter. Leaning out of the tent door whilst still standing in the grave, his arm resting on the ground, Harry Robinson was beckoning them to join him.

Stirling nudged Edwards. 'Come on, Harry wants to give us a treatise on the scientific removal of archaeological remains.'

Chuckling, Edwards followed him down the lawn.

Inside the tent they found Robinson standing alongside the half-exhumed skeleton. On the far side of the excavation, the SOCOs waited patiently, eyes smiling over their masks to Stirling and Edwards. Stirling could guess at what they were thinking. Harry was renowned for his enthusiastic nature.

Looking up as they entered, Robinson's glasses reflected the overhead lamp so that his eyes were momentarily lost to view. He spoke briskly as if addressing a pair of recalcitrant students.

'Ah, there you are! We're making *excellent* progress gentlemen. Although I'm not an expert, I've got one on their way here, I can say with *considerable* confidence this is a *male* skeleton. Although we'll need to do tests, judging by dental work done to several molars, the size and ossification of his bones etcetera, etcetera, I'd say he was past his twenties, probably into his thirties. That judgement is informed by the fusion of the clavicle which usually occurs mid to late twenties. He was interred fully dressed. There are fragments of rotted clothing here ... here ... and here, which *might* give us an understanding of what he was wearing when he died. There's a belt buckle here too and down here ...'

Robinson rattled on for a minute or so before Stirling interrupted him. 'Harry, just tell me how long he's been there?'

Behind one of the masks, a SOCO gave a soft snigger.

Harry looked up, beaming with pleasure 'Y*ears*, Stirling! *Donkey's* years! Can't be certain how many, mind you. Haven't had one of these for a little while but it's always good to refresh one's knowledge. We're going to stop now and wait for another specialist to arrive before going any further.'

Stirling thanked Harry and was turning to leave when Robinson gave a dry cough followed by silence. Turning back, Stirling saw Robinson was holding something out for him to look at. Disappointed that Stirling's excitement did not match his own, Robinson's voice had a peevish tone.

'You *might* be interested in this? It was lying amongst the remains. Badly corroded but I'd say it was a kitchen knife?'

⋘ ⋙

Day 10: Wednesday – 11.06 a.m.

The post mortem concluded that Carol Evans died of asphyxiation whilst heavily sedated by a combination of whisky and prescription sleeping tablets. Although toxicology would determine the amount of medication in her system, the pathologist had observed that from the residues in her stomach, she had taken enough to "render a horse insensible."

After arriving from the remand centre, Martin had spent an hour consulting with her lawyer. She now sat in the bare interview room with her customary poise and the lawyer at her side. Devoid of cosmetics, wearing a simple white T shirt over blue jeans and her hair pulled back into a pony tail, Stirling thought Katrina Martin looked every one of her years and wondered how she was getting on with her cell mates. Try as he might, he felt little empathy for her. At Stirling's side sat Helen, determined to present a professional façade, despite the events of recent days. Within arm's reach was a small table on which lay exhibit bags. After switching on the recorder and introductions for voice identification, Helen cautioned Martin and Stirling began the interview.

'I'm sorry you had to learn of Carol's death from us, but we had an obligation to inform you, formally.' He received a tight nod of acknowledgement as she watched him steadily.

'We must speak with you again about the murder of Michael Pemberton, and the death of your husband, Gérard Martin. You were arrested by DC Williams on suspicion of Mr Martin's murder when you arrived here. Do you understand?'

'Yes.'

'When you were interviewed previously you confessed to the murder of Michael Pemberton. In the light of your sister's death and the contents of her letter addressed to you, is there anything you wish to alter or add to that admission?'

Martin turned to her lawyer who nodded. 'I did not kill Michael Pemberton. Carol killed him. I was protecting her, as I have always done. Carol killed him for what he did to my daughter, Cassandra. And I'm not sorry she did, either.'

'In your own words, please tell us what happened.'

The lawyer intervened. 'It's a tangled tale Mr Stirling. It will help if my client starts at the beginning and explains things chronologically. The past gives understanding to the present.'

Happy for Martin to lead and see where it took them, Stirling agreed.

'Carol and I grew up in the house at Danes Green. I was Katy Evans then. Father died when we were both very young. Mother brought us up on her own until she died of a cancer when Carol was just fifteen, so I looked after her until she settled into art college when I left to work in London. I'd done well in my studies and had a job offer which gave me a good start in the City. In finance.

'Carol is ...' Martin stumbled, her voice cracking with emotion, '... was, a sensitive person and always lacked confidence. Even though she was by far the prettiest girl around and received a lot of attention from boys, and men too later, she never believed in herself. Losing Father so young left her insecure and, in my view, was the root cause of her many disastrous relationships. She was always looking for a kind man to take care of her but made a lot of poor choices. And men were all too willing to take advantage of her trusting nature.

'Carol was very artistic. Whether that had anything to do with her temperament I don't know, but they can be quite emotional, artistic types. Don't you think, Chief Inspector?'

Martin looked at Stirling, but he would not be drawn into an empathetic alliance of thought with her, thinking her sentiments had more to do with an impatience of anyone who lacked purposeful determination.

'Just the facts, as simply as possible please.' Stirling answered.

Martin studied him coolly over the table, calculating his impersonal reply before continuing.

'When Mother died, I was old enough to take over the tenancy and, years later, I bought the house from the Council as one could then, for Carol to live in. I was making good money. I was away for several years and although we kept in touch, we grew apart. Carol was a good artist but unfocussed. so I brought her down to London to live with me for a while, thinking it would be perfect with all the art galleries and museums and just the general buzz of the city, perfect for artistic stimulation. But she found the pace of life in London too fast for her hippy sensibilities, so she returned home to live alone in that dreary little house. And there she stayed,' sighed Martin, still disappointed at her sister's lack of ambition. 'I offered to buy her a nicer home elsewhere many times, but she always refused. Slowly, I came to understand she was genuinely content there, the house had too many memories for her to leave.'

Martin paused to sip from a plastic beaker of water on the table, appearing to drift away in some reminiscence for a moment, then continued.

'When I moved back up here with my husband, Gérard, she and I saw more of each other but by then she was living what I believe is called an *"alternative"* lifestyle, mixing with a group of unemployables and smoking too much dope. Apart from occasional low paid jobs and selling some paintings, she was often out of work and not fulfilling her potential. With hindsight, the dope only exacerbated her insecurities.

'I was appalled, but she wouldn't listen to big sister. So, that's how it was for a while. Gérard had little time for her, apart from ogling her of course. He could be charming and was very masculine, and Carol was an exceptionally attractive young woman with long blonde hair and a fawn like vulnerability that men find so appealing. They all wanted to protect her. And screw her of course!' Martin added cynically, looking pointedly at Helen. 'We know how men are, don't we?'

At her side, Martin's lawyer looked up and arched an eyebrow before returning to his notes. Helen said nothing. Martin smiled coldly, her eyes flitting between her and Stirling leaving him to wonder if her female intuition had picked up on some subtle behaviour between them at her home.

'Gérard spent the working week in London. I was busy up here building my new business, land holdings and property, and met Michael Pemberton in his capacity as the architect for our home. He was renting the cottage at The Wern and mentioned the land and buildings were coming up for sale, so I bought it with him as the sitting tenant. I rented the land to a local farmer and Pemberton stayed on in the cottage with the use of some outbuildings. He was very proud of that old Jaguar car. He already owned it when I met him and kept it in one of the outbuildings during the winter. He said he liked the solitude, but not for the reasons I first imagined.

'My fling with him began soon after I met him. Gérard worked for a French bank in London and spent a lot of time travelling between there and Paris, or flying to meetings around Europe. Pemberton created opportunities to seek me out about the design and the build but, in truth, he pursued me. He was an intelligent, charismatic man and attractive too, but he knew it and exploited it with an arrogance which had its own appeal. I was still relatively young and on my own too much, so I got involved with him quite happily. I wasn't in love with him. He was fun to be with and introduced me to a lot of people, many of them professionals and wealthy which was useful to my business. I knew of his reputation with the ladies but ...' she shrugged, '... it meant there was little risk of him falling in love with me and causing difficulties in my marriage. I'd made good money in London and Gérard was wealthy, so I had the best of both worlds. When Gérard was home he knew very few people up here, so it was easy to hide the affair from him.'

Arching her eye, Martin looked at Stirling, 'I suppose that makes me sound like a calculating bitch?'

Stirling gave her a wintry smile as Helen asked, 'We know about Pemberton's sexual tastes. What can you tell us of that?'

The smile in Martin's eyes died. 'I used to visit him at the cottage where there was little chance of discovery. It was an idyllic spot. Quiet and away from the world. We spent many afternoons and evenings there. There was some light spanking and some bondage too, but nothing serious and in the context of an illicit relationship, it was quite exciting. I was younger then and … curious, I suppose. And he was *very* persuasive. But, I never allowed him to do anything I was uncomfortable with. I controlled the relationship.'

Stirling could believe that to be the truth. Helen asked about photographs.

'He took some photographs of me without my agreement. He had an old-fashioned camera and liked black and white for what he called "artistic realism," whatever that meant. He had a reputation for being very discreet, so I decided to forget about them. Until, that is, he started asking for money in recent years and we've already talked about that.'

Martin paused as she thought for a moment. 'Through gossip I came to know that other women, before me and after, were treated more … severely. Which was why he liked the cottage, for the seclusion. A year later, well after the affair, Gérard and I were expecting our first child. With my business well established in the county we'd decided it was the right time to start a family. I quickly became pregnant and we were looking forward to the next chapter in our lives. Michael had another lover and I saw nothing of him.

'What I didn't know until after I became pregnant was that Gérard had been screwing Carol behind my back. I was in the north of the country for three weeks sorting out some problems with a complex investment I was involved in. Carol said Gérard seduced her whilst comforting her over another of her failed relationships. Personally, I think he was tempted by her ingénue beauty and couldn't resist the opportunity. Carol always needed a man to look after her and although she wasn't promiscuous, she could be quite spontaneous in her relationships.

'It becomes rather complicated now, but I'll explain as simply as I can. I've had many years to think about it. What I did *not* know was that Pemberton and Carol had been lovers for quite some time. Once my home was completed I saw nothing of him. He paid his rent to my company, not to me, so there was no reason for any contact. It transpired that he knew I was growing tired of him, so he'd taken an interest in Carol. We'd had a big housewarming party with many guests which is where they met.

'The surprise was that Pemberton fell in love with Carol. She told me, much later, he absolutely doted on her in the beginning. For the first time in her life she had an intelligent man who treated her well and was probably her first caring lover. For the better part of a year I wouldn't see her for weeks on end. I was busy and assumed she was back amongst her old crowd in Worcester when in fact she was, effectively, living at the cottage.'

Reaching over to the small table, Stirling lifted the photograph of the cottage from Pemberton's study and put it in front of Martin. 'Was that the cottage?'

Picking it up Martin gave a wistful smile. 'Yes, it was such a pretty place.'

'Who is that in the doorway?'

'It's Carol. I saw this picture many years ago, she had her own copy.' Turning it over she read the inscription. 'That's Carol's handwriting. She was utterly besotted with him and loved the cottage and its isolation. Carol had something of an artistic flowering whilst she was there, painting some good work and living out her hippy dream of a simple, rural life and walking about naked all day as nature's child. Quite pathetic, really, but the setting inspired her and she did paint some good work there. I believe he kept some of her paintings in his apartment. I think he was infatuated with her for a while.'

Helen put in front of her SOCO photographs of the paintings in Pemberton's apartment. Martin confirmed the indecipherable signature and paintings as her sister's work.

'So, what went wrong?' asked Stirling.

Martin's voice became cold. 'He reverted to type! He abused Carol's trusting and vulnerable nature. An intelligent man like Pemberton would have grown tired of Carol's simplistic thinking and narrow world view. However good the sex is, the brain must be nourished, too. It wasn't until years later that she could tell me everything he did to her. She was too ashamed and emotionally damaged to discuss it.

'His treatment of her was very different to my experience. I believe that as he lost respect for her, he went further and further to get his kicks and to see how far she would go to keep him. The silly girl complied because she was so in love with him. Slowly, she became completely dependent on him, accepting his coercion that it was what a woman should do for her man. She was far more vulnerable than I understood.

Martin's voice hardened. 'Carol described increasingly abusive and sadistic treatment. But things got even more sinister. He would take her up to a small wood above the cottage, naked, with her hands bound and leading her like an animal!'

'She said there was a big tree up there with ropes already fixed to it, so perhaps he'd taken others there before her. He'd tie her to the tree and photograph her in different poses, and ... well, you've seen photographs of the sort of things he liked to do. To start with it was no more than they'd done in the bedroom, but it gave way to something more brutal, ritualistic. She had marks on her body months later when she first began to tell me a bit about it, but not everything. The more submissive she became, the less Pemberton respected her and it became a self-perpetuating cycle. Had I known, I would have done whatever was necessary to get her away from him. Carol should have left him but didn't have the strength of character and he controlled her completely.'

Seeing Helen about to ask a question Martin held up a hand. 'That wasn't the worst of it! There was a brute of a lad, sixteen or so from a nearby village who spied on them. As time went on Carol concluded that Pemberton knew the boy was there but enjoyed the reckless voyeurism. He often blindfolded her and he …' struggling to speak, Martin paused to take a sip of water. 'The most disgusting part about it all was that he called the boy out, silently, and let him have sex with Carol whilst she couldn't protect herself. Apart from plead with Pemberton for it to stop which only heightened his enjoyment.'

There was silence in the room as each person reflected on Carol Evans's degradation. Stirling thought of the conversation with Osmand and his suspicion that he had not disclosed everything. He now understood why. The man was canny enough to know his involvement had amounted to rape. Vowing to settle with Osmand, Stirling waited as Martin lifted the cup with a trembling hand and sipped at the water before asking her to continue.

'Pemberton didn't love her!' she said contemptuously. 'He was infatuated with her beauty and the romance of it all for a while, but because she couldn't stand up to him, she lost his respect. Carol told me it became another of his games, this voyeuristic, third party sex. She had to perform other acts on the brute too, the details you can imagine for yourselves. Carol was so desperate to be loved, and by now completely dependent on him, she did whatever he wanted just to keep hold of him. It was too humiliating to tell me about and she had no one else to turn to, or so she felt.'

Helen asked, 'What happened to the photographs of Carol? They don't appear among those we've recovered.'

'When he tried blackmailing me I made it a condition of payment that he gave me all of the photos of Carol too. I couldn't be sure he'd given me them all, but I told him in no uncertain terms that I knew about his treatment of Carol and how much trouble I'd cause him if he didn't surrender them to me. When he introduced that boy, it was rape. He couldn't be certain that Carol would never be strong enough to make a formal complaint and he was so desperate for money he complied. As far as I know, anyway,' adding contemptuously, 'From what you've told me, he had plenty more to masturbate over!'

During a pause to collect her thoughts, the solicitor prompted Martin to return to the sequence of her story.

'The first few months of my pregnancy went well until at a social event, someone poured poison in Gérard's ear about me and Pemberton. Gérard was a proud, jealous and possessive man. Once that seed was planted, it began to consume him. He confronted me and, eventually, I admitted it, assuring him it had ended long before I conceived. Which was the truth, but he just wouldn't let it go. Men's usual double standards, as always. He'd fucked my sister and that was okay, but was insanely jealous when he discovered that *I'd* had an affair!

'Never mind the woman he was screwing in Paris, too. Like many successful French men, she might only have been his *"cinq á sept"* mistress but I knew there was someone else. Gérard was an attractive man, and wealthy too. That always helps. But, I'd had my fling, so I was no saint either.

'Whatever I said, Gérard's suspicions continued. Our rows, which had always been stormy, got more frequent and became violent too, with him hitting and slapping me. He would punch me sometimes if he was particularly angry. Domestic violence wasn't something I was used to and I couldn't fight back, he was too powerful. Especially as I was carrying the baby. Perhaps he wanted me to miscarry, I don't know, but it all contributed to a distancing between us.

'Then life got even more complicated. Unknown to me, Carol was pregnant too. The relationship breakdown Gérard had been comforting Carol over was hers with Pemberton who had got tired of her, or was interested in another woman more likely, and he'd thrown her out of the cottage. As I said, I was away on business and they had sex quite a few times. Stupidly, without any protection. I don't think Gérard could believe his luck, to be bedding his beautiful, blonde sister-in-law.

'But Carol and Pemberton got back together and two or three months later, after denying to herself the increasingly obvious, she knew she was pregnant with Gérard's child. Terrified of telling Gérard, me especially, or Pemberton and being abandoned again, she practiced the classic deception of letting Pemberton believe it was his child. For a few weeks, she told me, it changed his behaviour completely and they lived together quite normally with no abuse and she began imagining their family life together.'

So, thought Stirling, although he had omitted his own sordid involvement, Osmand's account corresponded with his description of the changed behaviour between the man and the blonde woman at the cottage.

'But neither leopards nor men change their spots, in my experience. With a lifetime of domesticity stretching ahead of him, Pemberton got fidgety as he realised how limiting fatherhood and nappies would be on his sex and social lives. Carol was painfully honest and couldn't lie if her life depended on it. Thinking it would be a good idea to make an honest start to their life together, Carol naïvely confessed her fling with Gérard. It was all the excuse Pemberton needed to throw her out of the cottage and dumped her at her home with a few possessions, but he kept her paintings. He probably thought they'd fetch some money!'

Having listened without interrupting for a long time, Stirling was becoming impatient. 'This is an interesting story of complicated private lives Mrs Martin, but it doesn't explain your husband's death, or Pemberton's for that matter?'

Martin, looked at her solicitor who cleared his throat and put down his notepad. 'Having gone through this with my client, Chief Inspector, I believe it is in Mrs Martin's interests, and those of a jury at some later date, to hear how things unfolded as sequentially as possible. It is complex, but bears listening to. I *assure* you.'

The emphasis caused Helen to turn to Stirling who gave a small shrug of acceptance. Intent on taking another sip of water, Martin's hand trembled as she lifted the paper cup to her mouth and spilt water into her lap. Setting the cup down, she looked at Stirling who was surprised to see her holding back tears.

'I miscarried before I reached ... at seven months.' Martin bent her head to stare at a point somewhere in the middle of the table and was silent for a while. 'It was a girl ... we were going to call her Josianne in memory of Gérard's younger sister who he had loved very much but had died at a young age.'

Recalling her lost child, Martin appeared to be in physical pain as long-suppressed emotions resurfaced and she gave a low moan of pain. Helen reached across the table to put her hand on Martin's and held it. Martin looked up at Helen and Stirling saw something unspoken pass between the two women. Watching the simple human gesture, the lawyer observed Helen with a discreetly veiled curiosity before hiding his thoughts in his notebook. Stirling saw something in Helen's face which raised a question he could never ask.

Taking a fresh tissue from the solicitor, Martin blew her nose several times and mumbled an unnecessary apology. Taking a deep breath and pulling herself upright, she faced them again, the mask back in place. Martin had repacked the pain and returned it to wherever she kept it.

'Gérard and I stayed together but it proved to be the death knell for our marriage. Something died in him too, with Josianne ...' Martin's voice faltered again at her daughter's name. 'He made me feel as if it was my fault, never countenancing of course that his violence and the stress might have caused my miscarriage. He became remote and the things he would say were like listening to his Mother, cold, aloof and sneering. Madame Martin was a *very* haughty woman. She died soon after we married. I wasn't sorry. She once called me "une chienne froid!"'

Martin spoke as if her character had been impugned. Stirling thought the old biddy had shown remarkable prescience.

'Gérard had no other family that I knew of. In the weeks after we lost the baby, he made sure he worked away a lot which was when I learnt of Carol's pregnancy, and that Gérard was the father. Pemberton had deserted her. Terrified of bringing it up on her own she confessed everything. More problematic, though, was her mental state. The stress of Pemberton's abuse, her isolation, her guilt at betraying me and the resulting pregnancy had brought her to the verge of a mental breakdown. She was clinically depressed.

'To me, the solution was obvious. After miscarrying, there was doubt about whether I could conceive again. I desperately wanted to save my marriage and to have a baby of my own, so I persuaded Gérard to adopt Carol's baby as our own. He was the father, after all, and Carol was my own blood, so it wasn't so far from what was intended. I was angry at him for his infidelity with my own sister, but I knew what she was like, so I forgave them both. And after my affair with Pemberton, it levelled the playing field with Gérard too.

'Gérard had insisted on me being near to the best physicians, so I was already spending a lot of time at our London apartment after the miscarriage. You can check the medical records if you wish. It took me a while to recover from the miscarriage, physically and emotionally. I'd been too traumatised to tell anyone up here in my small social circle and none of them was a close friend. I don't let people get close to me.

'Carol had neither the financial means nor the emotional resilience to cope with a child on her own, whereas I could provide a child with everything it would need or want. Gérard and I agreed to bring the child up as our own. Carol wasn't completely happy but had enough sense to understand it was the best thing for her child, and I promised her access to the baby. We fetched Carol down to live with us in London until the baby was born and although as a *ménage à trois* it was tricky, Gérard had to forgo the usual benefits, she stayed until the baby was weaned when she and I returned home. To the few people who knew either of us was pregnant, we simply reversed the tragedy. Carol was in such a poor state emotionally, so her distress was all too easy to misunderstand, especially among her social group of misfits and the brain dead. She stayed with me and the baby for a while until she was ready to settle back into her own home.

Martin had still not spoken the child's name, referring to it in the third person throughout. Stirling interrupted, 'To be clear, the baby was Cassie?'

'Cassandra,' Martin replied, correcting him as he imagined she had done many times over the years since.

'The gift of prophecy,' commented Stirling half to himself, wondering if Cassie could have foreseen such a tragic future for herself.

'You know something of Greek mythology, Chief Inspector?' asked Martin, looking at him thoughtfully, trying to engage him within the interview.

Side-stepping the digression, Stirling asked her to continue.

With a cool glance, she resumed. 'Pemberton was told that Carol had aborted due to the stress of his desertion. The only reaction we saw was relief that there would be no future call on his time, or his wallet. I didn't know then about his abuse of Carol so, as a sitting tenant with a legal entitlement to remain, he carried on living at the cottage. I detested him, but it was a business arrangement and I was happy to take his money, at an increased rent. I was surprised he wanted to carry on living there, but as time went by and gossip got back to me, I understood why. The seclusion was perfect for his proclivities.

'So, life went on. Cassandra - Carol always called her Cassie which they both preferred - grew up with me and had the best of everything. Independent schools, good holidays, whatever she needed. But, as she entered her teens, Cassandra became an increasingly quiet child. Carol came on holiday with us in the early years. We went to the south of France for a few years and had some very happy times.'

Martin smiled and shook her head at some recollection. 'It was after one of those holidays that she fitted those ridiculous faux shutters to her windows. Completely out of place in that street but she said they would remind her of happy times. Typical of Carol.

'A bond grew between Carol and Cassandra that I never had. Biology, I suppose, and she was much more relaxed in Carol's company. It was upsetting, but I learnt to live with it and as she entered her teens, Cassandra would spend occasional weekends with Carol.'

'Did she know that Carol was her biological Mother?' asked Helen.

'No. That was the pact between us. She was dear Auntie Carol who had never married. As far as I know, there were no men after Pemberton. I don't think she could ever trust a man again, believing they would all hurt her, physically or emotionally. Or both. Slowly, she came to understand that even before Pemberton, most of the men she'd known had taken advantage of her nature.'

Stirling felt a new sadness for Carol Evans as he thought of their meeting in the chapel, how she had pulled away from him, timidly asking permission to leave. What a waste of a life.

'We intended to tell Cassandra when we thought she was old enough to understand but it became increasingly difficult. Carol's self-confidence was low and, as time went on, she was happy not to take on the responsibility. She'd got used to playing the role of loving auntie, able to give a kind ear and uncritical support. However, Cassandra found out the truth for herself.'

After a break to change the tapes, the interview resumed. Martin described how, against her wishes, Cassie enrolled at the local sixth form college to study art. Martin had wanted her to study towards university and the professions, but having inherited some talent from Carol, who encouraged her discreetly, Cassie was determined.

Now sixteen, pretty but physically slight and often mistaken for being younger, she made good progress. There was a small circle of friends, but Cassie's shyness meant she was always at the fringe of things, overshadowed by more outgoing characters but seemed settled.

'To my intense frustration, she would dress down like some young people do and was often mistaken for a boy. I can't remember when she last wore a dress or anything feminine. It was a reaction against me. She was embarrassed by her wealthy background and was often teased about it by friends. Over the last year, Cassandra became increasingly secretive and withdrawn. I worried, but she wouldn't confide in me. I even suggested we meet with a child psychologist, but that was the wrong thing to have said. I felt she had inherited something of Carol's temperament. I lost patience and decided she would have to work her way through it. Last year she began to stay out, at friends' homes, she told me. I now know that wasn't always true …'

Noticing Stirling's restlessness, the lawyer put a hand on Martin's forearm and suggested she should explain her husband's death.

'Sorry, I've gone ahead. When Cassie was about six months old, Carol arrived unexpectedly one weekend in the middle of a violent row. Cassie was teething and very grizzly. I was exhausted with looking after Cassie, and supporting Carol, too. Gérard was increasingly unhappy with the arrangement we had reached, accusing me of having forced him into taking on Cassie. We were having terrible, violent rows. I was still suffering emotionally with the loss of my baby and was constantly exhausted. It was the most awful day. We'd argued, cried and raged all day. Cassie hadn't stopped screaming with her teething and was distressed by our arguments. We were fighting in the kitchen when, unnoticed by us, Carol walked in. I mean we were fighting, literally. Physically fighting.'

Martin's gaze had travelled to somewhere beyond the wall behind Stirling and Helen as she recounted the fight in a flat monotone voice. Her hand travelled to her throat as she relived the detail.

'Carol came into the kitchen to see Gérard sat across me, pinning me to the ground with his hands around my throat as we screamed hatred at each other. I was clawing at his face trying to get him off me and Cassie was sat in her high seat screaming. It was a terrible thing to stumble into, especially in her fragile condition.'

'He was choking me, I was struggling to fight him off … Suddenly, he stopped … just sat there looking down at me … confused. I don't think he could understand how I could have hurt him with both my hands in view. Then, as the pain hit him, he arched backwards … screaming … then he was at my side clutching at his back. His legs were kicking as he tried to reach the pain in his back … I was dazed, still trying to breath from being choked and couldn't understand what was happening or why Carol was there. It was a trance like experience, everything happening so quickly but sort of … in slow motion too … I saw her kneeling beside Gérard, stabbing him repeatedly. He couldn't protect himself and I just watched, stunned, trying to breath … unable to make any sense of it.

'By the time I *could* react, it was too late. Carol was slumped against the cupboard, panting and staring at the knife in her hand, holding her hands up to examine the blood running down her wrists and across her clothes. Gérard was lay there … eyes open … looking up at me, frightened … groaning quietly and gasping for air with blood frothing at his mouth. There was a sucking noise from a wound in his chest. She'd punctured his lung at least once. Then he just lay there, very still … quiet, with his eyes open. There was blood everywhere, across the floor, splashed up the cupboards. And through it all, Cassie kept screaming. It was hellish.'

Martin shuddered involuntarily at the recollection of the death, lost in thought.

'Tell us what happened next, please?' prompted Helen.

Martin looked at her distractedly, shaking her head. 'Sorry?'

'What happened next?'

'Oh, sorry. It's been a long time since I relived it in that detail and the first time I've ever been able to talk about it. Carol and I never discussed it afterwards. It was the albatross around our necks.'

Shaking her head, Martin leant her elbows on the table and put her head in both hands. 'Umm, we just sat there exhausted, stunned, both of us, with Gérard lying between us. Cassie was screaming so Carol went and lifted her from her high seat, brought her back over and sat down again, comforting her in a sort of trance so that Cassie got Gérard's blood on her too. His blood was spreading over the tiles so I started cleaning it up, sobbing with fear and screaming at her "What have you done?" and that sort of thing. Carol just sat there in a trance holding Cassie. It was a nightmare scene.'

'Why didn't you call for the police or an ambulance?' asked Helen. 'It wasn't you that had harmed him.'

Martin looked baffled by the question, 'Because he was already dead! Calling the police would only have seen Carol put in prison, both of us, possibly. She wouldn't have survived prison and who would have brought up Cassie then? The social care system? That would have completely ruined her life chances!'

Whatever empathy Helen might have shown earlier had been replaced by a dispassionate pursuit of the truth. Unable to conceal her scepticism, she asked, 'And all that was calmly going through your mind, immediately after your husband has been murdered, in front of you and your child?'

A spark flared in Martin's eyes. She knew how improbable it seemed. 'After a few minutes of her zombie like state, Carol began sobbing hysterically, saying "Sorry" over and over again, saying she would die in prison and never see Cassie again. I made her focus on Cassie, to get milk for her as I cleared up the mess. It was a scene of madness, but someone had to take responsibility'

'You didn't check his pulse to see if he was alive?' asked Helen.

Fixing Helen with an impatient look she replied, 'No! I knew he was dead, so I decided to do whatever I had to, to protect them both.'

Helen persisted. 'And the knife?'

'A kitchen knife. I was preparing food when the row started. After all the abuse from Pemberton, I can only guess at what went through her mind when she walked in. Carol picked it up from the work surface as she came over to help me. I replaced the whole set after,' adding with some irony, 'I should have done the same this time.'

As best as she could remember, Martin described the knife. Lifting a small box with a clear panel from the evidence table, Helen showed Martin the corroded knife. Flinching at the sight of it, Martin agreed it could have been the one used.

Martin described how she and Carol buried her husband's body and covered his disappearance. The base for the summerhouse had been prepared by Gérard before he died, and they had been waiting for delivery of the structure. Gérard had been at home for some weeks, scoping a new business venture, and had enjoyed the diversion of doing something practical with his hands. The garden was not overlooked by neighbours so, between them, they dragged and carried his body down the garden where Martin dug out the still soft earth and gravel from under some of the slabs and put him there, throwing the knife in with him. Two men from a large garden centre near Droitwich erected the summerhouse on site. With some mugs of tea and encouragement from Martin, they re-set the slabs that had been poorly replaced after burying him. Stirling made a note to find the delivery men, hoping that at least one of them might still be alive.

Asked how it was that neither Gérard's employers nor colleagues became concerned of his absence, Martin struggled to hide her satisfaction at having covered her tracks efficiently.

'Gérard had been restless for some time and was looking for a new business challenge. He had talked openly of travelling for a while, too. I knew through mutual acquaintances and some of his colleagues that he'd talked of being unhappy at home. He had time to prepare the slabs for the summer house because he'd left the company to prepare for setting up his own investment company.

'As a young man, Gérard had been a great one for the outdoors and yearned to recover some of that lost lifestyle. So, after he died, the few people who called were reminded circumspectly of how unhappy he had been in the marriage and had taken off abroad for an indefinite period, with a veiled inference of there being another woman. Some of them would have known about the woman in Paris so, through repetition and recycling, assumptions were made, and the calls got fewer and farther between.'

Stirling considered Martin's shrewdness and cold calculation. Enough truth and information to give the falsehoods credibility, whilst allowing people's imaginations and a desire to gossip to fill in the gaps, never having to provide a definitive account or to maintain one. And no family to ask awkward questions, either. Into her stride now, Martin continued with the back story.

'Gradually, the few calls asking for him dried up and the world moved on without Gérard in it. Not in the mortal sense.'

As the years went by and no one had come looking for Gérard Martin, she and Carol had built their lives around Cassie's needs, pushing Gérard further from their minds. Whenever Carol looked like spiralling out of control. Martin would remind her of what would happen to Cassie if Gérard was discovered. It controlled her, but added to her emotional frailty.

Martin looked at them across the table, 'Your next question might be, what happened to his wealth? I'm sure you're going to explore it anyway!'

A cold amusement danced in Martin's eyes as she waited for the question. Seeing Stirling and Helen waiting for her to continue, she continued with a hint of impatience.

'Everything he and I owned was in joint names, I'd made sure of that from the start. Even the apartment in London, which is now let on a long-term lease and has grown in value beyond belief. Slowly, I consolidated our shared assets into my company. If there was money in France under his own name, I don't know where they've been sending his statements to!'

Listening to her preening account, Stirling thought that with Croft's expertise, there might still be a chance to unpick this woman. Research of her business dealings from the moment of Gérard's death, subsequent asset disposals and consolidation might yet reveal an ulterior motive for her husband's death. It was interesting that Martin had yet to express a shred of remorse for Gérard's death. Stirling discreetly made another note.

Helen was concerned by something. 'To be sure we understand. We have photographs from Carol's home showing you, Carol and Cassie using the summerhouse over the years. Are you telling us that for sixteen years, you used the summerhouse as a place of family recreation, knowing that Gérard's remains, Cassie's father, were beneath you?'

The change in direction had caught her unawares and for a moment, Martin looked hunted. She turned to her solicitor for guidance who maintained a deep preoccupation with his notes.

Finding no encouragement there, and aware how it would sound to a jury, Martin answered, 'Yes.'

'Thank you. I just wanted to be sure I'd understood that correctly,' Helen said, pointedly. 'We still need to cover Pemberton's killing. How did Cassie come to meet Pemberton? That's not been explained.'

'Growing up without a father present left its mark on Cassie, I'm sure. She had some of Carol's emotional frailty, and I was an impatient Mother with high expectations of her. Looking back, I was tougher than I should have been and intimidated her gentle nature. As she entered her teenage years, Cassie wanted to know more about her father and was less content to accept that he had left and had no desire to meet her. I made a pretence of searching for him and told her I couldn't trace him, but she only became more curious. Carol was fearful of her curiosity so, to put an end to it, I told Cassie her father had died abroad.'

'How old was she when you told her that?' asked Helen.

'When she was fifteen. She appeared to accept it, albeit with some tears. Like all youngsters of her generation she was clever with computers and had her own laptop. Neither Carol nor I knew she'd begun her own research on one of those online ancestry sites. She was allowed to use my credit card for small purchases online and I didn't notice the annual subscription on my statement.'

'How had you dealt with parentage on Cassie's birth certificate?' interrupted Stirling.

'Gérard had arranged a home birth at our London apartment with a private nurse in attendance for the delivery. She had no idea who was who between Carol and me, and faithfully recorded the information we gave her. She thought she was delivering Mrs Katrina Martin, when in fact it was Carol. Once she was satisfied that Carol was well, she wasn't encouraged to hang around for long after the birth. Dishonest, yes, but a pragmatic solution which gave Cassie the security she needed and would fulfil our lives, or so we thought. Gérard registered Cassie's birth with the local Registrar and her official life began.

'Cassie couldn't find out anymore in the official records online than I'd already told her, but she was extremely curious to know what her Father had been like as a person, to hear stories about him, and frequently asked Carol to tell her. Carol deflected the questions as much as she could, and we thought Cassie would grow out of it, but Carol's ridiculous sentimentality undid us. Carol was a great one for memorabilia, photographs and the like. Whilst she was out one day, Cassie went rummaging and discovered Carol's so-called "Memory Box" where she kept lots of photographs, right the way back to when she and I were children.'

'How was that a problem?' asked Helen.

'Cassie knew what her father looked like, I'd given her photographs of Gérard when we first met and during our marriage, on holidays, of him holding her as a baby. The usual thing. She kept them on her dressing table.'

Martin confirmed some were tucked into the mirror frame which she had removed after Cassie's death.

'Carol had kept several photographs taken at the house warming party. Like all youngsters, Cassie was fascinated by looking at us when we were younger, the fashions and hairstyles of the day are always a hoot. I probably saw them at the time, but Carol was a memory hoarder.

'Carol had just started seeing Pemberton, secretly. In some of the pictures there was a proximity between them which, together with one of them seemingly brushing hands, might raise a question mark in a curious mind. And Cassie was a very bright girl. She asked Carol questions about the party and who she had been talking with. She described Pemberton as "just a man at the party" but, when pushed, told her he had been a "friend of the family" who had known Gérard. God knows why. She gave enough information for Cassie to know he was our architect too. Carol later believed Cassie had noticed her evasiveness when talking about Pemberton. Getting unsatisfactory information from us, Cassie thought a family friend from the past might tell her more about her father. One thing I always admired about Cassie was her determination when she set herself to something.

'Pemberton said she turned up at his door one afternoon last year, introduced herself and asked if he would tell her about Gérard. He made her welcome, told her stories about her father and overstated the extent of their friendship. I had much more to do with him over the house build than Gérard did, so it was a complete fabrication!

'Pemberton drew Cassie into his confidence by encouraging her art. He hated me and was contemptuous of Carol. Imagine! A pretty, naïve girl turns up at his door and she's the daughter of the woman he most detests, me? I'm sure he couldn't believe his luck. And all because of Carol's sentimentality in keeping those damned photographs.

'How long before he seduced, her I don't know, and I really can't think about it too much. He'd always had an incredible libido. He swore Cassie to secrecy, first by telling her I would stop her meeting with him when it was still a friendly connection and then, as the weeks progressed and she fell under his control, by threatening to reveal what they had done together and she would be disgraced. No doubt, if he took photos as well, he would have used them to coerce her. Once compromised, Cassie was increasingly dependent on him and obliged to keep it a secret.'

Martin hesitated over asking the question she was frightened of hearing the answer to, 'Did he take photographs of Cassie?'

Stirling wanted to lie to spare Martin some anguish, but it was pointless. The Inquest would reveal their existence.

'Yes, I'm afraid he did.'

'You've looked at them?' she demanded, tears welling in her eyes as she imagined Cassie's shame.

'Unfortunately, I have to.'

Martin clearly wanted to know more to understand how awful they were, yet not wanting to know.

Holding up a hand to stay her question, Stirling continued, 'I'll answer your questions honestly but, you should consider what you absolutely need to know.'

Stirling explained the measures he had taken to limit access to a small number of officers only, who must bring the evidence together for trial, or inquest. The lawyer reassured Martin it must be so.

Helen asked how Carol had made the connection between Cassie and Pemberton. Still troubled by the thought of the photos, Martin took a deep breath.

'It was many hours after Cassie died before we were contacted by the police. They didn't know who she was but when those terrible pictures were broadcast, someone recognised her and called them. It was the most awful thing to experience when the two officers knocked on my door. Naturally, I immediately feared the worst, but not in those circumstances. It was bewildering, we couldn't make any sense of it. Carol and I went to identify her body. They'd done their best to protect us from seeing the worst of the damage but ... it broke our hearts to see her like that. She looked so tiny lying there, stone cold, so alone, and so ... terribly damaged.'

Closing her eyes against the painful memory, Martin's voice choked as she stood in the mortuary viewing room again and wrapped her arms around her stomach for comfort. It was a full minute before she could continue. Stirling was reminded of sour, cold disinfectant and of Cassie's frail body broken on the road.

'Carol lost her mind for days afterwards. All the love we'd poured into Cassie's life, the things we did and the guilt we'd endured, to come to such a sad and inexplicable death! Carol spent a lot of time with me, always sleeping in Cassie's room. I was frightened she might take her own life too, so I kept her as close as possible. When she insisted on returning home, we spoke every day. But we were completely bewildered, unable to comprehend why she had been there, so alone and frightened. And who did the child belong to? Those terrible pictures in the newspapers and on the television only made it worse. The few friends we have thought we must have known *something* and, not knowing what to say, stopped calling so we felt even more isolated.

'No one would help us. As far as anyone was concerned I was her Mother and therefore, the point of contact for Ballard and his FLO. I've told you what I think of him, so I won't go over that again. I was told you wouldn't speak to me, Chief Inspector so, as the weeks passed and we got so little information from the police, we began to make our own enquiries amongst the few of her friends we knew about, but they couldn't help much.

'Then, a few days before the Easter holiday, I received the anonymous phone call I told you about. It was to my home number which was strange, because very few people have it. The woman appeared to know me and said Pemberton had been in an intimate relationship with Cassie. I refused to believe her, but she insisted. I asked how she could possibly know but she was extremely nervous and rang off. She'd withheld her number.'

'What did you do?' asked Helen.

'I was shocked to start with, then disbelieving. I thought someone was playing a cruel game with me. Few women like me but, even so, that would have been an extremely cruel thing to do. Both of us had been concerned about Cassie's growing withdrawal, but she'd refused to discuss anything. Carol thought there was a boy involved and had respected her privacy. I put it down to teenage angst and thought she must work it out for herself.

'It emerged that a few months before she died, when she was at Carol's home, Carol walked into the bathroom unexpectedly and saw a tattoo on Cassie's body. Cassie explained that all her friends were getting tattoos and made Carol promise not to tell me because

I would be upset. Cassie knew my views on tattoos, especially on young women.

'After she died, Carol spent hours in the bedroom Cassie used there, trying to keep some connection. Going through her things, she found a hand drawn design for the tattoo and decided to have one done in memory of Cassie. Of course, Carol needed to know if it had some spiritual meaning and traipsed around all the tattoo shops in town until a sniggering young man explained what it represented. A few minutes' internet research confirmed the appalling truth. That was the day after I received the anonymous telephone call.

'Carol came to my home and sobbed it all out, about the tattoo, what it meant, about the garden party photos Cassie had asked questions about and the questions about Gérard. That's when I searched her bedroom.'

'Just go through it again, please?' Helen prompted, searching for some disparity with the previous account.

'Hidden under her wardrobe were about a dozen letters from Pemberton to Cassie. He must have given them to her by hand because they didn't come through the post at either of our homes. They started innocently enough, encouraging her in her studies and complimenting her on her art, suggesting how she could improve. Quite innocent stuff really, but I was confused as to how or why she was in a correspondence with him.

'But, as they progressed, there were increasing inferences of intimacy, reminding her their "friendship" must be kept a secret because I would stop her meeting him. Reading between the lines, it was obvious they were having sex with him talking about her being over the age of consent at sixteen. The last two letters made veiled references that, knowing his tastes, I could interpret all too clearly. It was vile, and knowing of Carol's experience, I threw up imagining what poor Cassie might have been subjected to.'

'Where are the letters?'

'I destroyed everything that could link him to us. It was vile stuff anyway.'

Stirling needed to pin down the sequence of events. 'So, that was a couple of days before he died?'

'Yes. To start with I believed he had done it to hurt me, having my naïve sixteen-year-old daughter as his plaything. A sexual relationship between a man of his age and a child of sixteen would be bad enough, but the tattoo made it even more revolting. I wanted to kill him myself.'

'What stopped you?' asked Stirling.

Martin eyed Stirling steadily across the table, her jaw clenched. 'Once we understood the vile truth, Carol wanted to go and confront him, but I made her wait. To think through our options. Neither of us had any confidence in Ballard, and what could he have done anyway? Cassie was over the age of consent. Pemberton would have been made aware and become wary. I wanted to kill Pemberton but with a plan to get away with it, if I could, but not too worried if I didn't. But Carol cheated me of the satisfaction.

'She stayed with me that day and the next, crying most of the time whilst I just felt a numb, implacable hatred for the man. I hadn't been sleeping well since Cassie's death and was exhausted, so I took one of the pills my doctor had prescribed me. While I was asleep, Carol called him from my mobile on the Thursday evening to demand he meet early the next morning because she'd heard Cassie had contacted him. Typical of Carol's impulsiveness, she had not thought it through and overlooked phone-records. He thought I had called him.

'For business reasons, I've never changed my telephone numbers. Such was his arrogance, he agreed to meet "me" where the cottage had once been, believing I didn't know anything, or not everything, at least. It was weeks after Cassie had died so he must have been increasingly confident. For Carol, it fitted her sense of things. It was where he had abused her so badly, bringing things full circle. We'll never know if he took Cassie into that damned wood. I hope not. If she hadn't died, I'm sure he would have.'

'Couldn't you have stopped her, or intervened?' asked Helen.

'No, I was drugged out asleep. The first I knew about it was about quarter past eight on Good Friday morning. I was in the kitchen making coffee, unaware she had gone out, when she came back in my car with blood on her clothes and hands, completely hysterical and gabbling that she'd killed him. I thought she'd gone mad and was horrified when she pointed at the knife block and said she'd taken one and had left it behind. I got enough information out of her to realise she'd left a trail back to us, so I stripped her naked and sent her off to shower while I drove down there. It's only a few minutes' drive if you know the back lanes.'

As she talked about the killing, alert to every nuance and inflection, Stirling detected a subtle change in Martin's tone and in her delivery: a precise, slower pace, pausing before describing something or an action by her or by Carol. Was she having to think carefully to remain consistent to her previous account where it overlapped?

Helen probed exactly as Stirling wanted. 'Why didn't you call the police or ambulance? You couldn't be certain he was dead. You only had her account and you say she was hysterical.'

Martin looked taken aback, as if it had never occurred to her until now. Or had she not covered it off in her preparation, Stirling speculated? The story was very tidy, and Carol Evans was dead.

Martin shrugged, 'I could have. But Carol was certain he was dead when she left him. I suppose I acted on that presumption. I was afraid of the consequences as well.' Seeing Helen waiting for her to continue, she said, 'When I got there, he *was* dead. The knife was lying on the ground outside. I put it in the glove box of the car intending to throw it away but later thought it best to hide it in plain sight. So, after sterilising it and putting it through the dishwasher several times, I put it back in the block. Unfortunately, I didn't notice the damaged tip.'

She explained again removing the number plates to delay his identification, expecting him to have been burnt beyond recognition, and burning Carol's clothes at home with her own. Martin insisted she had ignited the rag with the cigar lighter. When asked how the plates were disposed of, she claimed to have dropped them into recycling bins in Pershore later that day on the way to the car valet and described the locations. In the monitoring room, Edwards noted the details and for CCTV in the town to be reviewed. It had already been seized at the start of the enquiry as being within the twenty-mile radius he and Stirling had decided on for the seizure of all CCTV.

'We asked you last time about the removal of a piece of jewellery from the body. Do you have anything more to add to that?' Helen asked.

Martin frowned in response to the question and looked warily from Helen to Stirling, asking cautiously, 'Wasn't it at Carol's home?'

Something in her tone pricked Stirling's instinct. Why was she being so cagey about this detail? Filing it away for later, Stirling put a brown evidence bag on the table and slid out the item inside so that it lay between them. Inside a clear plastic bag lay a gold signet ring, squashed as if it had been struck with a blunt object, the black stone inlay fractured but largely intact. Engraved into it was the symbol tattooed on Cassandra Martin's body.

Martin's hands recoiled from the table top as she stared at it coldly for long moments. The only noise in the room was the recording machine humming. Staring at the ring, she said, 'It was his. He didn't wear it all those years ago. When Carol and I were … involved.'

'Why would Carol keep something so reprehensible to her? It seems very strange that she would have kept something that represented her own suffering. It was tattooed on her daughter and she knew what it represented.' asked Stirling.

Martin seemed unsure what to say. Had she not expected this line of questioning?

'I … I'm not sure,' replied Martin, appearing to struggle to offer a rational explanation.

The questioning continued with Helen taking Martin through some previous answers to establish consistency, or the absence of it. Listening to her responding to some questions quickly and confidently, pausing over others to sift her options, Stirling knew he was still missing something. It was there, just out of sight, darting about amongst all the information they had gathered, the people they had talked to, and in Martin's careful delivery.

Or was it what she had *not* told them? What was Katrina "Katy" Martin holding back, and why? A girl from modest beginnings who had made a considerable success of her life. Was she trying to protect her reputation? How had she managed not to scratch his eyes out when he turned up at her home, and why? He thought of the tattoo on Cassie's body, the post mortem images and the tiny, lifeless foetus at her side, two innocent lives destroyed. Pemberton, impregnating the child of his erstwhile lover and her husband with his corrupt spawn. A calculated revenge, a dish eaten cold? The sadness in Cassie's eyes, consciously letting go of his hand, the enigmatic smile. She had intended to die, knowing her child would die with her. An unwanted pregnancy was a story as old as time, but would the shame have been so intolerable? Was Katrina Martin so formidable a mother that Cassie could not contemplate revealing her pregnancy?

Why would Cassie choose to kill her unborn child? Pemberton had rejected her. Painful, heart-breaking and treacherous yes, but however young, possibly the strongest instinct a woman can experience is to protect her unborn child. Or did she consider it with revulsion, thinking the baby would be unloved? Or unhealthy?

The photograph of the cottage. The frenzied attack. The bouquet, *"My sweet beautiful Cassie ... together soon."* The embittered regret in Carol Evans's letter to him: *"... everything was my fault, the mistakes and choices I made many years ago ... Cassie's life could have been so much better ... I can't live without her and must say sorry to her ... be with her to eternity."*

The look in Cassie's eyes.

A cold, sour chill ran through his gut as suddenly, all the oblique references coalesced and aligned. To the bitter end, Martin was trying to protect the last vestige of her daughter's dignity and, no doubt, something of her own.

It was the last thread.

Leaning forward, Stirling rested his elbows on the table and waited until he had Martin's attention. Looking her directly in the eyes and speaking softly, he said, 'Katrina. You have something else to tell us.'

From the corner of his eye, he saw Helen turn her head to look at him, curious. On the other side of the table Martin tried to maintain an impassive mask, but Stirling had seen the flash of fear as she guessed at what he was asking and stared at him dumbly.

'Katrina. I understand. Finally. We *will* do DNA tests.'

Stirling looked across to the solicitor trying to gauge what he knew. Had she confided in him?

Katrina Martin's eyes welled with tears as she turned to her lawyer in mute appeal. Putting a reassuring hand on her forearm, he advised her to answer truthfully.

Nodding weakly, Martin spoke faintly, the shame choking in her voice as she spoke.

'Cassandra was Michael Pemberton's daughter.'

The room was silent as each considered the appalling knowledge Cassie had been burdened with. Her trust debased. Her vulnerability exploited for revenge and sexual gratification. And all by her biological father who knew their true relationship and had consciously impregnated her with his incestuous bastard.

'Did you and Carol know that Pemberton was Cassie's true father?' Stirling asked gently.

With tears streaming down her face, Martin nodded and began to rock in anguish, her arms folded over her stomach to comfort the child once carried there.

After taking a few minutes to recover, Martin looked a broken woman. With the last deceiving veil pulled away, she had nothing left to protect.

Stirling re-opened the interview. 'Katrina, we can understand you trying to protect Cassie's memory, but the best way to do that is to help us understand the truth. Cassie was a victim of other people's choices. No one can reproach her actions, she was still a child.'

'But I should have protected her better!' she replied bitterly. 'Because of the decisions Carol and I took, before she was even born. We sowed the seeds of her unhappiness and her disgrace and, ultimately, her death. The Sins of the Mothers. A cruel twist on the proverb, don't you think?'

Stirling nodded sympathetically. He was rarely surprised at humanity's ability to inflict pain, particularly on those they claimed to love.

Breaking into the momentary silence, Helen asked, 'You said the past gave understanding to the present?'

'I wanted to protect Cassie's memory. it was all she had left. Before she was born, we truly believed Cassandra *was* Gérard's child. Taking her on was already difficult enough for him as it was, but Carol would insist on visiting most days of the week, even if I asked her to stay away when Gérard was home for the weekend. She always found an excuse to call in and Gérard resented her presence. It reminded him of his own infidelity and she was so timid in the company of men, he was contemptuous of her. Neither of us knew what she had suffered with Pemberton and I was caught in the middle.'

'Something changed?' Helen pressed.

'Yes … the truth revealed itself about six months after Cassandra was born. Like many babies, Caucasian babies, her eyes changed colour from the blue she was born with, the colour of Gérard's eyes, to a distinctive, dark grey. Gérard knew then that she could not possibly be his child and an already difficult situation for him became intolerable.'

'Sorry, Cassie's eyes?' asked Helen. She had not understood.

Martin looked at Helen, perplexed, and then to Stirling who understood but Martin had to explain it.

'She had his eyes! They were Pemberton's most striking feature. You've seen photographs of him and people have told you, surely?'

With a puzzled frown, Helen looked at Stirling and back to Martin. 'No. We struggled to find any good photographs of him. Those we have are several years old, poor quality newspaper articles and the like, and not good enough to show his eye colouring.'

'But what about the women you spoke to?' asked the solicitor, also surprised.

Helen thought back and shook her head. 'No. In the context of describing his looks generally, some mentioned he had nice eyes but didn't specify a colour and it wasn't relevant to the purpose of the interviews.'

The solicitor raised his eyebrows as Martin continued.

'Gérard was a proud man and as adorable as Cassandra was, looking into her eyes was a constant reminder of having been cuckolded by Pemberton. Worse still, a mocking presence at having been deceived into taking in his cuckoo. Pemberton had cuckolded him not once, but twice.

'There was a lot of bitter self-recrimination too because he knew he'd contributed to it through his infidelity with Carol.

However tragic the miscarriage, and the affairs, without Pemberton inside our family we would have got through it, with time. But with Cassandra there to constantly remind him, Gérard's pride was irretrievably wounded. He refused to believe Carol had made a genuine error about who the father was.

'Carol genuinely believed Gérard to be the father, but she was an emotional wreck, made worse by smoking too much weed. With all the stress, Carol's periods were often irregular. The silly girl lost track of her cycle and the sequence of her lovers. It was during a screaming row over the revelation of Cassandra's true paternity that Carol walked in. The rest I've told you.'

'Do you believe Cassie discovered Pemberton was her true father and that Carol was her biological mother?' asked Helen. 'If she'd found that out, I find it hard to believe Cassie could have kept that information to herself.'

Martin snorted contemptuously. 'You're confusing Pemberton with someone who had any scruples about other people's emotional needs! He was only interested in his own pleasures and in exercising control. He'd have known we would do whatever was needed to keep Cassie away from him and he would lose his control over her. The longer he kept that from her, the further she fell under his control as a supposedly sympathetic friend and, ultimately, the more he could hurt me and Carol. He revealed the truth to her during the weekend before she died. When she told him she was pregnant, only to discover the gross nature of an already intolerable situation.'

Stirling spoke. 'When I saw Cassie, she was deeply troubled.'

Martin nodded, staring vacantly at the wall behind him. 'He said he worked out she was his daughter quite quickly and claimed a genuine interest in her, at the start. To get to know her. But as they grew friendlier and he saw her prettiness, which reminded him of Carol as a young woman, he "gave in to temptation" was how he put it, smugly justifying his actions and that she had been an eager and willing participant. The filthy, lying bastard!' Martin spat the words out with hatred, 'She'd not even had a boyfriend to kiss, as far as we knew.

'He enjoyed telling the story, taunting. He said Cassie was with him that weekend, before you … spoke to her? She told him she was pregnant but instead of supporting her, he told her everything. Her world would have imploded. The two people she trusted, three if you count him, had lied to her all her life. Poor, poor Cassie. Seduced and abused by a man she thought was a friend, only to discover he was in fact her father, and now pregnant by him. She must have felt so alone. He told her to go home and tell me, a final insult aimed at me. He calculated I wouldn't trash Cassie's name by complaining to the authorities of his incest and would terminate the pregnancy discreetly. That was on the Sunday, so God alone knows where she spent that night. Wandering the streets, I expect. Her phone was never recovered so the police couldn't help in tracing her movements. They told me it was last registering in the city centre.

'How could Cassie deal with that? How could he do that to his own flesh and blood? It was so cruel! So, you can understand how we felt when we learnt that. Who wouldn't have wanted to hurt him? He abused and degraded his own daughter and then abandoned her, sending her to her death! I hope he rots in hell!'

Something about Martin's account of the conversation with Pemberton had caught Stirling's attention. 'Katrina. Your description of what Pemberton said, in the car. How he acted. You were talking in the first person. As though you were there?'

The solicitor's hand stalled over his notebook as he looked up sharply. Martin stared at Stirling with a new anxiety as she mentally reviewed her words before insisting, 'I'm telling you what Carol told me.'

Realising she sounded unconvincing, she added more forcefully, 'It's become very real to me in the last two weeks.'

Helen and Stirling pursued Martin for some time, pointing out her inconsistencies but she insisted resolutely she was only recounting Carol's description of the conversation until she fell forward over the table and broke down with wracking sobs.

Who Martin was crying for, Stirling wasn't sure.

Standing a safe distance along the corridor from the interview room, Helen and Stirling leant against the walls opposite each other, both deep in thought. Stirling wondered if he should have worked it out sooner. Possibly. Possibly not.

Helen stood with her arms folded, gazing down the corridor to nothing at all as she absorbed the life and death of Cassandra Martin. A steady clamour of steel doors slamming, and of obscenities being hurled between cells echoed down the corridor from the custody area. Pulling herself back to the moment, Helen looked at Stirling.

With a weary sigh, she said, 'My God Dougie, we do shovel society's deepest shit. That poor girl must have been so frightened. So confused and isolated.'

Stirling nodded but said nothing.

'You okay?' she asked, concerned.

Seeing her concern, despite all that had been said and done in recent days, he gave her a weary smile of gratitude. 'Yes. Thanks Helen.'

Edwards arrived with two chipped mugs of dubious looking coffee. 'Sorry, it's all that's available.'

Looking suspiciously at the fluid and taking a tentative sip, Stirling pulled a sour face. 'Better than nothing, I suppose.'

With occasional glances down the corridor to the red light over the interview room door, they quietly reviewed the key admissions and what still needed to be discussed.

'D'you believe her?' Edwards asked.

Helen had made up her mind before leaving the interview room. 'She's lying. Carol's not here to defend herself and there was something about her letter to Martin which seemed to allude to something they'd talked about. Saying everything was her fault and that she accepted responsibility. There was a subtle subtext about it if you ask me. Carol was emotionally unstable, wracked with guilt over the death of her own daughter. I think she was telling Martin to put it all onto her. They'd have talked in the week leading up to Martin's arrest and if Pemberton's murder was anything like she describes it, she's had plenty of time to transpose their actions, reversing their roles.'

'The same applies for Gérard's murder too,' said Edwards. 'D'you think she encouraged Carol to take her own life?'

Helen and Stirling looked at him. They had not considered the possibility.

'Actively encouraged her?' said Stirling. 'No, I don't think so. Under that tough shell, Katrina cared for Carol. She'd looked after her for all those years, even allowing for the fact they were bound by Gérard's murder. But we could imagine a scenario where Carol had expressed a wish to die to be with Cassie, telling her sister to blame everything on her.'

Stirling continued, 'If Gérard's murder happened in the way she describes, the kitchen's been refitted recently and with her wealth, once or twice before, probably. Any forensic retrieval is unlikely and what would it prove? That he died there, but not how. Her description of Gérard's death sets the precedent for Carol as an emotionally unhinged character capable of spontaneous and extreme violence.'

'She had considerable motive to hate Pemberton for his treatment of her,' said Helen, 'And then Cassie too, her own flesh and blood. The defence could easily represent Carol as capable of murder a second time.'

Edwards looked pensively into the middle distance. 'Katrina's had sixteen years to prepare for Gérard's discovery and would have rehearsed that story, thousands of times. Funny that Carol made no mention of Gérard in either of her letters?'

'When Carol wrote the letters,' said Stirling, 'as far as she knew we were only investigating Pemberton's murder. If we'd discovered Gérard sooner, I've no doubt Carol would have taken responsibility for that too. But we'll never know.'

With a disbelieving shake of her head, Helen cut in, 'So, she's putting both killings on to Carol, and we can't disprove it?'

Edwards pulled a shrug of his face, 'She's very cleverly put herself in the car with Pemberton's body, albeit after the murder, which explains away the presence of her DNA or fingerprints if recovered. We can charge her with assisting an offender and concealment but, beyond that, I think we'll struggle.'

'But who did Pemberton think he was meeting?' asked Helen. 'Carol or Katrina?'

Stirling reminded Helen of their first visit to Martin's home. 'She was genuinely surprised when you asked her about the call to Pemberton from her mobile. Personally, I think Carol, driven by her chaotic emotions, made the call and her sister took control and went to meet him. But, we can't prove it.'

Edwards cut in, 'The data from Katrina's satnav will show either one or two return journeys were made that morning. If Martin was the only person to go there, there'll be just one trip recorded, there and back. If Carol killed him and Katrina went there to clean up, as she describes, it should have recorded two return journeys. And even if Carol's car was used for one of the journeys, the satnav timings will give us the sequences of travel.'

'And we're certain there was no CCTV at any of those houses in the road leading to her house Bill? They're all wealthy people along there and will have alarm systems.'

'Nope.' replied Edwards. 'Every house was visited and we got nothing.'

Helen was puzzled by Martin's hesitation in discussing the ring. 'She's vague about the signet ring but I don't understand why? Do you?'

'If Carol killed him and took the ring,' said Edwards, 'it would explain Martin's surprise in the first interview. Claiming she'd killed him but unaware of that detail. But if Martin killed him and took it, why did Carol have it to give to you in the letter?'

Stirling had been mulling over the ring. 'What if Martin removed it and Carol took it away without her knowing, for some vengeful purpose? Martin may have been frightened of its discovery and tried to protect Carol, as she's always done. I can understand the damage to it but why keep something so abhorrent to them both? It might be something or nothing. Either way, it ties one or both of them into the murder so let's accept that for the time being.'

'And the cigar lighter?' asked Edwards. 'Where did that go? You say Carol had a cigarette lighter in her bag at the cathedral. Carol smoked weed when she was younger, but there was nothing at her home to suggest she was still a smoker.'

Stirling took another sip of the coffee and wished he hadn't. 'The controlled test at the Fire College yesterday suggests it's difficult, but possible, to ignite the cloth as she describes. There are several miles of lanes and hedgerows between the scene and her home. We can't do a fingertip search of every square inch, so the search teams can be forgiven it's not been found.'

Stirling tried to think of any more gaps or contradictions in Martin's interviews which they could unpack. He was inclined to think the worst of her. Highly intelligent, rigidly self-disciplined and other than when she had described the loss of her own child, seemingly devoid of sympathy or true empathy. She had still not expressed any remorse for Gérard's death. In the absence of hard evidence, a confection of truth, half-truths and lies would undermine a jury's confidence to deliver a verdict of guilt beyond all reasonable doubt. And in these circumstances, few juries would convict Katrina Martin of murder. Whatever he believed to be the truth, Stirling could not prove who had wielded either knife.

Swigging down the last of the coffee, he grimaced and handed the mug back to Edwards. 'Gérard could have died completely differently to how she tells it. The skeletal examination confirmed knife cuts on the bones which correspond broadly with her description of how he was attacked. Whether Carol was even in the house, I doubt we'll ever know. The only other witness, an infant of six months, is dead. House to house of past and present neighbours gave us nothing worth talking to her about. I doubt our enquiries with Gérard's past business associates will give us much after so many years, but we'll have to see. I'll get the satnav analysis expedited. Bill, go back in with Helen and take Martin through the fine detail to see if we can trip her up with any discrepancies. At the end of the day, it'll be for the jury to decide.'

Stirling was not even sure he would have enough to get Martin to trial.

3.39 p.m.

Stirling was hanging up his coat when a burst of raucous laughter from next door caught his ear. As he opened the door to the MCU, more laughter cloaked the noise of his entrance.

Stood around a desk with their backs to him were half a dozen of his team, all talking and laughing between themselves. Below them, out of sight, he could hear Geordie Heal's ripe language underpinning the humorous chatter. Intrigued, Stirling quietly joined the rear of the group. Presuming it was another colleague wanting a better view, someone shifted aside without taking their eyes from the computer screen everyone was looking at.

Looking at the screen, it took Stirling some seconds to understand what was provoking so much laughter. In front of four legs disappearing into white wellington boots, a man's body lay stretched across a tiled floor, its legs lost to view under a steel table pedestal. Recognising Ballard's pale, pudgy features, the story came back to him. The photo must have been taken by a SOCO officer at Cassie Martin's post-mortem.

The laughter around Stirling was fading away as a succession of elbow digs alerted others to his presence and an awkward silence fell over the room. Below him, an ebullient Heal continued cracking jokes until he realised no one else was contributing. Following the discreet nods in Stirling's direction, Heal looked around to see the boss stood behind him, staring intently at the screen.

Darting looks around him, Heal rose rapidly from his seat. Everyone was waiting to see how Stirling would react, ready to take their cue from him. Some were concerned, most were struggling to hide their amusement at Heal's predicament.

'Oh, hello boss. We weren't expecting you for a while yet.'

'Yes. I can see that,' replied Stirling flatly.

Unusually tongue-tied, Heal studied Stirling's face for a hint as to how much trouble he was in. He knew the photograph breached regulations and the sender could be easily identified. Inappropriate use of the email system was punished severely and, as a supervisor, he was now complicit in condoning it being seen by the team.

'It's um, Mr Ballard, sir,' Heal explained unnecessarily.

'Yes. I can see that, Sarge,' Stirling replied.

Around them people began drifting back to their desks. Stirling had said "Sarge" not "Geordie." Heal was in trouble.

Heal stumbled on, 'It came through a few minutes ago. A general email to every CID office in the force so it's not just us looking at it, but I take responsibility for the team, Sir. I shouldn't have shown it to everyone. Sorry boss.'

'My office, Sarge. Now!'

Turning to the team, Heal told everyone to get back to work. Worried for their Sergeant's position, everyone did as they were told, assuming the appearance of a deep interest in whatever was on their desks whilst glancing furtively at each other over the tops of their screens.

At the door, Stirling stood aside to let Heal pass in front of him towards his office. Pulling the door shut briefly, Stirling turned back to the room. Pressing a finger to his lips for silence, he gave an exaggerated wink. A spontaneous burst of laughter from someone was choked off as everyone shushed them quiet.

4.28 p.m.
When Edwards returned, Heal was still fending off good-natured barracking from the enquiry teams as they came in and heard about how Stirling had blagged him.

Claiming he had suspected Stirling's intentions all the time, Heal hadn't convinced anybody yet. And certainly not Edwards who listened with growing amusement as the story was recounted with growing embellishment of Heal's embarrassment as he went to the headmaster's study.

Edwards patted Heal's shoulder, 'You've been had Geordie. Sounds like you're buying the first round at the Twigs later!'

Settling into a seat opposite Stirling, Edwards was still chuckling. 'You've had some fun with Geordie, I hear?'

Stirling smiled. 'It will keep him on his toes in future when it comes to inappropriate emails. I don't give a toss for Ballard's embarrassment, I just hope the SOCO isn't in trouble.'

'She's denying any knowledge. The photographs belonged to Ballard's investigation, so it's got to have leaked from someone in there. That's her story so let's hope it stands up to scrutiny. Given Ballard's standing right now, if they do find out who sent it I doubt they'll get anything more than a reprimand.' Edwards was grinning.

'Let's hope so.'

'Consider it a measure of how well you're thought of. A lot of people were unhappy at how you were treated, and how our seniors allowed it to happen.'

Edwards continued, 'It's good to see the team with a smile on their faces. And well done. You've cleared up the murder *and* a killing we might never have known about.'

'*We* did, Bill, the team. The more we know about Pemberton, though, I'm still not certain there aren't any bodies at The Wern.'

They talked on, agreeing the many enquiries still to be completed for the prosecution case, fully aware that Martin could avoid indictment for either of the men's deaths for lack of evidence. Martin had given the date of her husband's death and, for the meantime, had been charged with concealment of his body and would be out on bail soon.

At the very least, Martin was an accessory to two killings and their concealment, but Stirling was not confident the CPS would prosecute her for any shade of homicide.

 number of them to be the team. The more we know about Pemberton, though, I'm still not certain there aren't any bodies at The Wern.'

They talked on, agreeing the many enquiries still to be completed for the prosecution case, fully aware that Martin could avoid indictment for either of the men's deaths for lack of evidence. Martin had given the date of her husband's death and, for the meantime, had been charged with concealment of his body and would be out on bail soon.

At the very least, Martin was an accessory to two killings and their concealment, but Stirling was not confident the CPS would prosecute her for any shade of homicide.

CB ぬ

Day 11: Thursday 10.11 a.m.

Stood in the gateway, she looked nervously up and down the street trying to see him. His text had said he was parked outside. A pair of headlights flashed and with a nervous smile, she began walking briskly towards his car. Clutching the light raincoat closed, she used her free hand to hold the collar up, supposedly against the wind but hoping it might hinder recognition too as she darted anxious looks around the square.

As she slipped into the passenger seat, the woman's coat parted to reveal a simple wool cardigan, blouse and skirt in a bland palette of greens. Watching her staring silently through the windscreen, Stirling saw someone who had withered under the weight of a personal burden, exacerbated by a life of sedentary routine.

Stirling broke the silence. 'Thank you for agreeing to meet me, Jenny.'

She twitched a smile in acknowledgement and continued to look anxiously at the building she had just left.

'Jenny, would you be more comfortable if I drove us somewhere more private than here?'

Jenny turned to him. 'Where?' she asked, uneasily.

Stirling gave her a reassuring smile. 'It's entirely up to you. I will only take you where you feel safe. We can stay here, but you are on show to the street if that's a concern. This is not a formal visit. It's off the record.'

After some thought, Jenny asked him to take her to a place she had not visited for many years. Surprised, Stirling asked if she was certain. Jenny nodded firmly and said she was. After some moments thought, Stirling started the car and drove out of the square.

Pulling to a stop at the centre of The Wern, Stirling switched off the engine and they sat in silence as Stirling waited until she was ready to talk.

Stirling thought back to twelve days earlier and reflected on how much violence this tranquil setting had harboured over the years. Under the encouragement of the spring rains and warm sun, the field grasses had grown quickly and now stood tall and lush, rising and dipping as a swell of wind rolled over it.

Above them, the trees in the copse swayed uniformly. He doubted Osmand would be up there for a long time. Stirling had considered arresting him for the rape of Carol Evans, but there wasn't a cat in hell's chance of taking that any further after so many years, and the victim dead. Following a meeting with the roads policing team and the local beat officer, new in post and very keen, Osmand was now awaiting appearance in the Magistrates Court after being intercepted on his way home from the village pub. As anticipated, he had failed the alcohol test by a long way and was arrested. Diligent enquiries found he had no insurance or road tax and several serious defects on his vehicle which was now impounded, awaiting disposal. Osmand had failed to heed Stirling's advice and had a loaded shotgun in the cab when he was stopped. A search of his home discovered other firearms for which he had no permit. Most surprising of all was the revelation that he had never passed a driving test. How he had never been prosecuted before seemed unbelievable, but the previous beat officer had been in post for too many years and was a weak character. Osmand had intimidated him along with all the other local men.

Interrupting his thoughts, Jenny said suddenly, 'It looks so different now.' She pointed across the clearing. 'The cottage was there.'

'Would you like to get out and walk around?'

Jenny looked around again and leaned forward to peer intently up at the copse. 'No. No. I'm quite happy here, with you. Thank you.'

She gave him a fluttering smile and continued to look around the clearing, repeatedly threading and unthreading her fingers in her lap.

The nervous behaviour and apologies reminded Stirling of Carol Evans. 'Jenny, are you sure you want to talk with me about it?' he asked. 'As I said on the telephone, I can arrange for you to meet with a female officer, if you prefer.'

Not having a female officer present was breaking the rules but he had his reasons and would deal with any criticism, if it ever came. He felt Jenny had suffered enough and too fragile to put through the justice mill, unless certain it was what she wanted.

Jenny stared at her feet. 'You've seen the photographs?' she asked.

Hearing no answer, Jenny lifted her head to look at him, her eyes wet with shame. Seeing Stirling's regretful confirmation, she instinctively pulled her coat closed against her remembered nakedness. Feeling foolish at the futility of the gesture, she began rummaging fruitlessly in a pocket for a tissue, wiping away tears with her free hand. Stirling handed her his clean handkerchief. Thanking him and apologising, she dabbed at her tears and blew her nose before apologising again.

Through her sniffles, she asked, 'How did you know it was me who made the calls?'

Reassuring her she was not in trouble, Stirling explained, 'In Pemberton's contacts, your home number was alongside Mr Jones's office numbers, which I thought unusual. Unless you were on friendlier terms than just a business acquaintance. We met when I came to meet Mr Jones. Later, as my investigation went on and I learnt of Pemberton's nature, I recognised aspects of your nervous manner as similar to those of Carol Evans and realised the pretty young woman photographed in his car was you.' He smiled kindly.

Blushing deeply, she turned her head away. 'What will happen to the photographs?' she asked quietly, 'Can they be destroyed?'

'You've not yet been formally identified in my investigation. Unless you want me to arrange a formal interview, they'll be filed away from prying eyes. I can't destroy them because they're stored on his computer, which is evidence. But only I know who you are. I will make a contact report of our meeting and of whatever you decide you want to happen, or not to happen, which will be filed discreetly.'

Jenny thought for a few moments. 'He took so many photographs Mr Stirling, I couldn't stop him. I've lived for so many years frightened he would do something with them. Are you sure no one will see them?'

'Only a small number of my people who must examine the evidence. Did Pemberton use them to extort money from you? He did with other women.'

'No, I've no money to speak of. I have a small home, but my income is modest and I've little in the way of savings. He knew that.'

Probing gently, needing to paint in the remaining blanks, he asked, 'David Jones knew of your relationship, I think?'

'Yes, but not the … intimate details.' Jenny cringed with the words, 'Mr Jones has always been very kind to me.' A thought seized her and she asked worriedly, 'He's not in any trouble, is he?'

'No, but when we met I thought he knew more than he was telling me.'

Silence fell between them as she looked out of the window.

'Can I ask some questions and see where that takes us, Jenny?' Seeing her nod, he asked, 'How long were you and Michael Pemberton lovers?'

Giving a deep sigh, she leant back into her seat and closed her eyes, happier to answer direct questions rather than have to describe it herself. 'Too many years, but it was always on and off. He picked me up and put me down depending on who else was available to him. I was extremely foolish, but I loved him very much. As did many other women, but whilst they all fell away, I was constant. However badly he treated me, I couldn't help but love him. I think he conditioned me to that. By the time I understood, it was too late for me to seek love anywhere else. I was washed out and too nervous around men. When I realised what had happened to that poor girl, it was the final straw.' Her voice died away, choking with emotion.

'Talk me through how it started and follow it from there, but only what you're comfortable to talk about.'

'I was nineteen when I first met Michael. I'd left secretarial college a year before and started working for Mr Jones. My parents were pleased I was working in a profession. Michael came in one day to see Mr Jones about a project they were involved in and paid me some compliments. I was young with no experience of men and he was so handsome, and very stylish. I began to look forward to his visits and he found excuses to drop by. Mr Jones warned me about his reputation but, like most foolish young women, I ignored his advice.'

Talking away from Stirling, she continued, 'We began meeting once a week and he swore me to secrecy, which I was happy to agree to for fear of being sacked for dating a client. I knew he had other women friends but persuaded myself it would be different with me. He took me to places I could never have experienced otherwise, spent money on me, always flattering me about being pretty and … oh,' she shook her head impatiently, '… it all sounds so stupid now, but I was *very* naïve.'

'You weren't alone Jenny,' he said, trying to offer reassurance.

She nodded, gulping for air as her stomach stewed noisily with nerves. Holding her tummy, she apologised. 'Sorry. I missed my breakfast. I was nervous about meeting you. Very soon I was completely love-struck. He was very kind to begin with, gentle too. He made me feel as if I was at the centre of his universe and as things became more intimate … I was a virgin and … well, he made it feel very special in that way too. He always made sure it was … satisfying, if you understand me?' Jenny fretted at her fingers in embarrassment and looked down into her lap. 'I'd never done anything more than light petting with boys before and from the few things my Mother told me, I grew up with very low expectations about sex, so what he taught me was a revelation and very exciting. To start with.'

Jenny blushed and turned away again. A long silence was broken by heavy taps of rain on the roof of the car, turning to a noisy thrumming as a squall passed through the clearing.

As the noise eased, Stirling resumed. 'But it didn't stay that way?'

She shook her head. 'No. He started doing things that I didn't feel were right, but he told me were quite normal. Ignoring my instincts, I let him do it because I loved him and wanted to please him. I didn't know any better and had no one I could talk to. I shouldn't have been seeing him in the first place and I certainly couldn't discuss it with Mother. She's very old fashioned. If I stayed with him overnight I had to invent a friend I was staying with, even in my twenties!'

Jenny gave a small mocking laugh and as the brief smile lit in her eyes, Stirling saw again the pretty young woman, saddened her life had come to this.

'With hindsight, I realised it was an incremental process. He was conditioning me to accept his behaviours as the norm. He just tied me up sometimes, to begin with. Then there were blindfolds and spanking. His hands to begin with but that escalated to other things and it got to the point, after a year or so, that he would often start with that and finish with sex. Sometimes he just liked to sit and watch me.

'He'd leave the room quietly and I didn't know if he was there or not. Twice, he left the house for hours leaving me tied to the bed and blindfolded. All I could do was lie there, frightened, not knowing when he would come back to release me and terrified I would pee on his bed. If I complained, he told me off and said I must trust him. Once, he came back smelling of another woman and was very aroused. I knew he'd had sex with her and came back to … do the same with me. He had a very strong appetite and risk excited him.

'You must think I was stupid not to walk out, but I was desperately in love with him and would have done anything to keep him. But, the more I submitted to him, the greater the hold he had over me so that emotionally, I felt constantly off-balance. Ecstatic when he told me other women meant nothing to him, that I was the only woman who could satisfy him and then, dejected when he rebuked me for any little thing that made him cross, for which I was punished.

'It was only when I got older and could look back with more detachment that I understood how, very subtly, and cleverly, he undermined my independence and self-confidence until I could barely make a sensible decision for myself without first consulting him. I became dependent on him.'

'Was marriage ever discussed?'

Jenny laughed bitterly. 'Oh, yes, often! But there was always a problem. It wasn't the right time, or after this project or the next. As the years passed I began to understand he would never marry, less still little old me. He and Mr Jones sometimes worked for the same clients so, occasionally, there was some professional overlap. He would tell his other women about me, in very patronising terms, I'm certain. I had to ring Katrina Martin once and when she realised it was me, she laughed down the phone and made it abundantly clear I was sharing him with her. She was older than me and talked down to me as if I were a child. She's a horrible woman, Chief Inspector. Cold and sneering. It was humiliating. I would challenge him about it but he'd get angry, saying I didn't trust him and turn it back on me, using it as an excuse to punish me. And then he'd be so kind that I'd get so terribly confused and believe I'd misunderstood, somehow.'

Stirling pointed to where the cottage had once stood. 'What's the significance of this place, Jenny?'

Jenny pointed to something. 'Was that where Michael died? I read the car was set fire to.'

Following her direction, Stirling saw the still blackened surface where the burning car had fallen onto its wheel rims, and confirmed it was. She sat looking at the burnt debris lying on the stones. The heavy shower had been brief and the sun was now warming the interior of the car, lifting the scent of her simple perfume. Across the stoned ground, wraith-like steam rose from the surface to be caught by the breeze and dragged away. A squabble of sparrows rose and fell around a large puddle of rainwater as they bathed their wings.

Pointing at them, Jenny laughed lightly. 'It was beautiful here, the cottage. So quiet and secluded, you could imagine anything for yourselves.' Looking at the scorched stones again, she continued, 'It was a lovely car, the Jaguar. I loved being taken out in it, sinking down into the seats and the smell of the old leather. He would take me out for long drives in it to all sorts of places, miles away from round here.' She paused, 'But that often involved doing things in it too. They've a special smell, old cars, haven't they?'

Stirling smiled and agreed as he thought of the old car his father would take out of the garage occasionally and the memories of childhood it brought to mind. Sitting in the gardens of quirky pubs his father always seemed to know about, throwing stones into a stream with his brother as a church bell measured out the remains of the weekend. His parents emerging beery and laughing in good humour before going home to a Sunday roast.

Stirling replied, 'We've never found out where he kept it through the winter.'

Jenny turned her head in surprise and said spontaneously, 'Oh, I know who can tell you where that is …' She stopped suddenly, as if she had revealed a guilty secret.

Masking his surprise, he asked, 'It's important we find it Jenny. Where is it, please?'

'When Michael lived here he kept it in an outbuilding but needed somewhere when he moved to the apartment. I once knew someone who had a big garage she didn't use and sold it to him. She's dead now, but her children still live in the area. I don't know where exactly it is, but they will.'

Noting down the details, Stirling realised he might never have found it if he had not taken a risk in meeting Jenny. She continued with her story.

'I'd not been in his car since I got too old for his tastes.' She shivered slightly. 'He locked me in the boot once, tied up and gagged, and drove around for hours with me like that to punish me for some petty offence. He was so angry, and I was very frightened. I can't even remember what it was I was supposed to have done but I was in there for so long I had to pee, so he punished me for that too! To my shame he photographed me like that. Michael was a very cruel man. A Jekyll and Hyde character in many ways.'

Stirling decided not to mention the photograph to Jenny. She had enough shame to carry.

'Whenever his car appeared, it was a sign of spring in the square. From my office on the top floor I can see his apartment. It was very painful to see women going to and from the apartment with him over the years and to still be in love with him.'

Jenny roused herself from some reverie. 'But early in our relationship we had many happy days here and, sometimes, I stayed overnight. I had to have permission to come here, you see, because of the other women.'

'But it didn't stay that way?' he asked, nudging her on.

She looked up at the copse. 'No, it didn't.' Jenny closed her eyes and a wincing frown suggested she was recalling some memory.

'You don't have to tell me about it, if you'd prefer not to.'

Opening her eyes, Jenny turned to him and studied his face. 'I believe I can trust you, Mr Stirling, and I need to tell someone about it. It's been bottled up inside me for all these years, the pain and the shame of it. It's why I wanted to come here. I need to try and banish it to the past, to see it differently with someone else, someone I feel safe with.' She looked down shyly before a sudden thought came to her and she looked at him frightened. 'But I can't give evidence! My mother is an old lady now and I … we couldn't bear the shame of it.'

'Pemberton and his alleged killer are both dead, and we don't need you for the case against Katrina Martin. But, I believe you were the victim of a crime against you, here. That *would* require you to be a witness, *if* it's something you want me to pursue?'

Stirling had not spelt it out, but Jenny knew what he was referring to.

Jenny's story was very similar to that of Carol Evans, who she had known of, but many years ago and had never met. She was shocked to learn there had been a baby. Believing Jenny had enough to think about for the moment, Stirling did not tell her who the baby had become.

Asking her only to tell him what she felt able to discuss, Stirling told Jenny he knew another man might have been involved. Smiling bravely, she repeated she wanted to talk it out, to exorcise the memories.

Tearfully, and circumspectly, she described two occasions of being blindfolded and bound to the tree. Jenny had never seen the man's face but could remember his calloused hands on her skin, touching and probing her body, faltering as she described his rank sweat. She never heard his voice properly, only his disgusting grunts as he rutted at her. Only Pemberton had spoken, directing everything and from the way Pemberton spoke to him, she had a feeling the other man was young. When she resisted, she was beaten.

The involvement of the stranger started a few years after they had started seeing each other and, she thought, his interest in her was waning. Because of the abuse by the other man, she had taken an overdose at the cottage which had frightened Pemberton badly and it didn't happen again.

When Stirling explained how he could investigate the rapes, Jenny shook her head violently saying that whatever protection the court could provide, they could not protect her from the shame.

When Jenny finished telling her story, the tension seemed to drain from her and she leant back into the seat, closed her eyes and rested as she steadied her breathing.

Stirling watched Jenny's face, pretty in repose, as he gave her time to recover. He doubted she would ever trust a man again and foresaw her shuffling into an early spinsterhood, taking up ever less space, ever less air, ever less of life itself and only regrets for company.

His own thoughts were interrupted at the touch of Jenny's hand on his forearm. 'Thank you for bringing me here, Mr Stirling.'

'I wasn't sure if I should. Has it helped?'

'Yes. You're the only person I've ever talked to about it. I couldn't tell anyone before, not while he was alive. It seems easier with you, somehow. I suppose you see all sorts of terrible things, and you know what kind of man Michael was. I didn't have to persuade you to believe me or need to justify myself to you. You've listened without judging me. That was important. Thank you.'

'Why did you make the anonymous phone calls?' he asked, explaining he needed to tidy things away.

'When I saw it on the news, I recognised the location and the car and called to give you his name.'

'Thank you. And the call to Mrs Martin?'

'Yes. Over the last year, I sometimes saw a teenage boy coming away from Michael's building. It's on the other side of the square, so some distance from me. Because it was a boy I gave it no thought and even when I saw the pictures of the girl who died, I still didn't make the connection. Many years ago, I stole a key to his apartment. When we still saw each other occasionally. I often work into the evening when we're busy and if it was dark and I'd seen him go out, I sometimes crept in there hoping to find my photographs. I was careful not to disturb anything and always made sure the woman downstairs didn't see me. I think some part of me still wanted to feel a connection to him.'

'How did you make the connection to Mrs Martin?'

'A week before he died I went in there. The woman who lives below him was away. I'd often see her going off in a taxi with her backpack and her curtains wouldn't move for weeks at a time. He'd left his computer open, in the study. On the screen were pictures of the person I'd thought was a boy but was in fact the Martin girl. He was doing to her …' Jenny flinched and shivered. '… the things he made me do. It was horrible. The media said she was nearly seventeen, but she looked much younger. He liked young women but even so, she was a child, really. I couldn't go to the police because I was trespassing and was simply too frightened. She was dead, so I wasn't sure what to do.

'I thought about it for a while and researched her death to be sure it was the same person. Katrina Martin's telephone numbers are still on our system from past business and even though I hate her, I thought she had a right to know. I telephoned her home number and told her what I knew. She was very demanding, but I wouldn't give my name. I got worried she would recognise my voice, so I hung up.'

Stirling worked through the information. It all made sense. 'What are your feelings about his death now, Jenny?'

She frowned and gave it a moment's thought. 'I'm not sorry he's dead. And I understand why she killed him. I couldn't have done it, but he *was* a bad man.' She paused, 'More than anything else, I feel free of him, at last.'

Jenny took a last look around The Wern and gave Stirling a weak smile. 'Thank you for bringing me here, it was something I needed to do. It's over, at last. May I go home now please, Mr Stirling?'

CG BO

Day 12: Friday - 9.35 a.m.

Around the room sat Edwards, Heal, Helen and the search team leader for the previous evening's search of Pemberton's garage.

The garage was at the end of a row of large, well built garages which formed part of, but separate from an apartment complex. Not overlooked, it explained why few people would have seen Pemberton making his occasional visits to it over the years and sufficiently far from any public thoroughfares to avoid the attention of opportunistic thieves. Two heavy duty floor bolts anchoring the up and over door were soon opened with an angle grinder.

Inside, an outline of dust spoke of where the Jaguar had stood, its dustsheet folded neatly upon a shelf. Along one wall, several shelves were cluttered with the usual paraphernalia of a man's garage; tins of polish, polishing cloths, touch-up paint tubes, part used pots of household paints and a rusting toolbox. A part worn spare tyre rested across one corner. In the other corner stood two, four-drawer metal filing cabinets that could have been sisters to the cabinet in Pemberton's study.

One cabinet contained motoring magazines stretching back fifty years. Another drawer held motoring documents which included the Jaguar's original log book together with tax discs and test certificates for every year since its construction.

A second cabinet covered in blankets to protect it from cold and damp held what they had been hoping to find. In the top two drawers hung rows of divider files, each neatly itemised with a woman's name, a year or years "from - to" and all sorted into chronological order starting when Pemberton had been in his early twenties. A quick glance through some of them revealed they contained many black and white photographs of women, some of which Stirling recognised as those stored on Pemberton's computer.

In the third drawer were two cameras: an inexpensive digital camera and an older camera with some film containers; some unused with sell-by dates that had expired several years ago. The bottom drawer contained more bondage equipment, including a black leather hood with zipped eye and mouth closures. To the side of the cabinet lay several coils of thin rope covered in a mantle of light dust.

Following fingerprinting and forensic examination to prove Pemberton's connection to the garage, the second filing cabinet was seized in its entirety and the garage re-secured. Heal, Helen and her colleague had spent the rest of the evening cataloguing its contents and creating a schedule, cross referenced to whatever information was already in the HOLMES system.

The purpose of the meeting was to review the content of the cabinet and consider what needed to be done. Heal opened with a summary of the schedule.

'When we lifted out the files there was a small notebook underneath which our man used to record payments received from various women. Most of them we know about but there's a few we don't, so there are more enquiries to be done, if you think we should?'

Replying to a question of how many more women there were and what sums of money, Heal said another eight women and a couple of hundred thousand extorted over a period of ten years. 'That's over and above what we knew about. Seems he got started on this caper a long time before we previously understood, boss.'

'I'm surprised he wrote it all down,' said Edwards. 'If a complaint had been made and it fell into our hands, it would have sunk him.'

Helen answered, 'Looking at the date order of entries, I think it was his way of keeping a tally of what he'd extorted from them and could "pace" his demands so they could bear the cost. Some entries end abruptly like the one from Martin. My guess is Martin wasn't the only one to stand up to him and he had others to fall back on who were more pliable.'

'Thing is,' interrupted Edwards, 'how far do we go with this? Whatever we think about whose hand was holding the knife, we've detected two murders. Pemberton's dead, so we can't prosecute the extortions, and as for the rapes involving Osmand, we've no complainants for those.'

Edwards was referring to new photos discovered in the cabinet which showed a burly young Osmand with his trousers at his ankles assaulting three women bound to the oak. The women's faces were not visible but two were almost certainly Jenny and Carol. The third woman was unknown to them.

There was silence as they all looked at Stirling. He was torn between wanting to pursue every possible line of enquiry against his responsibility to use precious resources sensibly and economically. Another murder could arrive at any moment and his team would be re-directed.

Looking around the table, Stirling said, 'I'm still concerned about whether all of those women went home safely. I think the public would expect us to take reasonable steps to be sure of that. So, scale everything back to prepare the prosecution file but leave two investigators working through Pemberton's files to identify each woman, so far as we can. If it turns up anything helpful to this investigation, it's a bonus. I propose we leave Helen and Lesley on it as they've been involved with all of the women and their collective knowledge will identify connections which two new people wouldn't. Sound reasonable?' he asked, valuing their views.

Everyone agreed, and the meeting began to disperse. Far from the investigation being over, there were still many weeks of hard work ahead to prepare the prosecution file.

Edwards lingered behind after everyone had left. 'Any thoughts on what to do with the photos of Martin and Evans?'

The seized cabinet had contained the original photos of Katrina Martin and Carol Evans. Stirling recalled the contrasting images: Katrina Martin, beautiful, young and naked in poses of contrived vulnerability, but in all of them looking at the camera provocatively, confident of her allure and challenging the viewer to linger over her; Carol progressively cowed and anxious.

Katrina, a willing participant. Carol, uncertain and submissive.

'Get Helen to show them to her to verify their identities and then see what CPS wants to do with them for evidence. At the end of the criminal process we'll seek a destruction order.'

2.01 p.m.
They were sat in front of the window again. Waiting for Tanner to finish reading his report, Stirling gazed out over the countryside, now fully garbed in spring green, towards the constant movement of the motorway beyond.

Unwinding the interwoven legacy of lies, deceptions and violence that led Cassie to her death had allowed him to find a degree of solace. Unable to save her, he at least understood. Despite that understanding, though, Stirling knew Cassie's eyes, Pemberton's eyes, would haunt him in the wee small hours of the night.

Stirling turned his attention back to Tanner as she continued reading. Dressed in her uniform of white shirt with its silver braided epaulettes and a black skirt, she sat with her legs slanted diagonally and sideways to the window so that afternoon sunlight illuminated the fine hair of her forearm and at her temple. Stirling found himself imagining an evening with Steph Tanner over dinner, pushing aside some unprofessional wanderings when she closed the file.

Putting the report down on the table, Steph Tanner gave Stirling an appraising look. He looked better than he did two weeks ago, she thought, the constant guardedness replaced by the energy she had noticed when she first transferred into the force. A successful investigation and Ballard's spectacular fall from grace had restored Stirling's professional reputation, not to mention McDonald's difficulties. Unfortunately, the Deputy would not be moving on anytime soon. Tanner had heard some gossip about Stirling having a new woman in his life and wondered if she was contributing to his improved demeanour, and then wondered why she was curious.

'Do we have the results on the knife yet?' asked Tanner.

'The formal lab report is on its way, but they say there's a perfect fit between the broken blade and the tip recovered from the body.'

Tanner pointed to the report. 'The loss of the satnav data is disappointing. I think I understand, but explain it to me?'

Seeing Tanner's brown eyes studying him candidly, Stirling thought there was a warmth in her voice he had not noticed before.

'Martin seems to have been planning thoroughly but Carol's telephone call precipitated the events of Good Friday morning. Martin's car was only a couple of months old. She'd already made some calls to the dealership complaining the satnav wasn't working properly and insisted the unit must be replaced. The work was scheduled for a week later. As one of their high wealth customers, they wanted to keep her sweet and had ordered it in ready for when the work would be scheduled. As soon as the dealership opened on Saturday, Martin was there demanding it was fitted immediately. Really played her face, we're told. The original unit was scrapped that day. We're trying to trace it but from what they've told us we don't hold out much hope of its recovery. We have statements from the dealership.

'It's possible that Carol's impulsiveness caused Martin to rush her planning. Until we told her, Martin was unaware the call to him was made from her mobile. She probably assumed Carol used her own mobile to call Pemberton. Carol claimed not to use one, but she did. Paid for by Martin, along with Cassie's. She could have over medicated Carol with sleeping pills and gone there to meet Pemberton herself. She said in interview she was planning to kill Pemberton, in her own time. Face to face with him, she could have lost control and murdered him in hot blood rather than the cold-blooded killing she was planning.'

Tanner nodded thoughtfully. 'Or Carol did? Do you think she coerced Carol into taking the blame?'

'That's my frustration, we'll never know! Only one person could tell us that and she's not likely to. The tone of Carol's letters was one of regret for all the problems she'd caused. Perhaps it was Carol's way of doing something useful for her sister, for a change.'

Handing the report back to Stirling, Tanner stood up and reached out to shake his hand. 'We'll see what the jury makes of it. Well done, Stirling. It's good to have you back.'

 (8 80)

Day 13: Saturday - 10.46 a.m.

Locking the cottage door shut, Ayesha heard a car engine start with a throaty bellow and settle to a steady rhythm. She turned to see Stirling drive out of the garage and park in the middle of the drive and cut the engine. Ayesha went and stood at the driver's door where Stirling sat looking up at her with a grin.

'Madam, your carriage awaits.'

'It's a beautiful car. Red too, perfect!'

Ayesha began a slow circuit of the car. Drawing her fingers along the polished paintwork, she liked the cool smooth metal under her fingertips and paused twice to stand back, arms folded, to look critically along the lines of the bodywork. At the passenger door, she leant over the open side to touch and smell the leather seat. Stirling got out and stood watching her pleasure in the car's styling.

Looking across at him, she asked, 'I love it, it looks like a proper old-fashioned sports car but what is it?'

'It? *She*, please!' replied Stirling with a look of mock offence.

Ayesha rolled her eyes. 'As beautiful as it is, *it's* a machine!'

Stirling laughed, 'Oh, stop being so modern and enter into the spirit of it.'

Poking her tongue out at him, Ayesha resumed her inspection around the car as Stirling talked. 'It's a 1960 Morgan convertible. They're handmade to order in Malvern. I'd wanted one since I was a kid and bought her ...' Ayesha looked at him archly '... *it*! a few years ago, but I was too busy working on the cottage, so it's been in the garage under a sheet. When I was suspended I got to work on it to keep myself sane.'

'You've done a good job. So, where are we going?'

From an outer earthwork of British Camp, Stirling and Ayesha sat in companiable silence looking over Herefordshire rolling and swelling away west to break on the foothills of the Welsh mountains, hazy under the midday sun.

Since arriving at Stirling's that morning, Ayesha had sensed an undercurrent of uncertainty between them after several days apart. There seemed to be a need to grow back into each other. She could see he was still preoccupied with the investigation but there was something else there too, a restlessness. Ayesha had her own concerns she needed to talk to him about.

'It's beautiful up here,' Ayesha murmured, leaning her head on his shoulder. 'Do you think she did it?' she asked.

Stirling put his arm around her. He had thought of nothing else in recent days, constantly weighing the competing hypotheses for and against Martin's guilt.

'We might never know. They both had motive and opportunity. As for the means, Carol was emotionally frail through his treatment of her in the past and now, through Cassie's suffering. If she *was* there and experienced some sort of emotional crisis and lost control, lashing out unexpectedly, she might have got lucky with the first knife strike and overwhelmed him. Once he was incapacitated and unable to escape, she could strike at will.

'On the other hand, Katrina was physically stronger and is intelligent. Her calculating, emotional detachment would have allowed her to plan it in a way that Carol couldn't. Our lucky break was the knife tip. Without that we could still be scratching our heads. And I might have been out of a job too!'

'Will she go to prison?'

Stirling shrugged. 'You're the lawyer. Your guess is as good as mine, but I doubt it. There are a lot of extenuating circumstances and she has formidable legal support. If we can't knock any holes in her story, she'll probably get away with a suspended sentence.

'If she was responsible, Carol is beyond the reach of justice for either killing. The few neighbours who remember Gérard confirm there was some tension between them at a few social gatherings, but the houses are so far apart they had no sight or hearing of the Martins' home. Even if we find a smoking gun amongst her financial history it will be an uphill task to get a safe conviction for murder. Without a realistic chance of gaining a conviction, there'll be some plea bargaining and she'll accept concealment of his body and aiding her sister. I think the court will take a dim view of the circumstances of Gérard's concealment all those years but, there'll be heavy mitigation. She'd thought that through, too!'

'But Pemberton was a depraved, predatory individual. Will society really care?'

'It's a fair point. Some will say society is safer without the likes of Michael Pemberton in it but, professionally, I'm irritated that I can't prove her guilt.'

They sat in silence, each preoccupied with their thoughts.

'We had some of your colleagues in our offices yesterday. A DI Croft from your financial crime team, or something like that, with some detectives from London. Do you know him?' Ayesha turned to watch for his reaction.

Without taking his eyes from the horizon, Stirling nodded.

'They arrested one of the senior partners, Parry, to do with serious fraud. They had a warrant and went through pretty much anything with his name on it. It had some connection with the murdered man, Pemberton? The partners were hopping mad. We had to cancel all but some essential appointments so that our clients wouldn't see anything of it.'

Getting no response, she asked, 'You knew it was going to happen, didn't you?' It was an accusation, not a question.

Turning to face her, Stirling replied, 'I couldn't say anything, and it was to protect you. If they had decided to talk to you, what you didn't know, you couldn't lie about. I was sure they wouldn't need to, but I had to remain impartial.'

Ayesha looked away. Did that mean he had been unsure of her involvement in a crime? Ayesha felt hurt that he might have doubted her integrity for one second. Her hurt turned to irritation. Would she have done the same thing?

'So, you didn't trust me, is that what you're saying?'

Stirling was surprised Ayesha had not grasped the limited choice he had been faced with. 'I trust you, completely! It was a professional decision.'

After a long silence, she said, 'The partners say he's unlikely to return. He's a cretin anyway, he's the touchy-feely one I told you about, so I won't miss him.'

'I wanted to say something, but I couldn't risk compromising the investigation, or you.' Seeing her watching him, he added, 'I thought you'd understand.'

'I suppose it's not as if we know each other well, is it?' she answered with an edge to her voice.

It was intended to sting. Ayesha didn't want to argue with him but could not shake off her smouldering resentment that he had not felt able to trust her. It also explained why he had avoided her for the last week.

Ayesha looked away so that Stirling could not see her troubled features. As much as she tried to be objective, she was doubting again if he cared for her. She had spent the journey down from her parent's home that morning analysing her feelings for him, wondering if she should get out before he hurt her too badly. And there was still so much about him she did not know.

When she had reached the cottage, Stirling had been playing classical music loudly. Recognising the piece but unable to place it, Stirling explained it was *"Enigma Variations"* by their "local" composer Elgar. How appropriate, she had thought, but with no idea how the day would end, had said nothing.

Ayesha was annoyed too by her own yo-yoing emotions. None of the men she had known previously had been meek, or they would not have appealed to her. But Stirling was different, both physically and intellectually. He always treated her with respect and, importantly, as an equal, but his occasional reserve both intrigued and frustrated her. And he could be very stubborn, like her father, a similarity which really grated. Not for the first time, Ayesha wondered if she was in love with him.

A cloud passing overhead blotted out the sunlight momentarily and Ayesha shivered. Whether from the cooler air or in anticipation of Stirling's response, she was not sure.

Neither of them spoke as they sensed each other's hesitation whispering between them. So, there it was, thought Stirling. The exit door, if he wanted to walk towards it. He could easily provoke a conversation to bring the relationship to an end, right here.

Following the course of cloud shadows tracking across the landscape, Stirling thought of their journey here; Ayesha's laughter at the wind dragging her hair about her face, her intelligent wit, good humour and easy company - when he wasn't upsetting her. Stirling smiled again as he remembered her naked fury in what was now referred to as "the knife incident."

He had given a lot of thought to telling Ayesha about Helen but had decided against it. To disclose it would fatally wound an already shaky relationship and it would not happen again. So, did that mean he wanted the relationship to survive, to develop into something enduring? His affection for Ayesha beckoned, but so too did his instinct to avoid more pain and unhappiness. Ayesha's as much as his own. A woman's face from the past came to mind, before he returned from London, and the sadness he had boxed up in the spare room at home.

He had adapted to, and enjoyed the flexibility of short-term relationships managed within the margins of his professional life. Of spending time with interesting women without concern for the longer term. But he knew that such relationships were essentially soulless. Without work to occupy his days and his mind, the last few months had revealed something to him which he had not experienced before. A corrosive loneliness.

Stirling turned his head to study Ayesha's profile discreetly as she stared out over the countryside, avoiding eye contact with him. He smiled. Her obstinacy amused him too. In that moment, Stirling decided he wanted to know this intelligent, funny woman much better. Taking her hand, he gave it a squeeze. Ayesha turned to look at Stirling, searching for a clue as to what he was thinking.

Standing up, he reached down to help Ayesha up to her feet. Seeing her hesitant smile, he cupped her face in both hands and kissed her before embracing her in an enveloping hug. Seeing the smile in his eyes, Ayesha relaxed and her doubts began to slip away.

Stirling took her hand. 'Come on, let's go. I have a plan for the afternoon and then I'm taking you to dinner.'

'Oh? And what *exactly* is your plan for the afternoon?' she asked, with half an idea.

'I think we should spend some time catching up with each other, don't you?' was all he said, a smile playing at the corners of his mouth. 'It's going to rain, anyway.'

'Really?' she asked, surprised.

Ayesha looked around at the horizon and saw only light clouds studding an otherwise blue sky. Turning back to Stirling with a bemused look on her face, her eyes narrowed on seeing his wide grin and she struck at him light-heartedly. 'Douglas!'

Feigning an affronted look, he replied, 'What? Trust me, I was a boy scout.'

Falling into step alongside Stirling, Ayesha felt happier and more relaxed than she had for some days. She doubted they would make it to dinner.

૯૪ ૪૦

EPILOGUE
Day 17: Wednesday - 12.37 p.m.

Stuffing his tools back inside the large bag at his side, the engineer called over to the customer and held out a slim aluminium case.

'What d'you want me to do with the old hard drive then Guv'nor?'

The customer winced at the term "Guv'nor," associating it with East End villains, wide-boy salesmen and TV cops. None of which chimed with his background as a retired investment advisor. He walked across the study to join the CCTV engineer who had spent much of the morning working on his home security master board. The movement-activated cameras at either side of the gated entrance to his home had failed recently. After lengthy circuitry testing, diagnostic analysis and more technical information than he needed to know, or understood, the engineer had advised an upgrade to more modern software which he had now fitted.

Handing over the old hard drive, the engineer continued in the irritatingly jokey manner which had grated all morning. 'It was good stuff in its day but like everything else, the technology's moved on. I can destroy it for you, if you like?'

The man turned it over in his hand, wondering if he should destroy it himself. There was no personal data on it, he thought, and it wasn't as if it was out of a personal computer. He asked the technician what data it contained.

Concentrating on writing out the job ticket, the engineer shrugged, 'The recording quality was excellent and would have captured whatever went past or arrived at your gate until it failed.

It had a rolling recording capability with automated deletion every twenty-eight days to ensure there was always sufficient memory to continue recording. The cameras at the gate were still working and the data recorder here has everything going past or approaching the gate for the last twenty-eight days. The problem was the data reader this end. It just wouldn't read the recording, which is why you only had the audio buzzer at the gate.' Jabbing over his shoulder with his pen, he added, 'That new system's got enough memory to get you to the moon and back,' and chuckled self-indulgently at his own joke.

Whistling tunelessly under his breath, the engineer continued to complete the form. Tearing the job sheet from the pad, he handed it across in exchange for the redundant hard drive.

'Say, wasn't there a bit of bother down here recently?' asked the engineer, his eyes lively for gossip. 'I heard the police was at the big house down the end. Body in the garden or something?'

Reluctant to fuel idle chatter, he offered vaguely, 'Yes, to do with someone's death, I heard. Are we finished then?'

Oblivious to the hint, the engineer ploughed on. 'A really nasty murder they say in the papers, reading between the lines, like. I read it in the local paper. Something to do with a dodgy housing scheme. And she'd buried her husband in the garden! There's no telling what folks will do, is there?' Holding up the hard drive he added, 'Anyway, better press on. Leave this with me Guv'nor, I'll destroy it for you and if you get any problems with the new system, just give me a call.'

Escorting the engineer to the door, keen for him to be gone and to take his overly familiar manner with him, something was bothering the man. His wife had told the police their CCTV was broken but she would not have understood what had failed, or when.

Holding out his hand, he said, 'I've changed my mind. I'll keep the hard drive, thank you.'

Returning to the study, he sat down heavily behind his desk and put the hard drive on the blotter in front of him. As he pondered its shiny aluminium casing, and what information it might contain, he thought back to when the police had called.

He had been ill in bed for several days when they had buzzed up from the electrically controlled security gate. Karen had let them through to drive up to the house, but she had not been able to help with any of their questions and had not disturbed him for fear of hindering his recovery. But Karen, his second wife, had only lived with him for a few years and her increasing forgetfulness was becoming a worry. He would have to insist on her seeing a specialist very soon.

Before his retirement and gaining the privacy he had looked forward to for so many years, he had travelled constantly, and often overseas, so he had barely known the people the officers had been asking questions about. He vaguely remembered going to a housewarming party at the Martin's home, many years ago, soon after they had moved in. He knew the Martin woman by sight as, sometimes, if he was waiting for the gate to open or to pull out into the road, he might see her drive past, and always in a top of the range Mercedes. But, apart from than that, he did not know her.

His first wife, Felicity, would have remembered the man who had lived at the end house. A French chap, he thought they'd said? Beautiful, gregarious Felicity, who had always taken an interest in other people. It was just one of so many things he had loved about her. His thoughts drifted away to memories of happier times, of Felicity's personality filling whatever room she was in, turning heads, of how people had moved towards her wishing to be part of that radiance and warmth, eager for the blessing of her smile. His eyes moistened as he remembered too, the lingering, painful disease which had wasted her body, robbing her of everything vital until death had been a serenely accepted blessing.

With a loud sniff, he wiped away his tears and returned his stare to the aluminium case. He knew from the television news and from reading the papers that the Martin woman had been charged with someone's murder and her husband's death. Surely, the Police must have enough evidence? He reached forward and put his hand on the telephone, hesitated, and sat back again as he thought about some of the people he had advised in the past, and of their disreputable connections. There would be a court case with a lot of media coverage. If the hard drive proved of interest to the police, what might be the consequences for him of the media spotlight?

He thought about his heart condition. Did he want the exposure?

END

About the Author

Ray Britain completed a highly successful policing career in the United Kingdom, serving in a variety of uniform and detective roles, but the investigation of crime and the camaraderie of investigators remained his preference. Grounded in the gritty reality of hard won, professional experience, Ray's debut novel *'The Last Thread'* puts the reader in the driving seat of a complex murder investigation with all the political and operational pressures that such investigations engage.

As a Senior Investigating Officer (SIO) Ray led many investigations and for many years was also a Hostage & Crisis Intervention Negotiator. In that voluntary role he attended hostage situations, many firearms incidents and numerous suicide interventions, not all of which ended happily. In both of those roles, Ray was active in national, specialist response arrangements, he trained with the FBI and led a large, multi-disciplinary team of several hundred people. His professional responsibilities took him to India, Europe, Australia and elsewhere, and he was awarded several Commendations in recognition of his work.

On leaving the police service Ray worked with other criminal justice organisations, including HM Government's Home Office, London. A Francophile who now writes full time, Ray's interests include mountain and fell walking, skiing, theatre, Dad dancing, reading and sailing.

You can connect with Ray Britain by visiting:

Website: http://www.raybritain.com/

Email: info@raybritain.co.uk

Twitter: https://twitter.com/ray_britain

GLOSSARY OF TERMS & ACRONYMS

All acronyms, terms and references used in *The Last Thread'* can be found in publicly available documents or by internet research. Any opinions perceived or implied are those of the author and do not belong to any professional body or other person(s).

ACC   Assistant Chief Constable - Most police forces have a Chief Constable, a Deputy Chief Constable and two to four ACC roles according to the size of the force, each with specific portfolio responsibilities. Typically, one with suitable career experience will lead for "Crime & Operations". The Metropolitan Police Service (Greater London) has additional roles due to scale.

ACPO   Association of Chief Police Officers - the former UK professional body which provided oversight to national policing policy and arrangements. Replaced in 2015 by the National Police Chief's Council. The term "ACPO" is still widely used, sometimes critically, to refer to a member of, or the collective executive of a police force.

Chassis Number   Prior to VIN numbers being introduced (1980) British cars had a manufacturer's serial number stamped into the chassis.

CID	Criminal Investigation Department - a generic, historical and common acronym for the investigative body of a police service.
"Cinque a sept"	French term for an after work social gathering or a tryst with a mistress before going home.
College of Policing	UK police service's national professional body, established 2012.
CoLP	Colloquial term for the City of London Police.
Dog - Cadaver Search	Trained to detect interred human remains. Also referred to as victim recovery or decomposition dogs, some are trained to detect the early stages of decomposition, others for the later stages of decomposition.
Dog - Historical Search	Trained to locate historical or archaeological graves.
DVLA	Driver Vehicle Licensing Agency - responsible for all driving related documentation and record keeping for the UK.
ECU	Economic Crime Unit - specialist Financial Investigators who investigate complex financial crime and trace/confiscate criminally obtained assets.

FLO	Family Liaison Officer - usually an investigator who provides support to a victim's next of kin and or, family.
FORCE (Police)	An historic term to describe a policing organisation, used less often now in favour of the term Service.
HMIC	Her Majesty's Inspectorate of Constabulary - responsible for independently assessing the efficiency of police services and promoting improvement. Each police service has a nominated 'lead' HMIC.
HOLMES	Home Office Large Major Enquiry System - introduced in 1985 following a critical review of the Yorkshire Ripper investigation. Superseded by HOLMES-2, an integrated information technology system used by all UK police forces for the management of complex and large-scale crime.
Lead Force	Many police forces are designated as having 'lead force' status in a specific discipline. (E.g. City of London Police - investigation of fraud.) A Lead Force leads in policy and procedure development and maintaining national professional doctrine, so avoiding conflicting and costly replication.

MO	Modus Operandi - the favoured means by which a criminal operates.
Murder Manual	An informal term for the UK national doctrine of good practice guidance for the investigation of homicide.
NCA	National Crime Agency - established in 2013, the UK's national law enforcement capability for tackling the most serious organised and cross border crime. Sometimes referred to as the "British FBI".
NFA'd	No further action - a term describing an enquiry as filed.
OCG	Organised Crime Group - Defined by the National Crime Agency as *"serious crime planned, coordinated and conducted by people working together on a continuing basis."*
OIC	Officer in Case/Officer in Charge - applicable to an officer at any rank who is responsible for a specific crime or enquiry.
PACE	Acronym for the Police & Criminal Evidence Act 1984 - together with Codes of Practice which provides a legislative framework for police and other law enforcement bodies in the exercise of their powers, the custody of suspects and the conduct of suspect interviews.

PNC	Police National Computer - introduced in 1974, a national data base containing millions of records which include: vehicles registered in UK, driver's records, criminal convictions, recorded stolen property and police intelligence.
PolSA	Police Search Advisor - specialist search advisor; a term often used to describe a planned, methodical search.
PCC	Police & Crime Commissioner - an elected official frequently belonging to a mainstream political party who is responsible for *"securing efficient and effective policing of a police area"*. PCC's replaced Police Authorities in 2012. With very low electoral turn out, reflecting public disinterest in the role, many consider PCC's as having a 'democratic deficit'.
Policy Book	Sometimes called a Decision Log - where an SIO records all key decisions on strategy and tactics, and the rationale for their decision making on why they are/not taking an action. Recorded for the benefit of any later scrutiny of the decision-making process to understand what the SIO knew, or should have known, when making their decision.

The quality of the SIO Policy Book can make or break careers.

Service (Police)   See Police Force above.

SFO   Serious Fraud Office - independent UK Government Dept. which investigates and prosecutes serious and complex fraud and corruption.

SIO Peer Reviews   Murder investigations are subject to regular peer reviews to ensure they are being led and managed efficiently and effectively, together with suitable and sufficient skills and resources. A 'hot' review may take place within 48 hours, with subsequent reviews taking place, if undetected, at 28-day intervals or as determined by a lead executive officer. The purpose of the review is to support the SIO to ensure s/he has sufficient resources and skills to run their investigation and to bring a fresh perspective to lines of enquiry.

Strategy Documents   A framework which records how specific lines of enquiry (e.g. house to house) will be conducted, how it is to be delivered, with role accountabilities and any contextual considerations e.g. risk assessments, community tension.

Task Force (TF)   Variously styled and structured from service to service with differing scope and capabilities. The author uses a model he is familiar with: a specialist firearms team with a surveillance capability and is also trained to support major crime investigations.

Une chienne froid	Derogative French term - a cold bitch.
VIN	A seventeen figure unique identifier number giving information of the manufacturer, the model and other unique information.
VRM	Vehicle registration mark.
Wounding/GBH	Serious injury as categorised in the Offences Against the Persons Act 1861 - a wounding and/or Grievous Bodily Harm.

- Section 18: where intent to harm is proven.
- Section 20: where intent to harm is not proven.

Book Club Discussion Notes

I know that many readers are members of Book Clubs which meet to discuss books they have read, to enjoy friendship and, I'm sure, a glass of wine … or two. Below are some discussion questions for *The Last Thread* which I hope could be helpful to you. Please feel free to share your discussions with me via www.raybritain.com I will be delighted to hear from you.

1. What did you like best about *The Last Thread*?
2. What did you like least about this book?
3. Did it remind you of another book(s)?
4. Which characters in the book did you like best?
5. Which characters did you like least?
6. If you were making a movie or TV drama of this book, who would you cast as the principle characters?
7. Who do you believe murdered Pemberton, and why?
8. Do you believe his killer should be shown any exceptional mercy?
9. Do you have a favourite quote from the book? If so, why did this quote stand out?
10. Would you read another book by this author?
11. What feelings did this book evoke for you?
12. What did you think of the book's length? What would you cut out or add?
13. If you got the chance to ask the author of this book one question, what would it be?
14. Which character in the book would you most like to meet?
15. Which places in the book would you most like to visit?
16. What do you think of the book's cover? How well does it convey what the book is about?
17. Did this story seem realistic?
18. How well do you think the author built the world in the book?
19. Did the book's pace seem too fast, too slow, or just right?
20. What was your initial reaction to the book? Did it hook you immediately, or take some time to get into?

21. Do you think the story was plot or character driven?
22. What made the setting unique or important? Could the story have taken place anywhere?
23. Did you pick out any themes, either overt or underlying throughout the book?
24. Did the structure of the book affect the story?
25. Did you relate to any of the characters? If so, what was it you connected with?
26. Did you like the ending?
27. What motivates the characters' actions? Are their actions justified, or ethical?
28. Do any characters grow or change during the novel? If so, in what way?
29. If you could insert yourself as a character in the book, what role would you play?
30. Did you expect the ending? Was it neatly wrapped up, or too neatly? Was the story unresolved, ending on an ambiguous note?

Printed in Poland
by Amazon Fulfillment
Poland Sp. z o.o., Wrocław

54903200R00315